THE WORLD'S MOST POWERFUL TANKS

THE WORLD'S MOST POWERFUL MACHINES

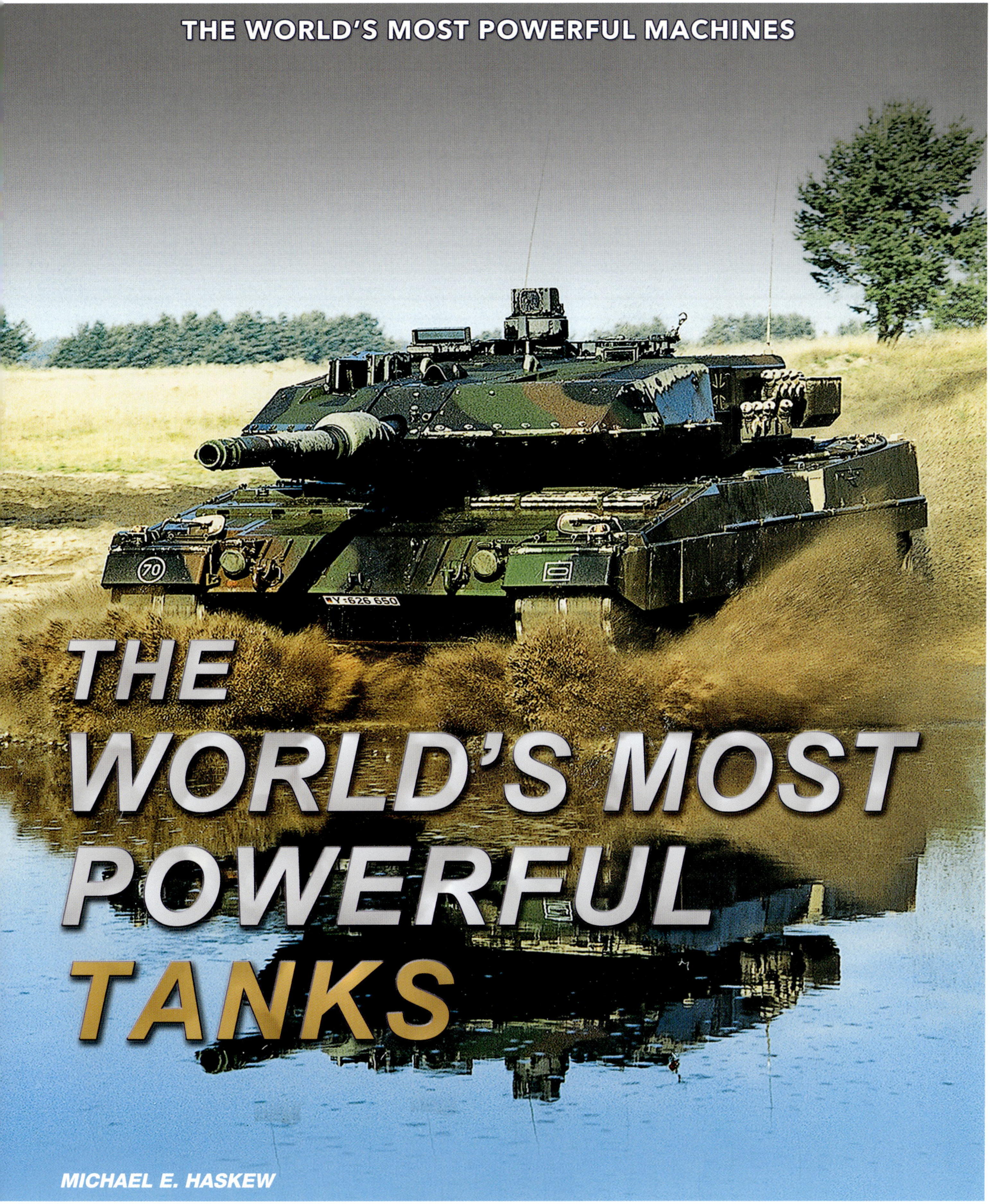

THE WORLD'S MOST POWERFUL TANKS

MICHAEL E. HASKEW

ROSEN PUBLISHING
New York

This edition published in 2017 by:

The Rosen Publishing Group, Inc.
29 East 21st Street
New York, NY 10010

Library of Congress Cataloging-in-Publication Data

Names: Haskew, Michael E., author.
Title: The world's most powerful tanks / Michael E. Haskew.
Description: New York : Rosen Publishing, [2017] | Series: The world's most powerful machines | Includes bibliographical references and index. | Audience: Grades 7-12.
Identifiers: LCCN 2016035767 | ISBN 9781499465587 (library bound)
Subjects: LCSH: Tanks (Military science)--History--Juvenile literature.
Classification: LCC UG446.5 .H3734 2017 | DDC 623.74/752--dc23
LC record available at https://lccn.loc.gov/2016035767

Manufactured in Malaysia

Contents

Introduction

Combining striking power and mobility, the tank has the potential to truly dominate the battlefield – a potential that has persisted during almost a century of warfare. As the technology of the tank evolves, its capabilities will only be enhanced.

Although its origin may be traced to Leonardo da Vinci, or even to the ancient Greek phalanx, the tank is today a thoroughly modern weapon. Its precision technology maintains the cutting edge of military land warfare doctrine. Admired for its combat capability and feared for its awesome capacity to deal death, the tank holds a grip on the collective psyche of military planners the world over.

From the beginning, the idea of armoured warfare drove innovation and those who conceived of the lumbering behemoths that rumbled over and through trench lines like fire-breathing dragons during World War I provided only a foretaste of the destructive capacity that was yet to come. Although primitive, the tanks of World War I set the stage for the future of armoured land battles.

Between the world wars, British officer and military strategist J.F.C. Fuller championed the development of the tank and others joined the inexorable tide of influence that slowly gained sway among the military establishments of great nations. Mechanization came to full flower during World War II and the legendary military minds of Heinz Guderian, Erwin Rommel, George S. Patton and Georgi Zhukov were among those who saw the potential for armour in rapid exploitation of an enemy weakness, acting as steel cavalry.

Armoured Advance

World War II itself was a global proving ground for advances in firepower, mobility and armour protection. Both the

The Bradley M2/M3 fighting vehicle was years in development and roundly criticized due to its cost and limited armour protection. However, it proved its worth as a combat troop carrier and in battle against Iraqi tanks during Operation Desert Storm and Operation Iraqi Freedom.

During the period of rapid rearmament under the Nazi regime in the 1930s, German soldiers load PzKpfw II tanks onto waiting transporters. The PzKpfw II and other German tanks provided the armoured ground thrust of the Blitzkrieg that conquered much of Europe in the early days of World War II.

Allies and Axis fielded ever more powerful tanks and the resulting clashes are remembered as epic struggles. Kursk, Arracourt, El Alamein and the Battle of the Bulge continue to resonate among historians and those few living veterans who remember the day of the Tiger, the Panther, the T-34 and the Sherman.

During the early days of the Cold War, the tank became a symbol of both freedom and repression. The Soviet Union exported its battle-tested tanks in great numbers to Warsaw Pact nations and client states, while the United States and Great Britain led the West in its search for an armoured vehicle that might stand up to an avalanche of armour from the East. Land warfare in the twentieth century became synonymous with the tank. It was inconceivable that a successful ground campaign might be waged without tanks and their supporting mobile infantry, riding into combat in armoured battle taxis. The day that had dawned in No Man's Land had reached high noon.

As early as 1918, German Field Marshal Paul von Hindenburg observed, "The fact that the tanks had now been raised to such a pitch of technical perfection that they could cross our undamaged trenches and obstacles did not fail to have a marked effect on our troops."

Awesome, Deadly Prowess

The thorough defeat of inferior Iraqi T-54/55, T-62 and T-72 tanks by the M1A1 Abrams, Challenger and other modern fighting vehicles of the coalition that ejected Saddam Hussein from Kuwait in 1991 and then toppled his regime in 2003 brought the absolute potential for the tank to determine the outcome of a land battle sharply into focus. The time, money and even lives that had been devoted to the advancement of armoured technology had suddenly seized the limelight.

Routinely weighing more than 50 tonnes (49.2 tons) and mounting fearsome weapons of 120mm (4.7in) or more, the main battle tank has become the focus of land warfare, first during an age of mutually-assured destruction at the height of the Cold War, then through the era of proxy wars in the Third World and eventually into the day of the despot, when civilized nations opposed the brutality of tyrants.

The tank has continued to evolve with the latest in fire control, weapons systems, thermal imaging, composite armour and computerization. Today's tank is capable of tracking multiple targets simultaneously, defending itself against the latest anti-tank weapons and ordnance fired by enemy armoured vehicles and bringing its crew home safely from the maelstrom of the modern battlefield.

From tank versus tank combat to urban warfare and counter-insurgency, the tank has adapted. In close quarters and facing low-technology weapons such as the improvised explosive device (IED), or on the open desert or plain confronting the finest military hardware of an enemy, the tank will continue to evolve, influence the tactical dialogue of ground commanders and endure.

From World War I to World War II

During two world wars and the quarter-century between them, the tank matured. Revolutionizing modern warfare, it brought firepower, manoeuvrability and armour protection to the battlefield. In the process, the tank itself became more heavily armed and armoured, swifter and more versatile in combat. On the ground, armour created and exploited the all-important breakthrough. The tank, in short, became a game-changer on the battlefields of the twentieth century, shaping the course of history.

This Tiger I heavy tank raises a cloud of dust along a dirt road. The Tiger performed extremely well against Allied tanks of all types. Its main weakness was its slow speed and lack of manoeuvrability.

Mark V Male (1917)

Entering production in late 1917, the British Mark V Male tank was a significant improvement over prior models, particularly the Mark I that had made history at the Somme in 1916. The service life of the Mark V Male spanned the inter-war years.

By the end of World War I, at least nine variants of the original British Mark I tank had between deployed on the battlefields of the Western Front. Among these, the Mark V Male, originally intended as a totally redesigned armoured fighting vehicle but eventually incorporating elements of earlier models, proved to be a significant technological advance over even its immediate predecessor, the Mark IV.

The Mark V Male was deployed late in the war and served with British, French, Canadian and American forces. Its combat experience was limited and primarily

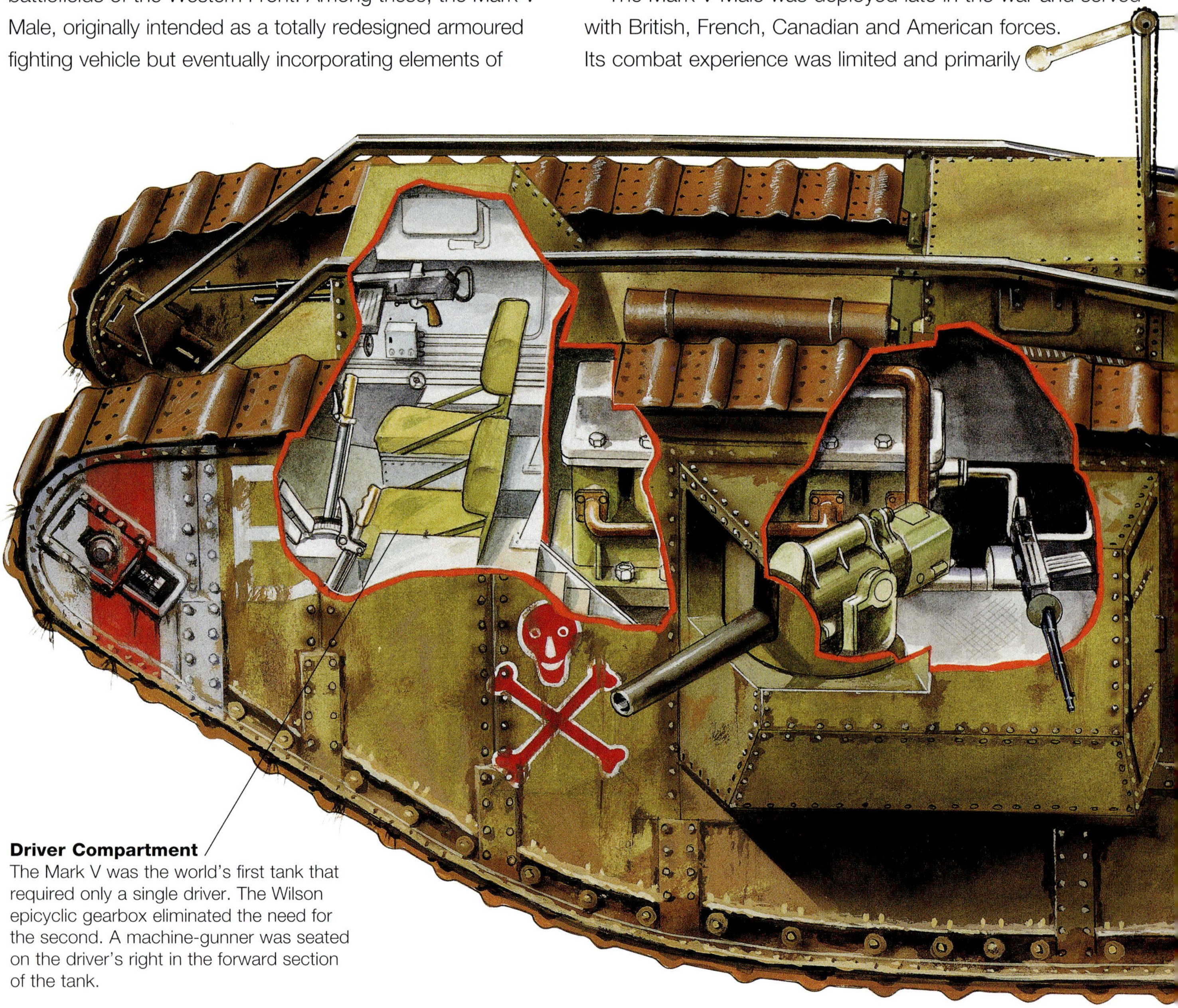

Driver Compartment
The Mark V was the world's first tank that required only a single driver. The Wilson epicyclic gearbox eliminated the need for the second. A machine-gunner was seated on the driver's right in the forward section of the tank.

occurred during the Battle of Le Hamel in the summer of 1918. In contrast to earlier tanks, the Mark V Male traversed ditches and trenches easily and its width of 4.11m (13ft 6in) cleared the way for infantry through the barbed wire that had previously been a significant obstacle to foot soldiers.

Technical Advances

Although the all-around track arrangement and its relatively heavy weight at 29.5 tonnes (29 tons) reduced the range of the Mark V Male to 72km (45 miles) and its combat endurance to 10 hours, the most up-to-date tank among the Allies late in the war included several operational enhancements. Among these was the six-cylinder 110-kilowatt

The rear view of the Mark V Male tank reveals the extended sponsons for the 6pdr guns, the characteristic all-around tracks of British tanks and the innovative unditching beam that assisted with movement through difficult terrain.

Although their traverse was limited, the pair of 6pdr sponson-mounted guns of the British Mark V Male tank provided formidable firepower, while the improved hull design facilitated movement across the uneven terrain of the battlefield. The enhanced mobility fostered cooperation between armour and infantry formations.

Specification

Dimensions	Length: 8.5m (27ft) Width: 4.11m (13ft 6in) Height: 2.64m (8ft 7in)
Weight	29.5 tonnes (29 tons)
Engine	1 x Ricardo six-cylinder petrol engine delivering 110kW (150hp)
Speed	7.4km/h (5mph)
Armament	Main: 2 x 6pdr (57mm/2.34in) QF guns Secondary: 4 x Hotchkiss 7.7mm (0.303in) machine guns
Armour	6–14mm (0.24–0.55in)
Range	72km (45 miles)
Crew	8

(150hp) petrol engine designed by Harry Ricardo, the world's first powerplant specifically designed for a tank. The new engine allowed for a maximum speed of 7.4km/h (5mph) despite the fact that it had to be cranked manually by four soldiers while a fifth pressed a magneto switch. Cold-weather starts were particularly difficult, with each of the cylinders needing to be primed and the spark plugs warmed.

The addition of the Wilson epicyclic gearbox eliminated the need for a second driver to steer the steel monster and the attachment of an unditching beam, carried atop the superstructure, afforded a means of extricating the tank from holes, ditches or thick mud, whereas older tanks might have had to be abandoned.

The firepower of the Mark V Male was enhanced substantially with two sponson-mounted 6pdr (57mm/2.24in) cannon and four 7.7mm (0.303in) Hotchkiss Mk 1 machine guns. The Mark V Female was slightly lighter weight and armed with four 7.7mm Vickers machine guns. These were enclosed in Skeens ball mounts that improved the firing radius from 60° to 90° while also providing greater protection for the single gunner than the firing slits of the Mark IV or the loopholes fashioned in the hulls of earlier tanks. The crew of eight included the commander, driver, two gearsmen and four machine-gunners.

Two significant variants of the Mark V appeared late in the war and saw limited service. The Mark V* incorporated a lengthened hull that enabled the tank to cross trench lines more easily, while the Mark V** added a more functionally sound length-width ratio for the longer hull. During its production run, 400 Mark V tanks – 200 Male and 200 Female – were manufactured. In total nearly 600 of the Mark V* rolled off British assembly lines; however, only 25 of the rare Mark V** were completed.

Battle at Le Hamel

When Australian and American troops assaulted a salient in the German line at Le Hamel on 4 July 1918, they were accompanied by 60 Mark V tanks of the 5th Brigade, Royal Tank Corps, supported by four supply tanks. The assault achieved its objective in a startling 93 minutes and prompted the Australian historian Charles Bean to observe that the action "furnished the model for almost every attack afterwards made by British infantry during the war."

Indeed, operating alongside the Mark V Male and Female tanks, Allied soldiers developed tactics to work in cooperation with the armour and rapidly exploited every opening created. Among the newly-discovered principles of the battlefield was the fact that infantrymen advanced more effectively while deployed in skirmish order around the tanks rather than clustering behind them for protection.

General J.F.C. Fuller, one of the foremost advocates of the tank during World War I and beyond, commented that the action at Le Hamel was a monumental achievement in terms of its rapid prosecution, short duration and the thorough nature of its success.

Between the Wars

Following the end of World War I, the Mark V tank continued to serve with British forces, most notably during their campaign in northern Russia and with White Russian forces during the Russian Civil War of 1917–1922. The Mark V remained in service with the Soviet Red Army into the 1930s and some indications suggest that it was active as late as 1941. One tale asserts that a long-captured Mark V was pressed into service by the Germans during the defence of Berlin in 1945.

Mark V on the Offensive

Following the Allied victory at Le Hamel, an Australian soldier remarked that the presence of the Mark V Male tank did not diminish the ardour of the infantry for combat and that they performed based upon their continuing sense of duty. Nevertheless, the tanks must have given the soldier and his comrades heart.

Although the timing of the combined-arms effort at Le Hamel was sometimes a bit awkward, the mere presence of the tanks resulted in the capture of a number of German prisoners. When a battalion of infantry was held up by direct fire from a German machine gun, a Mark V rolled forward and simply crushed the position under its treads. In the village of Hamel, the tanks blasted German soldiers out of buildings and swept the narrow streets with their machine guns.

The Mark V proved instrumental in the victory. Five tanks were damaged, while 13 crew were killed or wounded.

Right: Taking a moment to familiarize themselves with a new weapon of war, curious British infantrymen inspect the exterior of a Mark V Male tank during a lull in the fighting on the Western Front. Another tank appears to be canted in a ditch to the rear.

Sturmpanzerwagen A7V
(1918)

When British tanks reached the World War I battlefields in 1916, Germany rushed to keep pace with the technology that threatened the deadlock of trench warfare. The A7V, however, did not deploy until 1918 and then only in small numbers.

In the autumn of 1916, German infantry officers along the Somme battlefront encountered a new and potentially devastating weapon. The first British armoured fighting vehicle, which would become known universally as the tank, had appeared and immediately begun to alter the concept of entrenched infantrymen firing at one another across No Man's Land, occasionally going over the top to brave machine-gun fire and the shell bursts of artillery.

Senior German commanders quickly recognized the threat posed by the tank and on November 13, 1916, only weeks after the appearance of British armour on the Somme, they initiated the production of their own

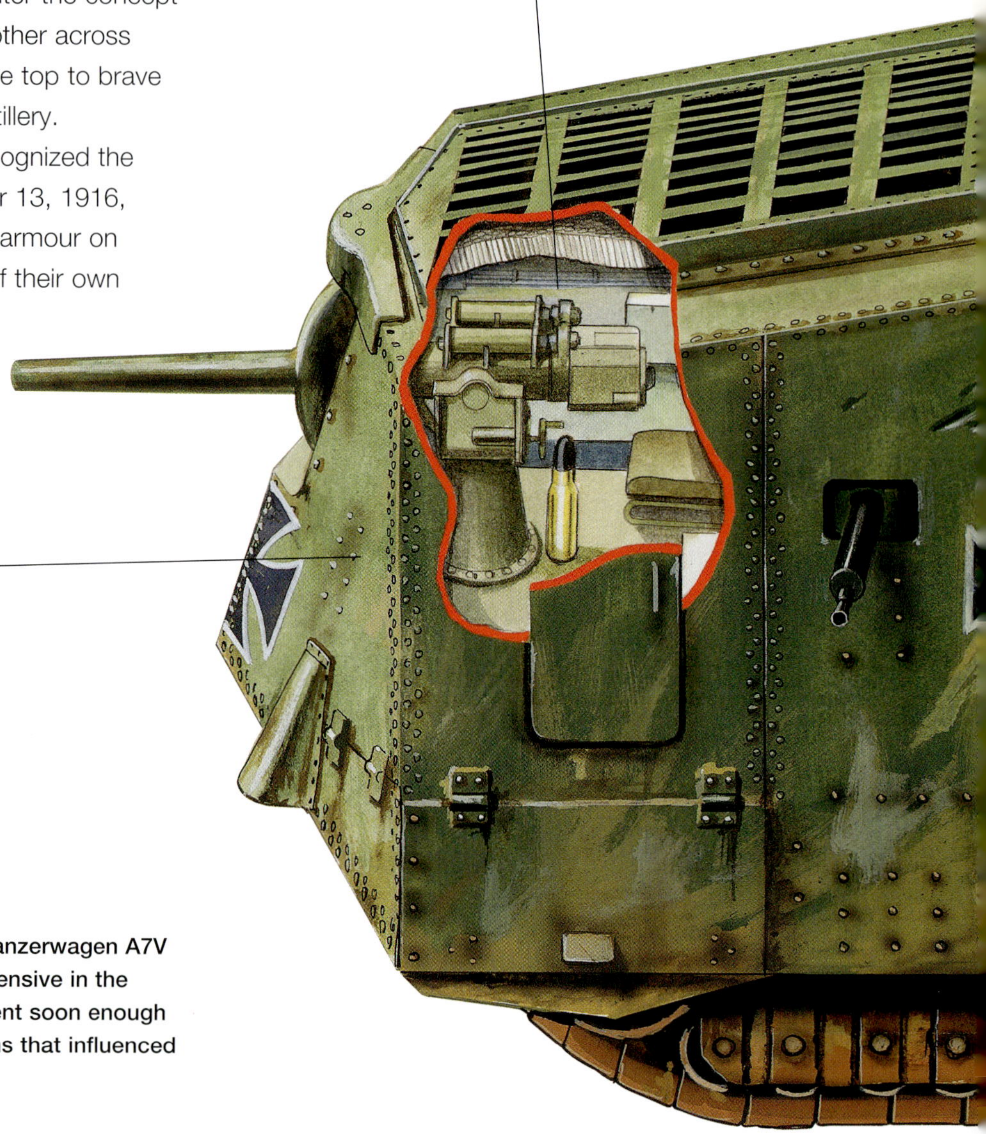

The first operational German tank, the Sturmpanzerwagen A7V initially entered combat during the Michael Offensive in the spring of 1918. Its shortcomings became evident soon enough and German engineers learned valuable lessons that influenced future designs.

tank. Although some research and development with armoured vehicles had been on-going since 1911, a design committee headed by Joseph Vollmer, a professional engineer and captain in the German Army, was formed. The resulting Sturmpanzerwagen A7V did not reach the front until the opening phase of the desperate Michael Offensive, Germany's last strategy for victory in World War I, which was launched on March 21, 1918.

A Box on a Tractor

In their scramble to achieve at least parity with their enemy's tanks, German engineers devised a 32.5-tonne

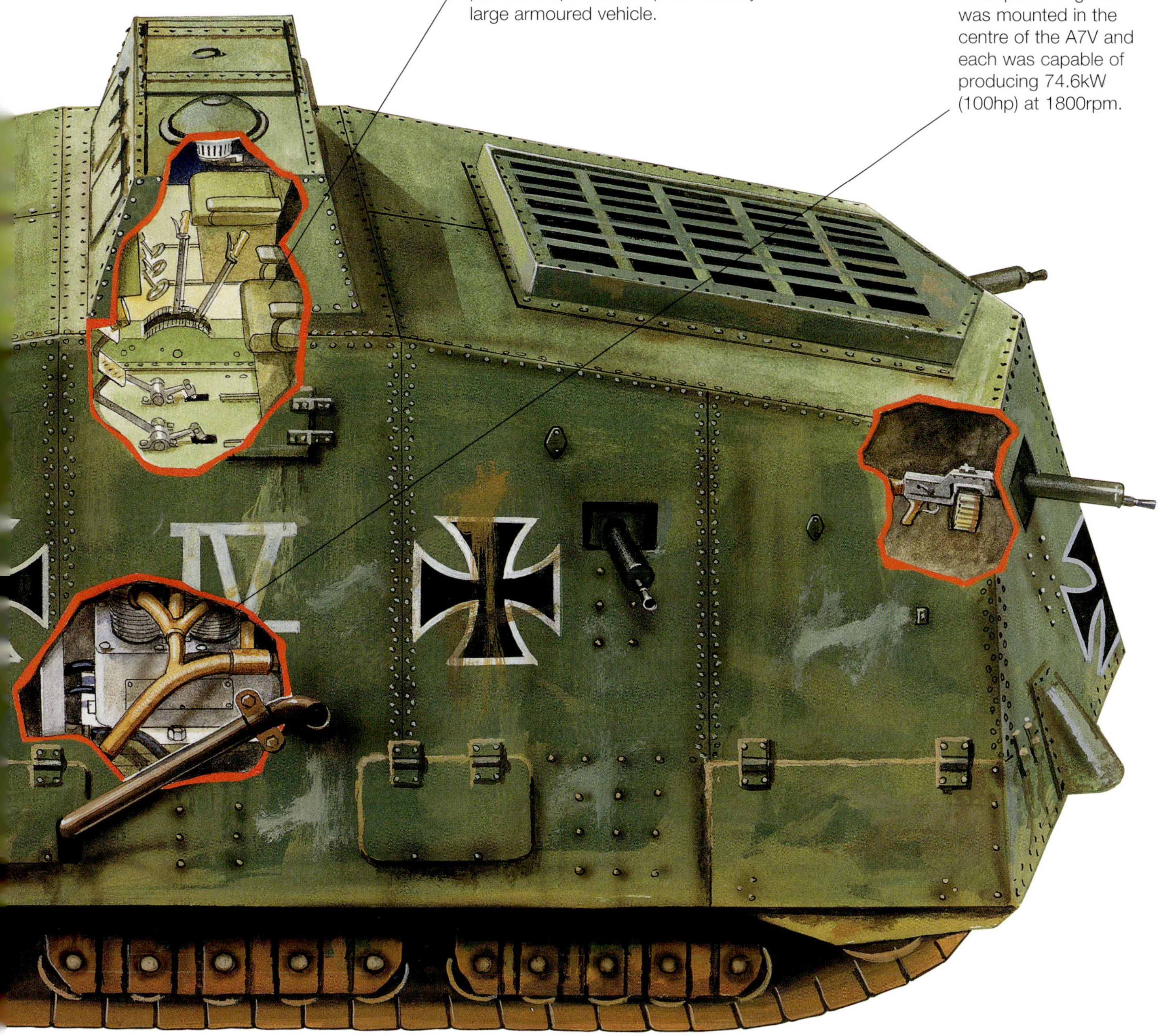

(35.8-ton) behemoth, a steel box on a tractor chassis. Designed to perform best on level ground, the A7V was handicapped on the cratered terrain of the Western Front from the beginning. The commander and two drivers were housed in a raised compartment centred on the vehicle and increasing its overall height to 3.5m (11ft 6in). Its ground clearance was a scant 40mm (1.5in), rendering the traverse of trenches, slight depressions in the terrain or even a small hill exceedingly difficult. The A7V was steered with a wheel and a system of levers. Two clutch pedals engaged the transmission gears.

Although the multiple machine guns and single heavy gun mounted aboard the German A7V tank were deadly to enemy infantry, the vehicle was an unstable platform for accurate gunnery and its high silhouette attracted hostile artillery fire.

Specification

Dimensions	Length: 8m (26ft 3in) Width: 3.2m (10ft 6in) Overall height: 3.5m (11ft 6in)
Weight	32.5 tonnes (31.9 tons)
Engine	2 x Daimler-Benz 4-cylinder inline 165204 petrol engines each developing 74.6kW (100hp) @ 1800rpm
Speed	8km/h (5mph)
Armament	Main: 1 x 57mm (2.24in) L/12 Maxim-Nordenfelt short recoil gun with 500 rounds Secondary: 6 x 7.92mm (0.31in) MG08/15 machine guns in flexible mounts with 18,000 rounds
Armour	20–30mm (0.78–1.1in)
Range	Road: 80km (50 miles) Cross-country: 30km (18 miles)
Crew	18

Thick armour of 20–30mm (0.78–1.1in) offered greater protection for the crew than that of British tanks; however, the A7V was ponderously slow and its high silhouette made the vehicle an obvious target for enemy artillery. Capable of providing significant firepower under favourable conditions, the tank mounted a single forward-firing 57mm (2.24in) Maxim-Nordenfelt gun with limited traverse and six or more Deutsche Waffen und Munitionsfabriken MG08/15 7.92mm (0.31in) machine guns. The cramped interior included space for 18 crewmen – the commander, drivers, machine-gunners, a gunner and loader for the cannon and ammunition suppliers.

Conceived as a multi-purpose vehicle, the A7V was also developed in four variants. The Überlandwagen was an unarmoured supply vehicle with an open top, while the A7V/U involved a proposed design with all-around tracks and a pair of 57mm guns, the A7V/U2 was a variant with smaller tracks and the A7V/U3 was a

"Female" version armed only with machine guns. Only the Überlandwagen and the A7V/U were actually built – 75 of the Überlandwagen were completed; the A7V/U only reached the prototype stage.

Only 20 of the A7V are known to have been deployed prior to the end of World War I. Coupled with its operational shortcomings, its feeble numbers made the tank an inadequate response to British production that reached more than 7700. Although several improved German tank designs were in development by late 1918, none were fielded before the Armistice.

Tank versus Tank

The first documented combat between opposing tanks occurred during a German effort to capture the French village of Villers-Bretonneux in the north of the country on 24 April 1918, as the Germans moved forward with infantry and 15 of the A7V tanks, pressing toward the Belgian city of Amiens. Three of the German tanks met three British Mark IV tanks under the command of Lieutenant Frank Mitchell. The lead British tank was a Male, mounting a 6pdr gun, while the other two were Female, armed with machine guns. Early in the fighting, the two Female Mark IVs were damaged and withdrew from the battle.

Mitchell continued his advance and took on the lead German tank, named Nixe, under the command of Second Lieutenant Wilhelm Biltz, who survived the war and went on to become a noted chemist and author. Nixe was damaged by three British hits and heeled over. Five German crewmen were killed as they exited the disabled tank. In turn, Mitchell's Mark IV was heavily damaged by a near miss from a German mortar round and abandoned. Both damaged tanks were subsequently recovered.

German A7V Tank in Action

Smoke and dust billow around this German A7V tank engaged near an abandoned farmhouse somewhere in France during the final major German offensive of World War I. The A7V was hurriedly designed and produced and only 20 were actually to become operational from the spring of 1918 to the Armistice in November of that year.

During the first recorded combat between opposing armoured forces at the French town of Villers-Bretonneux on 24 April 1918, one A7V was damaged along with one British Mark IV tank. Two other A7Vs withdrew under fire and four smaller British Whippet tanks were disabled.

The lone surviving example of a German Sturmpanzerwagen A7V, No 506, named Mephisto, is currently on display at the Queensland Museum in Brisbane, Australia. Mephisto is believed to be one of those German tanks that engaged the British armour at Villers-Bretonneux.

BT-5 (1932)

An upgunned transitional variant of the Soviet BT series of light or cavalry tanks, the BT-5 entered production in late 1932. It proved superior to the contemporary tanks of other world powers through to the end of the decade.

When examining the silhouette of the Soviet BT-5 light tank, the resemblance to the legendary T-34 medium tank of World War II and Cold War fame is unmistakable. In fact, the BT, or Bystrokhodny tank, was the forerunner of the T-34, one of the greatest tanks of all time. With its full name literally translating as "high-speed tank," the BT series lived up to expectations during a decade of production from 1930 to 1941.

Walter Christie

Ironically, the origin of the BT and the T-34 lay with the persistence of an American racing enthusiast and mechanic named Walter Christie. After the U.S. Army Ordnance Bureau declined more than once to produce Christie's prototype design, the Soviets managed to purchase blueprints and at least two turretless examples were then shipped to the Soviet Union as "agricultural tractors."

The Soviets enthusiastically produced working prototypes of Christie's tanks with various changes, designating them BT-1 through BT-4. A production version of the BT-2 began rolling off assembly lines at the Kharkov Komintern Locomotive Plant in the Ukraine early in 1932 and more than 600 were eventually built. The BT-2 featured a 37mm (1.45in) Model 30 main gun and a Model M5 petrol engine providing 298 kilowatts (400hp). Secondary armament consisted of a single 7.62mm (0.3in) DT machine gun. The overall weight of the BT-2 was 10.2 tonnes (10 tons) and armour protection ranged from 6–13mm (0.24–0.51in).

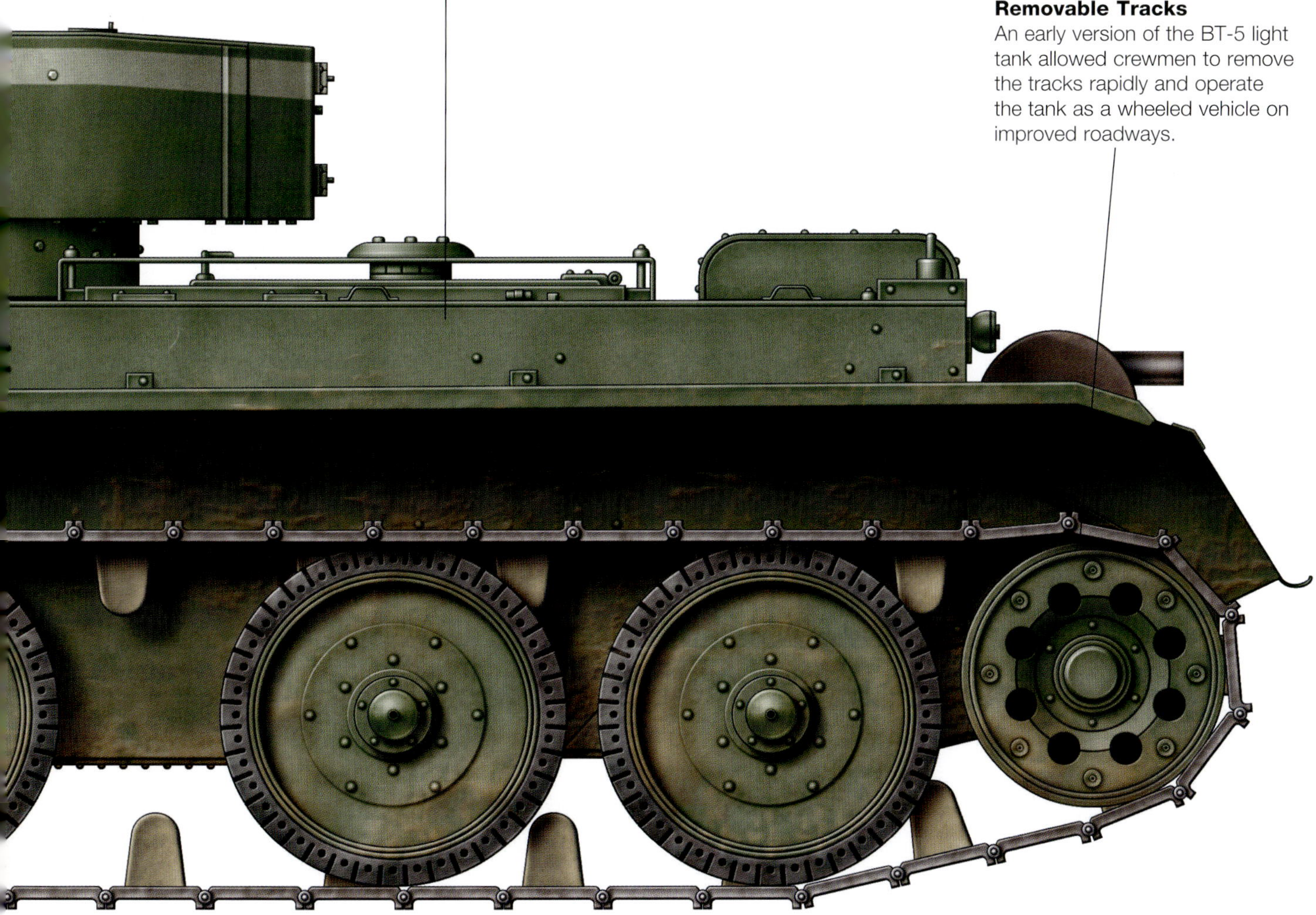

A variant of the original light tank design, the BT-7A mounted a 76.2mm (3in) howitzer. Only a relative few of these were adapted for field service. Note the coaxial machine gun atop the turret, which includes a prominent bustle.

The BT-2 was the first operational tank to truly demonstrate the genius of Walter Christie, and the foremost element of his design prowess was an innovative suspension system that included road wheels enclosed by rubber rings and mounted on long coil springs. The rubberized wheels absorbed some of the shock of cross-country movement and allowed the tanks to reach greater speeds. On improved roads, the Christie suspension could also operate the tank, with its tracks removed, as a wheeled vehicle. This innovation proved impractical in a vast, rural country such as the Soviet Union and was later abandoned.

Specification

Dimensions	Length: 5.58m (18ft 4in) Width: 2.23m (7ft 4in) Height: 2.25m (7ft 5in)
Weight	11.5 tonnes (11.3 tons)
Engine	1 x Model M5 12-cylinder petrol powerplant based on the American Liberty aircraft engine delivering 298kW (400hp)
Speed	72km/h (45mph)
Armament	Main: 1 x 45mm (1.8in) Model 32 gun Secondary: 1 x 7.62mm (0.3in) DT machine gun
Armour	6–13mm (0.24–0.51in)
Range	Road: 200km (120 miles) Cross-country: 90km (56 miles)
Crew	3

Enter the BT-5

Before 1932 was over, the Red Army sought improvements to the BT-2. The resulting BT-5 incorporated a larger cylindrically-shaped turret mounting a more powerful 45mm (1.8in) Model 32 main gun. The 7.62mm (0.3in) DT machine gun was mounted coaxially for better traverse. Communications were substantially improved with the installation of radio equipment. The larger turret provided more freedom of movement for the crew of three and greater ammunition capacity with 115 rounds of 45mm ammunition compared to the 96 rounds of 37mm carried by the BT-2. The BT-5 was slightly heavier at 11.5 tonnes (11.3 tons), although armour protection was unchanged.

The 12-cylinder M5 powerplant was based on the American Liberty aircraft engine and adapted for use with armour. It allowed the light tank to travel at speeds of up to 72km/h (45mph) on the road. Although impressive in

BT-5 tanks parade along a dirt track somewhere in the Soviet Union during the 1930s. The BT-5 and other tanks of the BT Series were the forerunners of the famed T-34 medium tank of World War II. The design resemblance is readily apparent.

its own right, this was considerably slower than the BT-2, which reached road speeds of up to 100km/h (62mph). The operational range of the BT-5 was 200km (120 miles), one-third less that of the BT-2. However, the better overall design and heavier main weapon of the BT-5 more than compensated for those decreases in some performance categories.

The BT-5 remained in production up to 1934 and was then supplanted by the BT-7. Several variants of the BT-5 were constructed, including the Model 1933 with twin turret hatches and a larger bustle, the prototype BT-5 flamethrower tank, the BT-5A self-propelled 76.2mm (3in) gun and the BT-5PKh with a snorkel added to assist in fording waterways. In total, 1884 BT-5 light tanks were reported to have been built.

The BT Tanks at Nomonhan

Although the BT-5 and BT-7 tanks deployed by the Red Army from May to September 1939 during clashes with the Japanese at Nomonhan possessed exceptional speed, the trade-off in light armour protection made them vulnerable. The Japanese destroyed a number of Soviet tanks with anti-tank guns and tank-killer squads that crept close and set the hot exhaust apparatus of the Soviet tanks afire with Molotov cocktails or explosives. Nevertheless, the Japanese developed a healthy respect for the 45mm (1.8in) guns of the BT tanks. These were capable of penetrating the armour of any Japanese tank then in service. Further, the classic double envelopment executed by Marshal Georgi Zhukov, sending the tanks on rapid flanking manoeuvres, sealed the Soviet victory at Nomonhan.

Tested in Combat

The most notable combat service of the BT-5 occurred during the series of clashes with the Japanese at Nomonhan, or Khalkhin Gol as it was known in Russia, in 1939. The superior tactics of Soviet Marshal Georgi Zhukov and the performance of the BT-5 and BT-7 tanks contributed to a decisive Soviet victory.

During the Spanish Civil War of 1936–39, a battalion of BT-5s fought with Republican forces and fared well against the German and Italian tanks deployed by the Nationalists. The Chinese Nationalist Army fielded four BT-5s against the Japanese during the Second Sino-Japanese War and the Soviets used the BT-5 during the Winter War with Finland.

With the outbreak of World War II, the BT-5 deployed during the Soviet offensive against Poland and in defence of the Motherland against the invading Nazis. Some BT-5s remained in service through to the end of the war.

Type 95 Kyugo Light Tank (1934)

When the Japanese Army called for a light or cavalry tank to support its infantry operations, the resulting Type 95 performed capably until confronted with the superior firepower and armour protection of Soviet, American and British tanks.

The Japanese Kwantung Army had been at war in China for three years by the time a prototype infantry or cavalry tank had been produced to support its operations on the Asian continent. Actively engaged against the Chinese Army and wary of the continuing threat from the Soviet Union, Japanese commanders nevertheless were compelled to wait until field tests and authorization were completed for the first production Type 95 light tank to roll off the assembly lines in 1936.

Turret
Characteristic of Japanese tank designs of the 1930s, the Type 95 turret was irregularly shaped and quite cramped, requiring the commander to direct the crew in combat and operate the main 37mm (1.45in) gun.

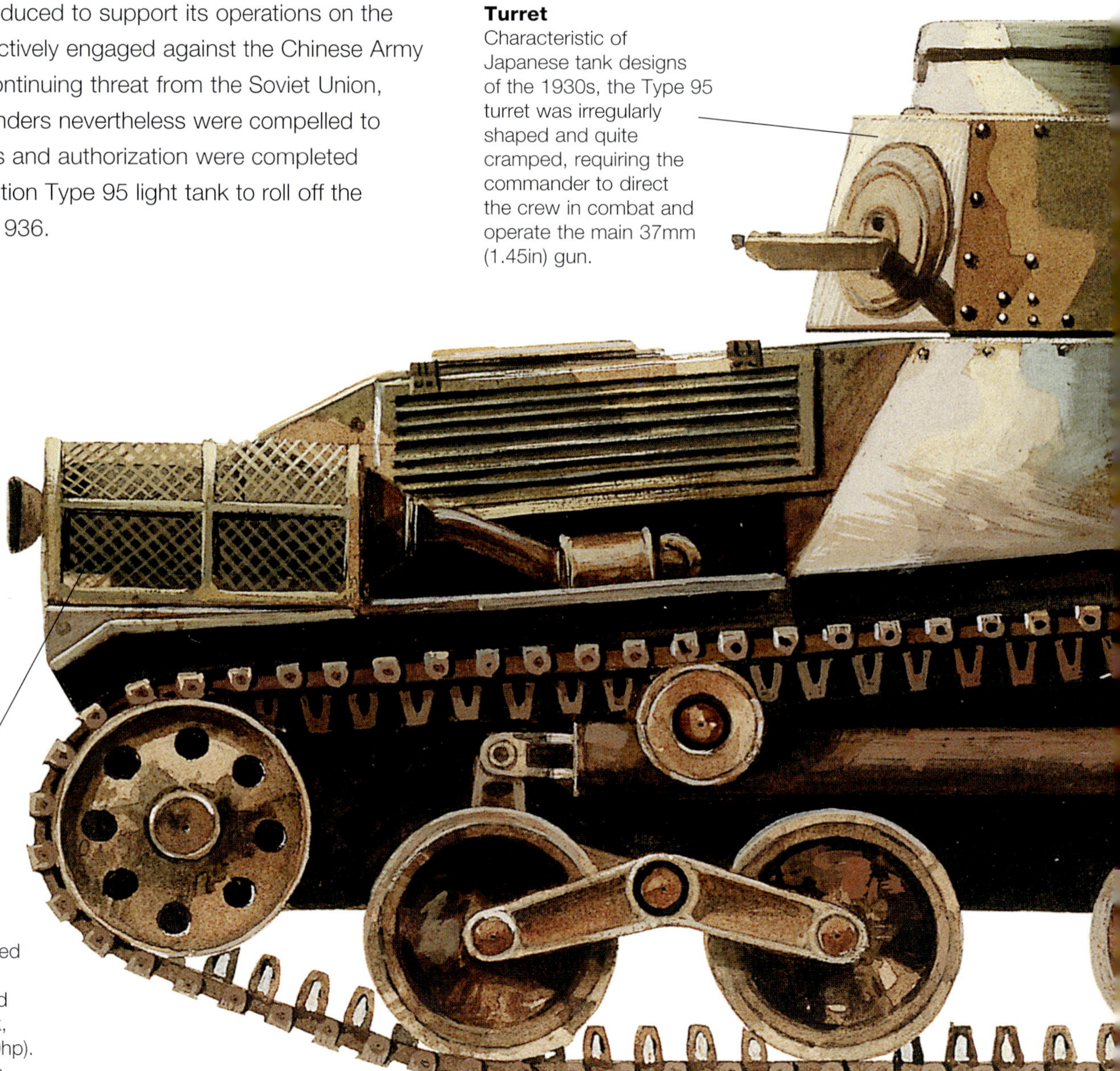

Engine
A six-cylinder air-cooled Mitsubishi NVD 6120 diesel engine powered the Type 95 light tank, producing 89kW (120hp). It was mounted at the rear of the hull.

Identified popularly as the Ha-Go, Ke-Go or Kyugo, the Type 95 was initially produced by Mitsubishi Heavy Industries. Subsequently, Hitachi Industries, the Kokura Arsenal, Kobe Seikosho and the Sagami Arsenal each produced the tank in quantity. Although there is some dispute as to the length of the Type 95 production run, either until 1943 or the actual end of World War II, up to 2300 are believed to have been completed. The standard Type 95 served throughout the war either as a mobile armoured complement to infantry operations or in a fixed pillbox-type defensive role, dug in with only the turret and main 37mm (1.45in) gun exposed.

This forward view of the Japanese Type 95 light tank shows the small size of the turret and its offset to the left, as well as the driver's view port to the lower right in the hull.

Main Armament
The Type 95 light tank initially mounted the Type 94 37mm (1.45in) gun; however, its disappointing penetrating power resulted in a transition to the Type 98 37mm gun, which supplied greater muzzle velocity.

Armour
The thin armour of the Type 95, only 6–14mm (0.24–0.55in) thick, offered little protection against the standard main weapons of opposing tanks. This weakness was discovered in battle against Soviet tanks in Manchuria and remained throughout World War II.

Suspension
The Type 95 employed a bell crank suspension with four rubber-edged road wheels on each side. The drive sprocket was at the front and the idler at the rear with two return rollers.

The high silhouette of the Type 95 tank was especially pronounced from the rear, adding to the tank's vulnerability in combat. Both the heavier weapons of enemy tanks and high-velocity anti-tank guns deployed by opposing armies took their toll on the Type 95.

Sceptical Commanders

Even as the tank entered production, some senior Japanese infantry commanders questioned the Type 95's lack of armour protection and firepower. While its armour ranged only from 6–14mm (0.24–0.55in) and its main weapon was the Type 94 37mm (1.45in) gun, cavalry officers asserted that both were adequate and won the day. Shortly after the Type 95 entered production, the main gun was upgraded to the Type 98 37mm gun with a higher muzzle velocity.

Capable of a top road speed of 45km/h (28mph), the Kyugo was of riveted construction, mounting a cramped turret from which the commander was required to load, aim and fire the main gun in addition to his other responsibilities. The turret was slightly offset to the left, and along with the main gun a 7.7mm (0.303in) Type 97 machine gun was positioned in the turret facing rearward at the tank's 5 o'clock. While the configuration was intended to allow the tank a wider field of fire, particularly against enemy infantry, it was a disappointment in practice.

The Type 95 hull positioned the driver forward to the right, while a machine-gunner was seated to the left and fired a second Type 97 gun. Along with 2970 rounds of machine-gun ammunition, the tank carried 119 high explosive and armour piercing rounds for the main gun.

Specification

Dimensions	Length: 4.38m (14ft 4in) Width: 2.06m (6ft 9in) Height: 2.18m (7ft 2in)
Weight	7.4 tonnes (7.2 tons)
Engine	1 x six-cylinder air-cooled Mitsubishi NVD 6120 diesel powerplant generating 89kW (120hp)
Speed	Road: 45km/h (28mph)
Armament	Main: 1 x 37mm (1.45in) Type 98 gun Secondary: 2 x 7.7mm (0.303in) Type 97 machine guns
Armour	6–14mm (0.24–0.55in)
Range	250km (156 miles)
Crew	3

Rough Ride

The Type 95 powerplant consisted of a rear mounted six-cylinder air-cooled Mitsubishi NVD 6120 diesel engine developing 89 kilowatts (120hp). The manual transmission utilized one reverse and four forward gears. The crew of three was often shaken considerably while traveling cross-country in rural China and an interior lining of asbestos was added to somewhat cushion the rough ride while also providing some relief from the extreme heat that developed inside the hull in tropical weather.

Limited Variation

The most significant variant of the Type 95 light tank was the Type 2 Ka-Mi amphibious tank, which was utilized by the Imperial Japanese Navy's Special Naval Landing Force both in offensive and defensive roles. The Type 2 required a fourth crewman to detach pontoons after the tank made landfall. An experiment with a 57mm (2.24in) main gun, the Ke-Ri, was quickly abandoned, while approximately 100 Ke-Nu tanks that

Japanese crewmen service a Type 95 light tank during a lull in the fighting somewhere in China. Introduced in 1936, the Type 95 was intended as an infantry support weapon and ultimately failed in confrontations with enemy tanks.

Pacific Peril for the Type 95

Although the Type 95 light tank participated in the victorious Japanese drive down the Malayan Peninsula and the capture of the British bastion at Singapore, tank versus tank encounters in Asia and the Pacific were rare. When they did occur, the Type 95 was often the loser.

The first contact between American M3 Stuart light tanks and the Type 95 occurred in the Philippines on 22 December 1941 and the skirmish was inconclusive. However, it was rapidly determined that the Stuart was more heavily armoured than the Type 95 and the advantage was later exploited.

Elsewhere in the Pacific, seven Type 95s were dug-in near the beaches of Tarawa to resist the U.S. Marine landings there in November 1943. In one short battle there, an American M4 Sherman tank took on a Type 95. The Japanese tank's 37mm (1.45in) shell turned the interior of the Sherman hull lemon yellow where it struck. No penetration occurred. The Japanese tank was dispatched by the American tank's 75mm (2.95in) cannon. The Type 95 fell victim to Stuart and Sherman tanks, as well as 37mm (1.45in) anti-tank guns and bazookas regularly on Saipan, Tinian, Guam, Peleliu and Okinawa.

paired the turret of the Type 97 tank with a 57mm gun were produced. A tank destroyer, the Ho-Ru, reached only the prototype stage while the Ho-To, an assault gun mounting a 120mm (4.7in) howitzer, never left the drawing board.

Disappointing Days

When the Kwantung Army clashed with the Soviets in Manchuria in 1939, the Type 95 achieved limited success; however, it was soon discovered that the heavier 45mm (1.8in) main guns of the Red Army's BT-5 and BT-7 tanks were capable of destroying Japanese armour at a standoff range. In contrast, the Type 95's 37mm (1.45in) gun could penetrate the Soviet armour but required closer combat.

Frankly, the Type 95 was functionally obsolescent with the outbreak of World War II. Improved Soviet tanks, the American M3 Stuart light tank and M4 Sherman medium tank and the British Matilda each easily outclassed the Type 95.

T-35 (1935)

The Soviet T-35 was the only tank with five turrets that reached deployment with the armed forces of any country. Its operational issues were numerous and the majority of the T-35's service life consisted of parade duties in Moscow.

The T-35 heavy tank proved to be a major inter-war disappointment for the Soviet OKMO Bureau. Influenced by the earlier triple-turreted T-28 medium tank, which was in turn influenced by the Vickers Independent multi-turret tank that never proceeded beyond a prototype stage, the T-35 was the only five-turreted tank that ever entered production.

The design of the T-35 dates to 1930 and the first prototype was introduced two years later. It is also possible

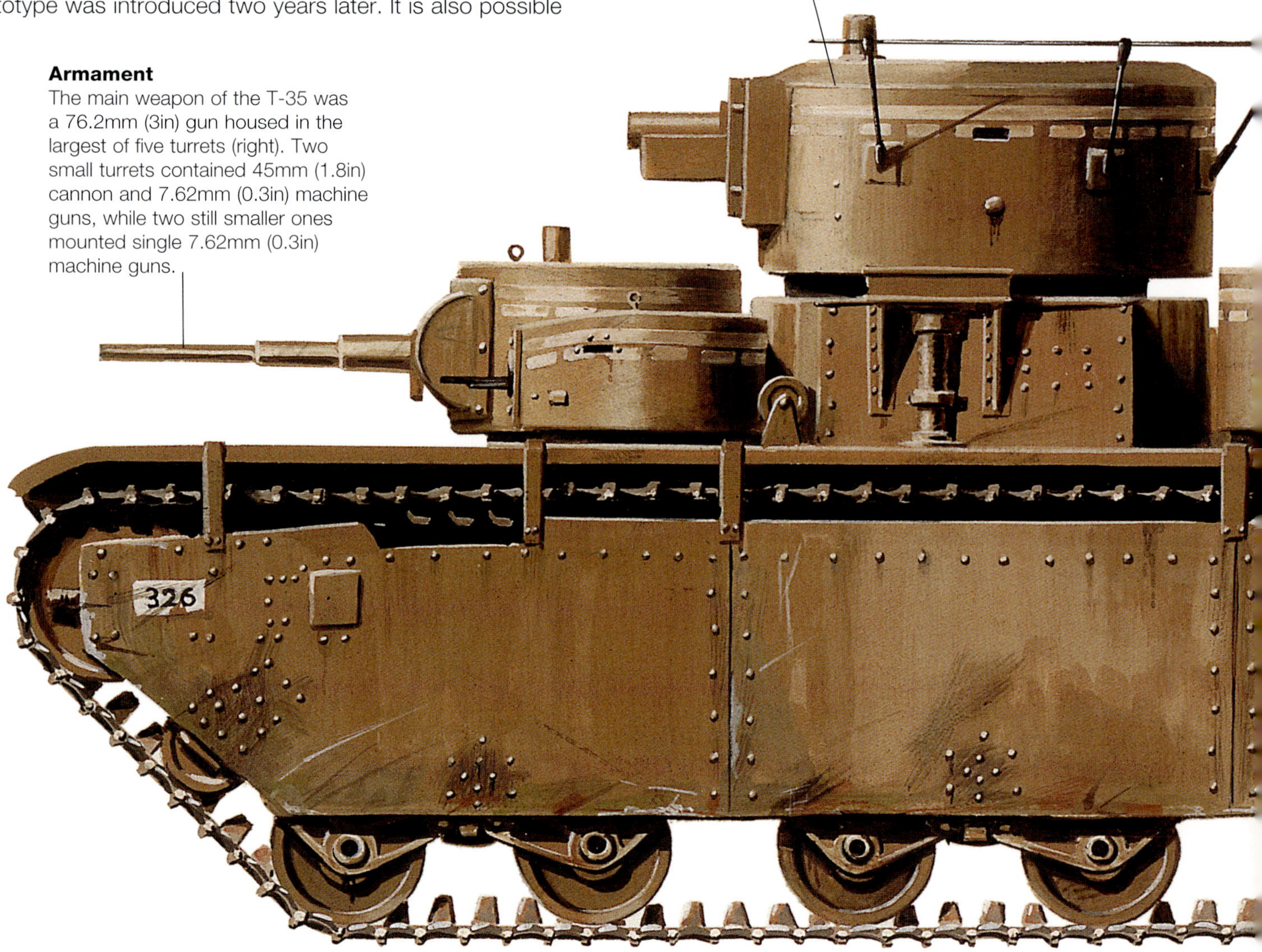

Main Turret
The main turret of the T-35 heavy tank was identical to that of the T-28 medium tank, as was the 76.2mm (3in) main gun. Later production models included a main turret with armour protection increased to 25mm (0.98in).

Armament
The main weapon of the T-35 was a 76.2mm (3in) gun housed in the largest of five turrets (right). Two small turrets contained 45mm (1.8in) cannon and 7.62mm (0.3in) machine guns, while two still smaller ones mounted single 7.62mm (0.3in) machine guns.

that German designers were involved in its conception during the late 1920s as they covertly developed tanks for the German Army between the world wars. Most of the 61 T-35s that were actually manufactured rolled off assembly lines from 1933 to 1938 and were longer than earlier models. Coupled with a considerable weight of 45 tonnes (44.2 tons), the additional length contributed to the already difficult task of steering.

Array of Armament

The main gun and turret, which initially housed a 76.2mm (3in) KT obr.1927/32 gun and later the improved KT-28

An overhead view of the Soviet T-35 heavy tank indicates a crowded configuration of five turrets. Although the T-35 presented a formidable façade, in truth the tank was lightly armed.

Armour
Armour protection for the T-35 heavy tank generally varied from 11–30mm (0.43–1.2in) and changed at times during production. Typically, the thickest armour was to the vehicle's front. Side skirts of 10mm (0.39in) plating were added to protect the tracks, wheels and coil spring suspension from anti-tank fire.

Engine
The mammoth T-35 heavy tank was powered by a 12-cylinder petrol Mikulin M-17M engine generating 370kW (500hp). Critics assert that the tank was underpowered for its prodigious 45-tonne (49.6-ton) weight.

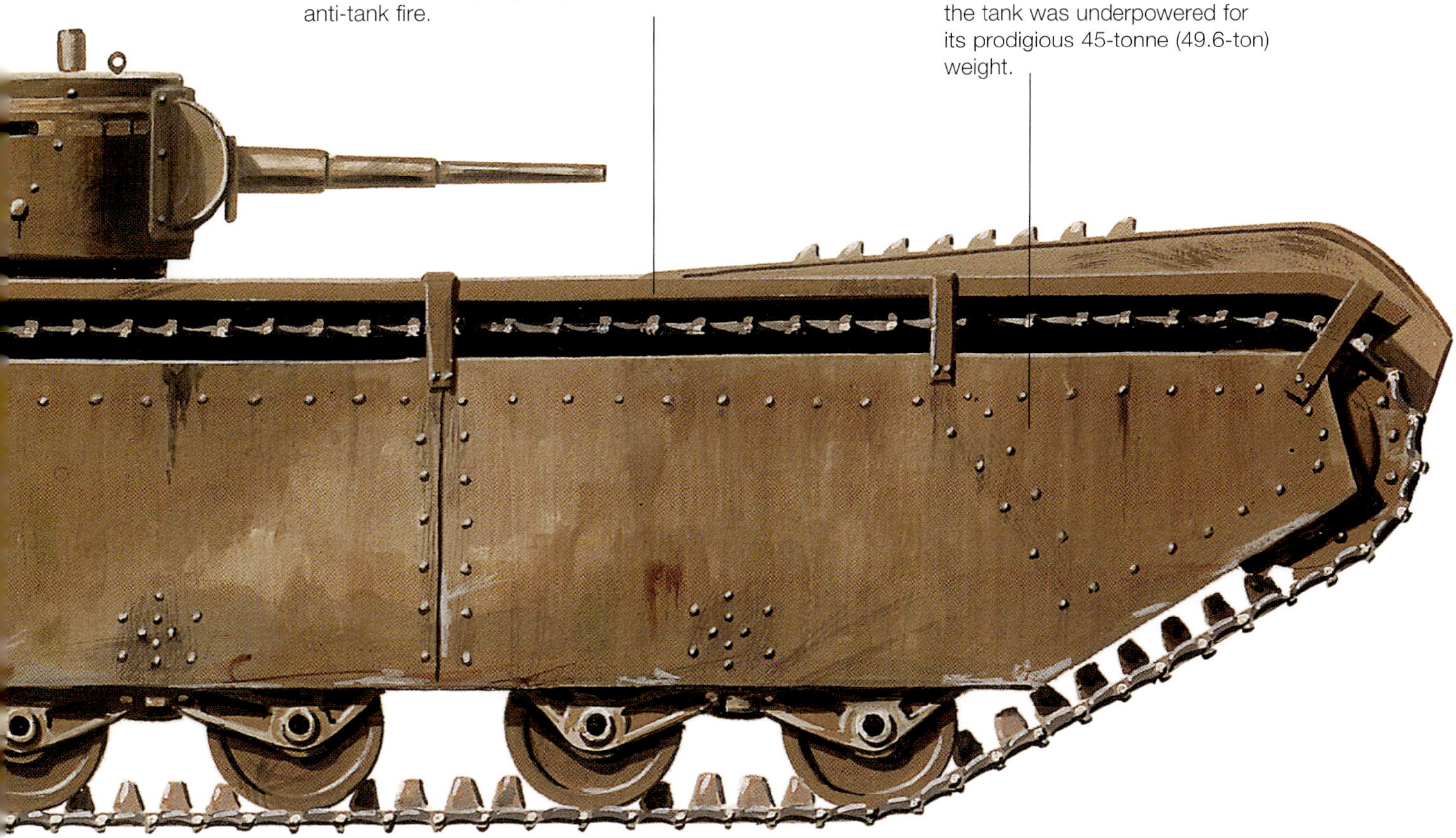

The T-35's main forward-firing 76.2mm (3in) gun was insufficient for tank-versus-tank combat.

cannon, were identical to those mounted on the T-28. Secondary weapons, mounted in two-seat diagonally situated turrets at the left rear and right forward quarters of the chassis, included 37mm (1.45in) guns in early prototypes that were replaced with 45mm (1.8in) weapons in later variants, along with a coaxial 7.62mm (0.3in) machine gun. A pair of small turrets each mounted a single 7.62mm (0.3in) machine gun.

Specification

Dimensions	Length: 9.72m (31ft 10in) Width: 3.2m (10ft 6in) Height: 3.43m (11ft 3in)
Weight	45 tonnes (42.2 tons)
Engine	1 x 12-cylinder petrol Mikulin M-17M delivering 370kW (500hp)
Speed	30km/h (18.64mph)
Armament	Main: 1 x 76.2mm (3in) KT-28 gun Secondary: 2 x 45mm (1.8in) 20K guns; 5 or 6 x 7.62mm (0.3in) DT machine guns
Armour	11–30mm (0.43–1.2in)
Range	150km (93.21 miles)
Crew	11 or 12

Confined Crew Compartments

Despite the formidable size of the T-35, its interior was quite cramped. The crew of either 11 or 12 were crammed into tight quarters, restricting efficiency during combat conditions, although at least one or two members were not actually stationed inside the vehicle. The tank commander was positioned in the main turret to the right of the gun, while the assistant commander was responsible for firing the 45mm gun in the forward No 2 turret and for the operational condition of the tank. A junior tank technician was responsible for driving the vehicle and was stationed forward in the driving compartment. Another crewman, actually referred to as the driver, fired the 7.62mm machine gun in the forward facing No 3 turret and assisted the junior tank technician with driving the T-35.

The commander of the main turret sat to the left of the 76.2mm gun and was responsible for firing the weapon, while the commander of the No 2 turret sat to the right of the 45mm gun and served as its loader. The commander of the rear-facing No 4 turret fired the second 45mm gun and sat to its left. A junior tank driver was positioned in No 4 turret and served as its loader. The commander of No 5 turret fired the rear facing 7.62mm machine gun. A senior radio operator sat in the main turret and also assisted with loading the 76.2mm gun. Outside the tank, a senior driver was responsible for the transmission and running gear, while at times a motor mechanic took care of the engine.

Protection and Production

Armour protection varied from 11–30mm (0.43–1.2in), increasing in 1936 to 50mm (1.97in) of frontal plating for the protection of personnel located forward in the hull. Construction was both welded and riveted and in 1938 a conical turret with 25mm (0.98in) frontal armour was introduced. Some vehicles were fitted with 10mm (0.39in) armoured side skirts for additional protection from anti-tank weapons.

Production was authorized on August 11, 1933, and minor improvements were made to the T-35 throughout

At 45 tonnes (42.2 tons), the mammoth Soviet T-35 heavy tank was difficult to steer, while its five turrets and lengthy chassis presented inviting targets for enemy gunners.

its five years of production, which proved to be slow and costly. The limited run of 61 tanks was extremely small compared to other Soviet armoured vehicles that were produced in significant numbers. Variants included the T-35B, a prototype with a different engine, and the SU-7, a prototype with various heavy weapons of at least 254mm (9.2in).

Poor Service Record

Ultimately, the T-35 heavy tank was deemed incapable of standing up to the German panzers that crossed the Russian frontier on 22 June 1941. Perhaps the Red Army high command had come to this realization prior to the outbreak of what came to be known as the Great Patriotic War. No record of deployment during the Winter War of 1939–40 with Finland exists and the evidence of involvement in World War II is scant.

The service record of the T-35 indicates that all models were initially assigned to the 5th Separate Heavy Tank Battalion in the vicinity of Moscow and from 1935 to 1940 the primary function of the unit was to roll through Red Square during parades. Some historians suggest that in the summer of 1940 the T-35s were reassigned to the 67th and 68th Tank Regiments of the 34th Tank Division with little expectation of success in combat.

Limited Deployment

Contrary to some reports, the T-35 was never confirmed to have been deployed with Red Army troops during the 1939–40 Winter War with Finland. In fact, the T-35 was initially issued only to the 5th Separate Heavy Tank Brigade near Moscow and was primarily employed in parades through Red Square, providing spectators, including foreign observers, with a false impression of overall Soviet tank strength.

Although photographic evidence reveals that at least one T-35 was captured by German forces during Operation Barbarossa in 1941, the tank's actual combat record is sketchy at best. Those T-35s that did face the German Army in combat were hampered by relatively light armament and limited mobility due to the design's extreme overall weight. Many were apparently lost to mechanical failure.

Panzer II Ausf F (1936)

Originally intended to bridge a gap in German tank design as heavier, more powerful machines were developed, the Panzerkampfwagen II became a mainstay of the German armoured force during campaigns in Poland and France.

The development of the Panzerkampfwagen II dates to 1934 and the covert modernization of the German armed forces, crippled on paper by the Treaty of Versailles. In that year, the government awarded a production contract for the PzKpfw II to Maschinenfabrik Augsburg-Nürnberg under the apparently nonthreatening label of "Industrial Tractor 100."

Main Armament
The main armament of the PzKpfw II was a light 20mm (0.79in) cannon. Experiments with heavier weapons were abandoned and the tank performed more in a reconnaissance role as World War II progressed.

Initially intended for training purposes, the PzKpfw II actually became the most numerous tank among the German panzer divisions, with more than 1000 in active service by the time of the May 10-June 22, 1940, offensive in France. Even as it was becoming obsolete with the arrival of the new PzKpfw III and PzKpfw IV, the PzKpfw II played a prominent role in the early German victories in Poland and during Operation Barbarossa on the Eastern Front as well.

Armour and Firepower

The first production model PzKpfw II, Ausf A, was introduced in 1935 mounting a 20mm (0.79in) KwK 30 cannon, which was also used by Luftwaffe aircraft in a

This frontal view of the PzKpfw II reveals the degree of the two-man turret's offset atop the chassis. The placement of the engine to the rear of the chassis afforded even distribution of weight throughout the tank.

Armour Protection
The armour protection of the PzKpfw II was initially 11–30mm (0.43–1.2in) thick; however, combat experience in the Spanish Civil War and the heavy guns of Allied tanks prompted progressive increases in armour as later variants were developed.

Engine
The original powerplant of the PzKpfw II was a 97kW (130hp) petrol engine. When this was deemed inadequate it was replaced by a six-cylinder Maybach petrol engine generating 104kW (140hp).

Suspension
The D and E variants of the PzKpfw II utilized a torsion bar suspension. However, the Ausf F, the final production model of the series, was reconfigured with a leaf spring suspension.

The rear view of the PzKpfw II shows the relatively high ground clearance that assisted with cross-country mobility. The Ausf F was fitted with a redesigned commander's cupola.

ground-attack role. The secondary armament was a single 7.92mm (0.31in) MG 34 machine gun mounted coaxially with the main weapon. The tank carried 180 rounds of 20mm ammunition and 1425 rounds for the machine gun.

Specification

Dimensions	Length: 4.64m (15ft 3in) Width: 2.30m (7ft 6.5in) Height: 2.02m (6ft 7.5in)
Weight	9.5 tonnes (9.3 tons)
Engine	1 x Maybach six-cylinder petrol powerplant delivering 104kW (140hp)
Speed	55km/h (34mph)
Armament	Main: 1 x 20mm (0.79in) KWK 30 cannon Secondary: 1 x 7.92mm (0.31in) MG 34 machine gun
Armour	35mm (1.37in) front; 20mm (0.79in) side; 14.5mm (0.57in) rear; 5mm (0.19in) underside
Range	200km (125 miles)
Crew	3

Experiments with both 37mm (1.45in) and 50mm (1.97in) main guns were abandoned as heavier tank designs rendered such increased firepower unnecessary. Initial testing and combat experience during the Spanish Civil War revealed that thicker armour and a more powerful engine were required for optimal performance.

Early armour protection consisted of 14mm (0.55in) steel plating to the front, rear and sides, and 10mm (0.39in) on the top and underside of the hull. With the Ausf B, frontal armour was slightly increased and the overall weight of the PzKpfw II was pushed to 8 tonnes (7.8 tons) with the addition of the Maybach six-cylinder petrol engine providing 104 kilowatts (140hp), replacing an earlier 97 kilowatt (130hp) powerplant.

A succession of variants introduced thicker armour protection and improved suspension for better cross-country performance, while the road speed of the Ausf D and Ausf E models, both deployed in 1938, reached 55km/h (34mph). The Ausf F, which made its battlefield debut in 1940, brought increased frontal armour protection of 35mm (1.4in) and side protection of 20mm (0.79in). The trade-off resulted in an increased weight to 10 tonnes (9.8 tons) and, therefore, a slower speed. However, with the significant presence of more powerful Allied tanks, it was considered necessary to increase the protection of the three-man crew of the PzKpfw II as its role evolved to more reconnaissance and command missions. The Ausf F also reintroduced a leaf spring suspension rather than the torsion bar suspension of the D and E variants.

The tank's turret was centred atop the chassis and offset slightly to the left while the driver sat forward in the hull and viewed the battlefield through small rectangular slits. The tank commander and gunner occupied the turret.

Continuing Versatility

As the PzKpfw II entered combat both east and west, its speed and light armour made the chassis an ideal platform for numerous other vehicles, including the Marder I and II self-propelled anti-tank guns and the Wespe self-propelled gun, which mounted a 105mm (4.1in) howitzer and was produced into 1944.

Another interesting variant of the PzKpfw II was the Flammpanzer II, equipped with a pair of flamethrowers. At least 100 of these were produced and entered service by 1942. An amphibious model was developed for the anticipated invasion of Great Britain in 1940. It was powered by a propeller shaft attached to the main engine and capable of a water speed of 10km/h (6mph).

Combat Character

During the opening months of World War II, the PzKpfw II proved to be the ideal combination of speed and firepower to execute the rapid ground advance of the German Blitzkrieg. Although its main gun was lighter than those of opposing armoured forces, particularly the French Char B1-bis, Somua S-35 and Renault R35, which mounted 75mm (2.95in), 47mm (1.85in) and 37mm (1.45in) weapons respectively, the PzKpfw II was fast and quite manoeuvrable in a cross-country advance.

The real advantage of the Panzerkampfwagen II early in the war resided in its superior mobility, which meshed well with the coordinated air, artillery and armour tactics developed by General Heinz Guderian, considered by some to be the father of the Blitzkrieg. The PzKpfw II was produced from 1935 to 1943 and nearly 1900 entered service in total.

Early Panzer Successes

When German armoured spearheads sliced deep into Poland in the autumn of 1939 and again into France in the spring of 1940, the Panzerkampfwagen II was among the most numerous tanks in action on the battlefield. The PzKpfw II mounted a 20mm (0.79in) cannon, upgunned from earlier German armoured fighting vehicles that carried only machine guns. It was light and relatively manoeuvrable in open country, suiting it well for reconnaissance missions and the deep, rapid penetrations of the Blitzkrieg doctrine.

As heavier tanks with greater firepower were introduced in growing numbers, the PzKpfw II remained an important forward observation, scouting and close infantry support tank. It was produced from 1935 up to 1943 and the final production version, the Ausf F, was introduced in 1940. From March 1941 to December 1942, a total of 524 examples of the Ausf F were produced.

In the photo below, a formation of PzKpfw II tanks advances cautiously through an open field and into a treeline during the opening weeks of World War II.

Char B1 bis (1937)

Several major French factories, including Renault, produced the Char B1 bis heavy tank for the French Army. The Char B1 bis was the final production version of the Char B1, entering service in 1937 as one of the most powerful tanks in the world.

Armament
The Char B1 bis heavy tank fielded greater firepower than any other contemporary armoured vehicle in 1940. A turret-mounted 47mm (1.85in) gun was serviced by the tank commander, while a 75mm (2.95in) howitzer was located in the hull. Highly-responsive steering compensated for the heavy weapon's lack of traversing capability.

Communications
The four crewmen of the Char B1 bis were dispersed throughout the tank, with the commander occupying the small turret. Communications, particularly in combat, were difficult at best.

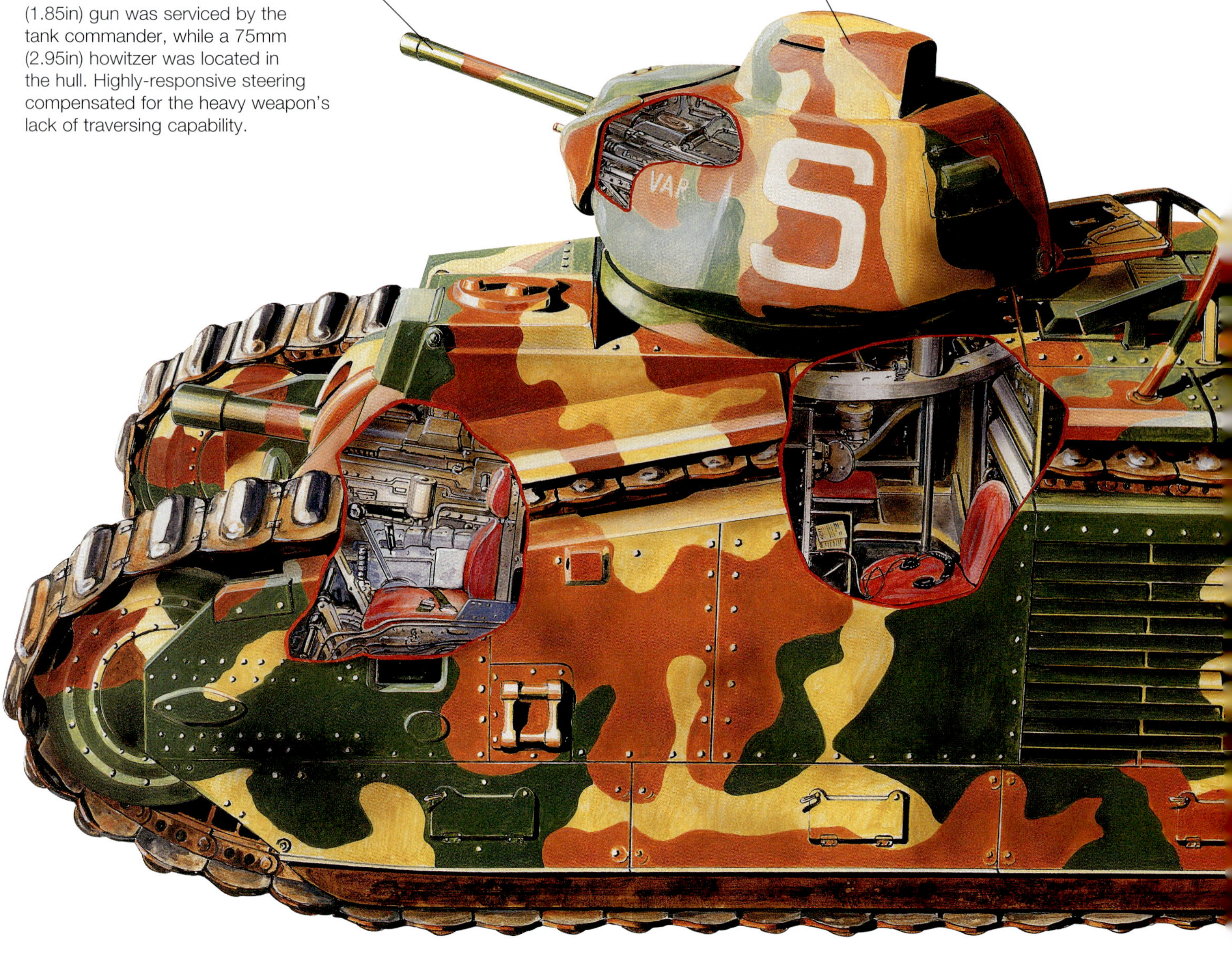

Despite the fact that the French economy had been ravaged by World War I and the devastation wrought by the Great War haunted the nation's military, relatively few officers of the French Army recognized the need for continuing modernization and mechanization of their forces. Soon after the war, General Jean-Baptiste Eugene Estienne began advocating the development of a French heavy tank.

By 1921, design work was underway; however, it would be 14 years before the resulting armoured vehicle, the Char B1, entered production. The final version of the Char B1, the Char B1 bis, was produced in limited numbers

The frontal view of the French Char B1 bis heavy tank presents a formidable array of firepower. The Char B1 bis was capable of destroying the best German armour in the field during the early months of World War II; however, it was not available in sufficient numbers.

Armour
French engineers combined welded and riveted construction along with some cast components in the Char B1 bis. Armour ranged from 14–60mm (0.55–2.36in) and was thickest toward the front of the hull.

Engine
The production powerplant of the Char B1 bis was a single six-cylinder inline Renault petrol engine, delivering superior performance to the engine installed in the earlier Char B1.

Air Intake
The air-cooled engine of the Char B1 bis required a substantial intake on the hull's flank. However, the 55mm (2.16in) side armour was considered adequate despite this potential weakness.

The track configuration of the Char B1 bis was reminiscent of World War I-vintage tanks; however, as this overhead view shows, the French heavy tank did incorporate innovations such as a rotating turret and 47mm (1.85in) gun with full traverse.

from 1937 to 1940, and when deployed properly on the battlefield it proved to be more than a match for the enemy tanks it confronted in the opening weeks of the German invasion in the spring of 1940.

Firepower and Fortitude

Although the influence of World War I-era tanks is unmistakable in the Char B1 design, the original French heavy tank and its successor, the Char B1 bis, did present several innovative technological advances. Among these were an electric starter and self-sealing fuel tanks. The heavy armament included a 47mm (1.85in) SA35 L/32 gun in a fully traversing turret, a formidable 75mm (2.95in) ABS SA35 L/17 howitzer fixed in azimuth in the front of the hull, a coaxially-mounted 7.5mm (0.3in) Chatellerault Mle. 31 machine gun and a second 7.5mm machine gun in a flexible mount. The tank carried 72 rounds of 47mm ammunition and 74 rounds for the 75mm howitzer. Armour protection from 14–60mm (0.55–2.36in) thick was provided by riveted and welded nickel-steel plating.

When the Char B1 bis entered production, its refinements to the original design included increased armour protection, an improved turret and a six-cylinder inline Renault petrol engine delivering 229 kilowatts (307hp). The production run was brief and on the eve of World War II only 400 Char B1 and Char Bi bis heavy tanks were in service. Production of the Char B1 bis was costly and from April 1937 to June 1940, only 369 of an original order for 1144 from the French Army had been delivered. When war broke out only 129 Char B1 bis tanks were in service.

Specification

Dimensions	Length: 6.63m (21ft 9in) Width: 2.52m (8ft 3in) Height: 2.84m (9ft 4in)
Weight	31.5 tonnes (31 tons)
Engine	1 x Renault six-cylinder inline petrol powerplant delivering 229kW (307hp)
Speed	Road: 28km/h (17.5mph) Cross-country: 21km/h (13mph)
Armament	Main: 1 x 75mm (2.95in) ABS SA35 L/17 fixed in azimuth in hull front Secondary: 1 x 47mm (1.85in) SA35 L/32 in fully traversing turret; 1 x coaxially mounted 7.5mm (0.3in) Chatellerault Mle. 31 MG; 1 x flexible mount 7.5mm (0.3in) Chatellerault Mle. 31 MG
Armour	14–60mm (0.55–2.36in)
Range	Road: 135km (85 miles) Cross country: 100km (60 miles)
Crew	4

Another variant, the Char B1 ter, which included a more powerful engine and thicker sloped armour, was slated for production in the summer of 1940. However, France fell to the Nazis before the project got underway.

Shortcomings in the Field

The Char B1 presented significant operational challenges as well. The tank commander occupied the confined, cramped turret and was responsible for both laying and firing the 47mm (1.85in) gun. The four crewmen were dispersed throughout the interior of the tank, making effective communications problematic. The tank weighed a hefty 31.5 tonnes (31 tons), contributing to a disappointing top road speed of 28km/h (17.5mph) and 21km/h (13mph) cross-country. The high silhouette of the Char B1 bis also presented an inviting target on the battlefield and the air-cooled Renault engine required a large intake on the tank's left flank, potentially weakening its armour protection.

Command and Control

When World War II began, the French Army was the world's largest and most powerful on paper. However, only three Divisions Cuirassees de Reserve, or armoured divisions, had been formed. A fourth division was quickly authorized within days of the outbreak of war. Although the main armament of the Char B1 and the Char B1 bis was capable of destroying any belligerent tank in service at the time – and the Germans were well aware of its potential as they initiated hostilities – the reality of combat worked against the success of the French tanks.

Once in the field, the tanks became prone to breakdowns and considerable routine maintenance was required to keep the Char B1 battleworthy. Prodigious fuel consumption drained the tank's three 400-litre (90-gallon) fuel tanks in as little as six hours. Perhaps the most difficult obstacle to overcome – and the most disconcerting – was the French tactic of committing the heavy tanks to battle piecemeal, primarily as infantry support, rather than the larger numbers that would allow their concentrated firepower to dominate the battlefield.

After the fall of France, the German Army pressed more than 160 Char B1 tanks into service, renaming the armoured vehicles the PzKpfw B1 bis 740(f). These were often used in garrison duty, such as the occupation of the British Channel Islands and for training purposes. The Germans converted a few to self-propelled guns and flamethrower tanks.

An apparently disabled Char B1 bis with a section of armour plating removed as attempts to repair the tank are undertaken.

Char B1 bis on the Attack

On 16 May 1940, a single Char B1 bis nicknamed Eure, commanded by Captain Pierre Billotte of the 1/41e BCC (Battaillon de Chars de Combat), proved that the French heavy tank was a formidable opponent. As Billotte's tank reached the streets of the village of Stonne, France, near the Belgian border, the commander took full advantage of his available firepower and destroyed 13 German tanks. Two of these were new PzKpfw IV models, while the rest were PzKpfw IIIs. Billotte also destroyed two 37mm (1.45in) Pak anti-tank guns. Although the tank was hit 140 times, no round penetrated the armour of the Char B1 bis.

Panzer 38(t) (1938)

After occupying Czechoslovakia, the German Army ordered production of the LT vz 38, the standard Czechoslovakian light tank, to continue. Redesignated the Panzer 38(t), the design proved one of the world's best in German service early in the war.

When Nazi Germany occupied the Sudetenland in 1938 and then the whole of Czechoslovakia in 1939, the spoils of Adolf Hitler's war of words included arms-manufacturing enterprises that were among the best in the world. The legendary Skoda Works and the engineering firm of Ceskomoravská Kolben-Danek (CKD) were among these and the Germans quickly adapted Czech ingenuity for their own purposes.

Stolen Property

One of the most notable weapons to emerge from the Czech arsenal emblazoned with the German cross was the LT vz 38 light tank, the standard armoured fighting vehicle

Main Armament
The Czech 37mm (1.45in) Skoda A7 gun turret mounted atop the Panzer 38(t) was heavier than the primary weaponry of other light tanks early in World War II, providing a definite edge in combat situations.

While the armour protection of the Panzer 38(t) exhibited some degree of slope, as seen in this frontal view, later production Axis and Allied tanks incorporated armour with a more pronounced slope in both chassis and turret designs.

of the Czech Army. The Germans redesignated the tank the Panzer 38(t), with the "t" designating tschechnisch, the German word for Czechoslovakian. An efficient design, the Panzer 38(t) was originally conceived following specifications issued by the Czech military in 1935 for a new light tank.

The Panzer 38(t) featured a leaf-spring suspension and armour protection of between 8–30mm (0.31–1.18in) on earlier versions, which was later increased to 50mm (1.97in) with additional plating. The Praga EPA six-cylinder inline petrol engine supplied 112 kilowatts (150hp) and generated a maximum road speed of 42km/h (26.1mph).

Armour
On early versions of the Panzer 38(t), armour protection varied from 8mm (0.31in) in less vulnerable areas to 30mm (1.18in) of frontal thickness. Later production models provided increased crew protection with armour up to 50mm (1.97in).

Riveted Construction
The turret and hull of the Panzer 38(t) were of riveted construction rather than welded and some ancillary components of the tank were bolted to the superstructure.

Engine
The Praga EPA six-cylinder water-cooled inline petrol engine delivered 112kW (150hp) and the Panzer 38(t) reached a top road speed of 42km/h (26.1mph).

This overhead view of the Panzer 38(t) reveals the rear placement of the engine with ventilation atop the chassis. The narrow turret was problematic for two men to occupy and the interior of the tank constrained movement for the crew of four.

Exposed portions of the exhaust system caused the Czech-designed Panzer 38(t) to be vulnerable to attack from the rear. However, high ground clearance of 400mm (16in) facilitated cross-country mobility.

Cross-country speed was a respectable 15km/h (9.32mph). The crew of four included a commander who also served as a gunner, and a loader/gunner in the two-man turret along with a driver seated forward in the hull to the right with the bow gunner/radio operator forward to the left.

Specification

Dimensions	Length: 4.61m (15ft 1in) Width: 2.135m (7ft) Height: 2.252m (7ft 5in)
Weight	9.85 tonnes (9.7 tons)
Engine	1 x Praga EPA six-cylinder water-cooled inline petrol powerplant delivering 112kW (150hp)
Speed	Road: 42km/h (26.1mph) Cross-country: 15km/h (9.32mph)
Armament	Main: 1 x Czech 37mm (1.45in) Skoda A7 gun Secondary: 2 x 7.92mm (0.31in) ZB-53 machine guns
Armour	8–50mm (0.31–1.97in)
Range	Road: 250km (160 miles) Cross-country: 100km (62.14 miles)
Crew	4

Foreign Firepower

The main weapon of the Panzer 38(t) was the Czech-made 37mm (1.45in) Skoda A7 gun, which the Germans redesignated the KwK 38(t) L/47.8. Some 90 rounds were carried in the turret and hull and handled by or passed to the loader during combat. The tank commander fired the main gun. Secondary armament included a pair of 7.92mm (0.31IN) ZB-53 machine guns, renamed the MG 37(t) by the Germans. The machine guns were routinely supplied with a total of 2550 rounds. In the turret, the ball-mounted machine gun could be fired by either the commander or loader. The hull machine gun was also in a ball mount, providing good traverse.

The Panzer 38(t) was more heavily armed and generally performed better in combat than its German counterparts, the PzKpfw I and II. Its operational road and cross-country range of 250km (160 miles) and 100km (62 miles) respectively made it a superb weapon of the Blitzkrieg, the rapid advance and combined arms tactic employed by the German Army during its early conquests of Poland, France and the Low Countries and the invasion of the Soviet Union.

German Accent

German engineers did make a few modifications to the original Czech LT vz 38 design, including a loader position in the turret that was accommodated with the reduction of 37mm ammunition to 72 rounds. Adjustable seats for the commander and loader were also installed.

As shells explode in their path and thick smoke obscures their vision, Red Army soldiers rush past an abandoned Marder III tank destroyer on the Eastern Front. The Marder III was a successful adaptation of the Czech-designed chassis that was primarily utilized with the Panzer 38(t) light tank.

Even as the tank was becoming obsolete by late 1941, production continued into the following year and more than 1400 Panzer 38(t)s were manufactured during a production run that began in 1939. The Germans also recognized the versatility of the Czech-designed chassis and modified it to produce several variants, both with open and closed turrets. These included the Marder tank destroyer, the Jagdpanzer 38(t) tank destroyer, popularly known as the Hetzer, the SdKfz. 138 Grille assault gun mounting a 150mm (5.9in) gun, the SdKfz 140 Flakpanzer 38(t) mounting a 20mm (0.79in) anti-aircraft weapon, and reconnaissance vehicles.

Hazardous Duty in the Panzer 38(t)

"I was the loader and we were all bursting with pride when we received our Czechoslovakian Panzer 38t's," wrote future Tiger tank ace Otto Carius as the 21st Panzer Regiment was formed prior to Operation Barbarossa. "We felt practically invincible with our 37-mm cannon and Czech machine guns."

Carius went on to describe a narrow escape when his Panzer 38(t) was hit by a Soviet 47mm (1.85in) anti-tank gun. In his book *Tigers in the Mud*, he wrote, "It happened like greased lightning ... A large piece of armour plating had been penetrated next to the radio operator's seat ... Not until I had run my hand across my face ... did I discover that they had also got me. Our radio operator had lost his left arm ..."

Extended Service

When the Germans occupied Czechoslovakia, 90 LT vz 38 tanks ordered by Sweden and slated for delivery in 1940 were commandeered and pressed into service with the Wehrmacht. Negotiations were initiated to build the tank under license in Sweden and the first of these were delivered to the Swedish military in December 1942. Licensed production continued into 1944, and 220 of the Swedish-built tanks were eventually completed.

The Swedes converted some of their tanks into self-propelled assault guns and armoured personnel carriers. All of their license built tanks, designated Stridsvagen m/41 S I and Stridsvagen m/41 S II (with improved armour and a more powerful engine), were retired from service in the 1950s.

During the mid-1930s, Peru purchased 24 LT vz 38 tanks from Czechoslovakia and these took part in the three-week border war that the Peruvians fought with neighbouring Ecuador from July 5 to July 31 in 1941.

Mk III Valentine Infantry Tank (1939)

Derived from a previous Vickers design, the A10, the Mk III Valentine Infantry Tank was available in large numbers at a critical time for Great Britain and the Commonwealth nations as a potential Nazi invasion of Britain loomed.

Initial discussions with Vickers to join the production effort for the new Matilda II tank ended due to the fact that the company already had facilities dedicated to its own cruiser tank, the A10. Instead, Vickers was asked to develop an infantry tank based on the A10 and the

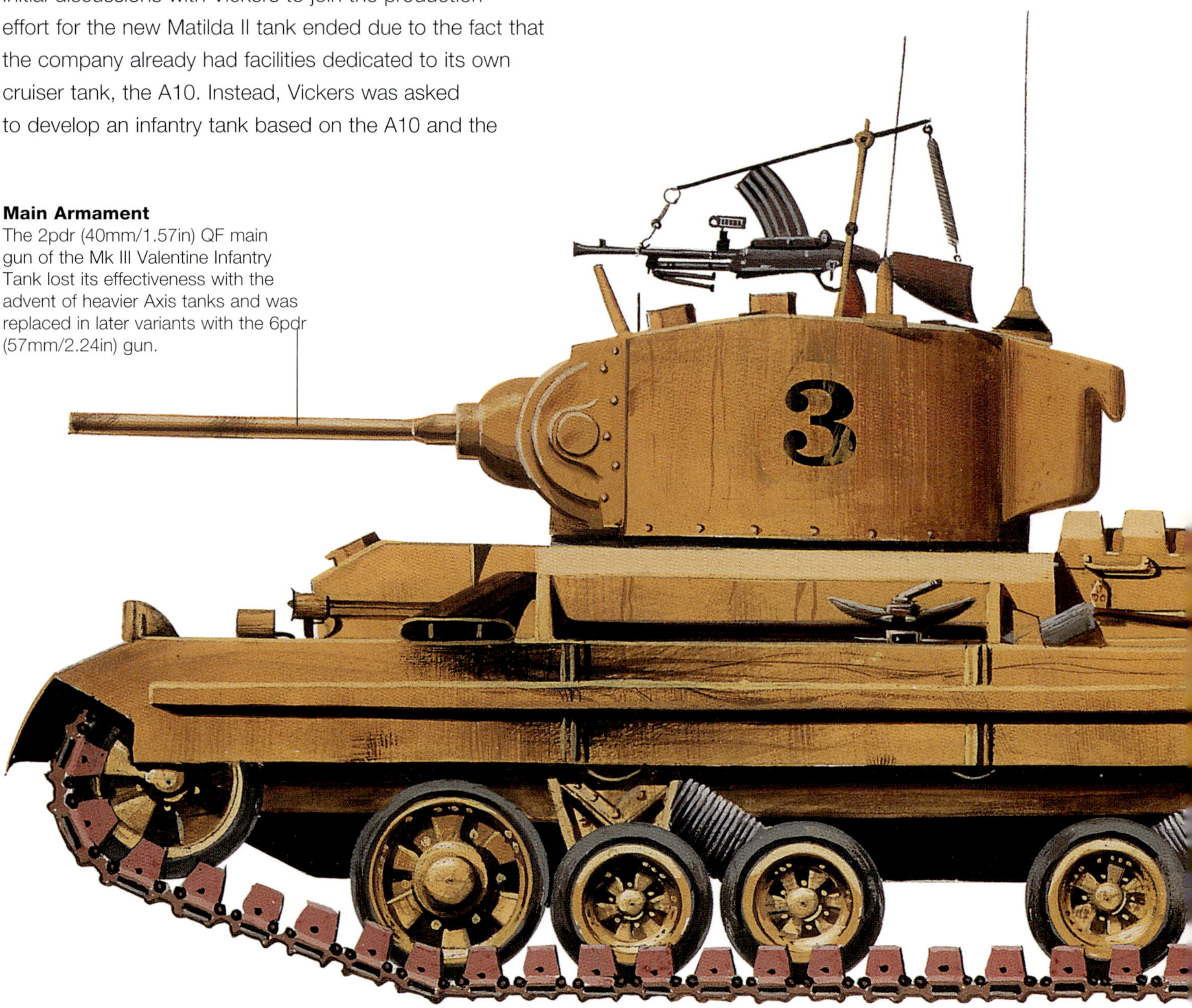

design was eventually approved for production in the summer of 1939.

Although some observers were sceptical of early Vickers designs, particularly due to small turrets that might not accept heavier armament easily, tanks were in short supply and World War II was going badly for Britain. With invasion by the Nazis a real possibility, tank production was critical. Quantity rather than quality was the order of the day and the Mk III Valentine entered production with little testing. It was a calculated risk, but the experience with the A10 assuaged some of the concern about the performance of the new tank, which, in fact, turned out to be quite reliable.

Valentines with Vickers Vigour

The first of the new Vickers tanks, the Valentine I, rolled off assembly lines in late 1940. From there, great quantities

Secondary Armament
The BESA machine gun was a British version of the Czech-made ZB-53 air-cooled machine gun and was utilized extensively by the British military during World War II.

Turret
The two-man turret of the Mk III Valentine Infantry Tank required the commander to serve as a loader for the 2pdr gun.

The Mk III Valentine Infantry Tank was rushed into production in 1940 without extensive field testing but proved reliable largely due to Vickers's experience with its forerunner, the A10 Cruiser Tank.

Armour Protection
The armour protection of the Mk III Valentine Infantry Tank varied from 8–65mm (0.31–2.55in), heavier than the A10 Cruiser Tank from which the Valentine was derived.

Engine
The AEC A190 six-cylinder diesel engine of the Mk III Valentine Infantry Tank generated 103kW (131hp). It was replaced in later variants with an American GMC diesel engine.

of the Valentine were produced and when the tank's production ceased in early 1944, nearly 8300 had been built. At one time in 1943, the Valentine was so numerous that it represented one quarter of total British tank production. The Valentine was also produced by other manufacturers in Britain, and Valentines built in Canada were primarily sent to the Soviet Union. Vickers production alone peaked at 20 tanks per week in 1943. Canadian built Mk IIIs totalled more than 1400, while those produced at various sites in Britain approached 6900.

The Mk III Valentine Infantry Tank, the most prominent in the series, benefited greatly from the Vickers experience with the A10. The numerous shortcomings discovered in the A10 were corrected in the Valentine, which was more heavily armoured with between 8–65mm (0.31–2.55in) of protection; it also experienced fewer breakdowns in the field.

The Mk III Valentine Infantry Tank was powered by an AEC A190 six-cylinder diesel engine generating 98 kilowatts (131hp). Its Meadows 22 transmission drove the tank with five forward and one reverse gear. A pair of three-wheeled bogies with coil spring suspension were mounted on each side. The Mk III

The Vickers-produced Valentine tank became one of the most numerous British armoured vehicles of World War II, as nearly 8,300 were built before production ended in late 1944.

Specification

Dimensions	Length: 5.41m (17ft 9in) Width: 2.63m (8ft 7.5in) Height: 2.273m (7ft 5.5in)
Weight	16.96 tonnes (16.6 tons)
Engine	1 x AEC A190 six-cylinder diesel generating 98kW (131hp)
Speed	Road: 24km/h (15mph) Cross-country: 12.9km/h (8mph)
Armament	Main: 1 x 2pdr (40mm/1.57in) QF gun Secondary: 1 x 7.92mm (0.31in) BESA machine gun
Armour	8–65mm (0.31–2.55in)
Range	145km (90 miles)
Crew	3

main armament consisted of a QF 40mm (2pdr) and the secondary armament was a single BESA 7.92mm (0.31in) machine gun.

The Valentine powerplant varied during production, as the Mk IV and Mk V, for example, utilized the reliable and quiet American GMC 6004 diesel engine along with an American-made transmission.

The Valentine carried a crew of three with the driver situated forward in the centre of the hull and separated by a bulkhead from the fighting compartment and turret, which held the gunner on the right and the tank commander, who also acted as loader, on the left. Another bulkhead separated the fighting compartment from the engine compartment at the rear of the hull.

Valentines Forward

In total, 11 different marks of the original Valentine were produced during World War II. One of the tank's greatest virtues was in fact its ability to accept substantially heavier weaponry. While I-VII mounted the 2pdr gun, the 57mm (2.24in) 6pdr QF was introduced with the VIII and continued up to the X. With the XI, a 75mm (2.95in) QF gun was mounted.

The Valentine tank saw extensive service with Commonwealth forces in the Mediterranean, the North African desert and in Burma, where it was superior to most Japanese tanks; however, it was relatively slow and inferior to newer tank designs entering service by 1943.

Valentine Variants

Numerous specialized vehicles were produced with the Valentine chassis, including the Bishop self-propelled gun that mounted a 25pdr QF main weapon, the Valentine Canal Defence Light, and bridgelaying, observation, command, mine-clearing, flamethrower and duplex-drive variants. The duplex-drive Valentine proved a success and for a time it was the standard amphibious tank of the British Army.

Although an attempt to develop a tank destroyer with an open turret and 6pdr gun protected by a shield was ultimately unsuccessful, the Valentine chassis did serve as the platform for the open-turreted Archer assault gun, which entered service in 1944. Production of all Valentine-related vehicles eventually ceased in 1945.

The Global Valentine

The Mk III Valentine Infantry Tank was deployed with British and Commonwealth troops around the globe during World War II. In this photo, tank crewmen allow a group of children to climb aboard and inspect their Valentine on the Mediterranean island of Malta during the local celebration of the birthday of King George VI.

Although the origin of the Valentine design predated the opening of hostilities, the tank provided firepower, armour protection and numbers that were substantial enough for Britain to defend itself and its far-flung Empire. The Valentine fought against the onslaught of the Japanese on the Asian continent from Malaya to Burma, against the Italian Army and subsequently the Germans in North Africa and with the Soviet Red Army following the opening of Operation Barbarossa on June 22, 1941.

By the end of World War II, more than 8000 Valentine tanks had been produced in Britain and Canada and numerous specialized vehicles utilized the Valentine chassis.

Panzer III Ausf F (1940)

The most numerous tank in the German arsenal at the time of the Soviet invasion, the PzKpfw III was developed as a lighter medium tank, equipping three companies of each armoured battalion, while a fourth was outfitted with the heavier PzKpfw IV.

Development of the durable Panzerkampfwagen III began in 1935 with an order from the German arms ministry for a medium tank that could complement the medium PzKpfw IV. During a four-year production run from 1939 to 1943, more than 5800 were produced and the role of the PzKpfw III evolved with the changing conditions of the battlefield.

During the course of World War II, no fewer than 11 variants of the original PzKpfw III production model, Ausf E, were built. Variants A to D were prototype models constructed in 1937 and 1938. With A to C the torsion-bar

The PzKpfw III served with the German Army on all fronts during World War II and was adapted from an armour versus armour role to infantry support as the conflict progressed. Its chassis was also used for assault guns, recovery and observation vehicles.

Armament
The main armament of the PzKpfw III was initially the 37mm (1.45in) KwK 36 L/46.5 gun, later supplanted by the 50mm (1.97in) KwK 38 L/42 gun. Secondary armament consisted of a pair of 7.92mm (0.31in) MG 34 machine guns, one in the turret and the other in the hull.

suspension was refined and with D and F, heavier armour, a higher-performance engine and an improved commander's cupola were installed.

The interior of the PzKpfw III was spacious compared to other contemporary tanks, although space was diminished as larger main weapons were installed in succeeding variants. The driver was positioned forward and to the left in the hull, while a radio operator/machine-gunner was seated to the right. Three crewmen – the commander, gunner and loader – occupied the turret, which was centred on the hull. The 12-cylinder Maybach HL 120 TRM petrol engine developed 224 kilowatts (300hp) and was positioned at the rear. The torsion bar suspension had six road wheels with a frontal drive sprocket, rear idler and three return rollers.

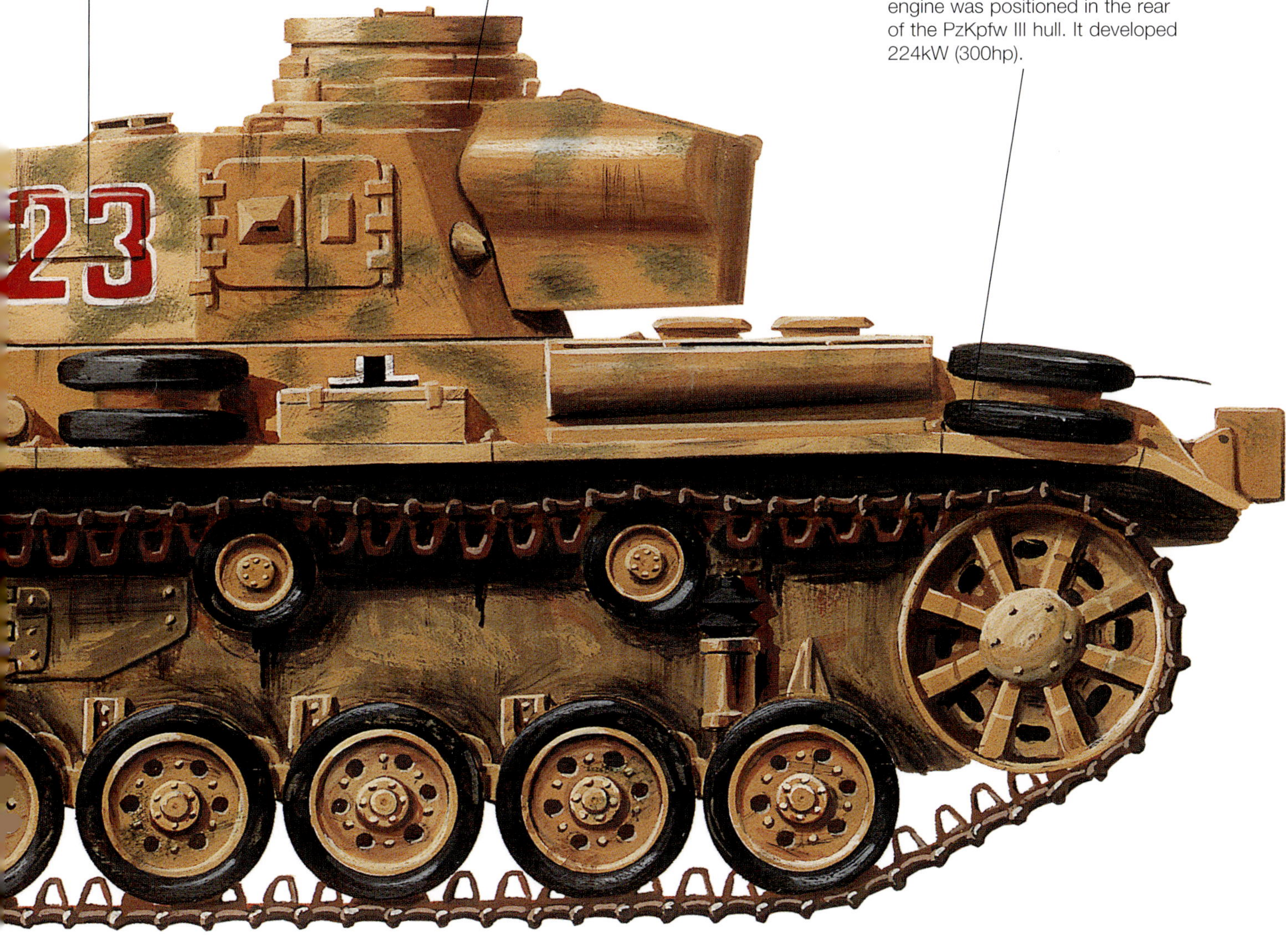

The imposing frame of the PzKpfw III was compact and efficient, actually incorporating turret armour with a slight slope to improve protection while the hull armour remained more square. As the main weapon was upgunned, the firepower was comparable to early Allied tanks.

Specification

Dimensions	Length: 5.38m (17ft 8in) Width: 2.91m (9ft 7in) Height: 2.44m (8ft)
Weight	17.41 tonnes (17.1 tons)
Engine	1 x 12-cylinder inline water-cooled Maybach HL 120 TRM petrol engine developing 224kW (300hp)
Speed	Road: 40km/h (25mph) Cross-country: 20km/h (12mph)
Armament	Main: Initially 1 x 37mm (1.45in) KwK L/46.5; later 50mm (1.97in) KwK 38 L/42 gun Secondary: 2 x 7.92mm (0.31in) MG 34 machine guns
Armour	15–50mm (0.59–1.97in)
Range	155km (96 miles)
Crew	5

Producing Panzer Power

When the Ausf E entered production in 1939, it was armed with a 37mm (1.45in) KwK 36 L/46.5 main weapon. In 1940, the Ausf F, virtually identical to the Ausf E, was introduced. The improvements with the Ausf F included a different engine ignition system, modified air intakes and improved torsion bar suspension. Approximately 300 Ausf F variants were produced with the 37mm main gun; however, as improving Allied tank designs rendered that weapon ineffective, 100 Ausf F tanks followed with the heavier KwK 38 L/42 50mm (1.97in) cannon. Throughout production, secondary armament included two or three 7.92mm (0.31in) MG 34 machine guns, mounted in the hull and in the turret adjacent to the main gun. By the time of the German invasion of France and the Low Countries on May 10, 1940, large numbers of the Ausf F had been deployed.

The G variant added armour to the gun mantlet, while armour protection for the front and rear hull of the Ausf H was increased with 30mm (1.18in) of additional bolted-on plating. Engine performance was increased with the Ausf H and wider tracks were added for greater stability in such conditions as the North African desert or the muddy terrain of the Eastern Front.

Following the shocking debut of the superb Soviet T-34 medium tank, the PzKpfw III Ausf J was introduced with a longer-barrelled 50mm (1.97in) gun to generate higher muzzle velocity. Subsequently, the L and M variants provided armour upgrades, nearly doubling the weight of the original PzKpfw III to more than 22.7 tonnes (22.3 tons). The Ausf M also included a chassis with greater stability.

German soldiers and tank crewmen sit atop PzKpfw III as it fords a stream early in World War II. Note the distinctive headwear of the Panzerwaffe on the crewman at far right. The PzKpfw III Ausf M, produced in 1942–43, included a deep-wading exhaust system.

Long Road Eastward

Even as the German Army rolled across the Russian frontier on June 22, 1941, the main battle tank capability of the PzKpfw III, the most prominent tank in its panzer divisions, was waning. The Soviet T-34 soon eclipsed other designs. Gradually, the PzKpfw III evolved into an infantry support tank while the PzKpfw IV, intended originally for the infantry support role, then shouldered the great weight of the tank versus tank fighting until the arrival of the PzKpfw V Panther in 1943.

The PzKpfw III Ausf N was modified as an infantry support tank and armed with a short-barrelled 75mm (2.95in) gun, which had originally been installed on the PzKpfw IV. A total of 64 rounds of 75mm ammunition were carried aboard the Ausf N, which was later also assigned to independent Panzer battalions as an escort for PzKpfw VI Tiger heavy tanks.

Champion Chassis

The PzKpfw III chassis proved to be quite versatile during World War II. Particularly with the improved torsion bar suspension of the Ausf F, the chassis gained a reputation as a steady gun platform, both in the tank and assault gun roles. The Sturmgeschütz self-propelled assault gun mounted a 75mm (2.95in) main weapon and was highly successful. Armoured recovery and observation vehicles also utilized the chassis, which were produced throughout the war.

Evolving Combat Role

Buildings blaze in the background as German soldiers, supported by a PzKpfw III, clear a war-torn street somewhere on the Eastern Front. The PzKpfw III was continually modified during World War II and evolved from a main battle tank to an infantry support vehicle as its firepower and armour protection were eclipsed by subsequent generations of Allied tanks.

The PzKpfw III was the frontline German tank during the early months of World War II. It was available in relatively large numbers and held its own for a time against the Soviets until the T-34 arrived in sufficient numbers to complement the older Red Army BT and T-26 models. In North Africa, the PzKpfw III was more than a match for British armour and dominated the battlefield until the arrival of the American M3 Grant/Lee and M4 Sherman medium tanks with their 75mm (2.95in) main guns.

KV-1A Heavy Tank (1940)

The KV series was often used in offensive operations, spearheading breakthroughs of defensive lines. Named for Klimenti Voroshilov, Soviet Commissar for Defence, the KV tanks were the foundation of Soviet heavy tank design for decades to come.

The Soviet fixation with multi-turreted tank designs died slowly. In 1938, when efforts were underway to produce a successor to the outmoded T-35 heavy tank, several design bureaus submitted multi-turret plans, while only one bureau went with a single turret and named the new tank after Soviet Commissar for Defence Klimenti Voroshilov.

This latest Soviet heavy tank was adopted and then deployed during the Winter War with Finland in 1940. Designated the KV-1, it was ordered into production in

Main Armament
The long-barrelled 76.2mm (3in) F32 main gun of the KV-1A replaced the shorter L-11 76.2mm weapon that had been mounted on the early KV-1 and seen action during the Winter War with Finland.

two variants. The first was the KV-1A, which was armed initially with a long-barrelled 76.2mm (3in) F32 main gun and 111 rounds of ammunition, substituted for the short-barrelled 76.2mm L-11 gun of early testing prototypes. The second model was the KV-2, a combination of the KV-1 hull, suspension and chassis with a huge turret mounting a 152mm (6in) howitzer.

Enduring Design

While only 141 of the original KV-1 tanks were produced in 1939 and the KV-2 foundered with a dangerously hefty turret and considerable weight with only 334 examples being constructed, the KV-1A became the mainstay of the Soviet heavy tank corps. In 1940, mainstream production shifted to the KV-1A, which was protected by armour of 37–78mm (1.45–3.07in), powered by a V-2K Series V-12 water-cooled diesel engine generating

The KV-1A heavy tank entered production along with the KV-2, an ill-conceived self-propelled assault gun with a tremendously oversized turret that mounted a 152mm (6in) howitzer. The KV-1A played a pivotal role in turning the tide of World War II on the Eastern Front.

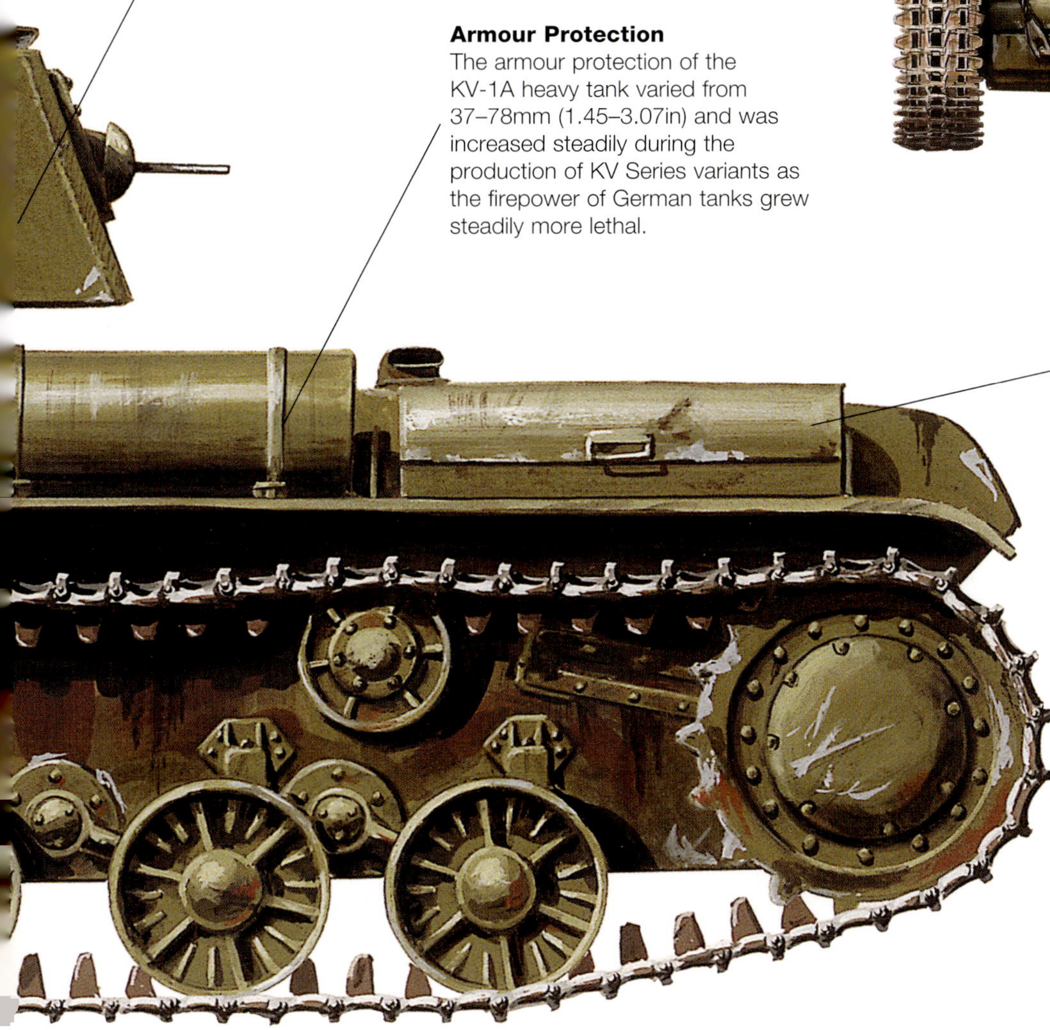

Although the KV-1A heavy tank was plagued with mechanical problems during its service life, it functioned well enough in its role as a breakthrough or assault tank, breaching enemy lines, striking rear areas and cutting off the retreat of enemy forces.

410 kilowatts (550hp) and achieved a maximum speed of 35km/h (22mph).

Secondary armament consisted of three 7.62mm (0.3in) DT machine guns with a total of 3024 rounds. One machine gun was mounted forward in the hull, while the second was coaxially mounted forward in the turret and the third faced the rear of the tank from the turret to defend against infantry attack from behind. A fourth 7.62mm machine gun was added on some KV models, mounted to the commander's cupola for defence against infantry and strafing aircraft.

Specification

Dimensions	Height: 2.75m (9ft) Width: 3.25m (10ft 9in) Length: 6.25m (20ft 6in)
Weight	46 tonnes (45.2 tons)
Engine	1 x V-2K Series V-12 water-cooled diesel engine generating 410kW (550hp)
Speed	35km/h (22mph)
Armament	Main: 1 x 76.2mm (3in) long-barrelled F32 gun Secondary: 3 x 7.62mm (0.3in) DT machine guns
Armour	37–78mm (1.45–3.07in)
Range	225km (140 miles)
Crew	5

Crew in the Confines

The KV-1A and subsequent variants of the original heavy tank carried a crew of five. The driver was seated forward in the centre of the hull, while a machine-gunner was seated to his left. The tank commander, gunner and the rear machine-gunner occupied the turret. One of the tank's major drawbacks was the fact that the commander served as the loader for the main gun. Therefore, he was often engaged in serving the weapon as the larger battle swirled around him.

Appreciable Armour Augmentation

As World War II progressed and German tanks were steadily increasing in armour protection and firepower, the KV-1A was improved to keep pace. Another 25–35mm (0.98–1.37in) of armour were added to the front and sides of the hull in the KV-1B, while the plating of the turret in earlier models was discarded in favour of a cast turret in the KV-1C. Subsequent steps to increase the firepower of the tank were less than successful. An attempt to fit the turret with a 107mm (4.2in) gun failed; however, in 1943 a number of KV-1s were fitted with the 85mm (3.35in)

DT-5 main gun and designated the KV-85. The armour protection of a relative few tanks was reduced in the hopes of increasing speed, but these, designated the KV-1S (skorostnoy, or fast) tank, did not achieve great success.

Mechanical Difficulties

Throughout its 1939–43 production run and its service life up to the end of World War II, the KV-1A and others in the series suffered from mechanical issues. Early models were plagued by a faulty transmission and clutch problems that at times made it impossible to change gears. With the exception of an engine upgrade that produced an additional 75 kilowatts (100hp) in the KV-1C, the increasing armour protection that was necessary for battlefield survivability was not accompanied by a better performing engine, leading to further problems with mechanical reliability. The lack of mobility was a profound weakness on the Russian steppes.

Although the KV tanks were prone to mechanical failure and some critics maintained that their main armament lacked the firepower of opposing heavy tanks, they were the product of sound design concepts and rendered vital service with the Red Army during the bleakest period following the German invasion. They also established a basis for the improved Stalin tanks that were to come.

Resurgent Red Army

The failure of German forces to capture Moscow in the winter of 1941 and again the following year, coupled with the Red Army's victory at Stalingrad in February 1943, allowed the Soviets to assume the offensive on the Eastern Front during 1943. Pictured below, Red Army soldiers, their banner whipping in the wind, have halted during a counteroffensive. Tank crewmen have joined infantrymen atop the hulls of KV-1 Model 1942 heavy tanks that were instrumental in stopping the Germans and seizing the initiative in the East.

Although the KV Series was criticized for having insufficient main armament and for its frequent mechanical breakdowns in the field due to transmission and clutch problems, the KV-1A proved adequate in combat against the German PzKpfw III and IV tanks it encountered. Meanwhile, Soviet designers learned their lessons well and developed the Josef Stalin series of heavy tanks that were deployed later in World War II and rolled through the streets of Berlin.

Panzer IV Ausf F1 (1941)

The workhorse of the German armoured forces during the war, the Panzer IV Ausf F1 was originally intended as an infantry support tank; however, it later assumed a tank-fighting combat role as Allied armoured vehicles became more powerful.

The most widely manufactured and deployed German tank of World War II, the PzKpfw IV was the mainstay of the German army's forces. The first rolled off the Krupp assembly line in the mid-1930s and from that date through 1945 more than 8800 were built. It was the only German tank in production throughout the war.

The PzKpfw IV was originally developed as an infantry support tank, while the concurrently produced PzKpfw III was envisioned as the primary tank versus tank weapon. The initial PzKpfw IV was constructed following specifications issued in January 1934 with a crew of five – the commander, forward machine-gunner/

The PzKpfw IV was produced in greater numbers than any other German armoured vehicle and its service life extended well beyond the end of World War II with the armed forces of numerous nations.

radio operator, loader, gunner and driver. It was armed with a short-barrelled 75mm (2.95in) main gun and two 7.92mm (0.31in) MG 34 machine guns, one mounted in the turret and the other forward in the hull.

When the PzKpfw III was authorized for production, its 37mm (1.45in) main weapon was deemed sufficient to take on enemy tanks. The heavier weapon of the PzKpfw IV was intended to neutralize gun emplacements, fixed fortifications and troop concentrations that could slow the progress of the German Blitzkrieg, the coordinated offensive action by aircraft, artillery, tanks and ground troops that swept

Turret
The asymmetrical construction of the PzKpfw IV included a turret that was offset 66.5mm (2.6in) for the tank's centre to allow the torque shaft to clear the rotary base junction.

Armour Protection
Throughout its service life, the armour protection of the PzKpfw IV was improved. Armour thickness ranged from 15–60mm (0.59–2.36in) and was of homogeneous rolled and welded nickel steel.

Main Armament
The main armament of the PzKpfw IV Ausf F included two sub-variants, the F1 and F2. The F1 mounted the short-barrelled 75mm (2.95in) L/24 gun and the F2 the long-barrelled 75mm L/43 gun (shown here).

The first examples of the PzKpfw IV Ausf F were designated the F1 due to the main 75mm (2.95in) L/24 gun. Later Ausf F tanks mounted the L/43 long-barrelled 75mm cannon and were designated F2.

The PzKpfw IV turret was power operated; however, manual controls were provided in the event of a loss of power. The tank's engine was placed in the rear of the chassis and operated with a manual transmission with six forward and one reverse gear.

across Poland and then France and the Low Countries in 1939 and 1940.

Continuing Upgrades

The first production model PzKpfw IV, Ausf A, was deployed with combat units in 1936. Within a year, improvements were made to the transmission and the Maybach 12-cylinder HL 120 TRM inline water-cooled petrol engine, resulting in the construction of relatively few B variants. The Ausf C, with turret armour increased to 30mm (1.18in), entered service in 1938, followed by the Ausf D that reintroduced the hull machine gun that had been removed earlier and reconfigured the turret's gun mantlet from an interior fitting to external. In September 1940, the Ausf E was introduced with augmented armour and a repositioned commander's cupola. Most existing PzKpfw IVs then in service were retrofitted to conform to the Ausf E configuration.

For nine months beginning in the spring of 1941, the Ausf F was in production and more than 500 were produced as both the German military and civilian manufacturers realized that the role of the PzKpfw IV had become dual – infantry support and tank engagement – and was likely evolving more into the tank fighting posture. With the Ausf F, hull armour was increased to 60mm (2.36in), while turret armour was upgraded to 50mm (1.97in). The hull machine gun was placed in a ball turret for a better field of fire and wider tracks provided improved stability in the varied climates where German armoured forces operated at the time.

The most significant improvement with the Ausf F was the introduction of a more powerful main weapon. The initial Ausf F was armed with the short-barrelled 75mm (2.95in) L/24 cannon. Then, numerous Ausf F models were armed with the long-barrelled 75mm L/43 cannon,

Specification

Dimensions	Length: 5.91m (19ft 5in) Width: 2.88m (9ft 5in) Height: 2.68m (8ft 10in)
Weight	22 tonnes (21.6 tons)
Engine	1 x 12-cylinder inline Maybach HL 120 TRM water-cooled petrol engine generating 220kW (296hp)
Speed	42km/h (26mph)
Armament	Main: 1 x short-barrelled 75mm (2.95in) L/24 gun Secondary: 2 x 7.92mm (0.31in) MG 34 machine guns
Armour	15–60mm (0.59–2.36in)
Range	Road: 240km (150 miles) Cross-country: 120km (75 miles)
Crew	5

The long barrel of the 75mm (2.95in) L/43 cannon of PzKpfw IV Ausf F2 was an imposing sight on the battlefield, here deployed for the Kursk offensive in July 1943.

The Most Plentiful Panzer

At peak production and deployment, the PzKpfw IV comprised fully 30 per cent of the active tank strength of the German Army. However, it took considerable time for the powerful tank to reach the front in substantial numbers after the outbreak of World War II. During the invasion of Poland in September 1939 and the conquest of France and the Low Countries in May 1940, the most prevalent German tanks engaged were the lightly armed and armoured PzKpfw I and II. When the German Army entered Warsaw, only 211 PzKpfw IVs had been deployed and only 278 were in action in the West the following spring.

Early in 1940, it became apparent that the PzKpfw IV was required in greater numbers. Although Krupp had been the sole manufacturer of the tank, production was expanded to other facilities and the PzKpfw IV began to replace the outmoded earlier models that had served since prior to the opening of hostilities. In 1939, an average of just under 40 PzKpfw IV tanks were produced monthly; however, that figure rose steadily to 83 in 1942, 252 in 1943 and 300 in early 1944 until some assembly lines were switched to other weapons. By the autumn of 1944, production had fallen to only 55 per month.

which produced greater muzzle velocity and penetrating capacity against enemy armour. Those PzKpfw IVs mounting the L/24 gun were designated the F1, while those with the L/43 were the F2. By June 1942, all production PzKpfw IV tanks were being armed with the L/43, reflecting the transition to the tank fighting role and these were designated Ausf G.

Rude Awakening

When the upgunned F2 was deployed to North Africa, it shook Allied tankers and higher echelon commanders with its L/43 gun, racking up an impressive combat record against British and American tanks. For a brief period on the Eastern Front, the F2 was the most powerful tank in the Panzerwaffe that was fielded in any appreciable numbers.

Although the PzKpfw IV was produced in great numbers, severe losses were experienced, especially from 1944 and right through to the end of the war when the Allies achieved mastery of the skies over Europe and the daylight movement of German armour became dangerous, if not virtually suicidal.

The final production variant of the PzKpfw IV, the Ausf J, entered service in the spring of 1944. It was of simplified construction compared to previous designs in an attempt to rapidly make good substantial battlefield losses. During its service life, the PzKpfw IV chassis served as a platform for several anti-aircraft weapons and tank destroyers.

Mk VI Crusader I Cruiser Tank (1941)

The British Crusader tanks were conceived between the world wars as rapid exploitation armoured vehicles that would exploit breaches in enemy defensive lines created by heavier weapons and then slash into rear areas to create havoc.

For British tacticians during the 1930s, the concept of the cruiser tank was logical. As heavy artillery and tanks blasted gaps in enemy defences, the cruisers would utilize speed to demoralize the enemy, striking deep behind the lines. This methodology would eliminate the spectre of trench warfare that had evolved on the Western Front in World War I.

However, along with the benefits of speed and mobility came a high price. Cruiser tanks, out of necessity, would have to sacrifice their armour protection to execute their mission efficiently. In addition, lighter weaponry was essential, as the additional weight of heavy guns would diminish combat effectiveness.

Armour Protection
The essence of the cruiser tank lay in its speed, which was achieved by the sacrifice of armour. Early Crusaders were thinly protected with up to 40mm (1.57in) of armour, while later variants were slightly improved to 50mm (1.97in).

Engine
The Nuffield 12-cylinder Liberty L-12 water-cooled petrol engine of the Crusader series was prone to overheating, while its Nuffield constant mesh transmission often broke down as well.

The Mk VI Crusader Cruiser Tank became a classic fighting vehicle of the desert war in North Africa. It was available in quantity, somewhat mitigating its lack of mechanical soundness, light armour protection and relatively weak firepower.

Nuffield's Crusader

The product of the design firm Nuffield Mechanization & Aero Limited, the Cruiser Tank Mk VI, which went on to become the Mk VI Crusader I Cruiser Tank and its follow-on variants, entered service in 1941. This was after design teams refined a two-turreted prototype, the A15 and put the new tank through gruelling trials that revealed shortcomings in mechanical function, particularly the cooling

The Crusader series of tanks were sleek, streamlined and looked to all the world like first-class armoured fighting vehicles. However, the harsh climate of the North African desert laid bare its shortcomings.

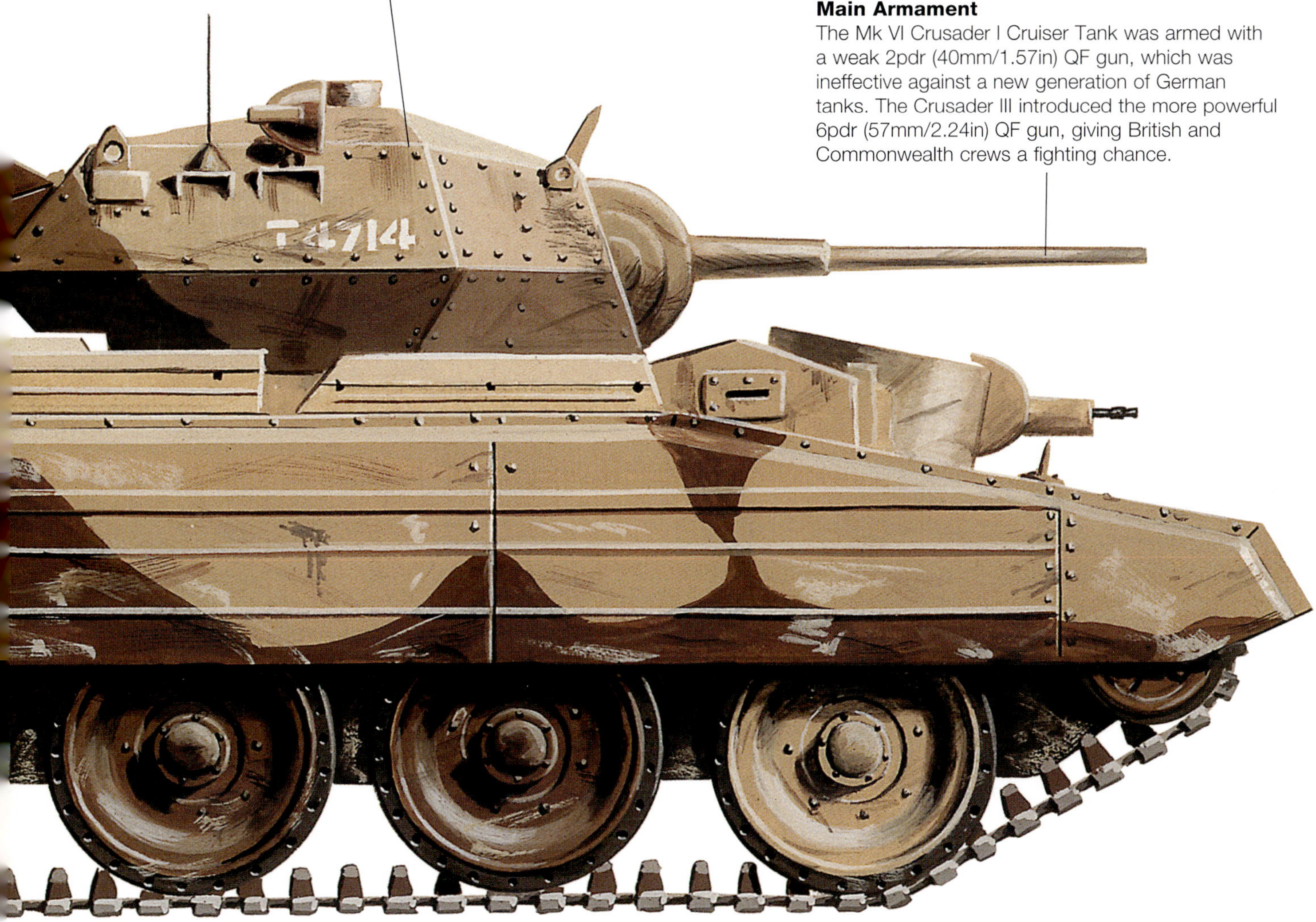

of the Nuffield 12-cylinder Liberty L-12 water-cooled petrol engine adapted for use with armour and the transmission, which often failed to change gears smoothly. One of the major faults of the Crusader series was the simple fact that several major issues such as these were never fully corrected and its unreliability dogged the tank throughout its service life. Still, more than 5300 Crusaders were built.

The first production model, the Crusader I, was true to the cruiser tank concept but from the beginning it was outclassed by heavier German tanks then in service. The Crusader I mounted a relatively weak 2pdr (40mm/1.57in) QF gun and was thinly armoured – only 40mm (1.57in) at its thickest. However, for all its faults the Crusader I looked like a fighting vehicle, but in actual combat the tank failed to live up to expectations. Within months, armour thickness was increased to a maximum of 50mm (1.97in) with the Crusader II. Astonishingly, the continuing problem with engine cooling was not rectified.

In its various upgrades, the Crusader series was crewed differently. The Crusader I and II included either four or five men, a commander, turret gunner, driver, loader and possibly a hull machine-gunner. Later, the Crusader III was reduced to a three-man crew due to a larger main weapon, the 6pdr (57mm/2.24in) QF gun.

Specification

Dimensions	Length: 5.99m (19ft 8in) Width: 2.64m (8ft 8in) Height: 2.23m (7ft 4in)
Weight	19.73 tonnes (19.4 tons)
Engine	Nuffield 12-cylinder Liberty L-12 water-cooled petrol engine generating 254kW (340hp)
Speed	Road: 43.4km/h (27mph) Cross-country: 24km/h (15mph)
Armament	Main: 1 x 6pdr (57mm/2.24in) QF gun Secondary: 1 x 7.92mm (0.31in) BESA machine gun
Armour	51mm
Range	204km (127 miles)
Crew	3

Secondary armament consisted initially of two BESA 7.92mm (0.31in) machine guns and then a single turret-mounted BESA machine gun. The tank's suspension was based on that of American inventor Walter Christie, originally conceived for rapid movement and stability with the addition of a bell crank and individually mounted road wheels.

Into the Desert

Regardless of its flaws, the Crusader was deployed to frontline British armoured units and became an icon of the desert war in North Africa. Well-trained crews compensated somewhat for the mechanical difficulties as best they could and coped with the Crusader's vulnerability

The angular slope of the Crusader III turret increased the effectiveness of the tank's armour protection, allowing the cruiser tank to more effectively fulfil its role of a swift, reasonably light fighting vehicle that exploited gaps in enemy lines.

to fire from German tanks and their superb 88mm (3.5in) flak gun converted to an anti-tank role.

The Crusader III, which became the definitive fighting variant of the series, made its combat debut at the pivotal battle of El Alamein in October 1942 and during the 1770-km (1100-mile) pursuit of the German Panzerarmee Afrika into Tunisia. About 100 of the Crusader III participated in the great El Alamein victory and the introduction of the 6pdr QF gun with 65 rounds of ammunition at long last gave the Crusader the ability to destroy the German PzKpfw III and IV tanks then deployed by the Germans in North Africa. The Crusader III was somewhat slower than its predecessors due to the weight of the larger gun; therefore, armour protection was largely unchanged. The maximum cross-country speed of the Crusader III was 24km/h (15mph), while its top road speed was 43.4km/h (27mph).

Performance Positive

The Crusader III endeared itself to its crews despite its penchant for mechanical breakdowns, and the series was available in sufficient numbers to counter the Axis threat in North Africa, although the British and Commonwealth soldiers who depended on it for survival did sustain substantial losses.

However, by early 1943 the reliable and highly-mobile American-built M4 Sherman medium tank was beginning to arrive in ever larger numbers and the Crusader was soon phased out of its combat role. The chassis, however, provided the mobile platform for several specialized vehicles. The Crusader IIC, for example, was armed with an effective 75mm (2.95in) howitzer, while anti-aircraft, recovery, bulldozer and prime mover vehicles were built around it as well.

Crusader Crossfire

With their 2pdr (40mm/1.57in) QF main guns, the first Crusader tanks deployed in North Africa were capable of taking on the German PzKpfw III with its short-barrelled 50mm (1.97in) gun. The short-barrelled 75mm (2.95in) gun of the PzKpfw IV was another story. The heavier German gun outranged the Crusader, a decided disadvantage in the desert.

The Germans also handled their anti-tank weapons skilfully, including the legendary 88mm (3.5in) gun and the 50mm (1.97in) Pak 38. They often lured the Crusaders into chasing their armour within range of concealed anti-tank guns and artillery. Once the British tanks were taken under fire, they had to either retreat out of range or run the anti-tank and artillery gauntlet to engage the German tanks. Neither option was usually favourable to the British.

Until the Crusader III, armed with the 6pdr (57mm/2.24in) gun, arrived in significant numbers, the greatest asset the early Crusaders possessed was speed. They were faster than any other tank in the desert; however, when hit they tended to burn furiously. In the photo below, a Crusader III has halted for its crew to rest while an ambulance has pulled to a stop nearby.

Churchill Mk IV (1941)

Conceived as an infantry support tank that would take on obstacles on a battlefield reminiscent of World War I trench warfare, the Churchill Mk IV evolved into a versatile fighting vehicle that fulfilled a variety of combat and support roles.

As British heavy tanks were designed initially with the single purpose of supporting infantry over rugged terrain, the Churchill Mk IV followed suit. When Harland and Wolff produced four prototypes of the A20 infantry support tank, the new vehicle was intended to advance at the same pace as the footsoldier, clearing man-made and natural obstacles.

In terms of production numbers among British tanks, the Churchill was second only to the Valentine. As for the number of variations on the original design concept, it was far and away supreme.

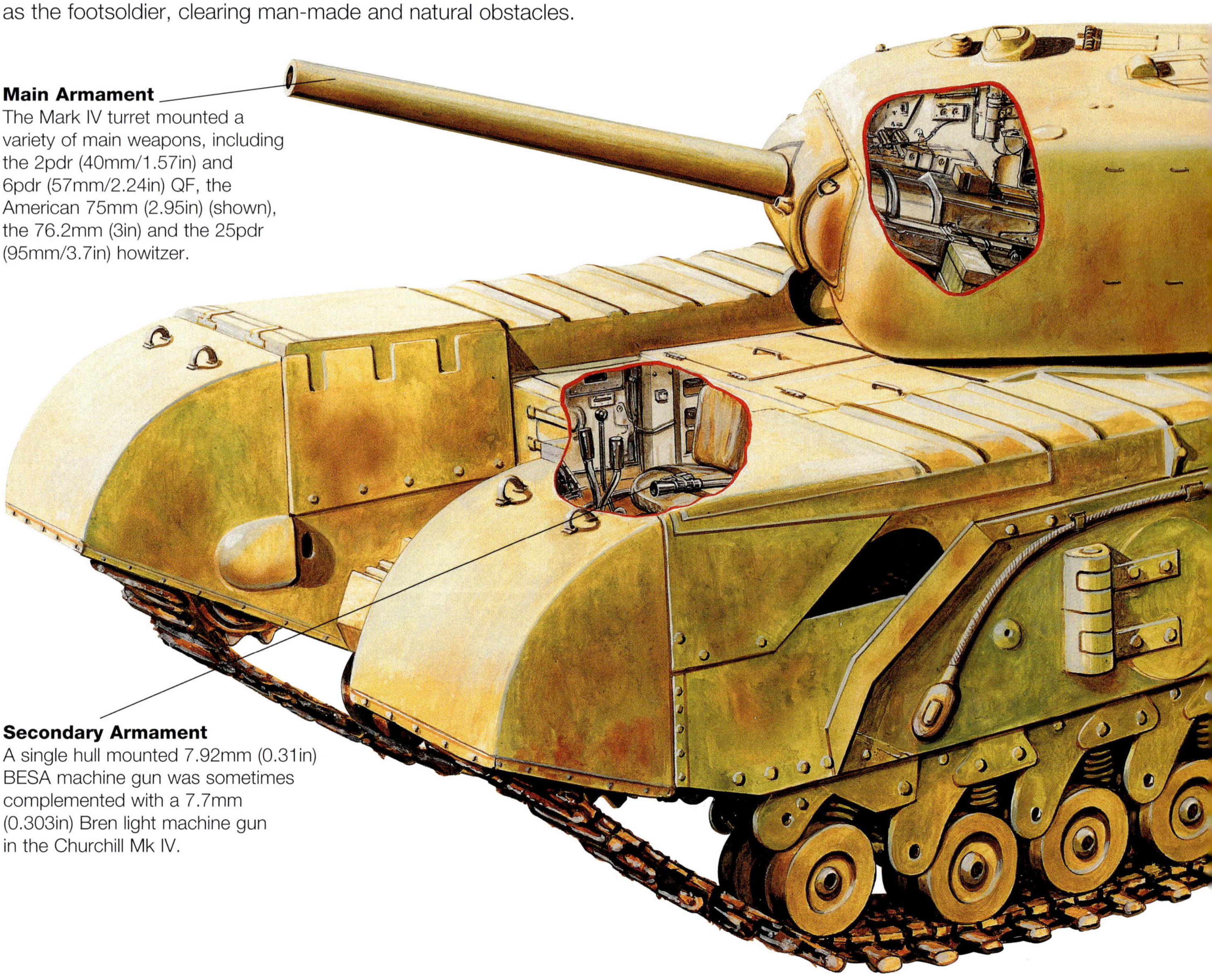

Main Armament
The Mark IV turret mounted a variety of main weapons, including the 2pdr (40mm/1.57in) and 6pdr (57mm/2.24in) QF, the American 75mm (2.95in) (shown), the 76.2mm (3in) and the 25pdr (95mm/3.7in) howitzer.

Secondary Armament
A single hull mounted 7.92mm (0.31in) BESA machine gun was sometimes complemented with a 7.7mm (0.303in) Bren light machine gun in the Churchill Mk IV.

The experimental Harland and Wolff models were completed in 1940, the same year that Nazi conquests on the continent of Europe rendered the advent of trench warfare unlikely. A mobile, hard-hitting war of movement would probably be required to dislodge the Germans from the conquered territory.

Whither the Churchill

With the fall of France in June 1940, the prospect of a Nazi invasion of Great Britain increased tremendously. The A22,

The box-like shape of the Churchill Mk IV hull and turret were unmistakable on the battlefield. As the tank's main armament was upgraded, it became more proficient in dealing with Axis armour.

Turret
The Churchill turret was of both welded and cast construction. When the 75mm (2.95in) gun was installed, it required a 90° rotation for loading from the left side due to the configuration of the crew inside the turret.

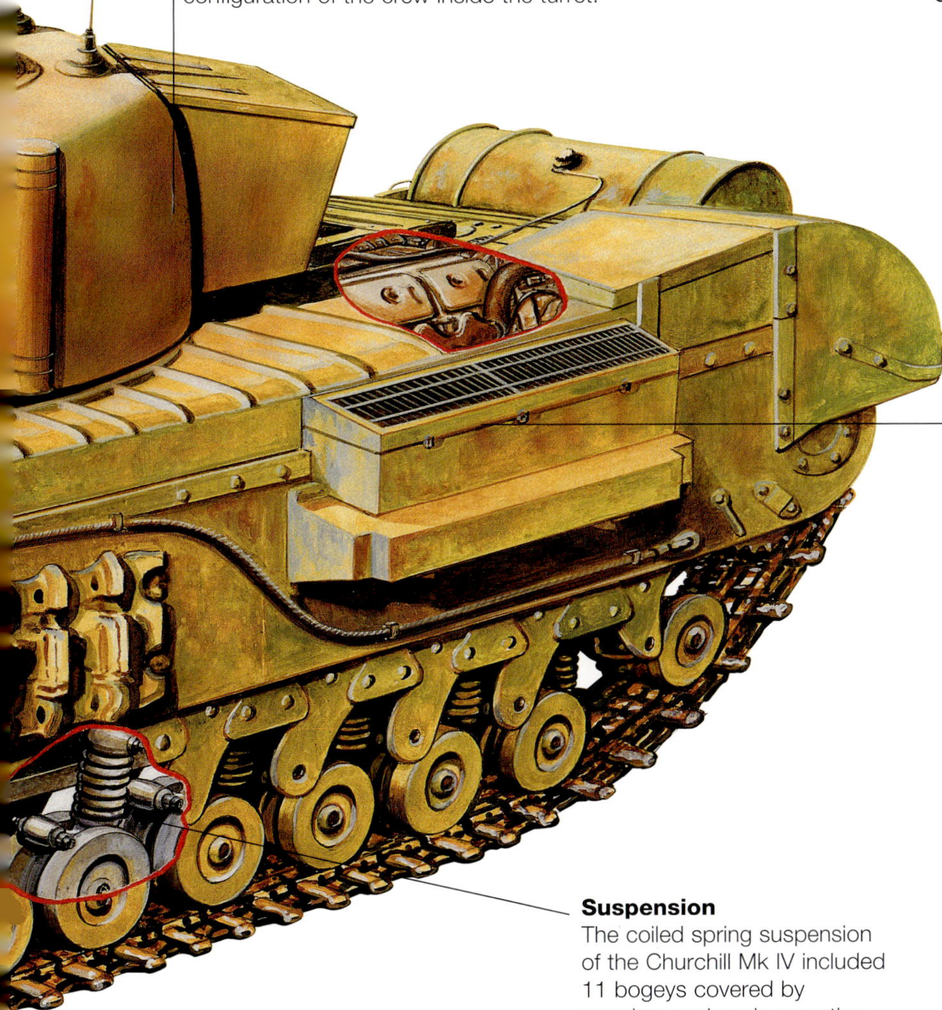

Engines
A horizontally opposed Bedford Twin-Six 12-cylinder petrol engine generated 261kW (350hp) and remained with the Churchill Mk IV throughout its service life despite the tank's increasing weight.

Suspension
The coiled spring suspension of the Churchill Mk IV included 11 bogeys covered by panniers and each mounting a pair of 254mm (10in) wheels. It proved most effective in providing traction on various surfaces.

an improved design of the original A20, was rushed into production in 1941 as time was of the essence. The tank was soon named "Churchill" in honour of Prime Minister Winston Churchill and designated the Infantry Tank Mk IV. Simply listing the number of variants, or Marks, that sprang from the original Mk IV would require several pages of text. In a confusing twist, the variants of the Mk IV were labelled with Marks of their own. In other words, the first combat version of the Churchill was the Mk I variant of the Mk IV.

Due to the exigencies of war, the early Churchill tank designs were produced rapidly and deployed without adequate field testing or refinement. One manufacturer admitted to the situation. A Vauxhall Motors spokesman related, "All those things which we know are not as they should be will be put right. Fighting vehicles are urgently required and instructions have been received to proceed with the vehicle as it is rather than hold up production."

The hefty Churchill Mk IV carried a crew of five and its hull was divided into four compartments with the driver forward beside a co-driver/hull gunner, the fighting compartment and turret in the centre with the commander, gunner and loader/radio operator and the engine compartment situated at the rear. The tank was powered by a Bedford Twin-Six horizontally opposed 12-cylinder petrol engine that generated 261 kilowatts (350hp). Originally, armour protection was between 16–102mm (0.62–4in); however, later versions beginning with the Mk VII increased it to 25–152mm (0.9–6in).

One of the most significant attributes of the Churchill Mk IV was its coiled spring suspension, which was contained under panniers on each side of the chassis with 11 bogeys carrying a pair of 254mm (10in) wheels. The configuration proved outstanding and contributed to the tank's ability to traverse uneven ground and negotiate steep grades.

Two iconic Allied tank types of World War II pass one another as crewmen shout greetings. On the left is the British Churchill Mk IV infantry tank. On the right is the American M4 Sherman medium tank. The types were workhorses of the Allied armoured forces during the war.

Specification

Dimensions	Length: 7.65m (25ft 2in) Width: 3.25m (10ft 8in) Height: 2.5m (8ft 2in)
Weight	40.6 tonnes (39.9 tons)
Engine	1 x Bedford Twin-Six horizontally opposed 12-cylinder petrol engine generating 261kW (350hp)
Speed	25km/h (15mph)
Armament	Main: 2pdr (40mm/1.57in) QF; 6pdr (57mm/2.24in) QF; 75mm (2.95in); 76.2mm (3in); 95mm (3.7in) Secondary: 1 x 7.92mm (0.31in) BESA machine gun; optional 7.7mm (0.303in) Bren LMG
Armour	16–152mm (0.62–6in)
Range	Road: 195km (120 miles) Cross-country: 100km (60 miles)
Crew	5

The unique suspension of the Churchill with its covering panniers is easily distinguishable from other contemporary tank suspension systems. The suspension was ideal for infantry support across broken ground and relatively steep gradients.

Advancing Armament

The tank was upgunned several times with the early Mk I and II mounting the 2pdr (40mm/1.57in) QF gun, the Mk III the 6pdr (57mm/2.24in) and the Mk IV NA75 the American 75mm (2.95in) gun. The Mk IV NA75 emerged from a battlefield experiment in North Africa. The heavier guns and mantlets of disabled American M4 Sherman medium tanks were placed into the turrets of Churchills. The success was immediate and by the summer of 1944 more than 200 of these conversions had been completed. Many of the Mk IV NA75 tanks went on to do great service in Italy.

The Mk I also mounted a 76.2mm (3in) howitzer in the chassis; however, this proved unwieldy and was removed in favour of a hull-mounted 7.92mm (0.31in) BESA machine gun in the Mk II and later variants. Some Churchills also carried an optional 7.7mm (0.303in) Bren light machine gun.

Remarkable Versatility

During the course of World War II, nearly 7400 Churchill infantry tanks of all Marks were produced. The specialized vehicles derived from the original included several that were instrumental during the Allied landings in Normandy on 6 June 1944 and the ensuing campaign in Western Europe, including the AVRE (Armoured Vehicle Royal Engineers), which carried a 290mm (11.4in) spigot mortar, the flamethrower-equipped Crocodile, the Kangaroo personnel carrier, the AVRE/CIRD mine clearing vehicle, the ARV (Armoured Recovery Vehicle) and the ARK (Armoured Ramp Carrier) bridging tank.

Production of the Churchill Mk IV infantry tank continued throughout World War II and the various specialized vehicles spawned by the design remained in service with the British Army until 1952.

Dieppe Disaster

Despite its innovative and largely effective suspension system, the Churchill Mk IV tank met with disaster during its combat debut. Operation Jubilee, a raid against the French port city of Dieppe carried out on August 19, 1942, ended disastrously and with heavy loss of life among the primarily Canadian forces.

The Churchill Mk I and II tanks that took part in the raid suffered great losses as well. A total of 30 Churchills of the 14th Tank Battalion, some armed with flamethrowers, became bogged down in the sand on Dieppe's beaches. Another 30 tanks of the Calgary Regiment landed behind schedule. Only a few of the tanks managed to get off the beaches and move inland to support the infantry.

As a result of the shifting sand and concentrated German fire, every Churchill was either destroyed or abandoned, and every crewman killed or captured. However, the disaster of Dieppe was not in vain as many of the hard lessons resulted in better planning for the Normandy invasion two years later.

M3A3 Stuart (1941)

The American Light Tank M3 was developed as an infantry support vehicle with excellent speed and effective armament and served with the U.S., British and Soviet armies in both the European and Pacific theatres during World War II.

The American Light Tank M3 entered production in the spring of 1941 as it was becoming more apparent that the United States might ultimately be drawn into the widening conflict in Europe and the Pacific. The M3 replaced the existing M2, already deemed obsolete and which epitomized the inter-war American interpretation of the role of the tank in combat – speed, mobility and infantry support.

The Light Tank M3 was reliable in the rugged conditions of the battlefield and gained tremendous popularity with its British and American crews. The British considered the M3 somewhat large for a light tank but recognized its strengths in infantry support and reconnaissance roles. This model served with the British 7th Armoured Brigade in the North African desert in 1942.

Main Armament
Throughout the service life of the Light Tank M3, the 37mm (1.45in) M6 gun was its main armament, unsuitable for tank versus tank combat, but adequate against other targets in infantry support.

Suspension
The vertical volute spring suspension was characteristic of American armoured vehicles of the World War II era. It featured rear idlers that were on the ground, reducing pressure and providing better support for the rear of the M3A3.

Power and Improvements

Most tanks in the M3 series were powered by the Continental W-670-9A radial petrol engine, which was also in great demand for other vehicles. Therefore, the Guiberson diesel T-1020 was fitted in some M3 chassis, as were twin Cadillac V-8 engines in a modified hull that required raised decking and resulted in designation as the M5, or Stuart V as the British referred to it, naming the tank for Confederate Major General J.E.B. Stuart, a dashing cavalry commander during the American Civil War.

Secondary Armament
The M3A3 Stuart mounted at least a pair of 7.62mm (0.3in) M1919A4 Browning air cooled machine guns, one coaxially in the turret and a second ball-mounted in the hull. Some models included an anti-aircraft machine gun at the turret hatch.

Engine
The Continental W-670-9A air-cooled, seven-cylinder radial engine generated 186kW (250hp) in the M3A3. Other M3 powerplants included a pair of Cadillac V8 engines and a Guiberson diesel.

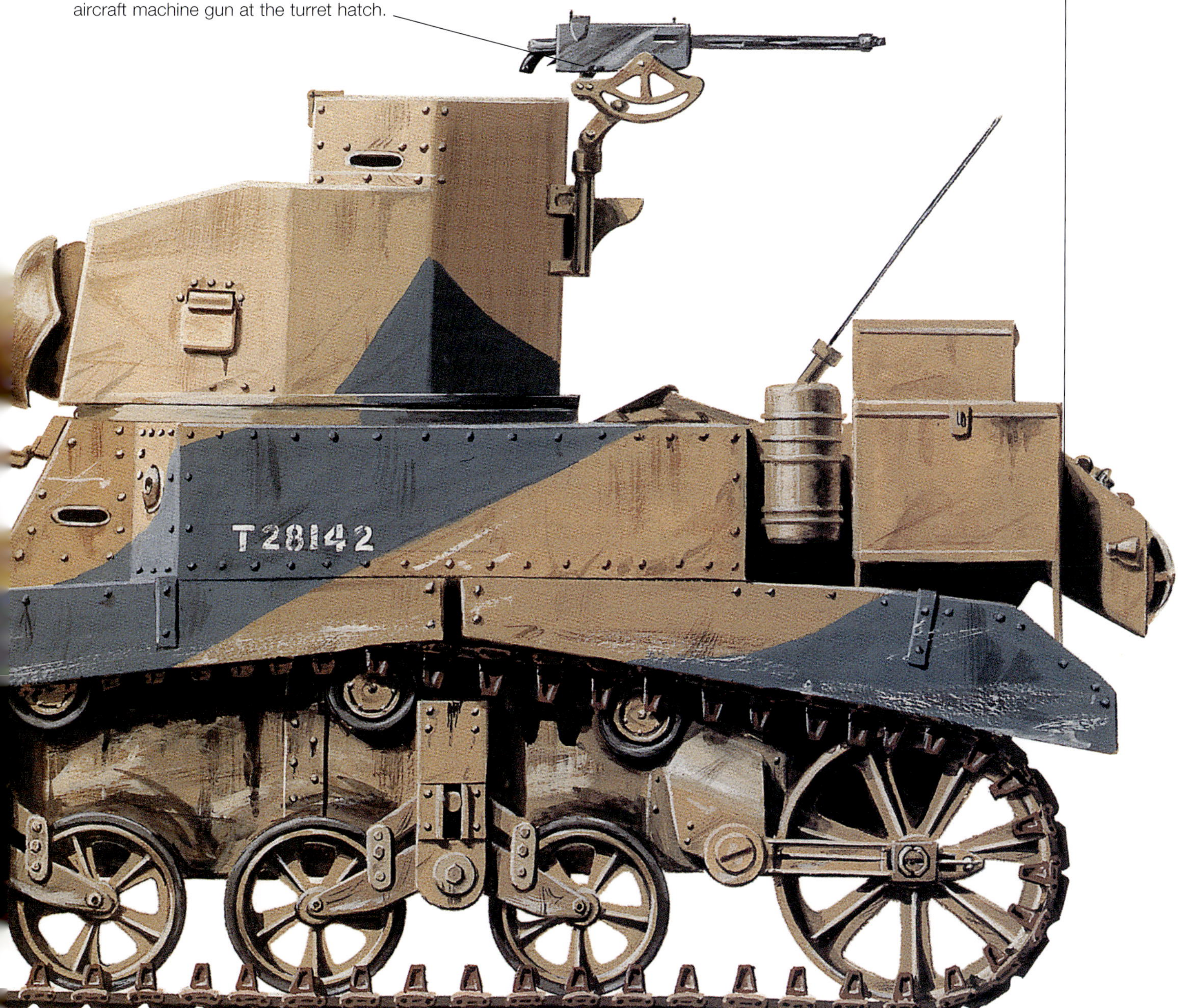

The relatively high silhouette of the M3 Light Tank made concealment difficult; however, speed was the primary advantage the tank possessed in the face of superior enemy forces. Thicker sloped armour increased the survivability of the M3A3.

The most common variants of the M3 were the M3A1, referred to by the British as the Stuart III or IV depending on whether its powerplant was petrol or diesel, and the M3A3, or Stuart V. The main armament throughout the M3 production run from 1941 to the end of World War II was the 37mm (1.45in) M6 cannon, already ineffective against the new generation of Axis armour emerging with the onset of the conflict, but it was still lethal against other types of targets. Secondary armament consisted of up to five Browning 7.62mm (0.3in) M1919A4 machine guns.

The accuracy of the main gun was improved with the M3A1, which included a gyro-stabilized mount in a power traverse turret with basket. Sloped armour with thickness increased from 43mm (1.6in) to 51mm (2in) was introduced with the M3A3, the driver's compartment was enlarged and a pair of sponson-mounted machine guns were removed, reducing the number of Brownings to three. The basic M3 layout was considered spacious for a light tank with the driver forward in the hull to the left, the co-driver to his right and the commander and gunner occupying the two-man turret.

Specification

Dimensions	Length: 4.53m (14ft 10in) Width: 2.23m (7ft 4in) Height: 2.52m (8ft 3in)
Weight	14.7 tonnes (14.4 tons)
Engine	1 x Continental W-670-9A air-cooled, seven-cylinder radial engine generating 186kW (250hp)
Speed	58km/h (35mph)
Armament	Main: 1 x 37mm (1.45in) M6 gun Secondary: 2 x 7.62mm (0.3in) M1919A4 air-cooled Browning machine guns
Armour	10–65mm (0.39–2.6in)
Range	Road: 120km (75 miles) Cross-country: 60km (40 miles)
Crew	4

Speed versus Power and Protection

During the course of World War II, thousands of M3 light tanks entered service with the British Army and the Soviet Red Army through the American Lend-Lease programme. Although they were intended for infantry support and reconnaissance, inevitably the M3 became involved in uneven fights with heavier German tanks and anti-tank weapons. Its shortcomings in firepower and armour protection became painfully apparent. Therefore, some military observers offered negative views of the tank's performance. Nevertheless, functioning in its primary roles the M3 was more than adequate in both Europe and the Pacific.

British crews in North Africa grew fond of the diminutive 14.7-tonne (14.4-ton) tank and nicknamed it the "Honey." Along with the M3 Grant and M4 Sherman tanks supplied by the U.S., the M3 light tank helped the British and later American forces to win the North African campaign.

In the Pacific, the M3 light tank was effective as an infantry support vehicle, penetrating thick jungle and negotiating terrain that heavier tanks could not. Japanese armour development was significantly behind that of the United States and the M3 was powerful enough to neutralize Japanese tanks, machine-gun nests, bunkers and troop concentrations as American troops fought their way, island by island, across the Pacific.

End of Days

Although the M3 light tank remained in production up to the end of World War II, by the autumn of 1944 its successor, the M24 Chaffee, was being deployed. A profound example of the rapid increase in armoured firepower during the war, the new M24 light tank mounted a 75mm (2.95in) gun. Subsequently, some M3 tanks were modified as command vehicles for armoured formations or had their turrets removed entirely with more machine guns mounted for direct infantry fire support.

Experimentation with specialized M3 vehicles was ongoing, including an anti-aircraft version with 12.7mm (0.5in) machine guns, a flamethrower variant and a few mounting a 75mm (2.95in) howitzer, but none of these ever reached anything beyond the production stage. In total, more than 25,000 M3 light tanks were built between March 1941 and October 1943 and the reliable design remained in service with the armed forces of numerous countries long after World War II. In fact, some were reported to still be active into the 1990s.

Strident Stuart

Despite its lack of firepower and armour protection, the American-built Light Tank M3 was nevertheless effective against softer targets such as troop concentrations, machine-gun emplacements and other enemy positions that might threaten Allied infantry. A pre-World War II design, the M3 series was rapidly becoming outdated when the United States entered the war, but thousands had already reached the Eastern Front and North Africa with British and Soviet forces through Lend-Lease.

In the absence of significant enemy anti-tank weapons or armour, even the predecessor of the M3, the M2, proved battleworthy in the Pacific. During a crucial stand by U.S. Marines at the Tenaru (actually Ilu) River on the island of Guadalcanal in the Solomons, a platoon of M2 tanks responded to attacks by charging Japanese troops. Firing canister and with machine guns blazing away, the American tanks cut the enemy troops to shreds.

Right: The riveted construction of the hull of this early M3 series light tank is clearly visible as this M3 negotiates a steep hill during training exercises. Note the hull mounted 7.62mm (0.3in) Browning machine gun.

M3A3 General Lee (1941)

In the rush to provide additional armoured firepower to counter German tanks in North Africa, American designers adapted an existing hull to carry a sponson-mounted 75mm (2.95in) gun.

For American designers hurriedly seeking to upgun existing tanks as the Germans deployed armoured fighting vehicles with 50mm (1.97in) and 75mm (2.95in) weapons to North Africa, necessity was truly the mother of invention in the summer of 1941. When the M3 medium tank entered production that August, no American turret available in quantity could mount a heavier weapon than 37mm (1.45in).

Main Armament
The M3 medium tank carried a 75mm (2.95in) gun mounted in a sponson in the hull and a 37mm (1.45in) cannon in the turret. The configuration was expedient for U.S. factories during a time when new tanks were badly needed to replace British losses in the North African desert.

The solution was a rolling contradiction, an anachronism that indeed also featured aspects of up-to-date design. The M3 medium tank was clearly influenced by World War I designs with its sponson-mounted 75mm cannon. Yet, the vertical volute suspension was characteristic of United States armoured vehicles of the 1930s and was utilized throughout World War II.

Bridging the Gap

As British tank losses in North Africa approached levels that could not be replaced without assistance, the U.S. rejected overtures to make British-designed

The M3 turret was offset to the left, shifting the weight for balance with the installation of the 75mm gun in the tank's hull.

The unorthodox appearance of the American M3 light tank was largely due to the urgency with which the tank was produced. The need for firepower was addressed with a 75mm (2.95in) sponson-mounted gun in the tank's hull.

More than 4,200 M3A3 and M3A5 American-built medium tanks were shipped to Great Britain and the Soviet Union. In the North African desert and on the Eastern Front, the M3 series helped bridge the shortage of Allied tanks until the arrival of the M4 Sherman.

Specification

Dimensions	Length: 5.64m (18ft 6in) Width: 2.72m (8ft 10in) Height: 3m (10ft)
Weight	27 tonnes (26.5 tons)
Engine	1 x General Motors 6046 12-cylinder diesel combining two GM 6-71 engines and generating 313kW (420hp)
Speed	40km/h (25mph)
Armament	Main: 1 x 75mm (2.95in) M2 L/31 cannon in sponson hull mount Secondary: 1 x 37mm (1.45in) M6 turret-mounted cannon; up to 3 x 7.62mm (0.3in) Browning M1919A4 machine guns
Armour	12.5–76mm (0.49–3in)
Range	Road: 240km (160 miles) Cross-country: 150km (90 miles)
Crew	6 or 7

tanks in American factories. The alternative was the rapid development, manufacture and deployment of the M3, demonstrating the ability of American industry to respond to an urgent need. Although the design was obviously flawed, the M3 filled an immediate need and offered some relief to a growing shortage of British armour in the desert.

The M3 utilized the suspension and drivetrain of the early M2. It stood approximately 3m (10ft) high with its crew compartment elevated to accommodate the angle of the drivetrain, while a small turret and commander's cupola capped the earliest models. Its high silhouette made the M3 vulnerable to enemy fire and prevented the tank from operating well in a hull-down position. It was relatively slow with a cross-country speed of only 26km/h (16mph). However, the tank was durable in the harsh desert climate.

American Desert Armour

A total of 6258 M3 medium tanks were produced from August 1941 to December 1942 and many of these were completed at the Baldwin Locomotive Works in Philadelphia, Pennsylvania. The British purchased great numbers of these and some were modified with the removal of the commander's cupola in favour of an elongated turret to hold radio equipment. These were nicknamed the General Grant by the British, while those M3s that were not modified were referred to as the General Lee. These were references to Union General Ulysses S. Grant and Confederate General Robert E. Lee, who opposed one another during the American Civil War.

The Soviet Red Army also received the M3 and the tank was apparently unpopular as it was dubbed the "coffin for seven brothers." Regardless, the appearance of an Allied tank mounting a 75mm weapon took the Germans somewhat by surprise.

Basics and Modifications

With a hull that stood more than one and a half times as tall as the average man, the M3 medium tank appeared ungainly and top-heavy. While it was less than streamlined and obviously drew from the designs of a bygone era, the M3 was capable of delivering a strong punch. Its significant firepower lay with the 75mm gun mounted in a sponson on the right side of the hull. This mount was accepted simply because time was of the essence.

The limited traverse of the big gun was a handicap when duelling with enemy tanks; however, it was handy in providing mobile artillery support and in reducing Axis strongpoints. The availability of both armour piercing and high explosive ammunition increased the tank's effectiveness. Meanwhile, the 37mm (1.45in) M6 cannon mounted in the tiny turret offered little in the way of support against enemy armour. Secondary armament included up to four 7.62mm (0.3in) Browning M1919A4 machine guns in the hull and turret. Armour protection ranged from 12.5–76mm (0.49–3in).

Early M3 medium tanks were somewhat underpowered with the Wright Continental R975 EC2 engine that generated 253 kilowatts (340hp) to move the 27-tonne (26.5-ton) vehicle. As modified examples came into the line, performance improved. The M3A1 was of welded construction rather than riveted. Armour protection was upgraded and a General Motors 6046 12-cylinder diesel engine generated 313 kilowatts (420hp) in the M3A3. The M3A4 utilized the Chrysler A57 engine, generating 276 kilowatts (370hp). The M3A5 was identical to the M3A3 but of riveted construction, and over 4200 of the M3A3 and M3A5 were shipped to the Soviets.

Sherman Ascendant

Although the tank served its purpose, the career of the M3 medium tank was destined to be short. Even as M3 production was gaining momentum, its successor, the legendary M4 Sherman medium tank, was rapidly moving toward deployment.

M3 in Combat

The combat debut of the M3 medium tank occurred at Gazala in North Africa in 1943. The Germans had no warning that a heavier Allied tank mounting a 75mm (2.95in) gun was in the field and were startled at the appearance of the M3. The Grant tanks at Gazala quickly added substantial firepower and actually engaged German tanks while remaining safely out of range of the towed 50mm (1.97in) Pak 38 anti-tank guns deployed by the Germans.

The M3 was reliable and less prone to breakdowns due to the infiltration of blowing desert sand into moving parts than other Allied tanks. However, it was slow and its high silhouette offered an inviting target for enemy guns when the tank did venture within range. The riveted construction of some M3s presented an additional hazard for Allied crewmen. When an enemy round hit the tank, it was not uncommon for the rivets to fracture and fly about the interior of the vehicle with devastating results.

T-70 (1942)

Although the Soviets largely abandoned light tanks as World War II progressed, the T-70 was manufactured by small factories and combined the reconnaissance and infantry support functions.

By the end of 1941, Soviet tank design had shifted almost entirely to the medium T-34 and heavier KV-1 tanks. The performance of light tanks called their future value into question even though some opportunity remained for an effective reconnaissance and infantry support armoured fighting vehicle. Small factories that were unable to manufacture components for the T-34 and KV-1 could build the light tank in sufficient numbers.

Main Armament
The 45mm (1.8in) L/46 Model 38 gun of the T-70 light tank was more powerful than the 37mm (1.45in) weapon of the preceding T-60. Along with heavier armour protection, the tank increased in weight to more than 9 tonnes (9 tons).

In contrast, during the 1920s and 1930s the Soviets had invested substantially in the development of tankettes that were manned by a single soldier, and light tanks that were crewed by only two. The tankette design was finally abandoned and in the late 1930s a prototype T-40 was authorized for production following at least six modifications that had begun more than a decade prior and were based on the early T-27.

Following the Nazi invasion of the Soviet Union on 22 June 1941, light tank production was stepped up considerably even though much of the Soviet industrial capacity was disassembled and moved east of the Ural

The T-70 light tank entered production in March 1941, at a time when the importance of such vehicles was obviously eroding in the Soviet military and attention was focusing on the T-34 medium and KV-1 heavy tanks.

Turret
The multi-sided angular turret of the T-70 light tank was offset substantially to the left, while heavier components and ammunition storage compensated with even weight distribution and stability.

Engine
A pair of tandem six-cylinder GAZ 202 petrol car engines delivered 104kW (140hp) and drove the T-70 at a maximum speed of 45km/h (28mph).

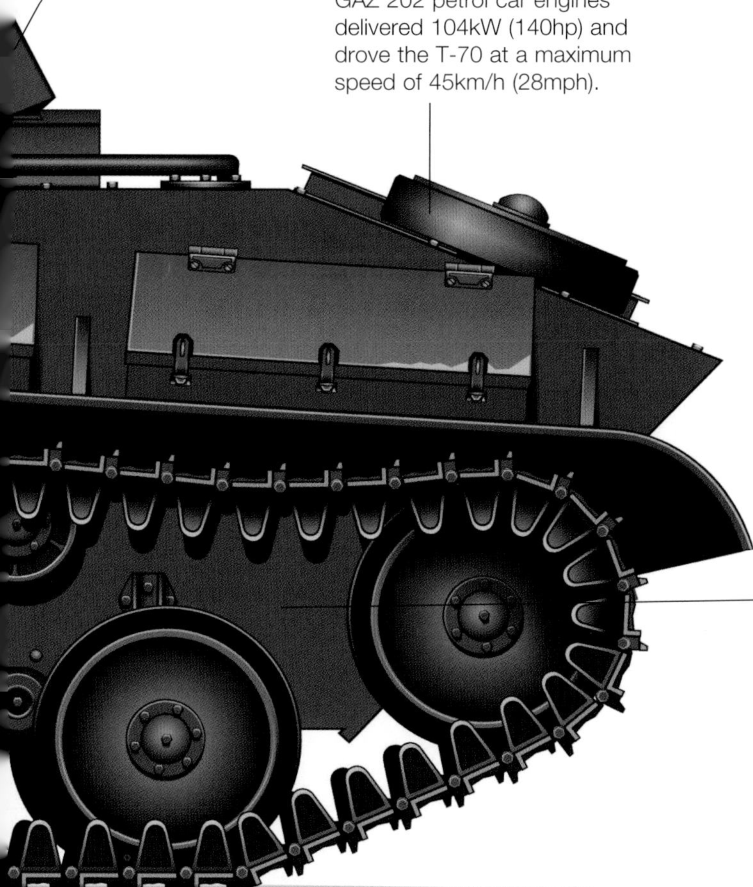

Suspension
Later T-60 and T-70 light tanks utilized solid rather than spoked wheels in the durable torsion bar suspension.

Mountains to avoid being overrun by German spearheads. The T-40 was renamed the T-60. In 1942, the T-60A emerged with limited improvement in armour protection and a change to solid rather than spoked wheels in the torsion bar suspension.

Then, as German armoured strength grew, it became apparent that the early 20mm (0.78in) and follow-on 37mm (1.45in) gun and light armour protection of the T-60 could not stand up to the German panzers in combat. Therefore, the T-70 was designed to combine both scouting and infantry support roles in a compact fighting vehicle weighing only 9.2 tonnes (9 tons) with a crew of just two, a commander and driver.

With their hatches open and infantrymen riding on the hulls, T-70 light tanks of the Soviet Red Army churn across a frozen landscape somewhere on the Eastern Front. The T-70 was the last viable production model Soviet light tank of World War II. Only 120 of the subsequent T-80 were built.

Re-evaluated Specifications

The T-70 was designed at Factory No. 38 in Kirov and powered by a pair of tandem six-cylinder GAZ 202 petrol automobile engines delivering 104 kilowatts (140hp). The early twin powertrain was deemed inadequate and revised in production. Protected by 10–60mm (0.3–2.3in) of armour, the T-70 was deemed impervious to 37mm anti-tank fire. It was more than three tonnes heavier than the T-40 and its 45mm (1.8in) L/46 Model 38 gun was more substantial than the 20mm and 37mm main weapons of the T-40 and T-60. On board were 94 rounds of 45mm ammunition and the tank also carried a 7.62mm (0.3in) DT machine gun mounted coaxially in the turret.

The T-70 driver was positioned forward in the hull, while the commander occupied the wide turret that was offset to the left to a pronounced degree. The commander was also required to fully operate the main weapon, greatly diminishing his effectiveness during combat situations. The T-70 entered production in March 1942 and by September production at Factories 37 and 38 had shifted entirely to the T-70 as the last T-60s were completed. Production of the T-70 ceased in October 1943 and the remarkable number of 8226, including the T-70A with enhanced armour protection, were completed.

In late 1943, the Soviets initiated production of a successor, the T-80, but even then the combat value of the light tank was being seriously questioned by the Soviet military and civilian authorities. The T-80 was shelved not long afterward and only 120 examples of it were actually completed. Other light tanks, such as the American M3 Stuart, were available through Lend-Lease. Light tank production ceased in the Soviet Union late in 1943 and Soviet resources were directed toward a more practical weapon, the self-propelled gun.

Specification

Dimensions	Length: 4.29m (14ft 1in) Width: 2.32m (7ft 7in) Height: 2.04m (6ft 8in)
Weight	9.2 tonnes (9 tons)
Engine	2 x tandem six-cylinder GAZ 202 petrol car engines generating 104kW (140hp)
Speed	45km/h (28mph)
Armament	Main: 1 x 45mm (1.8in) L/46 Model 38 cannon Secondary: 1 x 7.62mm (0.3in) DT machine gun
Armour	10–60mm (0.3–2.3in)
Range	360km (220 miles)
Crew	2

Although the T-70 light tank combined the best attributes of years of Soviet research and development, its combat relevance was already waning when it entered production in March 1942. The T-70 was successful on a limited basis as a reconnaissance and infantry support tank.

Self-propelled Gun Successor

The remaining inventory of T-70 chassis was earmarked for production of the SU-76 self-propelled gun. The SU-76 mounted a highly effective 76mm (3in) gun that was well suited for infantry support and more than 14,000 were completed between 1942 and the end of the war. The SU-76 was open-turreted and was unpopular with its crews due to a lack of armour protection and exposure to the elements during inclement weather. In terms of numbers, the SU-76 was produced in greater quantity than any other armoured vehicle deployed with the Red Army, except the legendary T-34 medium tank.

Another self-propelled weapon that utilized the light tank chassis was the open turreted T-90, the first mobile anti-aircraft vehicle fielded by the Red Army, mounting a pair of 12.7mm (0.5in) DShK machine guns. The ZSU-37 followed in 1945 with a 37mm (1.45in) anti-aircraft gun and was manufactured until 1948.

T-70 in Harm's Way

The T-70 was truly the last of its kind in terms of Soviet armoured production. Only 120 of its successor, the T-80, were actually completed prior to the end of light tank production in late 1943. The T-70 had evolved from numerous preceding light tank types and a research programme that dated back to the 1920s. Light tanks had been conceived in part to fulfil the role of infantry support rather than engaging enemy tanks, and early Soviet models were equipped with the 37mm gun, later improved to the 45mm gun of the T-70.

However, as World War II progressed it became apparent that light tanks were encountering heavier enemy armoured vehicles and newer tank designs were capable of handling both infantry support and tank versus tank duties. Although the T-70 remained in service through to the end of the war, its exposure to combat operations was greatly diminished. In this photo, snow-covered T-70s pause in a forest on the Eastern Front as soldiers clad in winter camouflage gear trudge forward.

T-34 Model 1943 (1942)

The T-34 medium tank is one of a few weapons that may, quite literally, be credited with winning World War II. The T-34 reached the battlefield in large numbers in 1941 and quickly evened the odds for the Red Army against German tanks.

Perhaps one of the most iconic images of World War II is that of a Red Army T-34 medium tank, soldiers aboard and on foot nearby, speeding westward toward the frontier of the Third Reich and the Nazi capital of Berlin. Indeed, the T-34 medium tank, which first entered production in 1940 and the service of the Red Army in the same year, changed the course of the war in the East.

Until the T-34 reached the battlefield in large numbers, German armour, particularly the PzKpfw III and IV, had reigned supreme. The appearance of the T-34 proved

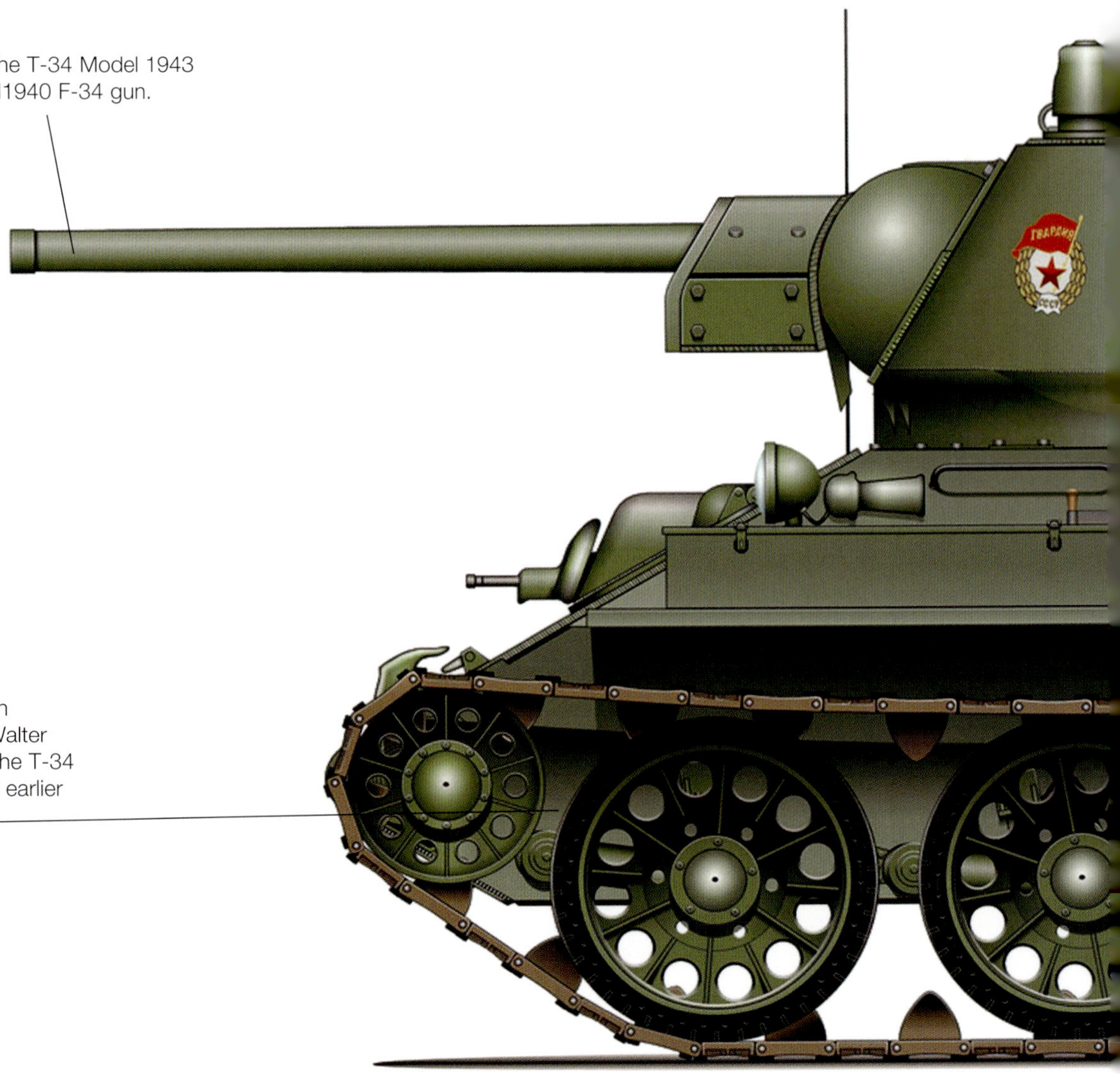

Main Armament
The main weapon of the T-34 Model 1943 was the 76mm (3in) M1940 F-34 gun.

Suspension
The coil spring suspension developed by American Walter Christie and utilized with the T-34 was carried over from the earlier BT series of tanks.

shocking to the German tankers who encountered it for the first time in November 1941 near the Russian village of Mzensk. However, the tank itself had been in the design and prototype phases of development since the mid-1930s. While it was intended to replace the outmoded T-26 and BT series tanks, the T-34 bore an unmistakable family resemblance. Its sleek profile with the turret forward and its low silhouette with sloped armour were true to the design

The high ground clearance and proven Christie suspension of the T-34 medium tank made it ideal for mobile warfare across the vast Russian steppes as the Red Army pursued the Germans westwards towards Berlin in 1944 and 1945.

Turret
Earlier model T-34s had a very cramped turret, but the Model 1943 had an enlarged cast hexagonal turret, which gave welcome extra space for the crew.

Engine
The T-34 incorporated a V-2-34 V-12 38.8-litre diesel engine that generated 375kW (500hp).

An aerial view of a T-34 Model 1942, with its cast two-man turret. The main difference between the Model 1942 and Model 1943 was the larger turret of the latter. The hull and chassis remained essentially the same for all models.

perspective that would rule Soviet production for decades to come.

Belligerent Breakthrough

While it borrowed from earlier Soviet tank designs, the T-34 broke new ground with speed, mobility, firepower and armour in a lethal combination. Its V-2-34 V-12 38.8-litre (8.5-gallon) diesel engine generated 375 kilowatts (500hp) and enabled the 26.5-tonne (26-ton) tank to reach a top speed of 53km/h (33mph). It maintained the Christie suspension of the earlier BT series, which was already proven superior in cross-country operation over broken terrain. Armour protection ranged from 15mm (0.59in) on the bottom of the hull to 60mm (2.4in) on the turret front. The effectiveness of the hull armour was increased by its slope, reducing penetration and sometimes deflecting enemy shells.

The four-man crew included a commander, driver, loader and gunner. Early production T-34s were armed with the 76.2mm (3in) ZIS5 F 34 gun and the commander was still required to serve the weapon. Radios were in short supply and only command tanks received them – all other tanks still communicated with flags. The interior of the T-34 was painfully tight, restricting the combat efficiency of the crew. The driver, for example, was the lone occupant of the forward hull compartment and his visibility was quite restricted in early-production T-34s.

By early 1944 the T-34/85 had incorporated several improvements, such as a more spacious three-man turret, relieving the commander of responsibility for laying and firing the main weapon. The newly-installed 85mm (3.35in) ZIS-S-53

Specification

Dimensions	Length: 6.68m (21ft 11in) Width: 3.0m (9ft 10in) Height: 2.45m (8ft)
Weight	26.5 tonnes (26 tons)
Engine	1 x V-2-34 V-12 38.8-litre (8.5-gallon) diesel engine delivering 375kW (500hp)
Speed	53km/h (33mph)
Armament	Main: 1 x 76.2mm (3in) ZIS5 F 34 gun Secondary: 2 x 7.62mm (0.3in) DT machine guns
Armour	15–60mm (0.59in–2.24in)
Range	400km (250 miles)
Crew	4

provided the Soviet tank with greater range against the heavy German PzKpfw V Panther and PzKpfw VI Tiger, mounting high-velocity 75mm (2.95in) and 88mm (3.5in) guns. The ZIS-S-53 gun influenced Soviet tactics, allowing Red Army tank commanders to rely less on the need to rapidly close with the Germans in order to get within range for their main guns to fire effectively. The T-34/85 still lacked a rotating turret basket on which the gunner and loader could stand during combat, negatively impacting the tank's rate of fire.

Panzers Surprised

When the Soviet T-34 medium tank reached the front lines in the East, the long domination of the battlefield by powerful German tanks was finally over. The Germans were amazed at the performance of the T-34 with its powerful 76.2mm (3in) gun, later upgrade to 85mm (3.35in), its speed and its cross-country mobility.

After German tanks of Panzergruppe II under the command of General Heinz Guderian met the T-34 in battle for the first time, the general wrote, "Numerous Russian T-34s went into action and inflicted heavy losses on the German tanks at Mzensk in 1941. Up to this time, we had enjoyed tank superiority, but from now on the situation was reversed. The prospect of rapid, decisive victories was fading in consequence. I made a report on this situation, which for us was a new one ... I described in plain terms the marked superiority of the T-34 to our PzKpfw IV and drew the relevant conclusion as that must affect our future tank production."

Silhouetted against a barren landscape, three Soviet T-34 medium tanks pause, their hatches open, before moving forward to the frontlines. The overwhelming numbers and performance of the T-34 doomed the German Army to defeat on the Eastern Front.

Strength in Numbers

In total more than 57,000 T-34 medium tanks were produced in Soviet factories during World War II, which is a remarkable achievement considering the disruption of heavy industry after the Germans launched Operation Barbarossa on 22 June 1941, and many facilities were dismantled and moved to safety east of the Ural Mountains. During the war, over 22,500 T-34/85 tanks were produced and better efficiency cut production time in half and sharply reduced the overall cost per unit. During the pivotal battle for the city of Stalingrad on the Volga River, some tanks were said to have rolled directly off the factory floor and into active combat against the Germans. While Soviet tactics were refined slowly and many T-34s were lost during mass charges against German armour and anti-tank weapons, the Red Army could make good its combat losses with numbers the Germans could never hope to match. The over-engineered German Tiger and Panther tanks were plagued by mechanical failures, costly to build and never available in sufficient numbers to sustain a protracted war effort.

T-34 variants included self-propelled assault guns and flamethrower, bridging and recovery vehicles. The T-34 continued in production until 1958 and more than 84,000 were eventually built. Some upgrades continued into the 1960s and a few T-34s are said to continue in service today.

Panzer VI Tiger Ausf E (1942)

The most feared and respected tank of World War II, the formidable Panzerkampfwagen VI Tiger was in production for two years, but only slightly more than 1300 were ever completed.

While the PzKpfw IV was in production in the late 1930s, plans were already underway to develop a successor. The German armaments ministry issued initial specifications for a 36.5-tonne (36-ton) tank in early 1941 and Henschel set to work, developing a prototype in a relatively short period of time. Abruptly, the development of the 36.5-tonne tank was halted as specifications were issued for an even larger tank – a 45.7-tonne (45-ton) behemoth – in May of the same year.

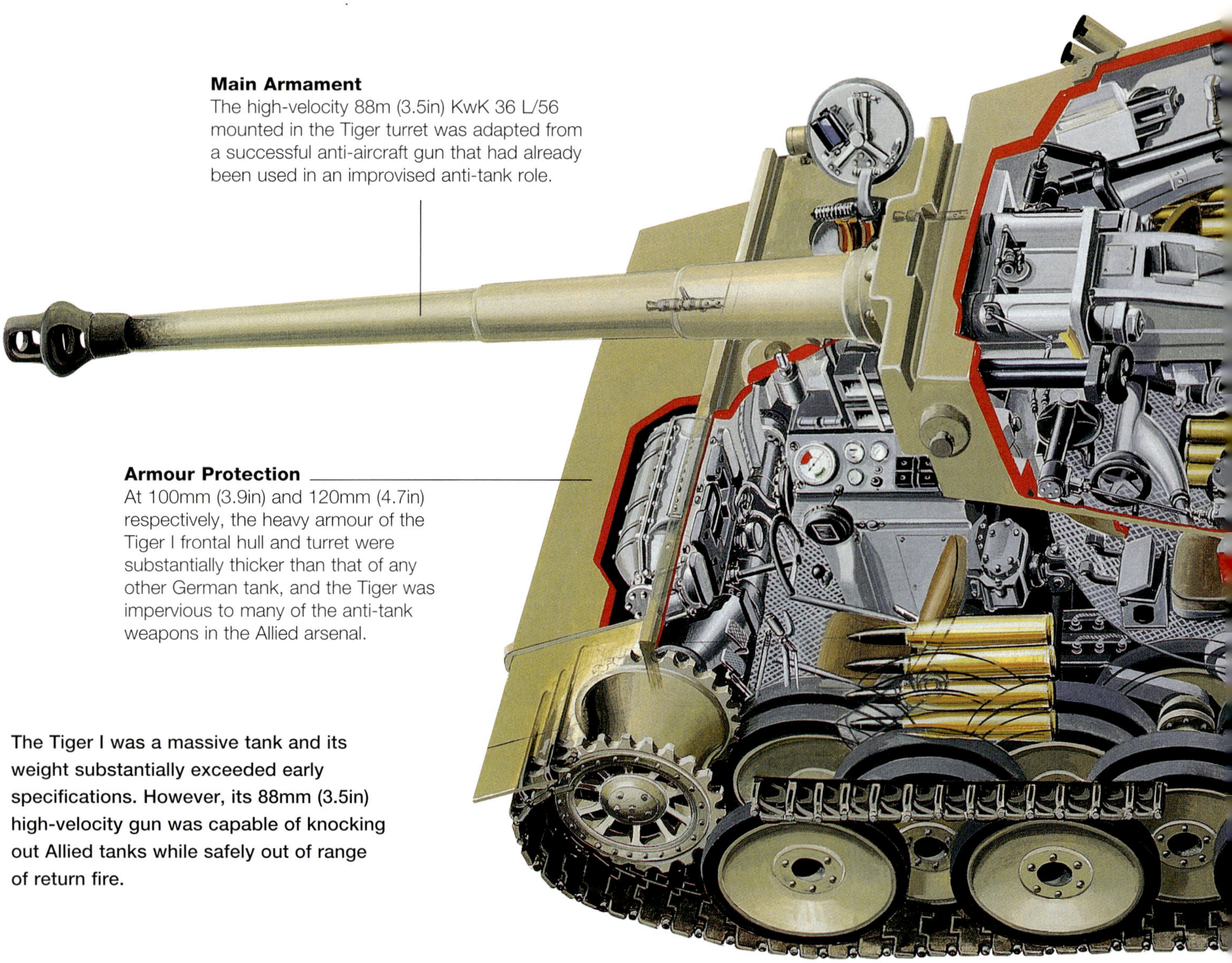

Main Armament
The high-velocity 88m (3.5in) KwK 36 L/56 mounted in the Tiger turret was adapted from a successful anti-aircraft gun that had already been used in an improvised anti-tank role.

Armour Protection
At 100mm (3.9in) and 120mm (4.7in) respectively, the heavy armour of the Tiger I frontal hull and turret were substantially thicker than that of any other German tank, and the Tiger was impervious to many of the anti-tank weapons in the Allied arsenal.

The Tiger I was a massive tank and its weight substantially exceeded early specifications. However, its 88mm (3.5in) high-velocity gun was capable of knocking out Allied tanks while safely out of range of return fire.

One of the most innovative aspects of the new tank was the requirement that it mount a version of the 88mm (3.5in) anti-aircraft gun adapted for use with armour. It had already achieved notoriety in its role as a tank killer when the weapon was used against armour rather than aircraft. Both Henschel and Porsche forged ahead with prototypes and the two contractors were told that the tanks had to be ready for demonstration on Hitler's birthday, April 20, 1942.

The tracks of the PzKpfw VI Tiger tank were changed depending on whether the vehicle was operating on roadways or cross-country. Wider cross-country tracks resulted in lower ground pressure and better mobility.

Turret
The three-man turret of the Tiger I weighed 9.9 tonnes (9.7 tons) with the gunner forward on the left, the loader seated on the right facing the rear and the commander placed behind the gunner.

Engine
After 250 Tigers were produced, the early 12-cylinder Maybach HL 210 P45 engine was replaced by the Maybach V-12 HL 230 P45 engine, generating 522kW (700hp).

Suspension
The torsion bar suspension of the PzKpfw VI Tiger included eight bars on each side of the vehicle with interwoven wheels. The wheels were 800mm (31.4in) in diameter and evenly distributed the tank's great weight. However, they required continuous maintenance.

Henschel borrowed from its 36.5-tonne prototype and developed the VK 4501(H). Porsche produced its own design and came up with the VK 4501(P). Both tanks were presented on time for the Führer's review and in August the Henschel design was chosen and designated the PzKpfw VI Ausf E. Later, it also came to be known as the Tiger I. When the initial production authorization was issued to Henschel, an order for 90 of the Porsche design was also awarded in the event of a setback with the Henschel during trials. These vehicles were actually completed as the Panzerjäger Tiger (P) Ferdinand, a massive tank destroyer named for Dr Ferdinand Porsche, the head of the company.

Tiger Tracks

The new Tiger tank entered production in August 1942 and over the next two years only 1350 were completed. Nevertheless, when production ended in August 1944, the Tiger had earned a fearsome reputation. However, the tank was over-engineered and had to be built to such exacting specifications that technical difficulties were common. The cost of production was extreme as well – twice that of the PzKpfw IV.

The Tiger I weighed 56.9 tonnes (56 tons) and it was powered by the Maybach HL230 P45 12-cylinder petrol engine, developing 522 kilowatts (700hp). The three-man

Specification

Dimensions	Length: 8.45m (27ft 8in) Width: 3.7m (12ft 1in) Height: 2.93m (9ft 7in)
Weight	56.9 tonnes (56 tons)
Engine	1 x Maybach V-12 HL 230 P45 engine, generating 522kW (700hp)
Speed	38km/h (24mph)
Armament	Main: 1 x 88m (3.5in) KwK 36 L/56 high-velocity gun Secondary: 2 x 7.92mm (0.31in) MG 34 machine guns
Armour	25–120mm (0.98–4.7in)
Range	140km (80 miles)
Crew	5

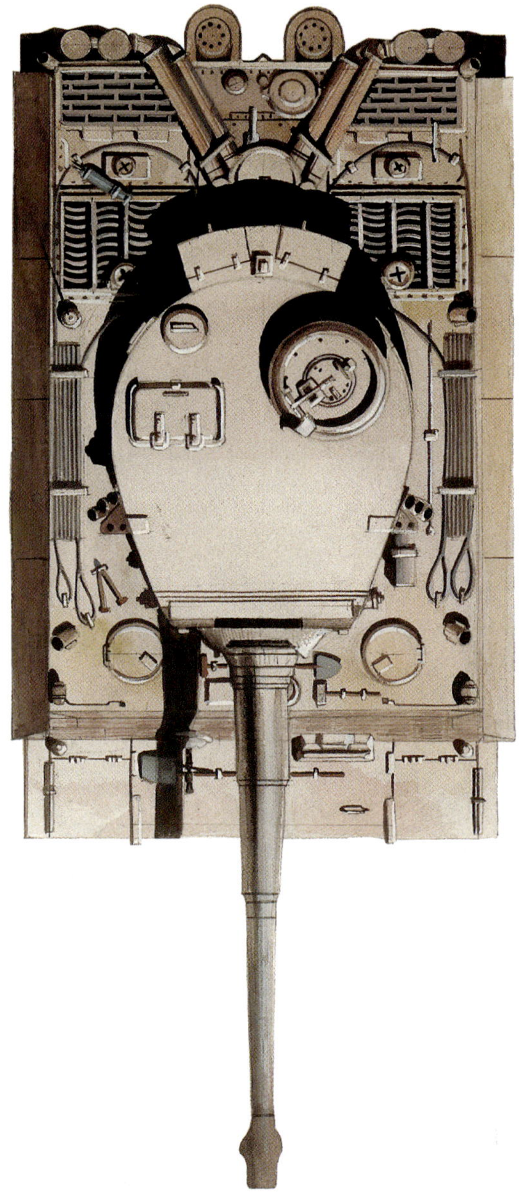

During two years of production only 1,350 Tiger I tanks were completed due to complex and expensive manufacturing processes. The cost of a single Tiger was double that of the earlier PzKpfw IV.

turret alone weighed 9.9 tonnes (9.7 tons) and housed the massive 88mm (3.5in) Kwk 36 L/56 gun modified to fit. It was sighted and fired with precision optics that made the weapon even more deadly in skilled hands. Inside the turret, the gunner sat forward and to the left with the commander behind and the loader occupying a folding seat on the other side, facing to the rear. The driver and radio operator/gunner were located forward in the hull with the transmission gear box between them. Secondary armament consisted of two 7.92mm (0.31in) MG 34 machine guns, one mounted

The PzKpfw VI Tiger tank was hurriedly deployed and suffered from inadequate trials and field testing. Early Tigers were particularly prone to mechanical failures, particularly with the Maybach powerplant and the complex interwoven wheels and suspension system.

coaxially in the turret and the other in a ball mount in the hull.

The tank's torsion bar suspension was divided equally with eight bars on each side and interwoven wheels that actually created mobility problems at times. The wheels often became clogged with rocks, mud and debris which could cause the wheels to seize. Operations in freezing temperatures were also difficult as the Tiger's tracks and wheels, caked in mud, often froze solid, immobilizing the tank completely. When the vehicle travelled on roadways it utilized tracks 515mm (20in) wide, and when moving cross-country a change was made to a 715mm (28in) track.

Field Operations

The Tiger first saw action on the Eastern Front near Leningrad in September 1942. In late 1942, the Tiger also entered combat in North Africa near the town of Rabaa, Tunisia. Few Tigers actually reached North Africa due to the priority of the Eastern Front and the interdiction of German convoys by Allied aircraft, warships and submarines in the Mediterranean.

Due to pressure from Hitler and the exigencies of war, the Tiger was placed in service somewhat prematurely. It was plagued by mechanical problems early in its service life and some reports indicate that the tank was underpowered for its size, further impeding efficient movement. The Tiger was often simply too heavy for effective mobility and its ground clearance was sometimes too low to traverse difficult terrain. For long-distance travel, the Tiger was loaded onto flatbed railway cars, an arduous and time-consuming task.

For all its drawbacks and difficulties in the field, the basic design of the Tiger was outstanding. The tank struck fear into the hearts of Allied soldiers who encountered it, becoming one of the iconic weapons of World War II.

SS-manned Tiger I Ausf E tanks advance through snow-covered forest somewhere on the Eastern Front, 1943.

Victor at Villers-Bocage

During World War II, the PzKpfw VI Tiger tank was reported to have achieved a six-to-one kill ratio against Allied tanks. Its overwhelming firepower and heavy armour protection allowed the Tiger to dispatch enemy vehicles from safe distances and ward off shells from most Allied anti-tank weapons. Despite several drawbacks, it was a formidable weapon in combat – as demonstrated by SS Hauptsturmführer Michael Wittman at the French village of Villers-Bocage on 13 July 1944.

In minutes, Wittman's single Tiger of SS Heavy Panzer Battalion 101 destroyed 13 tanks, two anti-tank guns and up to 15 troop carriers of the British 22 Armoured Brigade. Accounts of the action at Villers-Bocage vary, but one fact remains undisputed to this day. The Tiger tank was virtually without equal on the battlefields of World War II. Wittman, a holder of the Knight's Cross with Oak Leaves and Swords who was killed in action two months after his amazing feat of arms, was only one of at least 12 tank commanders who are believed to have recorded more than 100 kills with the Tiger.

M4A4 Sherman (1942)

The American Medium Tank M4, popularly known as the Sherman, reached the battlefield in great numbers during World War II and essentially overwhelmed the technologically superior German tanks in North Africa and Western Europe.

The ubiquitous Medium Tank M4, produced in greater quantity than any other tank during World War II with the exception of the Soviet T-34, tipped the balance of victory in favour of the Allies through adequate performance in the field and sheer weight of numbers. From 1941 to the end of the war, approximately

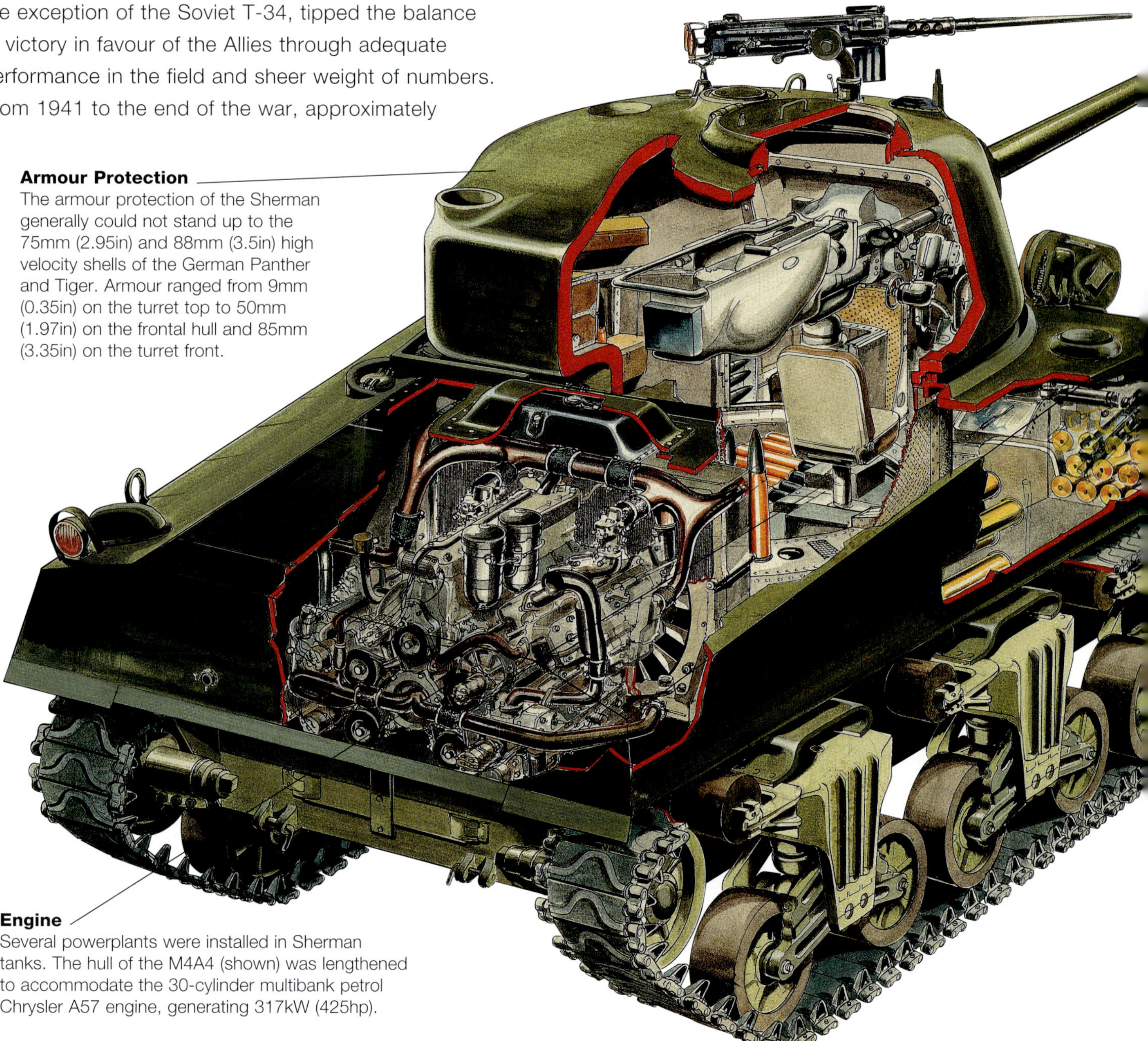

Armour Protection
The armour protection of the Sherman generally could not stand up to the 75mm (2.95in) and 88mm (3.5in) high velocity shells of the German Panther and Tiger. Armour ranged from 9mm (0.35in) on the turret top to 50mm (1.97in) on the frontal hull and 85mm (3.35in) on the turret front.

Engine
Several powerplants were installed in Sherman tanks. The hull of the M4A4 (shown) was lengthened to accommodate the 30-cylinder multibank petrol Chrysler A57 engine, generating 317kW (425hp).

53,000 Sherman tanks were produced by American factories. Sherman production run ended in the 1950s and the tank remained in service with armies around the world for half a century.

Even as the M3 Grant/Lee medium tank was rolling off U.S. assembly lines and deployed against the Axis, designers were painfully aware of the tank's shortcomings and a hurried effort to develop a successor was underway. The object was to field a medium tank mounting a 75mm (2.95in) gun that bettered the M3 in performance but used as many of the components of the older tank as possible. In September 1941, the prototype M4, known at this stage as the T6, was completed and ready for quick evaluation.

Mass Production

The story of the Sherman, conceived, manufactured and deployed in a matter of months, demonstrates the capability of American industry to produce war materiel on a scale that not only equipped the U.S. armed forces but allowed

Secondary Armament
The M4 Sherman was armed with a 12.7mm (0.5in) Browning machine gun for defence against enemy aircraft, and a pair of 7.62mm (0.3in) Browning M1919A4 machine guns, one mounted coaxially in the turret and the other forward in the hull.

Main Armament
Originally, the M4 Sherman medium tank was armed with a 75mm (2.95in) gun that produced insufficient muzzle velocity to penetrate the armour of some German tanks. It was later upgunned with a high-velocity 76mm (2.9in) and with the British 17pdr (76.2mm/3in) QF.

Ammunition Storage
Up to 90 rounds of 75mm (2.95in) ammunition were carried aboard the M4A4 Sherman in wet storage, reducing the potential of a catastrophic explosion if the tank took a serious hit.

The American Medium Tank M4, commonly known as the Sherman, sacrificed armour protection for speed. Although it was vulnerable to the fire of German tanks and anti-tank weapons, the Sherman was available in large numbers and contributed significantly to victory in World War II.

The M4A4 Sherman tank incorporated the Chrysler A57 engine along with greater separation of the road wheel for better traction. The hull of the M4A4 was 280mm longer than other Sherman variants.

The M4 Sherman medium tank used the same hull and suspension system as its predecessor, the M3. However, its main weapon was mounted in a turret rather than sponson mounted in the hull, a vast improvement that gave the 75mm (2.95in) gun 360° traverse.

Specification

Dimensions	Length: 6.06m (19ft 1in) Width: 2.9m (9ft 6in) Height: 2.84m (9ft 4in)
Weight	31.62 tonnes (31.1 tons)
Engine	1 x Chrysler A57 30-cylinder multibank petrol engine generating 317kW (425hp)
Speed	47km/h (29mph)
Armament	Main: 1 x 75mm (2.95in) M3 L/40 gun Secondary: 2 x 7.62mm (0.3in) Browning M1919A4 machine guns; 1 x 12.7mm (0.5in) Browning M2HB machine gun
Armour	9–85mm (0.35–3.35in)
Range	Road: 160km (100 miles) Cross-country: 100km (60 miles)
Crew	5

the nation to serve as the great "arsenal of democracy," sending thousands to Great Britain and other allies through Lend-Lease.

When the Sherman entered combat with British forces at the pivotal battle of El Alamein in North Africa in the autumn of 1942, it was quickly determined that the main 75mm (2.95in) M3 L/40 gun was capable of holding its own against the German PzKpfw III and IV tanks deployed with *Panzerarmee Afrika*. However, it was soon proven wholly inadequate when confronting the next generation of German tanks, the PzKpfw V Panther and PzKpfw VI Tiger. The muzzle velocity of the weapon was simply too low to penetrate the thick enemy armour. Therefore, a new high-velocity 76mm (2.9in) weapon was later introduced in American tanks, while the British installed the 17pdr (76.2mm/3in) QF gun on many Shermans, resulting in a variant nicknamed the Firefly.

The Sherman was easily recognizable with its high profile that stood nearly 3m (10ft). Although the tank's hull armour was sloped to deflect enemy shells, it remained a highly visible target for German tanks and anti-tank gunners while in open country. In addition to its numerical superiority, the Sherman enjoyed the advantage of mobility with a top speed of 47km/h (29mph).

However, a portion of this speed was derived from thin armour protection that ranged from 9–85mm (0.35–3.35in), woefully inadequate against the high velocity Rheinmetall Borsig 75mm (2.95in) and 88mm (3.5in) cannon of the German Panther and Tiger respectively. Both were often able to deliver lethal shots against a Sherman from standoff distances, out of range of the Allied tank's 75mm (2.95in) main weapon.

Sherman Swarm

Despite its disadvantage in direct tank versus tank combat, the Sherman won a battle of attrition as American factories could make good their losses while German production could not keep pace due to the over-engineered precision production required with the perspective that quality could eventually overcome quantity. Sherman tankers developed effective tactics to take on the heavier German vehicles. For example, a platoon of four Shermans might attack a Tiger from different directions, using speed to manoeuvre to the vulnerable rear of the enemy tank.

One or more Shermans might well be sacrificed in the process, but the Tiger would be conclusively overwhelmed and defeated.

Multiple Models

During the war, the Sherman was continually improved. Several variants were in simultaneous production but successive designations such as M4A1 to M4A4 did not necessarily mean that one outclassed the other. These production models differed primarily in their powerplants. These included the Wright Whirlwind, Continental R975, Caterpillar nine-cylinder diesel, General Motors 6-71 diesel, Ford GAA III and the Chrysler A57.

The M4A4 hull was lengthened 280mm (11in) to accommodate the Chrysler engine and its road wheels were placed further apart for better traction. Other variations on the M4 included a hull that was entirely cast on the M4A1 rather than a combination of cast and welded construction and the replacement of the vertical volute suspension on the M4A3 with a horizontal system. In total, the Sherman was a reliable medium tank available in great numbers. Despite its shortcomings, the M4 ultimately became a war winner.

Sherman Diversity

Perhaps no other chassis produced during World War II, with the possible exception of the British Churchill, was modified for so many specific purposes as the American Medium Tank M4. In the basic tank, the crew of five included a commander, driver, loader, gunner and assistant driver/ machine gunner. Three crewmen occupied the turret, while the driver was forward in the hull to the left with the assistant driver on his right.

Along with specialized tanks came specially-trained crews to operate them. The Sherman variants ranged from the duplex-drive (DD) tanks that were conceived to negotiate water and roll onto contested beaches to provide fire support for infantry, ammunition carriers, mine-clearing flail tanks, flamethrower tanks and recovery vehicles. In the Pacific, the Sherman was superior to any Japanese armoured vehicle.

In the photo below, American infantrymen hug the flank of a Sherman tank as they proceed cautiously through a small French village. Note the plough-like appendages on the front hull of the Sherman used to negotiate the French bocage (hedgerows).

Panzer V Panther Ausf D (1943)

After overcoming early mechanical problems, the Panzerkampfwagen V Panther with its high-velocity 75mm (2.95in) gun became, in the opinion of some, the best all-around tank of World War II.

Although research and development of a medium tank that would eventually replace the PzKpfw IV had been ongoing since 1937, the pace quickened sharply after the Soviet T-34 began to arrive on the Eastern Front in late 1941. Several top German manufacturers, including Henschel, Porsche, Daimler-Benz and Maschinenfabrik Augsburg-Nürnberg AG (MAN) submitted prototypes at various times.

The Henschel and Porsche designs ultimately evolved into the heavy PzKpfw VI Tiger, while Daimler-Benz and MAN competed for the medium tank contract, which was

Panzer V Panther Ausf D

offered by the German armaments ministry with specific requirements for a tank that could mount the long-barrelled 75mm (2.95in) KwK 42 L/70 cannon, employ sloped armour of sufficient thickness, mount larger wheels and tracks for improved mobility and maintain certain weight specifications.

Panther Progress

The MAN design, designated the VK 3002, won the competition officially in the spring of 1942 after considerable

The wide tracks and double torsion bar suspension with interwoven road wheels allowed the PzKpfw V Panther to handle varied types of terrain with relative ease.

Turret
A three-man turret had already been developed when the Panther was being evaluated, and several modifications were introduced. Among these were the addition of a cast commander's cupola and a bracket for an MG 34 anti-aircraft machine gun in later models.

Main Armament
Manufactured by Rheinmetall-Borsig, the main weapon of the PzKpfw V Panther medium tank was the long-barrelled high-velocity 75mm (2.95in) KwK 42 L/70.

Armour Protection
Armour thickness in the Panther Ausf D was up to 80mm (3.14in) thick and sloped at 55° to improve its effectiveness in protecting the five-man crew. Side armour generally varied in thickness from 40mm to 50mm (1.57in to 1.97in).

deliberation. After the first prototype of the new PzKpfw V Panther was completed that September, a limited production run of 20 units gave way to the first substantial production model, the Ausf D, which was built beginning in November. It was hoped that at least a few of the new tanks might be operational for combat in early 1943, and the sense of urgency to supply a tank that could counter the T-34 was immense.

A total of 842 examples of the Ausf D were produced from January to September 1943 with MAN, Daimler-Benz, Henschel and Niedersachen assembling the new tank. The short interval from prototype to production would come back to haunt the Panther for a time, and when the Ausf D entered combat during the series of ferocious battles around the Kursk salient in July 1943 the results were less than dazzling. More Panthers were lost due to mechanical failure than enemy action, and Panzer General Heinz Guderian remarked tersely, "They burnt too easily, the fuel and oil systems were insufficiently protected and the crews were lost due to lack of training."

Rapid Maturity

The harsh reality of combat laid bare the weaknesses in the Panther, including transmission and drive train breakdowns, oil and petrol leaks that caused fires in the crew compartments, an engine that was prone to overheating and suffered from bearing and connecting rod problems, and more. While the confidence of the crews was minimal with the early production Panthers, most of the problems were corrected and the tank became quite popular with veteran panzer troops.

Specification

Dimensions	Length: 8.86m (29ft) Width: 3.4m (11ft 2in) Height: 2.95m (9ft 8in)
Weight	47.4 tonnes (46.6 tons)
Engine	1 x V-12 Maybach HL 230 P30 petrol engine generating 514.5kW (690hp)
Speed	46km/h (28.6mph)
Armament	Main: 1 x long-barrelled high-velocity 75mm KwK 42 L/70 gun Secondary: 2 x 7.92mm (0.31in) MG 34 machine guns
Armour	15–80mm (0.59–3.14in)
Range	200km (124 miles)
Crew	5

The long barrel of the main 75mm (2.95in) high-velocity gun was an imposing sight for Allied tanks and troops that encountered the German Panther on the Western Front in the summer of 1944. After the Normandy landings, the Ausf A was deployed to France in significant numbers.

In August 1943, an improved Panther, designated Ausf A in a rather odd sequence, entered production and nearly 2200 were completed. Armour protection was increased from a maximum of 80mm (3.15in) in the Ausf D to 120mm (4.7in), while the tank's weight increased slightly as a result. The most numerous Panther variant was the Ausf G, which incorporated improvements to the exhaust system, introduced tapered armour on the upper hull and installed a rotating periscope that improved the driver's field of vision. The Ausf G entered production in the spring of 1944 and nearly 3000 were completed by the end of the war.

The Panther was initially powered by the Maybach HL 210 P45 petrol engine, later upgraded to the V-12 Maybach HL 230 P30 petrol engine generating 514.5 kilowatts (690hp) and delivering a top speed of 48km/h (28.6mph) with an exceptional range of 240km (150 miles).

Limited Production

Despite its ultimately superb battlefield qualities, the Panther was costly to build and its exacting specifications contributed to a relatively lengthy production process. Originally, it was hoped that production would reach 600 new Panthers per month; however, in reality production peaked at 330, hampered by both the German penchant for engineering and incessant Allied bombing. By the spring of 1945, only about 6000 Panthers had been built.

A handful of the Panther were adapted to the tank destroyer role and were known as the Jagdpanther, while others were built as command, observation and recovery vehicles, although never in quantity. The Panther proved a remarkably capable combat tank and some remained in service with the armed forces of various countries long after the war, the last reported being with the Syrian army in the Six-Day War of 1967. Perhaps the combat record of the Panther is overshadowed by the lesson that sheer quantity tipped the battlefield balance of victory in favour of the Allies during World War II.

Anticipating a review by senior officers, the commander and driver of a PzKpfw V Panther emerge from the hull and turret of their tank. Note the Zimmerit anti-magnetic mine paste on the tank's exterior, the black Panzerwaffe uniforms and the anti-aircraft machine gun bracketed to the commander's cupola.

Prowling Panther

The leading Panther tank ace of World War II was SS Oberscharführer (Technical Sergeant) Ernst Barkmann. Already a decorated tanker, Barkmann halted his Panther in a thick stand of oak trees near the French village of Le Lorey one day in late July 1944 and set about a mission of destruction that validated the reputation of the Panther as a cold, efficient engine of war. As a column of 15 American M4 Sherman tanks and auxiliary vehicles approached, Barkmann waited for the appropriate moment and opened fire.

In quick succession, Barkmann knocked out the first two Shermans in the column. He then destroyed a fuel truck further back. As other Shermans attempted to get around the wreckage and deploy for combat, he destroyed seven more along with several support vehicles. A tactical air strike damaged his Panther, but Barkmann was able to withdraw to safety at Neufbourg. For his action, he received the Knight's Cross.

KV-85 Heavy Tank (1943)

Although it was few in number, the KV-85 heavy tank entered service in 1943 as a bridge from the older KV series of Red Army tanks to the Josef Stalin series that spearheaded the Soviet victory in the Great Patriotic War.

The KV series of Soviet heavy tanks was developed in the late 1930s to replace the slow and unreliable multi-turreted T-35, which had rapidly grown obsolete. Named in honour of Soviet Defence Minister Klimenti Voroshilov (1881–1969), the KV tanks represented a break from earlier multi-turret designs and set the stage for the next half-century of Soviet tank research, development and construction.

Armed with a 76.2mm (3in) gun, the KV-1 emerged as a primary Red Army assault and breakthrough tank.

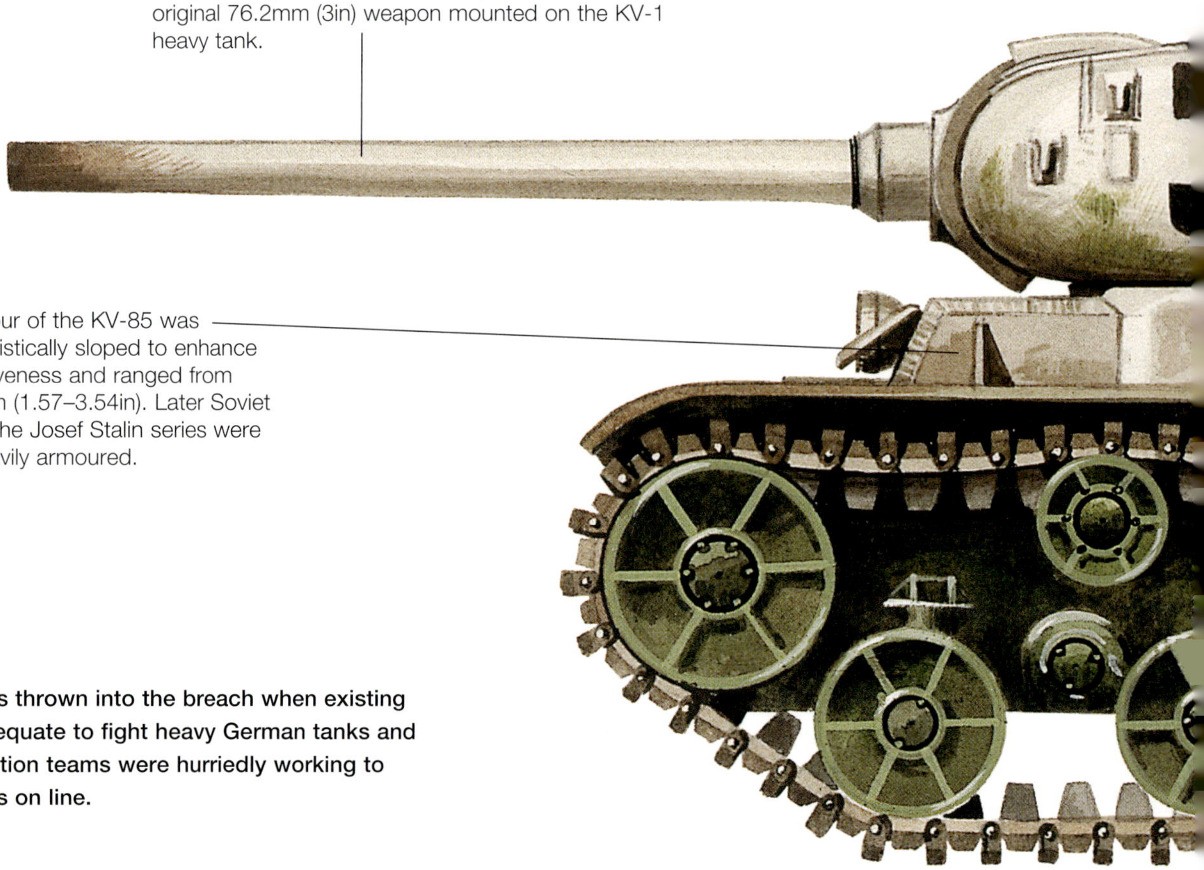

The KV-85 heavy tank was thrown into the breach when existing KV-1s were deemed inadequate to fight heavy German tanks and Soviet design and production teams were hurriedly working to bring the new Stalin series on line.

Following the German invasion of the Soviet Union on June 22, 1941, the KV-1 underwent numerous upgrades and modifications, including additional armour protection and an improved turret that originally had been constructed of armour plating but transitioned to a stronger cast production method.

The turret and main gun of the new IS-85 tank were paired with the chassis of the existing KV-1S heavy tank to create the stopgap KV-85, deployed in small numbers during the autumn of 1944 to battle German tanks on the Eastern Front.

Turret
The KV-85 turret was actually a new tank component, originally designed and manufactured for the IS-85, one of a new generation of Soviet heavy tanks in the IS series.

Engine
The 12-cylinder V-2K diesel engine generated adequate power for the 43-tonne (42.3-ton) KV-85. The tank's top speed, in turn, was 42 kilometres (26mph).

As German tanks increased in size and strength, reports from the battlefield indicated that the main 76.2mm (3in) weapon of the KV-1 was insufficient in tank versus tank combat. Therefore, several attempts were made to upgun the tank. An experiment with a 107mm (4.21in) gun was abandoned, while the installation of a 152mm (6in) gun in a larger turret, the KV-2, ended in failure.

Bridging the Gap

Meanwhile, Soviet tank designers were vigorously working on a new series of heavy tanks, the Josef Stalin (IS) series. However, while completion of the design for the new Stalin tank and its production remained several months in the future something had to be done on an interim basis to achieve a measure of parity with the German PzKpfw V Panther medium and PzKpfw VI Tiger heavy tanks that were in action on the Eastern Front.

The most practical solution at the time was to marry the turret of the new IS-85 heavy tank mounting the 85mm (3.35in) DT5 gun, originally deployed as an anti-aircraft weapon, to the chassis of the KV-1S, a variant of the original KV-1 with a smaller turret and thinner armour protection to gain some speed and mobility. The KV-1S turret was also the first to incorporate vision blocks in a 360° arc, providing the tank commander with a broad view of the field.

Specification

Dimensions	Length: 8.6m (28ft 2in) Width: 3.25m (10ft 8in) Height: 2.8m (9ft 2in)
Weight	43 tonnes (42.3 tons)
Engine	1 x V-2K V-12 diesel engine generating 448kW (600hp)
Speed	42km/h (26mph)
Armament	Main: 1 x 85mm (3.35in) DT5 gun Secondary: 2 x 7.62mm (0.3in) DT machine guns
Armour	40–90mm (1.57–3.54in)
Range	330km (205 miles)
Crew	4–5

Only 148 KV-85 tanks were built during a brief production run in 1943–44. However, the KV-85 played a significant role in bridging the performance gap between the KV series of heavy tanks and the superior Josef Stalin series.

The resulting hybrid heavy tank was referred to originally as Objekt 239 and later as the KV-85. The main weapon of the KV-85 was a proven entity, already adapted from the towed anti-aircraft role to the T-34/85 medium tank and the SU-85 tank destroyer. The KV-85 was rapidly produced during the autumn and winter of 1943–44 and due to its short-lived purpose only 148 were completed. A major contributing factor to the low production rate of the KV-85 was the significant demand for the DT5 gun, given its multiple roles. The first KV-85 entered combat in September 1943. By the following spring, the IS-2 heavy tank was entering production, rendering the KV-85 at best redundant. Therefore, its production virtually ceased by early 1944.

Stopgap Specifications

Like the KV-1 before it, the KV-85 carried a crew of four, including a commander, driver, mechanic and gunner, although in some cases a fifth member was added to the already crowded interior. As with other Soviet designs, the commander occupied the cramped two-man turret and was required to serve the main gun, restricting his ability to direct the tank in combat. Secondary armament included two 7.62mm (0.3in) DT machine guns, one mounted in the hull and the other facing forward in the turret coaxially with the main weapon. The KV85 was powered by a single V-2K V-12 diesel engine that generated 448 kilowatts (600hp). The tank's top speed on road was a respectable 42km/h (26mph).

KV-85 in Combat

The combat record of the KV-85 is mixed. While the tank offered comparable firepower to German armoured fighting vehicles, its armour was susceptible to the high-velocity rounds of enemy tanks and anti-tank weapons. During one engagement in the Ukraine in November 1943, the 34th Guards Heavy Tank Regiment lost seven of its 20 KV-85s to fire from German PzKpfw IV tanks and Marder tank destroyers. The following day, a German attack was repulsed with no losses to the remaining KV-85s.

The legacy of the KV-85 "bridge" tank ultimately did not reside with its actual deployment, but in its glimpse of the powerful IS heavy tank series, the shape of things to come.

KV-85 Versus Panther and Tiger

In the photo below, a KV-85 tank sits silently today, a monument to the service of its crews during World War II. Many KV-85 tanks were deployed in the Ukraine, holding their own against German armour. On January 28, 1944, near the Telman collective farm, KV-85s and SU-122 tank destroyers took on 15 Tigers and 13 other enemy tanks according to a report.

The narrative reads: "... Our tanks and SP-guns opened fire and broke up the enemy combat formations, destroying six tanks (of these, three Tigers) and up to a platoon of infantry. The KV-85 of Senior Lieutenant Kuleshov was designated to liquidate the German infantry ... He fulfilled this assignment with fire and his tracks. A tank group (three KV-85s and two SU-122s) under the command of company commander Guards Sr. Lieutenant Podust defending Telman ... prevented German forces from shifting to other areas ... suffer(ing) almost no losses while inflicting significant losses on the enemy."

Five Tigers, 14 other tanks and armoured vehicles and six anti-tank guns were reported destroyed in the engagement.

Churchill AVRE (1943)

The Churchill AVRE was developed in 1943 for a variety of uses as combat engineers overcame natural and man-made obstacles, paving the way for Allied troops across the beaches of Normandy and onto the Third Reich.

Following the disastrous raid on the French coastal town of Dieppe in 1942, the abortive dress rehearsal for the Normandy landings that were to come two years later, it was apparent that the machines of war and the infantry who worked in concert with them sometimes encountered obstacles for which no immediate solutions were available.

At Dieppe, a number of the new Churchill tanks had bogged down on the soft beaches. The armoured vehicles overcame a seawall only with great difficulty. The Royal Engineers engaged at Dieppe encountered difficulties in attempting to clear minefields and destroy tank obstacles while continually under enemy fire. Clearly, one of the lessons of the Dieppe Raid centred around the ability of the Royal Engineers to do their vital job when the time came for the full-scale invasion of Nazi-occupied Europe.

Engineering Expertise

The solutions to many of the problems encountered at Dieppe and those anticipated in Normandy were found,

Main Armament
The main armament of the Churchill AVRE was a 290mm (11.4in) spigot mortar that used a powerful spring to hurl an 18.1kg (40lb) projectile at enemy fixed emplacements more than 73m (239ft) away.

The log carpet variant of the Churchill AVRE was an ingenious attempt to provide traction for armoured and wheeled vehicles by deploying logs to form a temporary road. Wet spring and autumn weather in Western Europe often delayed Allied offensive operations.

to a great extent, in the Churchill AVRE (Armoured Vehicle Royal Engineers). The simple concept of the Churchill AVRE was that it could transport Royal Engineers with an additional measure of safety, protecting them against enemy fire, particularly from small arms, so that they could function. The AVRE also mounted a 290mm (11.4in) Petard spigot mortar that hurled an 18.1kg (40lb) projectile dubbed the "flying dustbin" a distance of slightly more than 73m (239ft).

The concept of the AVRE has been credited to Lieutenant J.J. Denovan of the Royal Canadian Engineers, who was attached to the Special Devices Branch of the British Department of Tank Design. Denovan envisioned a tank with as much interior space

Log Carpet
The AVRE Log Carpet variant carried 100 logs measuring 152mm (6in) in diameter and 4.26m (14ft) in length. The logs were tied together with wire and carried on an overhead frame. When deployed they fashioned a temporary road across difficult terrain.

Crew Compartment
The interior of the Churchill AVRE was modified to allow room for Royal Engineers and their array of gear, including tools, equipment and explosives used to clear obstacles, deploy bridging and other tasks.

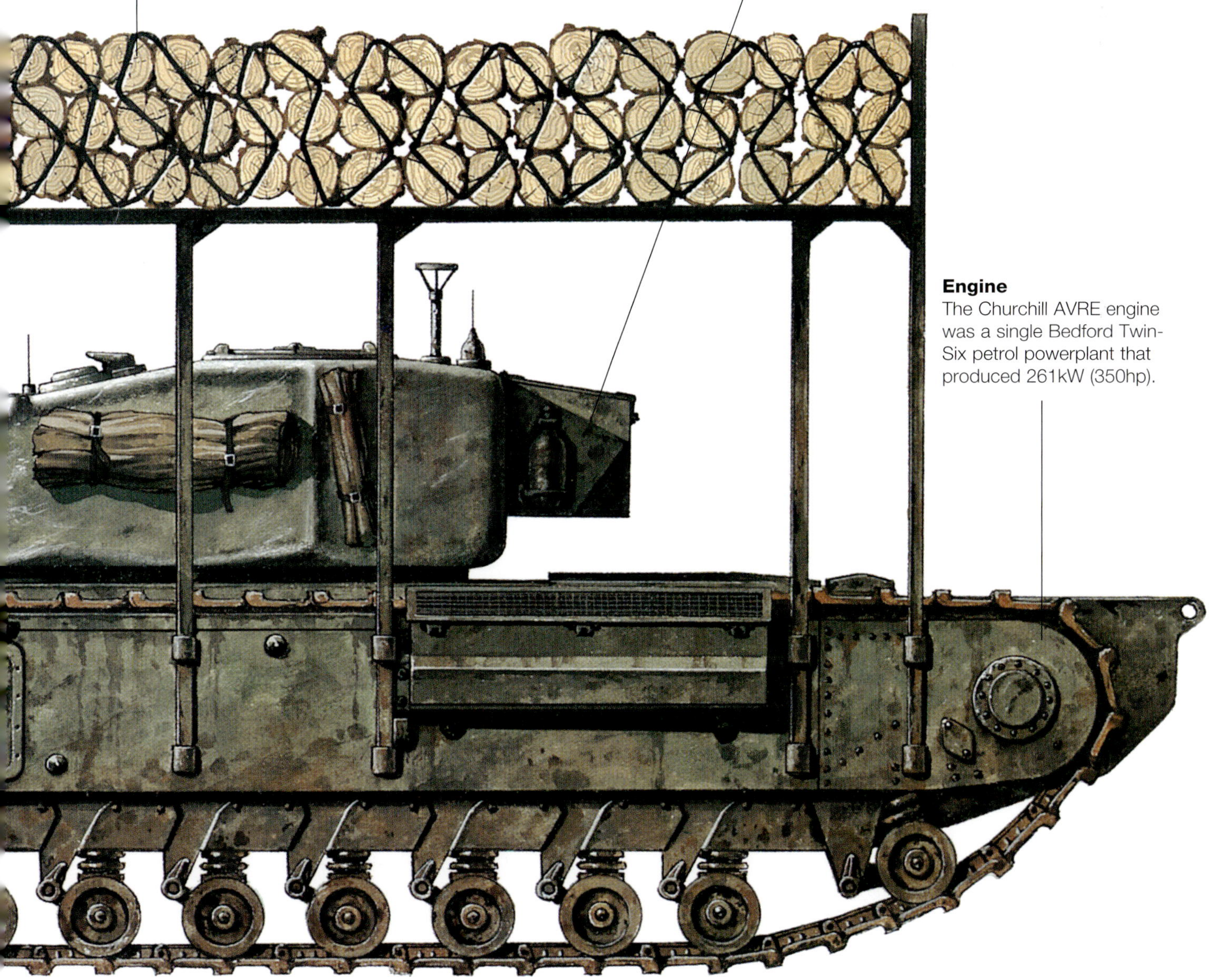

Engine
The Churchill AVRE engine was a single Bedford Twin-Six petrol powerplant that produced 261kW (350hp).

Some Churchill AVRE were designed to carry large bundles of logs at either end of the hull. In this configuration, the tank was able to extend logs or fascines in more than one location.

as possible to transport the engineers and their array of explosives, tools and equipment. The comparatively spacious interior, armour plating and side access door of the Churchill tank made it an ideal candidate.

By late 1942, the prototype AVRE was under construction by the 1st Canadian Mechanical Equipment Company. On 25 February 1943, a demonstration was held during which Royal Engineers emerged from the converted Churchill and blew a large hole in a concrete wall. Meanwhile, the huge spigot mortar was being developed on its own. Lieutenant Colonel Stewart Blacker had previously designed a mortar that was used by the Home Guard. His adaptation of the spigot mortar for use with armour was attached to the mantlet of the main gun on the Churchill turret.

Specification

Dimensions	Length: 7.44m (24ft 5in) Width: 2.44m (8ft) Height: 3.45m (11ft 4in) with log carpet mounted above tank
Weight	40.72 tonnes (40.07 tons)
Engine	1 x Bedford Twin-Six petrol engine developing 261kW (350hp)
Speed	Road: 20km/h (12.5mph) Cross-country: 12.8km/h (8mph)
Armament	Main: 1 x Petard 290mm (11.41in) spigot mortar Secondary: 1 x 7.92mm (0.31in) BESA machine gun
Armour	16–102mm (0.62–4in)
Range	144.8km (90 miles)
Crew	5

Invasion Preparation

The spigot mortar and the Churchill tank adapted for use by the Royal Engineers came together at a crucial time during World War II. Preparations were underway for D-Day, the Normandy invasion of June 6, 1944. Even as plans for the AVRE were being finalized, it was apparent that variants of it could provide close support for advancing troops in a number of ways. Production of the Churchill AVRE began in mid-1943 and continued through the end of the war. At least 700 were produced from the conversion of Churchill Mk III and IV tanks.

The inventive frame that carried sizable logs above the Churchill AVRE log carpet tank was quite possibly the only workable solution to the need for lengths of temporary roadway. A tracked vehicle was best suited to reach the area where the logs were needed, and overhead was the sole workable location for the bundles bound by wire.

This Churchill AVRE demonstrates its ability to traverse challenging obstacles during field testing. Note the large bundles of fascines that have been dropped at the foot of the obstacle to assist in negotiating its formidable height.

Sanity Questioned

During the D-Day landings, the Churchill AVREs played a significant role in clearing German strongpoints on Gold, Juno and Sword Beaches. Along with each of the three British and Canadian divisions that hit these beaches, two squadrons of the 5th and 6th Assault Regiments, Royal Engineers, landed.

At Gold Beach, "Hobart's Funnies" of the 79th Armoured Division went to work. AVRE Bobbin tanks covered areas of soft sand and clay with canvas to allow tanks and troops to pass, while fascine tanks dropped their loads of wooden bundles into shell holes. Within an hour of landing, the specialized assault tanks had been credited with opening four exits from Gold Beach near Le Hamel. Petard mortars destroyed numerous German positions. The strongest of these was a nearby sanatorium. The Germans defended the building until mid-afternoon, when it was literally pounded flat by the 290mm (11.41in) spigot mortars of several Churchill AVRE tanks.

About 180 AVREs were completed prior to the Normandy invasion and assigned to the 1st Assault Brigade, 79th Armoured Division, under the command of General Sir Percy Hobart. The 79th Armoured Division had been formed to provide command structure for an array of specialized tanks that were expected to perform critical tasks on D-Day and beyond. These specialized tanks were nicknamed "Hobart's Funnies."

The AVRE was modified with numerous attachment points that were capable of carrying a variety of equipment. Variants included the AVRE Bobbin with a canvas mat on a spool that was deployed to supply better traction for vehicles; the AVRE Log Carpet device that carried 100 logs 4.26m (14ft) long and 152mm (6in) in diameter, bound together by wire and deployed from an overhead frame to create a makeshift road; AVRE tanks that carried a variety of explosives; AVRE tanks that carried fascines that could be dropped into ditches or low areas for tanks and troops to traverse more easily; and mine-clearing tanks, bridging tanks and more.

On the battlefield, the concept of the Churchill AVRE proved so sound that specialized tanks have remained in service throughout the world for decades since it was withdrawn from service. The Churchill AVRE also saw action during World War II with the 25th Armoured Assault Brigade during the Italian campaign.

T-34/85 (1944)

The improved firepower of the T-34/85 medium tank came about following analysis of the T-34 performance during the Battle of Kursk. Three 85mm (3.35in) weapons were considered before a decision was made to mount the ZIS-S-53.

Following the victory at Kursk in July 1943, thwarting the German offensive Operation Citadel, the Soviets began to assess the performance of their T-34 medium tank in combat with the German PzKpfw V Panther and PzKpfw VI Tiger tanks. The T-34 was equipped with a 76.2mm (3in) main weapon, while the German tanks mounted high-velocity 75mm (2.95in) and 88mm (3.5in) guns respectively.

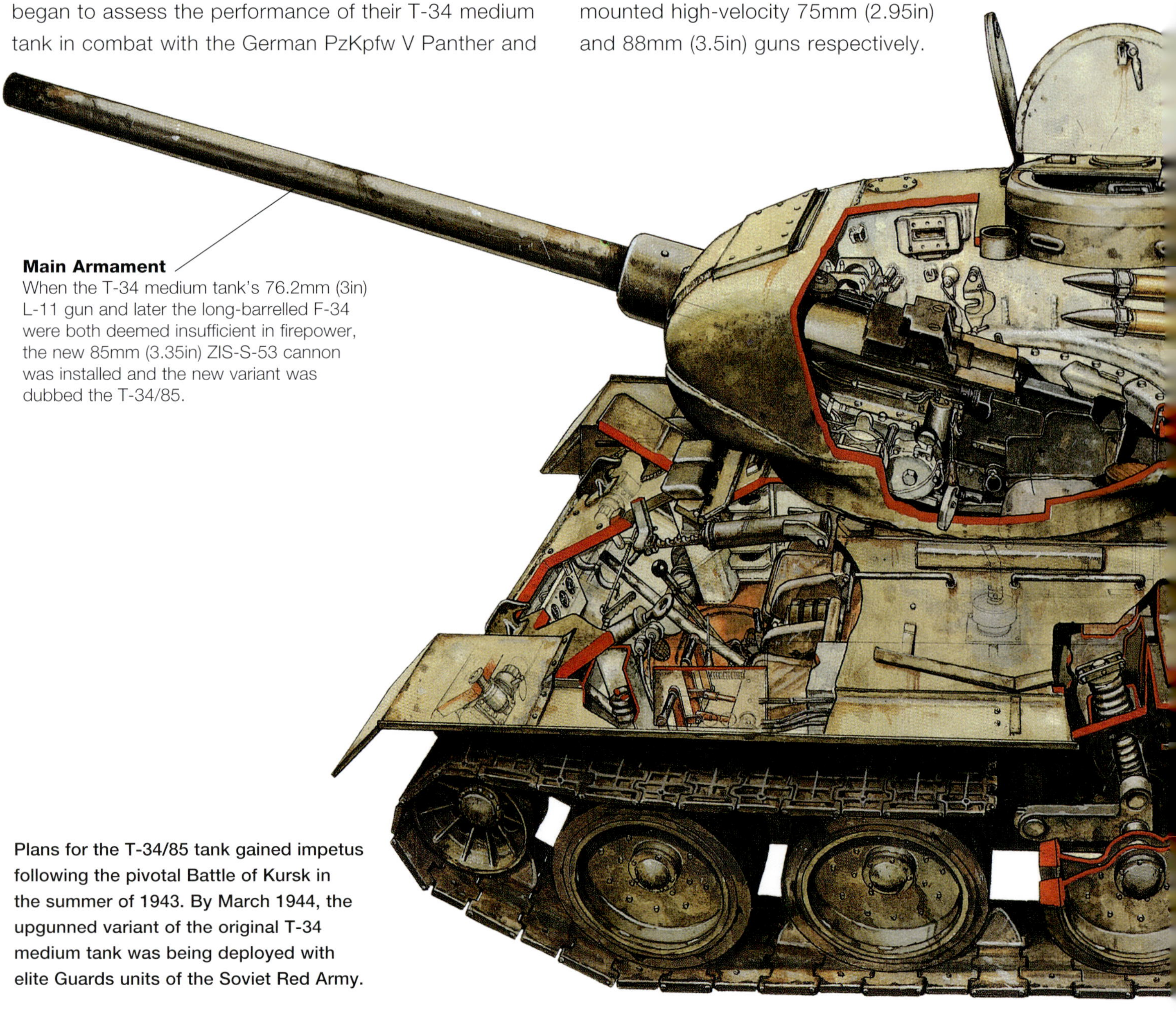

Main Armament
When the T-34 medium tank's 76.2mm (3in) L-11 gun and later the long-barrelled F-34 were both deemed insufficient in firepower, the new 85mm (3.35in) ZIS-S-53 cannon was installed and the new variant was dubbed the T-34/85.

Plans for the T-34/85 tank gained impetus following the pivotal Battle of Kursk in the summer of 1943. By March 1944, the upgunned variant of the original T-34 medium tank was being deployed with elite Guards units of the Soviet Red Army.

Both sides lost tanks in great numbers, but it was determined that the T-34's main weapon did not provide sufficient muzzle velocity to penetrate German armour at a reasonable distance, compelling the Soviets to execute mass charges to close rapidly with the Germans in something resembling a Wild West shootout.

The initial conclusion was that the T-34 required more armour and additional plating was affixed to a small number of the tanks. During testing it was determined that the additional armour so eroded speed and manoeuvrability that the experimental model, the T-43, was discarded.

The Power of Suggestion

The designers came to the realization that the answer to enhancing the T-34's combat capability laid in a new main weapon. Soviet records indicate that during a meeting on August 25, 1943, V.G. Grabin, the chief designer at Artillery Factory No 92, suggested arming the T-34 with a more powerful 85mm (3.35in) gun. Three separate designs

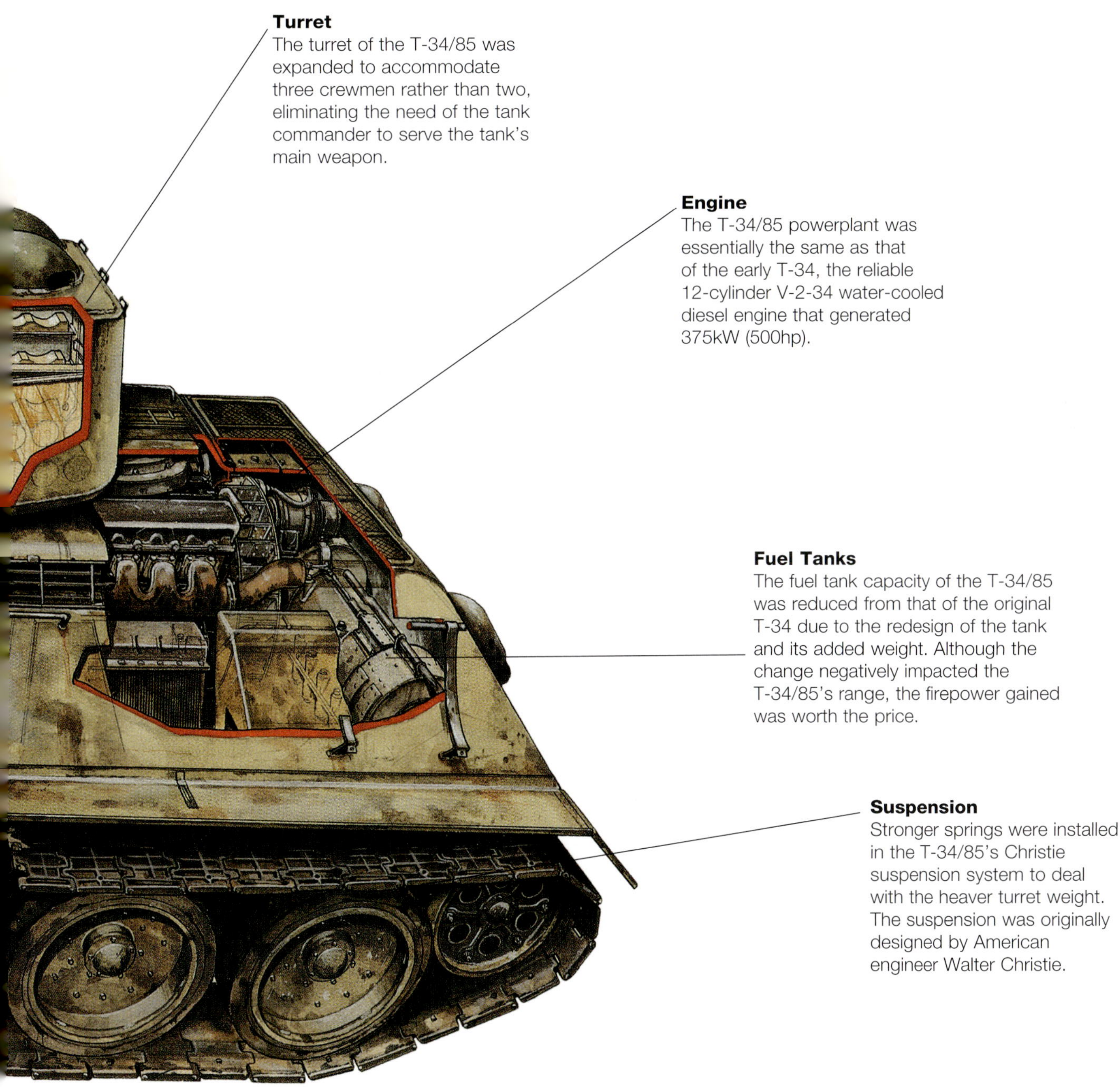

The long barrel of the high-velocity 85mm (3.35in) ZIS-S-53 gun enhanced the sleek, streamlined profile of the T-34/85 medium tank with its turret forward atop the hull. The design was characteristic of Soviet tanks for decades to come.

were tested before the ZIS-S-53 gun, sponsored by General F.F. Petrov, was accepted. The gun was also used in the KV-85 and IS-2 heavy tanks, as well as the SU-85 tank destroyer.

The one-piece cast turret was enlarged to accommodate a third crewman, bringing the total to five, with the commander no longer required to serve the main gun in combat. The new configuration substantially improved the combat efficiency of the T-34/85. The commander was positioned in the rear of the turret to the left with the gunner in front of him and the loader on the right. The driver and a second machine gunner were positioned forward in the hull. The basic turret redesign was completed within weeks at Production Works No 112 in Gorky.

Specification

Dimensions	Length: 6m (19ft 8in) Width: 2.92 metres (9ft 7in) Height: 2.39 metres (7ft 10in)
Weight	32 tonnes (31.4 tons)
Engine	1 x 12-cylinder V-2-34 water-cooled diesel engine developing 375kW (500hp)
Speed	55km/h (34mph)
Armament	Main: 1 x 85mm (3.35in) ZIS-S-53 gun Secondary: 2 x 7.62mm (0.3in) DT machine guns
Armour	20–55mm (0.78–2.1in)
Range	300km (188 miles)
Crew	5

Other changes to the T-34/85 from the original T-34 included a commander's cupola atop the turret with five vision slits. A hatch was installed in the turret roof for the loader and included ventilation slits to evacuate fumes from the main weapon and a turret-mounted 7.62mm (0.3in) DT machine gun. A second machine gun remained in the hull. Pistol ports were placed on the turret sides.

Due to space restrictions, the size of the fuel tanks was reduced, slightly curbing the T-34/85's range compared to the earlier T-34. The heavier turret also required that stronger springs be introduced to the Christie suspension to adjust for the additional weight.

Prescribed Production

The exigencies of war greatly influenced the hurried production of the T-34/85. By December 15, 1943, on the strength of proven hull designs – three of which were in production with only slight differences between them – the Soviet State Defence Committee ordered production of the T-34/85 to commence. The turret itself, however, had not been finalized and its designers were required to catch up with the pace of hull production.

Production Works No. 112 actually began manufacturing the new tank in January 1944 and the first T-34/85s were delivered to elite Guards armoured units in March 1944. During the spring, two more manufacturing facilities, in Omsk and Nizhnij Tagil, were assigned to produce the T-34/85. Most of the new tanks actually were produced in Nizhnij Tagil. Throughout wartime production, the turret and other components of the tank were refined and improved. At one time, the three factories were producing three slightly different turrets.

Battlefield Improvement

The T-34/85 indeed brought better combat survivability to Soviet armoured forces. The greater range of the new main weapon and its muzzle velocity of 780 metres per second (2559 feet per second) improved penetration of German armour plating with armour-piercing ammunition. Combat experience revealed the need for additional protection against German anti-tank weapons such as the shoulder-fired Panzerfaust. Additional thin plating or wire mesh was welded into areas around the hull and turret that were susceptible to "trapping" shells or hollow charges. These were often successful at deflecting otherwise damaging strikes.

Approximately 22,500 T-34/85 tanks were produced during the war and production continued into the late 1950s. Variants included the OT-34/85, mounting an AT-42 flamethrower instead of the hull machine gun. The flamethrower was capable of emitting a stream of fire up to 100m (327ft).

T-34/85 Ambush

In the photo at right, Soviet crewmen relax while their column of T-34/85 medium tanks travels through a forest. On August 12, 1944, a lone T-34/85 under Lieutenant Aleksandr P. Oskin of the 53rd Guards Tank Brigade employed its 85mm gun against the latest German heavy tank, the Tiger II.

Oskin observed three Tigers along a dirt road and realized that from his concealed position he could fire at their flanks. At a range of 200m (656ft), Oskin ordered his gunner, Abubakir Merkhaidorov, to fire at the second tank in line. The shell penetrated the turret. Two more hits were scored. The fourth shell set the Tiger alight. As the first Tiger in line rotated its turret, Oskin got off four rounds. Three did little damage, but the fourth set the Tiger ablaze.

Blinded by smoke and fire from the other two German tanks, the third Tiger began to withdraw, but Oskin manoeuvred behind it. A single round destroyed the tank. Oskin had demonstrated what the T-34/85 could do in combat and was decorated as a Hero of the Soviet Union.

Sherman Crab Mine-Clearing Tank (1944)

The Medium Tank M4, popularly known as the Sherman, has been adapted for specialized service more than any other tank. The Sherman Crab Mine-Clearing Tank utilized a flail to detonate land mines, clearing a path for troops that followed.

As their troops struggled with extensive German minefields in North Africa, British and Commonwealth inventors and engineers continually laboured with limited resources to develop an effective means of clearing these lethal obstacles for the safe passage of soldiers and vehicles. During the Battle of El Alamein in October 1942, minefields sown on the orders of German Afrika Korps commander General Erwin Rommel had been proved to be quite troublesome, delaying the British advance considerably. Rommel had referred to these mine-strewn areas as the "Devil's Gardens."

The Sherman Crab was the result of extensive research by British engineers and designers who operated with limited resources. The Crab was developed in time to accompany British assault troops ashore during the D-Day landings.

Main Armament
The Sherman Crab mining tank mounted the standard 75mm (2.95in) gun and was sometimes employed in the infantry support or tank versus tank role. When the flail was in use, the gun faced to the rear.

Hydraulic Apparatus
The right arm of the Sherman Crab flail was hydraulically powered, raising and lowering the apparatus as needed. The Mk II variant included a jib that was weighted and balanced to follow the contour of the terrain.

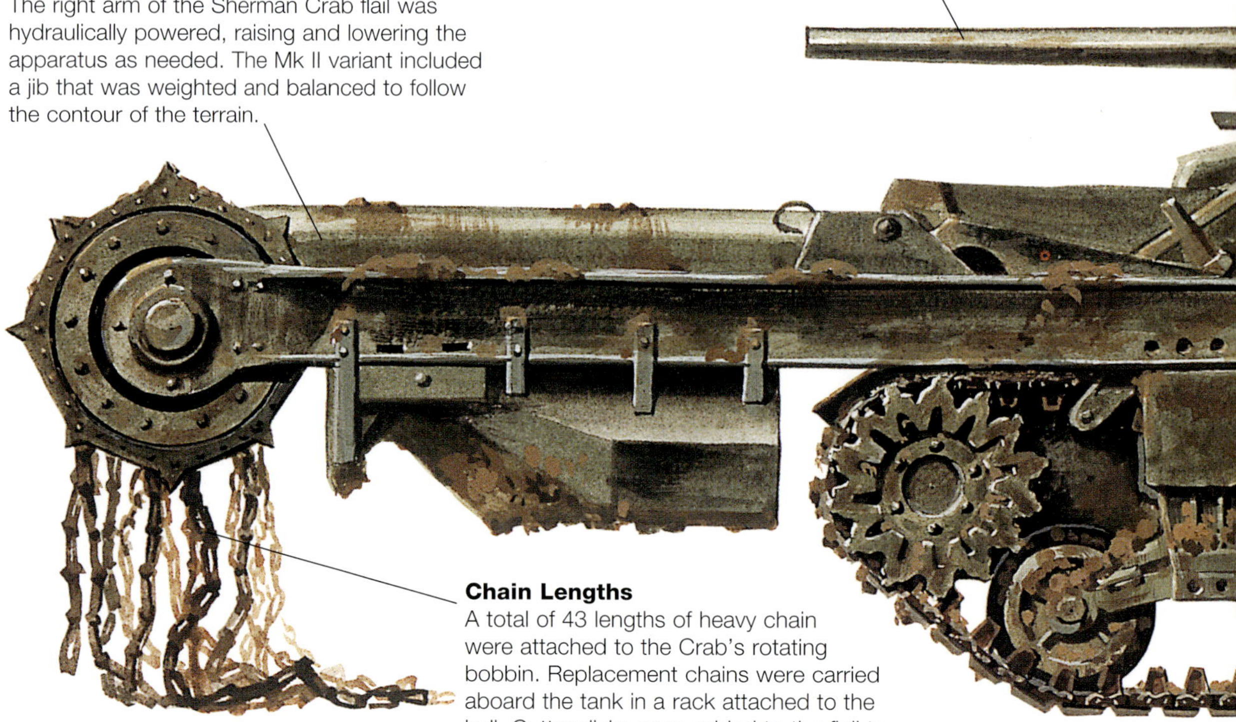

Chain Lengths
A total of 43 lengths of heavy chain were attached to the Crab's rotating bobbin. Replacement chains were carried aboard the tank in a rack attached to the hull. Cutter disks were added to the flail to destroy barbed-wire entanglements.

Early efforts to develop a workable flail tank that would destroy mines with a system of rotating lengths of chain, beating the ground in front of the vehicle, had resulted in some promising prototypes. However, resources were limited.

Flailing Away

In the spring of 1942, a South African officer, Captain Abraham du Toit, had experimented with flail technology. His ideas were then presented to Major Norman Berry, Assistant Director of Ordnance Stores at British XIII Corps headquarters. Berry supported the research and in October 1941 du Toit was promoted and ordered to Britain to

Sherman Crab Mine-Clearing Tank

Using a rotating bobbin and 43 lengths of chain, the Sherman Crab detonated land mines in its path and marked the passage through a minefield with coloured chalk, smoke or luminous poles periodically fired into the ground automatically.

Engine
The Sherman Crab's Ford GAA V-8 petrol engine was modified to accept the drive shaft that powered the flail. Operating the flail off the main tank engine was a decided advantage over an external engine that was prone to breakdowns.

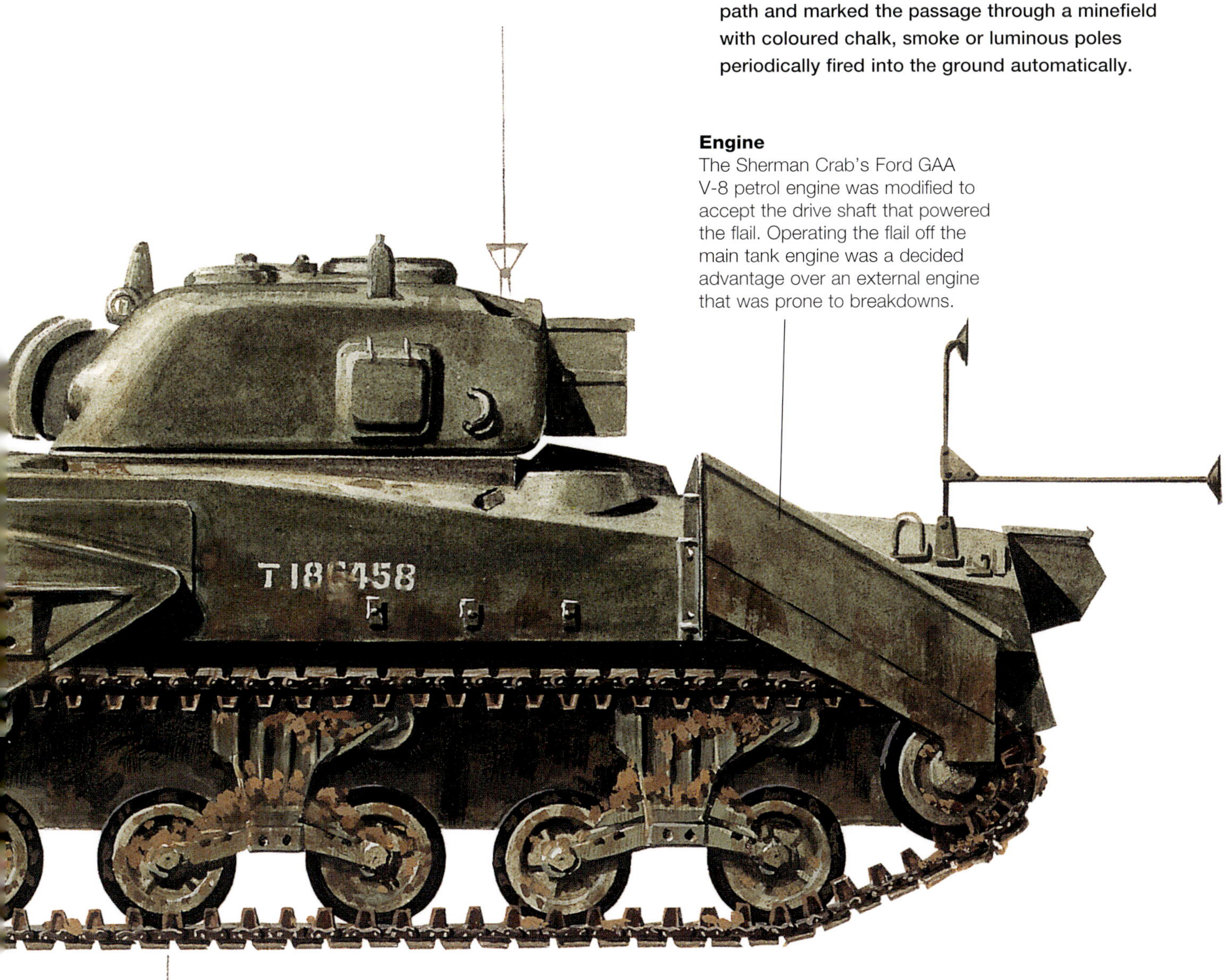

continue his work. Concurrently, experiments with the Matilda tank resulted in the Matilda Scorpion. At El Alamein, 25 Matilda Scorpions were deployed in mine-clearing activities, but the results were disappointing.

Meanwhile, du Toit continued working with other flail tank designs. British engineers experimented further with the Valentine tank and produced the Valentine Scorpion, while the M4 Sherman was also fitted with a flail. Sherman designs were designated the Crab, Lobster and the Mk IV and Mk V Scorpions. The Crab design proved exceptional. One significant improvement over other designs was that the Crab flail operated off the main engine of the tank rather than an external engine that might be prone to breakdowns – particularly from clogged air filters due to the massive amounts of dust and earth that were kicked up by the flail.

General Sir Percy Hobart, commander of the 79th Armoured Division, observed the Sherman Crab during testing and pressed for its approval for production. Hobart's command fielded a number of specialized tanks that served varied purposes during the Allied offensive in Western Europe and the Italian Campaign. Collectively, these specialized armoured vehicles were known as "Hobart's Funnies." Hobart knew that a reliable flail tank would be crucial to the rapid movement of Allied troops across the Normandy invasion beaches as the D-Day landings of June 6, 1944 approached.

Specification

Dimensions	Length: 6.35m (20ft 10in) Width: 2.81m (9ft 3in) Height: 3.96m (13ft)
Weight	32.28 tonnes (31.7 tons)
Engine	1 x Ford GAA V-8 petrol powerplant generating 373kW (500hp)
Speed	46km/h (28.75mph)
Armament	Main: 1 x 75mm (2.95in) gun Secondary: 1 x 7.62mm (0.3in) Browning machine gun (removed from some tanks)
Armour	15–76mm (0.59–2.9in)
Range	62km (100 miles)
Crew	5

Crab Configuration

The Sherman engine was modified to accept the second drive shaft to operate the large flail that was, in essence, a rotating bobbin with 43 lengths of chain attached. Initially the bobbin was lowered and raised by two arms that extended forward from the hull. A hydraulic

Sherman Crabs often operated in groups of up to five, formed in echelon to clear a wide area through a suspected minefield. While the Crabs cleared mines, other tanks often provided cover in case of an enemy attack.

apparatus incorporated in the right-hand arm powered the raising and lowering of the bobbin and controlled its 142rpm speed. The bobbin height could be adjusted based on the suspected depth of any mines that lay ahead of the Crab. Cutter disks were also added to the bobbin to strip away barbed wire that might otherwise entangle and damage or destroy the chains.

Crabs at War

During the Normandy landings on June 6, 1944, the Sherman Crabs of the Westminster Dragoons, 22nd Dragoons and 1st Lothians and Border Yeomanry were with the first wave of British and Canadian troops to land on Gold, Juno and Sword Beaches, clearing mines and engaging German machine-gun nests and bunkers. The Crabs saw service throughout the rest of World War II and American observers were impressed with their battlefield capabilities, eventually deploying a few to the battlefield.

During the winter of 1945, the 51st Royal Tank Regiment received a squadron of 15 Sherman Mk II Crabs and these were utilized on the Italian front.

Since the Crabs were often at the leading edge of an Allied advance, their role could change quickly from mine clearing to direct combat with the enemy. From D-Day through to the end of the war, the 1st Lothians and Border Yeomanry lost 36 Sherman Crabs in action.

The flail of a Sherman Crab kicks up a cloud of dust and dirt while undergoing extensive testing in April 1944. British designers and engineers used the American M4 medium tank as the basis for the most effective Allied mine clearing tank of World War II.

Creeping Crab

The Mk II variant of the Crab introduced a counterbalanced and weighted jib that automatically adjusted the height of the bobbin to further ensure that deeply-buried mines were detonated. Known as the Contouring Crab, this version required a system of gears that maintained the speed of the flail as the tank traversed uneven terrain, particularly while the vehicle was climbing.

For the protection of the crew, a blast shield was installed on the forward hull of the Crab. While the flail was engaged, the main gun pointed directly to the rear and the vehicle moved quite slowly at only 2.01km/h (1.25mph). The hull machine gun was removed since the vision of the gunner was often obscured by the operating flail. Extra chains were carried in a container attached to the hull. The addition of the flail increased the Crab's weight by approximately 32 tonnes (31 tons), while the standard M4 Sherman weighed 31 tonnes (31 tons).

Sherman Crabs were among the first tanks to reach the invasion beaches on D-Day. Although they were vulnerable to enemy fire while the flail operated, they were actually effective combat vehicles with their 75mm (2.95in) guns and served a dual purpose at times.

Sherman VC Firefly (1944)

Intended as a short-term solution to the need for additional firepower, British designers replaced the main gun of the M4 Sherman with the heavier 17pdr QF and produced a tank that was effective against German Tigers and Panthers.

Sobering lessons learned in North Africa and Italy convinced British tank designers that a heavier main weapon was critical to any future success against German armour and anti-tank weapons. Although a new generation of British tanks was on the drawing board, the Cromwell and Challenger models would not be ready for many months, and delays and setbacks, which had become routine for weapon development programs during wartime, could also be expected.

The American-built M4 Sherman medium tank was available in large numbers; however, its 75mm (2.95in) and later 76mm (2.9in) main weapons were deemed insufficient in combat against the German PzKpfw V Panther and PzKpfw VI Tiger, whose 75mm and 88mm (2.95in and 3.5in) high-velocity guns could destroy the Allied tanks at extended ranges, theoretically before an Allied gun could be brought to bear.

Main armament
The 17pdr (76.2mm/3in) QF anti-tank gun was the most powerful weapon of its kind built by the British during World War II. Modified to fit the M4 Sherman turret, it proved an equalizer in combat against German Tiger and Panther tanks.

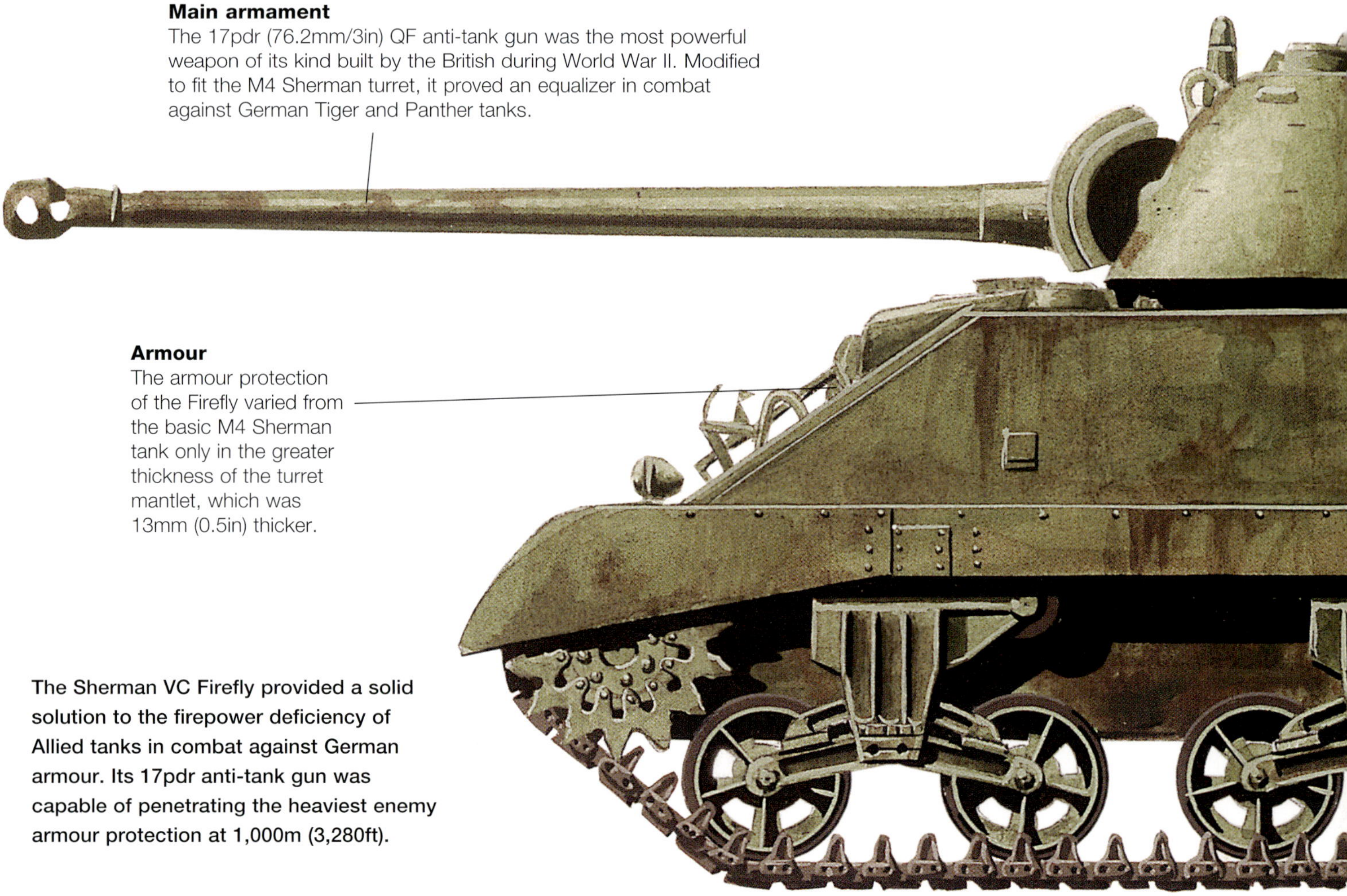

Armour
The armour protection of the Firefly varied from the basic M4 Sherman tank only in the greater thickness of the turret mantlet, which was 13mm (0.5in) thicker.

The Sherman VC Firefly provided a solid solution to the firepower deficiency of Allied tanks in combat against German armour. Its 17pdr anti-tank gun was capable of penetrating the heaviest enemy armour protection at 1,000m (3,280ft).

Unofficial British efforts to upgun the Sherman with the 17pdr (76.2mm/3in) QF anti-tank gun had been underway since late 1942. However, design issues appeared insurmountable. The small turret of the Sherman could not accommodate the lengthy recoil of the 17pdr and one solution that removed the gun's recoil system altogether would have required the entire tank to absorb the recoil, eventually shaking it apart.

Engineering Effort

An engineering team led by Vickers designer W.G.K. Kilbourn set to work on the necessary M4 modifications that would make the 17pdr operational. First, the recoil cylinders were shortened and moved to the sides of the gun so that the

By D-Day, June 6, 1944, nearly 350 Sherman Firefly tanks were in service with British forces. As the campaign in Normandy came to an end, the number of Fireflies in service topped 400.

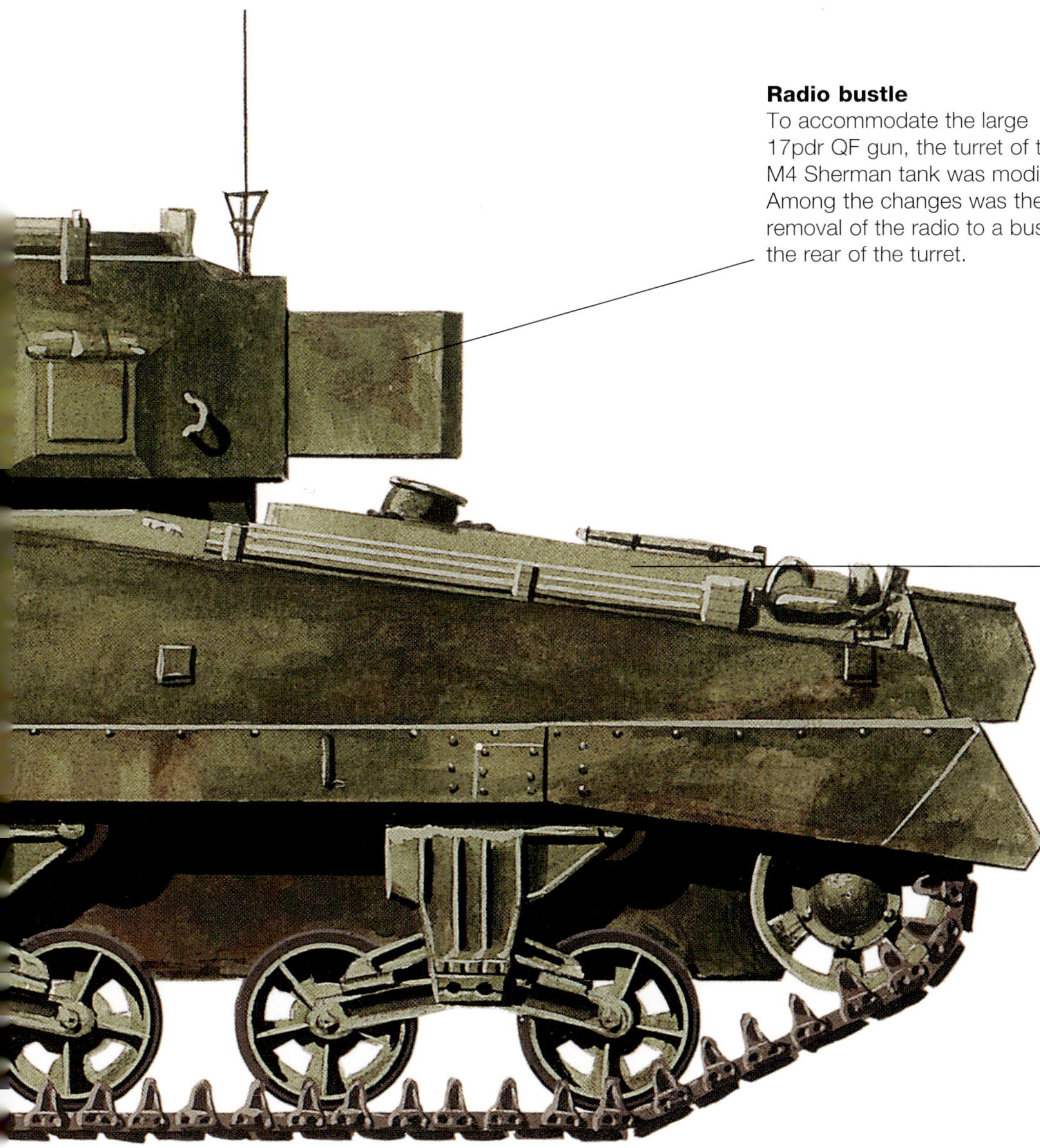

Radio bustle
To accommodate the large 17pdr QF gun, the turret of the M4 Sherman tank was modified. Among the changes was the removal of the radio to a bustle at the rear of the turret.

Engine
The Firefly powerplant varied with the version of M4 Sherman that was being modified. Those that were M4A4 conversions were powered by the Chrysler A57 30-cylinder petrol engine.

width of the Sherman turret could be fully utilized. Then, the engineers rotated the breech of the gun 90° to allow for loading on the left side rather than from the top. The gun cradle was shortened to fit into the Sherman turret, a second hatch was cut in the turret top to allow the gunner to exit the tank quickly if necessary, the radio was removed to a bustle on the turret rear and a new mantlet was developed for the 17pdr and its cradle.

The gun itself was modified with a longer section at its base to improve the stability of the entire gun platform, while the hull machine gun prominent in other versions of the M4 was removed to allow for greater storage of 17pdr ammunition, reducing the crew from five to four – the commander, driver, gunner/loader and radio operator. The reconfiguration of the gun itself was extensive enough that those 17pdrs intended for mounting atop the Sherman were constructed specifically for that purpose.

Although the Firefly packed a heavier punch, it retained the armour protection of the standard Sherman with the exception of the new mantlet, which was 13mm (0.5in) thicker. The Chrysler 30-cylinder multibank A57 petrol engine powered the M4A4 Shermans that were converted to Fireflies. Other standard powerplants included the Continental R975 radial petrol engine and the Ford GAA V-8 petrol engine.

Specification

Dimensions	Length: 7.85m (25ft 9in) Width: 2.67m (8ft 9in) Height: 2.74m (8ft 11in)
Weight	33 tonnes (32.4 tons)
Engine	1 x Chrysler A57 30-cylinder petrol powerplant generating 350kW (470hp)
Speed	40km/h (25mph)
Armament	Main: 1 x 17pdr (76.2mm/3in) QF gun Secondary: 1 x 7.62mm (0.3in) Browning machine gun
Armour	15–100mm (0.59–3.9in)
Range	Road: 201km (125 miles) Cross-country: 145km (90.1 miles)
Crew	4

The Sherman VC Firefly was easily distinguishable from the closely-related M4 medium tank. The barrel of its main gun was substantially longer than the earlier 75mm (2.95in) gun mounted on the turret of the basic Sherman.

Preferred Production

With preparations for the D-Day landings in Normandy proceeding, the availability of the new Firefly was received with enthusiasm and in February 1944, an initial order for 2100 was placed by the British Army. By D-Day, 342 Fireflies had been delivered to General Sir Bernard Montgomery's 21st Army Group. Several variants of the basic Sherman were modified as Fireflies, depending on which were available to the British.

The Sherman VC Firefly entered production in the autumn of 1943 and was available to British forces during the Normandy campaign. Its 17pdr QF gun substantially improved the odds of survival in combat with German tanks.

Stinging Firefly?

When the Sherman VC Firefly entered service with the British 21st Army Group under the command of General Sir Bernard Montgomery in the spring of 1944, the Germans quickly grew to respect the new Allied tank mounting the QF 17pdr gun. The Firefly proved its worth in combat rapidly as well. In several documented actions, the Firefly got the best of the heavy German Tiger and medium Panther tanks, particularly when firing from concealed positions.

One such event occurred on August 8, 1944, near the French village of Saint-Aignan-de-Cramesnil. Fireflies of the Northamptonshire Yeomanry destroyed three Tigers in a matter of minutes, one of them reported to have been commanded by SS Tiger tank ace Hauptsturmführer (Captain) Michael Wittman.

As the Firefly became available in greater numbers, British armoured units were equipped with a complement of both the upgunned tank and the standard Sherman armed with the 75mm (2.95in) gun. By the end of the war, production was scaled back somewhat with the arrival of new tanks designed from the beginning to accommodate heavier weapons. Eventually, between 2000 and 2300 Fireflies were produced, including a small number that were delivered to American forces. The official designation as either VC, 1C or 1C Hybrid indicated that the Sherman was armed with the 17pdr gun.

In combat, the Germans quickly realized that the Sherman with the long barrelled weapon was a formidable foe and made it a priority target. The 17pdr, the most powerful anti-tank gun produced by the British during World War II, was capable of penetrating the frontal armour of either the German Tiger or Panther. Armour-piercing ammunition actually penetrated nearly 200mm (7.8in) of armour at a distance of up to 1000m (3280ft).

Interestingly, the Firefly was not considered as effective against machine-gun positions, troop concentrations or other soft targets as the earlier Sherman with the 75mm gun and high-explosive ammunition. Nevertheless, some degree of firepower parity with German armour was indeed welcome on the Western Front.

Cromwell Mk VIII (1944)

Perpetuating the British line of cruiser tanks but finally accounting for the need for a more powerful gun and increased armour protection, the Cromwell Mk VIII made great strides in combat effectiveness against German tanks.

Although British military tacticians were reluctant to let go of the concept of the cruiser tank, lightly armed and armoured but with excellent speed that would exploit breaches in enemy lines and achieve deep penetrations, as World War II progressed it became apparent that the survivability of such armoured vehicles on the battlefield was questionable.

German tanks were more heavily armed and armoured than the British cruisers that were available at the outbreak of war, and experience in the North African desert revealed the inherent weaknesses of the early cruisers that sacrificed both armour and armament for speed. By 1942, a replacement for the inadequate Crusader tank was actively being developed to address these issues. Two prototypes emerged, the A27L, which became the Centaur, and the A27M, which developed into the successful Cromwell Mk VIII.

The Cromwell Mk VIII provided a considerable improvement in firepower and armour protection over previous cruiser tank designs. The Cromwell entered combat with British armoured units during the Normandy campaign in 1944.

Engine
The V-12 Rolls-Royce Meteor petrol engine provided power that preserved the Cromwell's speed advantage despite the added weight of a heavier main gun and enhanced armour protection.

Powerplant Particulars

The primary difference between the Centaur and the Cromwell was in their engines. The Centaur retained the Nuffield Liberty Mark V petrol engine, while the Cromwell was fitted with the more powerful V-12 Rolls-Royce Meteor petrol engine. The Rolls-Royce engine was better able to maintain acceptable speed while carrying the heavier weight of increased armour and the all-important main weapon that would serve as something of a battlefield equalizer in combat with German tanks.

In other aspects of their development, the Cromwell and Centaur were quite similar. The Cromwell Mk III, for example, was simply a Centaur I with the Rolls-Royce engine installed. The first three Cromwell variants each

The Cromwell Mk VIII cruiser tank represented a significant improvement in combat performance and crew survivability over previous British tanks. The enhanced performance was based on lessons learned in battle against German armour.

mounted the 6pdr (57mm/2.24in) QF gun. The Cromwell I included two 7.92mm (0.31in) BESA machine guns, while the Cromwell II added wider tracks for stability and one of the machine guns was removed.

Future Firepower

By 1943, the British were well aware of the prowess of the German 75mm (2.95in) and 88mm (3.5in) high-velocity guns mounted on a new generation of armoured fighting vehicles. It was obvious that the 6pdr could not stand up to the range and muzzle velocity of the enemy tanks. Therefore, the new 75mm QF gun was seen as a logical alternative. In short order, production of the newly upgunned Cromwell Mk IV was initiated. The first of these tanks were delivered to armoured units in Great Britain in October 1943.

Cromwell designers did not embrace the benefits of sloped armour and the turret is easily recognized by its flat lines and box-like appearance. The Cromwell silhouette was considerably less conspicuous than the American M4 Sherman, which was available in large numbers, actually somewhat inhibiting the production and deployment of the new British tank. A 1942 field exercise comparing the Cromwell, Centaur and the Sherman revealed that the American tank was superior in reliability and gunnery. The exercise spelled the demise of the Centaur and resulted in improvements to the Cromwell and its preparation for full-scale production and deployment in its final form.

Early Cromwells were valuable to British units as training tanks and helped to familiarize crews with the attributes of the new cruiser tank prior to the campaigns in Western Europe. Along with the 75mm gun, the Cromwell Mk IV had thicker armour up to 76mm (2.9in) in vital areas and the Meteor engine delivered a top speed of 61km/h (37.9mph).

The Cromwell Mk VIII was easily distinguished from other tanks on the battlefield due to its box-like turret and straight lines. Although its silhouette was considerably lower than the American M4 Sherman, the Cromwell did not incorporate sloped armour for added protection.

Specification

Dimensions	Length: 6.35m (20ft 10in) Width: 2.9m (9ft 6in) Height: 2.49m (8ft 2in)
Weight	29 tonnes (28.5 tons)
Engine	1 x V-12 Rolls-Royce Meteor powerplant generating 447kW (600hp)
Speed	61km/h (37.9mph)
Armament	Main: 1 x 75mm (2.95in) QF gun Secondary: 2 x 7.92mm (0.31in) BESA machine guns
Armour	8–76mm (0.31in–2.9in)
Range	Road: 278km (173 miles) Cross-country: 128.75km (80 miles)
Crew	5

Cromwell Configuration

The interior of the Cromwell was functional with the driver forward in the right side of the hull and separated from

The Cromwell Mk VIII mounted the 75mm (2.95in) QF gun, providing firepower that could hold its own against German tanks. The Cromwell power-traversed turret could also be turned manually.

the hull machine gunner by a steel bulkhead, while the commander, gunner and loader occupied the three-man turret with the engine positioned in the rear. In February 1944, final specifications for the Cromwell were issued, including the addition of 6mm (0.23in) of armour below the compartments housing the crew and the welding of all rivets on the front hull and the seams of the turret's steel plating to improve structural integrity and aid in the tank's water proofing.

Although more than 4300 Cromwells were built during the course of the war, the predominant tank among British armoured formations remained the American M4 Sherman. However, the Cromwell did enter combat during the Normandy campaign and was well received by its crews. Further tank development was to result in the Comet, which arguably was the best British tank of World War II. Cromwell variants included the Mk VIII with a 95mm (3.74in) howitzer, as well as armoured recovery, artillery observation and command vehicles.

Cromwell Combat

The Cromwell Mk VIII entered combat in June 1944 and primarily equipped units of the British 7th Armoured Division – the famed Desert Rats. At full strength, the armour complement of a Cromwell regiment included the Mk IV with its 75mm (2.95in) gun, the 95mm (3.74in) howitzer-equipped Mk VIII and the Sherman Firefly, an upgunned British variant of the American M4 Sherman medium tank.

Although its main gun was still inferior to those of the German Tiger and Panther tanks, it was a considerable improvement over previous British cruiser tank models. The bocage country of Normandy inhibited the Cromwell's advantage of speed, but once the breakout from the hedgerow was achieved the tank kept pace with the rapid movement of infantry across France and into the Third Reich. In the photo below, Cromwells display their speed, raising clouds of dust during a swift advance.

Tiger II "King Tiger" (1944)

Even as production began on the initial Tiger, the Henschel and Porsche companies were working to develop an even more formidable heavy tank. When Henschel won the contract in October 1943, the result was dubbed the Tiger II or "King Tiger."

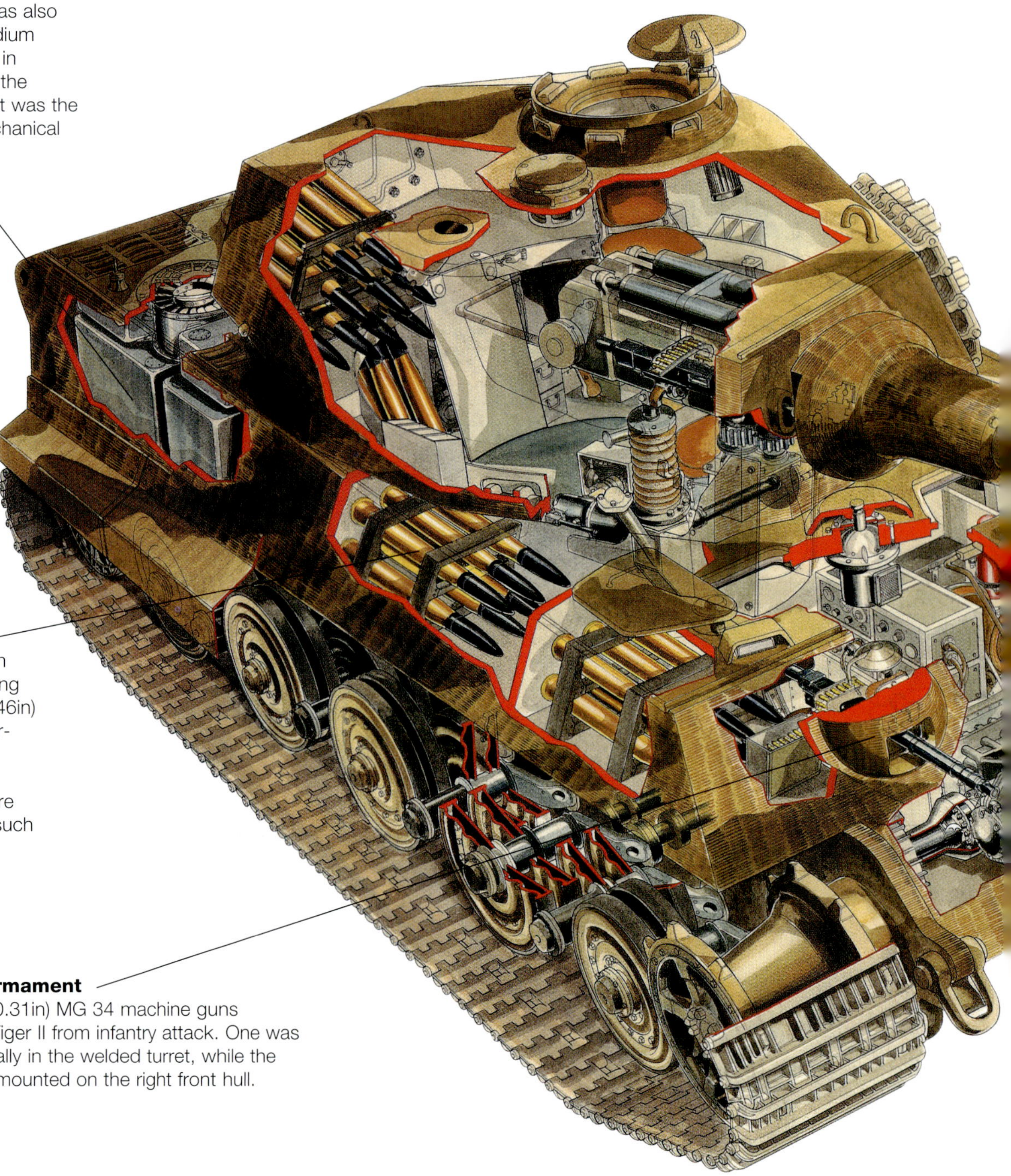

Engine
The V-12 Maybach HL 230 P30 petrol engine was also used in Panther medium tanks produced late in the war. In the field, the Maybach powerplant was the source of many mechanical breakdowns.

Ammunition Stowage
The Tiger II carried a minimum of 80 rounds of armour-piercing and high-explosive 88mm (3.46in) ammunition. While the armour-piercing rounds were for hard targets such as enemy tanks, the high-explosive rounds were devastating to softer targets such as troop concentrations.

Secondary Armament
Two 7.92mm (0.31in) MG 34 machine guns protected the Tiger II from infantry attack. One was mounted coaxially in the welded turret, while the other was ball-mounted on the right front hull.

The heaviest tank produced during World War II, the Tiger II was also known as the King Tiger in literal translation of the German Königstiger, or Bengal tiger. At 63.5 tonnes (62.5 tons), it outweighed any other heavy tank deployed in appreciable numbers. Its 88mm (3.5in) KwK 43 L/71 high-velocity gun was the finest implement of warfare of its kind in the German arsenal when production began in earnest in mid-1944.

The impact of the Tiger II on the battlefields of Europe may best be measured in its psychological effect on Allied soldiers who encountered the armoured giant, or those who believed they had. The Tiger II was never available in great numbers owing to the German penchant for perceived quality over quantity and the damage inflicted on the country's industrial capacity by continuous Allied bombing. Through the course of World War II, fewer than 500 Tiger IIs were actually completed and deployed during a brief production run from late 1943 through the spring of 1945.

The Tiger II heavy tank resulted from a design competition between German defence contractors Henschel and Porsche. Krupp actually designed and manufactured both turrets that were produced for the tank.

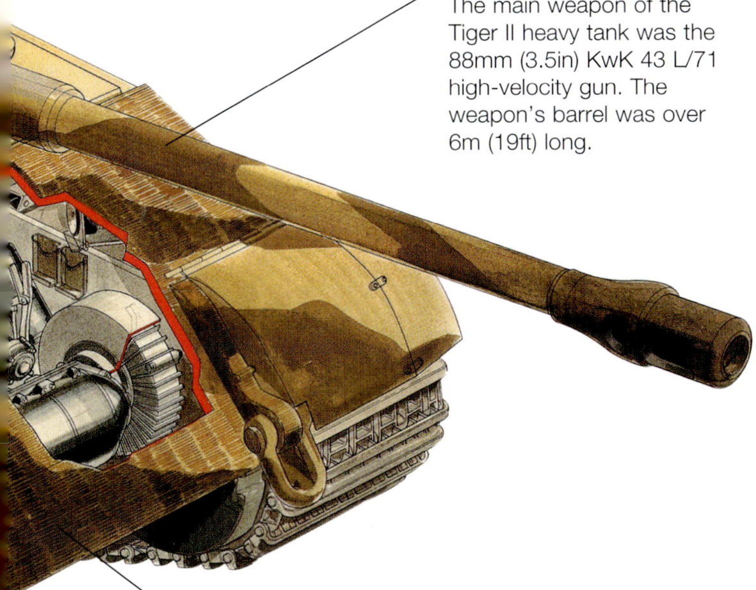

Main Armament
The main weapon of the Tiger II heavy tank was the 88mm (3.5in) KwK 43 L/71 high-velocity gun. The weapon's barrel was over 6m (19ft) long.

Armour Protection
The frontal armour of the Tiger II was 150mm (5.9in) thick and sloped 50mm (1.97in), while armour protection for the front of the turret increased to 180mm (7in). Side armour was 80mm (3.15in) thick and sloped at a 25° angle.

Although the Tiger II was a formidable foe in combat, fuel shortages and mechanical failures resulted in a number of the massive tanks being abandoned in the field or destroyed by their crews to prevent capture.

Henschel Initiative

The Tiger II carried a crew of five with the commander and gunner positioned in the turret to the left of the main gun and the loader to the right. The driver and hull machine-gunner/ radio operator were forward in the hull to the left and right respectively. The V-12 Maybach HL230 P30 petrol engine was positioned in the rear. The interior layout of the Tiger II was similar to the production version of the PzKpfw V Panther medium tank, while the distinctive sloped armour of the hull was also characteristic of the medium tank's design.

The Henschel-designed hull was all welded, while two turrets were actually utilized. Although Henschel was the primary contractor, the great German arms manufacturer Krupp had a hand in the design and production.

The first turret, erroneously known as the Porsche turret, was rounded and presented a potential shot trap for enemy shells fired at the weaker area where the turret joined the hull. It also had a distinctive bulge on the left side to accommodate a commander's cupola. Only the first 50 production Tiger IIs were equipped with this turret. The remainder were topped with the so-called Henschel turret, flatter and more angular, eliminating the prominent bulge and the shot-trap issue.

Armour protection was significant, ranging from 40mm (1.57in) to 180mm (7in). The tank's traverse torsion bar suspension included nine overlapping road wheels on either side of the hull. These were sometimes prone to trapping stones, mud and other debris in the field and required regular inspection and cleaning. In cold temperatures, the wheels might also be frozen together and require thawing or chipping away at the constraining ice.

With its muzzle velocity of up to 1000m (3280ft) per second, the main gun was capable of destroying Allied tanks at a range of up to 2.4km (1.5 miles), a standoff range at which most Allied guns could not effectively reply. Secondary armament included a pair of 7.92mm (0.31in) MG 34 machine guns, one mounted forward in the hull and the other coaxially in the turret.

Specification

Dimensions	Length: 7.25m (23ft 10in) Width: 3.72m (12ft 2in) Height: 3.27m (10ft 9in)
Weight	63.5 tonnes (62.5 tons)
Engine	1 x V-12 Maybach HL 230 P30 petrol engine producing 514kW (690hp)
Speed	38km/h (24mph)
Armament	Main: 1 x 88mm (3.5in) KwK 43 L/71 high-velocity gun Secondary: 2 x 7.92mm (0.31in) MG 34 machine guns
Armour	40–180mm (1.57–7in)
Range	Road: 170km (105 miles) Cross-country: 120km (70 miles)
Crew	5

Mammoth Mechanical Malfunctions

Although many features of the Tiger II were actually ahead of their time, the tank was plagued by mechanical issues. Many of the problems stemmed from an unreliable drivetrain. Its tremendous weight strained the Maybach powerplant and resulted in frequent breakdowns, while the suspension was also suspect in varied weather conditions. The weight of the Tiger II contributed to difficulties with cross-country movement, particularly over marshy terrain and across rivers. Long-distance travel was accomplished on railway flatcars.

The cost of Tiger II production was prohibitive as well, several times greater per unit than that of other German tanks. Each Tiger II further required the investment of 300,000 man-hours to complete. Fuel consumption was extreme and limited the range of the Tiger II, particularly during the crucial hours of the Battle of the Bulge in late 1944.

Battlefield Statement

Despite its shortcomings, in experienced hands the Tiger II was capable of dominating the battlefield. It was initially deployed on the Eastern Front in the spring of 1944 and later in Normandy, the Ardennes Offensive and the defence of Berlin. The advanced technology of the Tiger II set the standard for main battle tanks of the post-war era and significantly influenced the future role of armour in combat.

The Tiger II reached the battlefield on the Eastern Front in the spring of 1944 and was to play a pivotal role in Hitler's Ardennes Offensive in the West. However, fuel shortages and mechanical problems crippled its performance in the field.

Tiger Tales

The highest-scoring German armour ace of World War II, Feldwebel (Warrant Officer) Kurt Knispel destroyed 168 enemy tanks before his death at the early age of 23 while commanding a Tiger II on the Eastern Front. Meanwhile, SS Hauptscharführer (Master Sergeant) Karl Körner, who survived the war and passed away in 1997 at the age of 77, remembered attacking a large number of Soviet Stalin tanks.

"On the road from Bollersdorf to Strausberg stood a further 11 Stalin tanks and away on the edge of the village were around 120 to 150 enemy tanks in the process of being refuelled and rearmed," Körner recalled. "I destroyed the first and last of the 11 Stalin tanks on the road ... My own personal score of enemy tanks destroyed in this action was 39."

In the photo below, the menacing barrel of a Tiger II heavy tank's main gun casts a long shadow.

Jagdpanzer VI Jagdtiger (1944)

Although the Jagdtiger, or Hunting Tiger, was the most heavily armed and armoured vehicle deployed during World War II, its ponderous weight, high fuel consumption and inadequate powerplant limited its worth on the battlefield.

Somewhat curiously, it was a policy of the German Armaments Ministry from 1943 until the end of the war that the introduction of a new tank design would be accompanied by that of a similar tank destroyer mounting a main weapon of limited traverse. Late in 1943, just as the Tiger II heavy tank was about to enter production, the Jagdpanzer VI Jagdtiger was in development.

In October 1943, an iron model of the Jagdtiger was completed and production began in July 1944. By the end of the war only about 70 had been completed and deployed. All of these were assembled at the Nibelungwerk in St Valentin, Germany. The reasons for the limited production were numerous, including Allied bombing that continually impeded progress, the high cost of and time

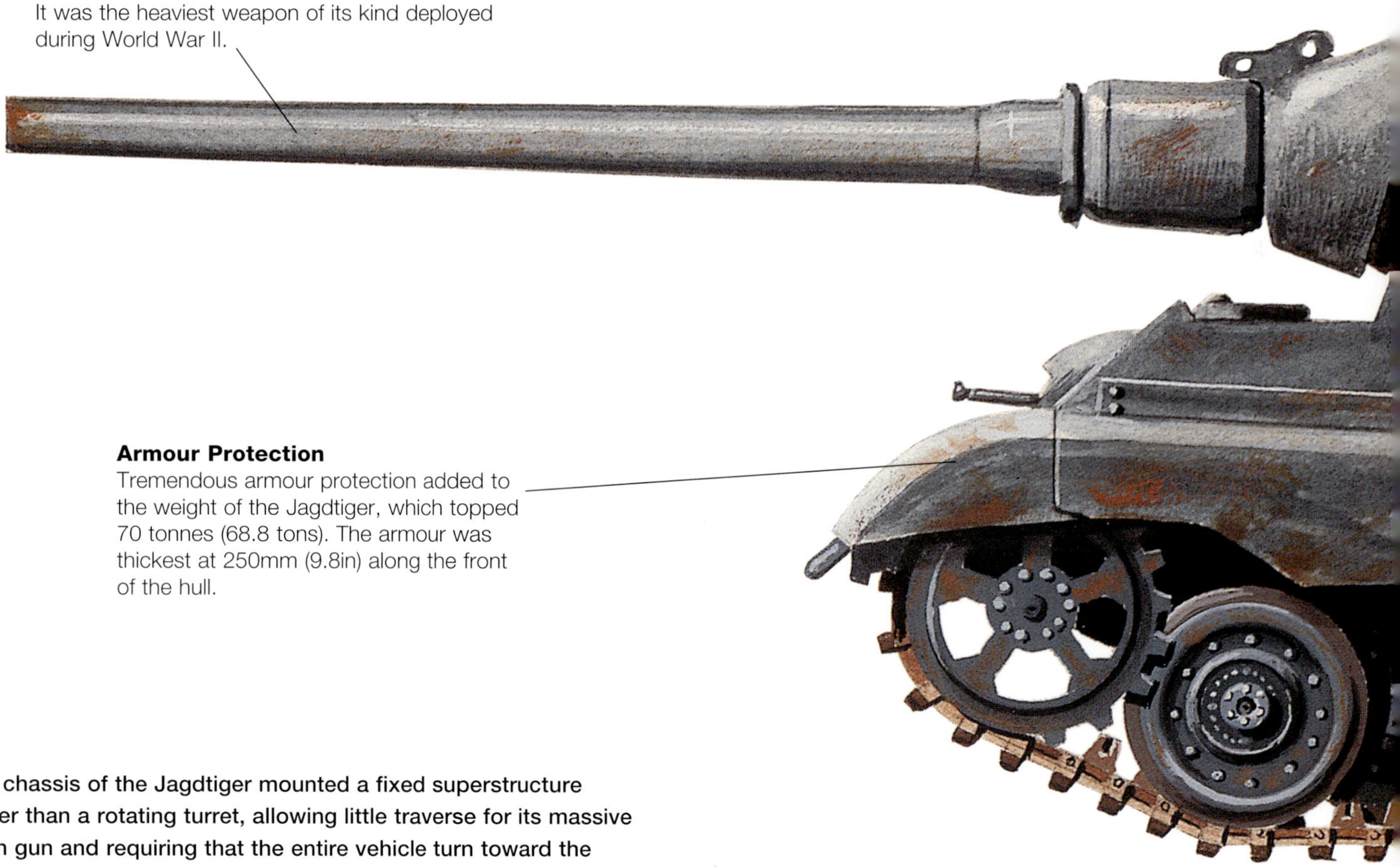

The chassis of the Jagdtiger mounted a fixed superstructure rather than a rotating turret, allowing little traverse for its massive main gun and requiring that the entire vehicle turn toward the target to fire accurately.

involved in production, the requirement that the hull of the Tiger II be lengthened 260mm (10.2in) to accommodate the Jagdtiger's massive 128mm (5in) Pak 44 L/55 gun and the availability of the gun itself.

Jagdtiger Construction

Although the Jagdtiger closely resembled the Tiger II, its chassis supported a superstructure rather than a turret, giving the tank destroyer a higher profile. The main gun had limited traverse of only 10° left and right and the

The high silhouette of the Jagdtiger made it a conspicuous target on the battlefield. Aside from vulnerability to tank-killer squads, infantry mounted attacks from several directions simultaneously and the Hunting Tiger became the hunted when Allied fighter bombers prowled.

Superstructure
The turret of the Tiger II was removed in favour of a high superstructure in the Jagdtiger, while the hull of the heavy tank was lengthened to accommodate another crewman and the heavy main gun.

Engine
The V-12 Maybach HL 230 P30 petrol engine was used in Panther medium tanks and the Tiger II heavy tank. The engine was inadequate to efficiently power the Jagdtiger, the heaviest armoured vehicle deployed during World War II.

The massive hull of the Jagdtiger resembled that of the PzKpfw V Panther medium tank with its sloped armour and descending side skirts that partially protected the suspension and wheels. The hull itself was lengthened 260mm (10.2in) in the tank destroyer configuration.

entire vehicle had to be oriented toward the target for it to fire effectively. The Jagdtiger was produced with two suspensions, one by Porsche that utilized eight road wheels and another by Henschel that utilized nine road wheels. Only 11 examples with the Porsche suspension were fielded. The armour protection of the tank destroyer was substantially greater than any other vehicle then in service. It was thickest at 250mm (9.8in) along the frontal hull.

The Jagdtiger's V-12 Maybach HL230 P30 petrol engine also powered the Tiger II and the PzKpfw V Panther medium tank and Jagdpanther tank destroyer. Although the powerplant was insufficient for the Tiger II, the situation was exacerbated by the extreme 70.6-tonne (69.5-ton) weight of the Jagdtiger. As a result losses to mechanical failure were often greater than those to enemy fire. One company of 10 Jagdtigers lost one in combat, one to friendly fire and eight abandoned or destroyed by their own crews due to malfunctions.

Specification

Dimensions	Length: 10.65m (34ft 11in) Width: 3.63m (11ft 11in) Height: 2.95m (9ft 8in)
Weight	70.6 tonnes (69.5 tons)
Engine	1 x V-12 Maybach HL230 P30 petrol engine generating 522kW (700hp)
Speed	38km/h (24mph)
Armament	Main: 1 x 128mm (5in) Pak 44 L/55 gun Secondary: 2 x 7.92mm (0.31in) MG 34 machine guns
Armour	25–250mm (0.98–9.8in)
Range	Road: 120km (75 miles) Cross-country: 80km (50 miles)
Crew	6

Weapons Wanted

The 128mm (5in) Pak 44 L/55 anti-tank weapon was the heaviest gun of its kind fielded during World War II. Due to its size, the Jagdtiger could carry only 38 to 40 rounds of armour-piercing or high-explosive ammunition. The Pak 44 was also utilized with the failed Maus supertank project. It was so powerful that one German commander reported a round traveling through four walls of a house and maintaining enough velocity to destroy an American tank on the other side; however, it was extremely heavy and had to be locked down during transit in order to prevent the sights from being jolted out of calibration. At times, the Pak 44 was not available in sufficient quantity and the 88mm (3.5in) Pak 43/3 was substituted. A few Jagdtigers were also armed with the 128mm (5in) Pak 80.

American soldiers examine a captured Jagdtiger somewhere in Northwest Europe, late 1944. Note the open doors of the hatch at the rear of the superstructure, the Zimmerit anti-magnetic mine paste applied to the hull and the spare tracks attached to the superstructure.

Initially, a single 7.92mm (0.31in) MG 34 machine gun was installed for defence against infantry attack. A second MG 34 was later added for anti-aircraft defence. Although the machine gun was generally effective against infantry, it was mounted in the hull with limited traverse, making the Jagdtiger vulnerable to tank-killer squads. Compounding the problem was the fact that the Jagdtiger was ponderously slow and often overwhelmed by enemy troops approaching from numerous directions. Its lack of speed largely prevented any movement during daylight hours, as Allied mastery of the air would have made attack by enemy fighter bombers a near certainty.

Mobile versus Stationary

In theory, the Jagdtiger was to have been a mobile tank destroyer without equal. However, in practice it became something more akin to a static pillbox or gun platform for its heavy weapon. The number of available Jagdtigers was sufficient only to equip two heavy tank destroyer battalions, 512 and 653. Most of these were destroyed or abandoned, while roughly 20 per cent were lost to enemy action. The Jagdtiger saw action in Hungary and during the defence of Berlin in the East, and in the West during the Battle of the Bulge and defensive operations along the German frontier in the spring of 1945.

Jagdtiger in Combat

Although only about 70 examples of the Jagdpanzer VI Jagdtiger were produced by the Nibelungwerk in St Valentin, Germany, the mammoth tank destroyers managed to get into the fight. The results were mixed.

Mechanical failures accounted for numerous losses among the Jagdtigers and the inexperience of some crews resulted in disaster. Tiger tank ace Otto Carius remembered a Jagdtiger commander turning broadside rather than toward the enemy and absorbing several hits that resulted in the deaths of all six crewmen. During a January 1945 encounter, however, a company of Jagdtigers destroyed 11 Sherman tanks, 30 trucks and other vehicles.

M-24 Chaffee (1944)

True to its heritage as an armoured vehicle for reconnaissance and infantry support, the M24 Chaffee light tank was a vast improvement over its predecessor, the M3 Stuart, mounting a 75mm (2.95in) main gun and a trio of machine guns.

The first M24 Chaffee light tank reached the U.S. Army in Europe in November 1944, just days before the Germans launched their Ardennes Offensive. During the Battle of the Bulge, two troops of cavalry utilized 34 of the new tanks in reconnaissance and to support infantry operations. Indeed, the Chaffee was a light tank and its 75mm (2.95in) main gun was a major improvement in firepower over the 37mm (1.45in) gun of the Stuart. However, with its light armour the M24 remained vulnerable to German tank and anti-tank gunfire as well

The M24 Chaffee light tank reached the battlefields of Europe in November 1944. Its numbers were too few to make a definitive impact on Allied operations before the German surrender.

Main Armament
The 75mm (2.95in) M6 gun, adapted from the modified weapon that served aboard the B-25 Mitchell bomber, provided the firepower that had long been lacking in American light tanks.

Armour Protection
The thin armour of the M24, only 38mm (1.5in) at its thickest on the front of the hull, meant that the speedy and upgunned tank was still vulnerable to a variety of German anti-tank weapons.

as the shoulder-launched anti-tank weapons issued to German troops.

Named after U.S. General Adna R. Chaffee, who had been an advocate of armoured forces in the American military during the inter-war years, the M24 was developed in response to the need for a more heavily-armed light tank to counter improving German weaponry. In the spring of 1943, Cadillac undertook the design challenge and by the end of the year its prototype, the T24, was ready for evaluation.

Compared to its predecessor, the Stuart light tank, the M24 Chaffee appeared more modern and streamlined in design. The tank offered both speed and firepower but sacrificed armour protection to deliver the two positive aspects of its performance.

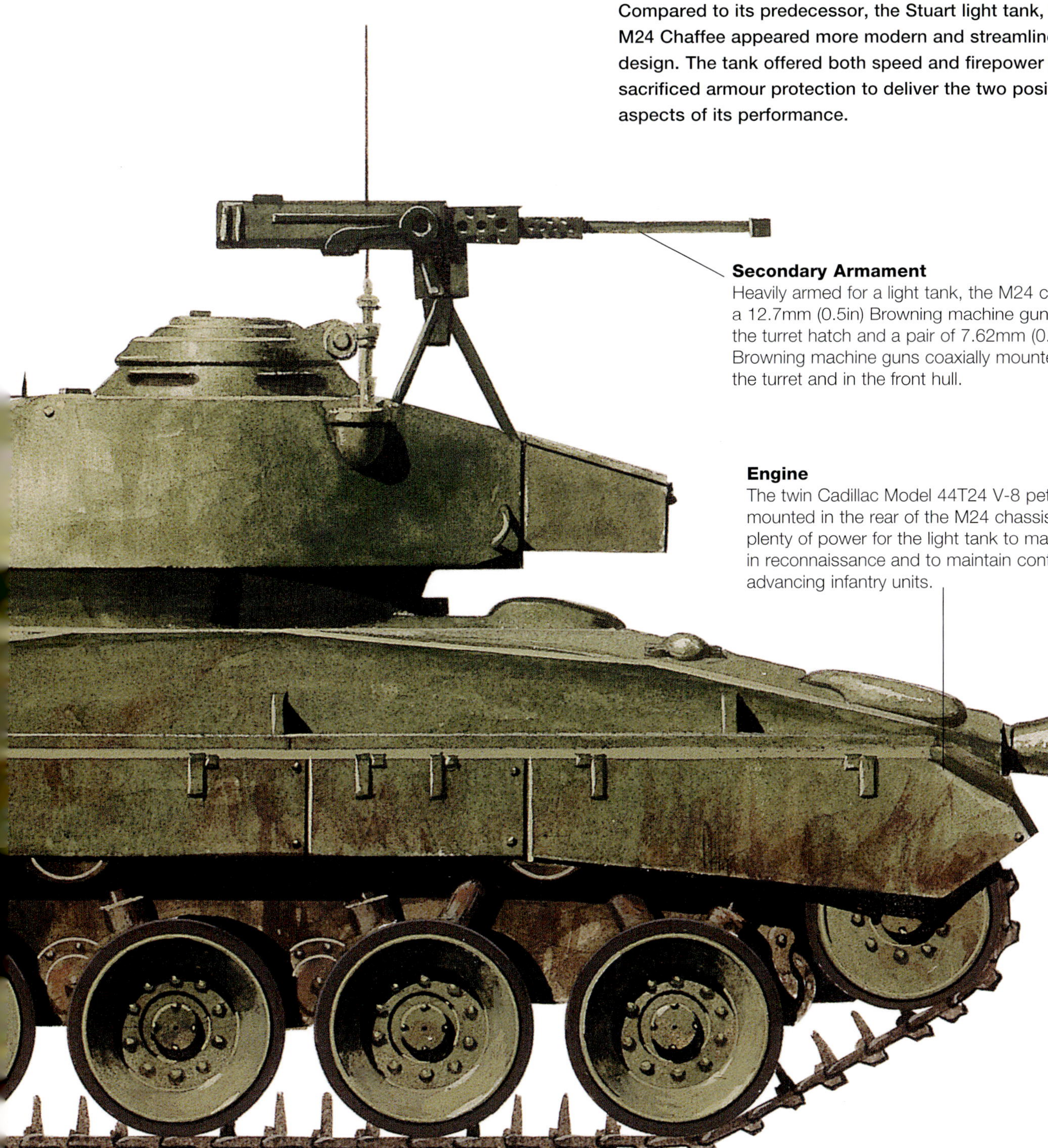

Secondary Armament
Heavily armed for a light tank, the M24 carried a 12.7mm (0.5in) Browning machine gun on the turret hatch and a pair of 7.62mm (0.3in) Browning machine guns coaxially mounted in the turret and in the front hull.

Engine
The twin Cadillac Model 44T24 V-8 petrol engines mounted in the rear of the M24 chassis produced plenty of power for the light tank to manoeuvre in reconnaissance and to maintain contact with advancing infantry units.

Specification

Dimensions	Length: 5.49m (18ft) Width: 2.95m (9ft 8in) Height: 2.46m (8ft 1in)
Weight	18.4 tonnes (18.1 tons)
Engine	Twin Cadillac 44T24 V-8 petrol engines generating combined 164kW (220hp)
Speed	56km/h (36mph)
Armament	Main: 1 x 75mm (2.95in) M6 gun Secondary: 2 x 7.62mm (0.3in) Browning machine guns; 1 x 12.7mm (0.5in) Browning machine gun
Armour	9.5–38mm (0.37–1.5in)
Range	161km (100 miles)
Crew	5

The successor to the Stuart series of light tanks, the M24 Chaffee incorporated a heavier main weapon, modern hull and turret designs and wider tracks for better mobility in difficult terrain. The tank came into its own during the Korean War of 1950–53.

Chaffee and Change

Efforts centred on the modification of an existing 75mm (2.95in) gun for use in the newly-designed T24. Eventually, the basic French gun that predated the turn of the twentieth century and had recently been modified to assume an anti-shipping role aboard the B-25 Mitchell medium bomber was further adapted for the new tank and designated the M6. Secondary armament consisted of a pintle-mounted 12.7mm (0.5in) Browning machine gun on the turret hatch and a pair of 7.62mm (0.3in) Browning machine guns coaxially mounted in the turret and forward in the hull.

Accepted as the M24, the Cadillac tank entered production in April 1944. When production ceased in August 1945, more than 4700 of the tanks had been built. For a light tank, the Chaffee interior was somewhat spacious for its crew of five, which included the commander, gunner and loader, who occupied the three-man turret, and the driver and radio operator/assistant driver forward in the hull. The M24 was powered by twin Cadillac Model 44T24 V-8 petrol engines that allowed the 18.4-tonne (18.1-ton) tank to achieve a top road speed of 56km/h (35mph). Its torsion bar suspension supported the M24 well during cross-country manoeuvres. Its light armour ranged from only 9.5mm (0.37in) to 38mm (1.5in).

Compared to the latest Stuart variant, the Chaffee was virtually a complete redesign. The tanks shared the same drivetrain, but the sleek lines of the M24 had ushered in a new era of armoured vehicle development in the United States. Actually, the M24 could be considered the first tank in a family of armoured vehicles that shared the same chassis but were utilized for numerous purposes, including self-propelled artillery, anti-aircraft and command duties.

Playing a Role

While the additional firepower of the 75mm gun was welcome, it remained apparent that the M24 was no match for German tanks such as the Panther or Tiger. It was, however, effective in its reconnaissance role, in reducing soft targets such as machine-gun nests and troop concentrations and as mobile artillery. The problem for the Americans was that it simply did not become available in sufficient numbers before the end of the war. The Stuart remained the primary light tank of the U.S. armoured forces for the duration. A small number of M24s were delivered to the British Army as well.

The greatest combat contribution of the M24 Chaffee came during the Korean War of 1950–53. In the early days of the conflict, the Chaffee was available in quantity and it delivered excellent performance in the reconnaissance and infantry support roles. Again, however, it was sometimes compelled to serve in tank versus tank combat and was overmatched by the superb Soviet-built T-34 medium tanks deployed by North Korean forces.

The French Army deployed the M24 during the fighting in Indochina and a number were in service during the debacle at Dien Bien Phu. During its 1971 war with India, the Pakistani Army also used them. The Chaffee proved to be a versatile light tank – by far the best of its kind to be developed by the Allies during World War II. The design has in fact been so durable that the armies of a number of small countries continue to operate modernized M24s today.

Delayed Justification

The M24 Chaffee light tank represented a new generation of American tank development; however, its combat debut in World War II did little to enhance its reputation. Due more to its lack of numbers than inferior performance, only a few dozen Chaffee tanks reached the front prior to the end of the war. The proving ground for the M24 was, though, on the other side of the world. During the Korean War of 1950–53, the Chaffee served as valuable mobile artillery during the defence of the Pusan Perimeter and worked well in a reconnaissance role in company with heavier tanks that could take on the Soviet-made T-34s in service with Communist forces. In the photo below, Chaffee crewmen talk with other soldiers as their column of tanks and trucks pauses to rest somewhere in Germany.

10011

Modern Tanks

Tanks of the modern era graphically illustrate the astonishing pace of advancing technology. Since World War II, the tank has evolved to an impressive frontline weapon of war, exhibiting the latest in firepower, laser, digital and thermal imaging, global positioning and precision instrumentation technology. In an ironic twist, soldiers operating such sophisticated military hardware often find themselves in counter-insurgency combat, facing the constant threat of low technology weapons.

The T-72 main battle tank has come to symbolize the waning military influence of the former Soviet Union around the globe. Originally intended for the export market, the T-72 has remained in service with the armed forces of various nations for nearly half a century.

IS-3 (1945)

The last Soviet heavy tank to enter production before the end of World War II, the IS-3 became operational too late to influence the outcome of the war but nevertheless became a symbol of the Red Army's military might.

The combat record of the Soviet IS-3 heavy tank is somewhat shrouded in mystery. Although reports of it being deployed against the Japanese in Manchuria in 1945 have surfaced, the consensus in the West is that it became operational too late for active military deployment during World War II.

While the IS-3 may have been a late arrival, its predecessors in the Josef Stalin series of heavy tanks did exert significant influence on the outcome of the Great Patriotic War. The Red Army victory during more than a month of fighting that swirled around the Kursk salient came at a tremendous price. More than 6000 Soviet tanks had

Engine
The IS-3 was powered by a 12-cylinder, V-2 diesel engine, generating 447 kW (600 hp).

been lost at Kursk and a special commission was convened to determine the cause of the horrendous losses.

In response to the commission's findings, it was determined that a new heavy tank, one that could perform on par with the legendary T-34 medium tank, was needed. The older KV-1 heavy tank had already given way to the KV-85, mounting a heavy 85mm (3.35in) gun. Still, continuing reengineering of the KV-85, including improving the transmission and redesigning the hull and suspension, gave rise to the new IS-1 heavy tank with a lower silhouette and lighter weight than the KV-85.

Leninist Lineage

With the design improvements came the realization that the IS-1 was capable of mounting an even heavier weapon. Both a 100mm (3.9in) and 122mm (4.8in) gun were installed

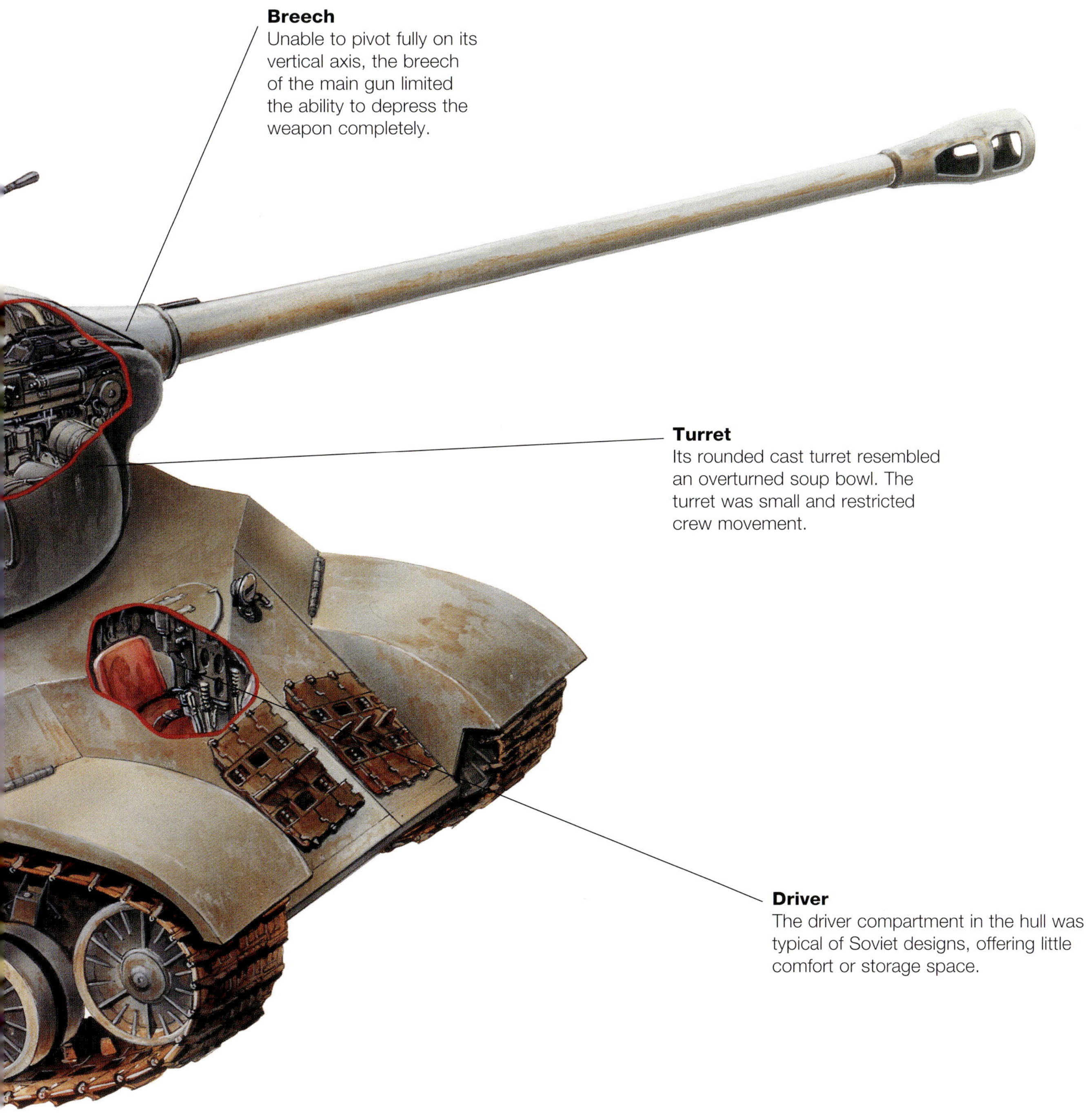

in experimental models, with the former demonstrating better armour penetration. The 122mm, though, was available in quantity and its high-explosive round was deadly in an anti-personnel role while its armour-piercing ammunition was considered adequate.

Therefore, in 1944, the first IS-2 mounting the long-barrelled 122mm (4.8in) A-19 went into production. It was later supplanted by the 122mm D25-T, with a better rate of fire and improved fire coordination capabilities. The D25-T was recognized by its distinctive double-baffle muzzle brake.

Specification

Dimensions	Length: 6.77m (22ft 2in) Width: 3.07m (10ft 1in) Height: 2.44m (8ft)
Weight	45.8 tonnes (45 tons)
Engine	1 x V-2-IS V-12 diesel powerplant generating 447kW (600hp)
Speed	37km/h (22.9mph)
Armament	Main: 1 x 122mm (4.8in) D25-T gun Secondary: 2 x 7.62mm (0.3in) DT or DTM machine guns; 1 x 12.7mm (0.5in) DshK machine gun
Armour	20–230mm (0.78–9in)
Range	Road: 160km (100 miles) Cross-country: 120km (75 miles)
Crew	4

With the IS-3 heavy tank, improvements over its predecessor, the IS-2 (aerial view shown here), included enhanced armour protection, a reduced frontal area and a lower silhouette.

The First and the Last

The final production tank of the Stalin series, assembly of the IS-3 began in May 1945 under the engineering supervision of M.F. Balzha at Experimental Plant No 100. With its roots firmly in the recent past, the IS-3 may also be considered the first heavy tank of its kind, or perhaps a bridge between the old and new. Regardless of how it is perceived, the IS-3 influenced Soviet and Eastern Bloc tank design for the next half century and became an early icon of the Cold War military prowess of the Red Army.

Although the IS-3 bears something of a family resemblance to preceding Soviet tanks, its design was distinctly different. At the end of World War II, fewer than 30 of the new tank had been completed, but by mid-1946 the number in Red Army service exceeded 2300. Despite the fact that its combat participation in World War II is doubtful, a regiment of the 45.8-tonne (45-ton) machines participated in a victory parade through Red Square on 7 September 1945.

Several notable improvements were included with the IS-3. The armour protection arrangement that had provided greater protection for the IS-2 but resulted in a lighter tank was retained. The welded hull with its rolled steel plating was sloped to the maximum possible degree, while the frontal area of the tank was actually reduced in width and overall size. The D25-T gun was state of the art among Soviet weapons manufacturers. The thickness of the frontal hull

and turret armour were raised to 120mm (4.7in) and 230mm (9in) respectively and the turret was dramatically rounded and flattened to resemble an overturned pan or soup bowl. The angular design of the hull prompted tank crewmen to nickname the IS-3 "Shchuka," or "Pike."

The rounded and flattened turret, intended to reduce the silhouette of the IS-3, was to become a hallmark of Soviet tank design for the next half century. However, two consequences, perhaps unintended, were the subsequent inability of the main gun breech to pivot fully on its vertical axis and depress completely, and although the internal controls allowed the commander to rotate the turret, the very size of the interior severely restricted the crew's freedom of movement.

The long barrel of the D25-T gun protruded well beyond the hull of the IS-3. The presence of the IS-3 heavy tank in Soviet armoured units was startling to Western observers.

The appearance of the powerful IS-3 shook Western military men and politicians alike. For years to come, the Soviet heavyweight was considered the finest war implement of its kind in the world.

Cold War Icon

The service life of the IS-3 heavy tank extended well into the 1950s, equipping the armoured forces of the Soviet Red Army and of the Eastern Bloc and client states around the world. Egypt became a primary recipient of the IS-3 and the tank was prominent in exercises with the Egyptian military of the period. Some IS-3 tanks were lost during confrontations with Israel. Many of these captured heavy tanks were repaired and placed in service with the Israeli Defence Force (IDF), some of them even upgraded with the engines of captured later-production T-54s.

In the photo at right, the distinctive turret of the IS-3, which was said to resemble an overturned soup bowl or skillet, is easily distinguished. The narrow frontal area and low turret of the IS-3 theoretically reduced the probability of detection and the drawing of enemy fire.

Centurion A41 (1945)

Developed as a cruiser tank during World War II, the British Centurion A41 arrived too late to see action against the German tanks it was intended to defeat. Nevertheless, its service life has lasted more than half a century.

Days after the end of World War II in Europe in May 1945, the Centurion A41 main battle tank, built to 1943 specifications, arrived on the Continent. Developed by the British Directorate of Tank Design as a heavy cruiser tank that was capable of defeating the powerful German armour that had cost the Allies so many lives, the original mission of the Centurion was unfulfilled.

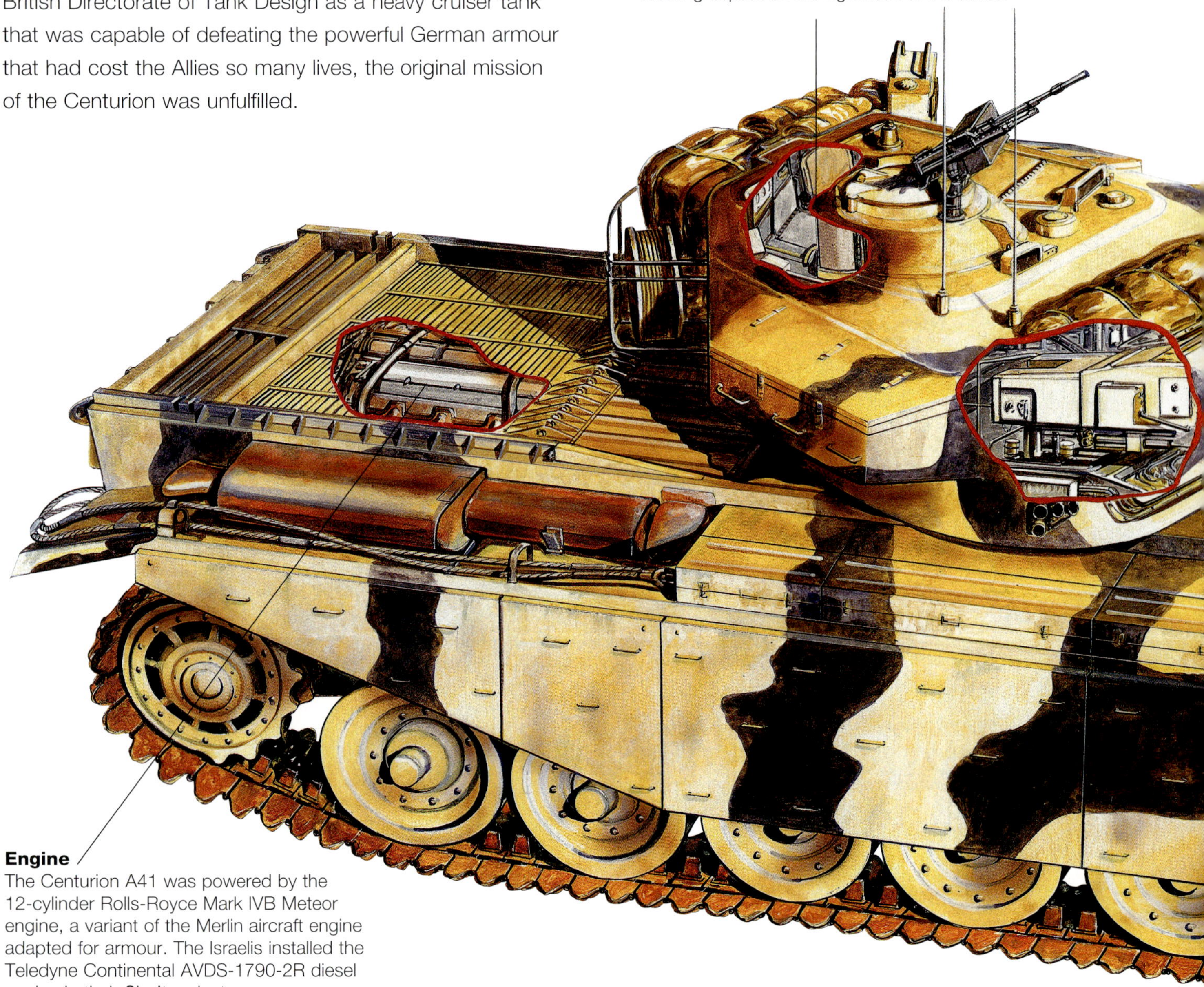

Commander Position
To pinpoint a target, the Centurion commander used periscopic rangefinding sights that were mechanically linked to the sights of the gunner. The commander was positioned beneath a rotating cupola on the right side of the turret.

Engine
The Centurion A41 was powered by the 12-cylinder Rolls-Royce Mark IVB Meteor engine, a variant of the Merlin aircraft engine adapted for armour. The Israelis installed the Teledyne Continental AVDS-1790-2R diesel engine in their Sho't variant.

Given the rather dismal performance of their armour during the war, British designers had set about improving the Comet cruiser tank with a new model that was more reliable in the field, heavily armoured to withstand a hit from the dreaded German 88mm (3.5in) gun, maintained reasonable road and cross-country speed and protected its crew against anti-tank mines. The comprehensive requirements put forward by the War Office were a tall order. However, in the case of the Centurion, the developers were equal to the task.

The Centurion A41 main battle tank reached the front lines in Europe just days after World War II ended. However, its design proved practical and adaptable, contributing to a long service life and impressive combat record.

Main Armament
The 105mm (4.1in) L7A2 rifled gun served as main armament on the majority of Centurion tanks, although a limited number were produced mounting the 17pdr and 20pdr QF guns.

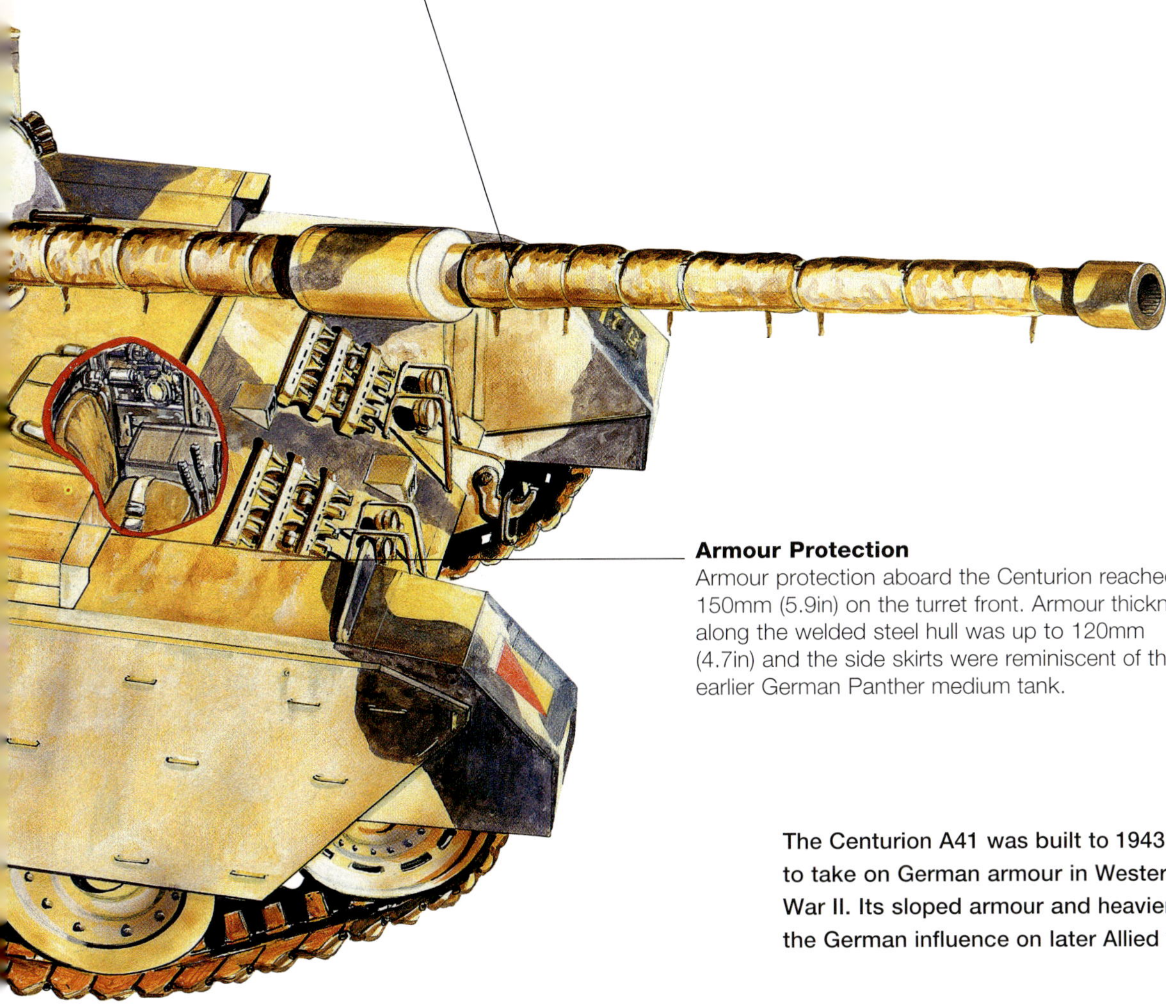

Armour Protection
Armour protection aboard the Centurion reached 150mm (5.9in) on the turret front. Armour thickness along the welded steel hull was up to 120mm (4.7in) and the side skirts were reminiscent of the earlier German Panther medium tank.

The Centurion A41 was built to 1943 specifications particularly to take on German armour in Western Europe during World War II. Its sloped armour and heavier gun were indicative of the German influence on later Allied tank designs.

The Centurion A41 exhibited few shortcomings compared to contemporary main battle tanks. Among these were a somewhat limited range, relatively slow speed and average cross-country capabilities.

Enduring Centurion

Although the Centurion did not debut in combat until the Korean War of 1950–53, it was clearly a vast improvement over earlier British tanks. The design proved highly adaptable to upgrades and no fewer than a dozen Marks were produced during a post-World War II service life that has lasted more than half a century. A total of 4423 Centurion tanks were produced by the Royal Ordnance Factory, Leyland, Vickers and other defence contractors from 1945 to 1962 and a number of these remain in service with the armed forces of various nations even today.

The Centurion proved such a versatile design that upgraded variants with increased weight might otherwise have resulted in the development of a new main battle tank. However, as the Centurion exceeded its initial weight limitation of 36 tonnes (35.4 tons), a new trailer was ordered to haul the tank instead. In fact, the Centurion was deemed exceptional in virtually every other category of performance and referred to by some experts as the "universal tank."

Specification

Dimensions	Length: 7.6m (25ft) Width: 3.38m (11ft 1in) Height: 3.01m (9ft 10.5in)
Weight	52 tonnes (57 tons)
Engine	1 x 12-cylinder Rolls-Royce Mark IVB Meteor engine generating 485kW (650hp)
Speed	34km/h (21mph)
Armament	Main: 1 x 105mm (4.1in) L7A2 rifled gun Secondary: Up to 2 x 7.62mm (0.3in) Browning machine guns; 1 x 12.7mm (0.5in) Browning M2 machine gun
Armour	17–152mm (0.67–6in)
Range	Road: 185km (115 miles) Cross-country: 96km (60 miles)
Crew	4

Lasting Layout

The Centurion featured an expanded welded-steel hull that placed a driver forward and to the right with ammunition stored to his left. The three-man turret seated the commander on the right beneath a rotating cupola, along with the gunner and loader. The armour was sloped to ward off projectiles and the thickness of the hull armour was substantially improved to 120mm (4.7in) in an effort to defeat the German 88mm shell. Turret armour increased over the years to 150mm (5.9in).

The external horizontal springs of the Horstman suspension replaced the Christie suspension that had equipped earlier British tanks and the 12-cylinder Rolls-Royce Mark IVB Meteor engine was installed. The Meteor was adapted for tanks from the highly successful Merlin aircraft engine.

Early Centurions mounted the 17pdr (76.2mm/3in) QF gun, originally a towed anti-tank weapon. This was followed by

a relative few mounting the 20pdr (84mm/3.3in) QF gun. Ultimately, the 105mm (4.1in) L7A2 rifled gun was chosen to equip the majority of the tanks. Secondary armament varied depending on the Mark from a single 7.62mm (0.3in) Browning machine gun mounted coaxially in the turret to three machine guns, including the turret mounted Browning, a second 7.62mm (0.3in) Browning in the forward hull and a 12.7mm (0.5in) M2 Browning anti-aircraft machine gun atop the turret.

Holding the Line

The Centurion A41 main battle tank was effective in both offensive and defensive combat roles during the Korean War. When Chinese and North Korean forces attacked the defensive line held primarily by the British 29th Infantry Brigade along the banks of the Imjin River north of the South Korean capital of Seoul in April 1951, Centurions of the 8th King's Royal Irish Hussars were instrumental in covering the withdrawal of the British and United Nations troops.

Following the success of the delaying action at the Imjin River that compelled Communist forces to slow their offensive, General John O'Daniel of the U.S. I Corps remarked on the British tankers' handling of their machines, saying that the "8th Hussars ... taught us that anywhere a tank can go is tank country – even the tops of mountains."

The Centurion A41 main battle tank compiled an impressive service record during more than half a century with the armoured forces of nations around the world. Its armour protection and accurate 105mm (4.1in) rifled gun made it an enduringly effective weapon.

Military Longevity

The Centurion A41 served not only during the Korean War but also in Vietnam. Centurions of the Indian Army destroyed many U.S.-built M24 Chaffee light tanks deployed by Pakistani forces during brief wars in 1965 and 1971. The Israeli Defence Force utilized the Centurion effectively during the Six-Day War of 1967 and the 1973 Yom Kippur War. Centurion variants are still active as modified recovery, bridgelaying and troop carrier vehicles.

The Israelis modified the Centurion to produce the Sho't variant, which served into the 1990s. The Sho't regularly prevailed during the Yom Kippur War in single combat with Soviet-made Syrian T-54/55 and T-62 tanks. One report indicated that during the course of a 30-hour battle along the hotly contested Golan Heights two damaged Sho't tanks took on more than 100 Syrian tanks and destroyed 60 of them – the equivalent of an entire Syrian armoured division.

The major Israeli modifications to the original Centurion design included sophisticated fire-control equipment and the introduction of the Teledyne Continental AVDS-1790-2R diesel engine, which considerably improved the tank's overall performance.

T-54/55 (1947)

The Soviet T-54/55 main battle tank was produced in greater numbers than any other tank in history. More than 65 years later, it remains in service with the armed forces of numerous small nations and Third World countries.

During the last days of World War II, Soviet engineers deemed the experimental T-44 medium tank an inadequate replacement for the T-34, which became the stuff of legend during the victory over Nazi Germany. With the failure of the T-44, it was decided to top the hull with a new, sleek turret that resembled an overturned soup bowl or small dome.

The prototype T-54 had been constructed and with many modifications the tank would go on to be built in

The T-54/55 main battle tank was in production for nearly 40 years and equipped the armoured forces of the Soviet Union and other Warsaw Pact armies. The tank's longevity may be attributed to its ease of modification.

Main Armament
The T-54/55 was originally armed with the 100mm (3.9in) D10T gun. This was later upgraded to the improved D10T2S with a bore evacuator and improved gun-laying system.

NBC Protection
With the dawn of the Nuclear Age, it became necessary to improve survivability of tank and crew in the event of an atomic detonation. A nuclear, biological and chemical (NBC) defence system was installed in the T-54/55 in the 1950s.

greater numbers than any other tank in military history. The T-54 main battle tank was built in the Soviet Union and the Communist Bloc nations of Poland and Czechoslovakia, beginning in 1945 and ending as late as 1983. During a 38-year production run, an estimated 86,000 or more were built. An unlicensed copy of the T-54 was also produced in China.

Many Modifications

By the late 1950s, modifications to the original T-54 had become so numerous that a new designation, T-55, was approved. Outwardly, the T-54 and T-55 were virtually identical. The primary differences between the two basic tanks were in the more powerful engine, improved main weapon of the T-55 and the improvement of basic nuclear,

The T-54/55 main battle tank evolved from a failed project to replace the T-34 medium tank. Therefore, it was somewhat lighter than contemporary purpose-built main battle tanks that it might encounter in combat.

biological and chemical (NBC) weapons protection.

Powered initially by the 12-cylinder Model V-54 diesel engine, the T-54 was constructed with a modified Christie suspension and mechanical synchromesh transmission. Its armour protection ranged from 30mm (1.18in) on the hull top to 170mm (6.7in) at the front of the hull. Such thicknesses were altered many times over the years. At 36 tonnes (35.4 tons), the T-54 was lighter than other main battle tanks and the weight differential was owed somewhat to its origin as a medium tank.

The original main gun, the 100mm (3.9in) D10T, was adapted from a dual-purpose naval gun and limited in its effectiveness due to the lack of a computerized fire-control system. The gun was loaded from the top, a difficult job in combat made more so because the seats in the original T-54 were welded to the hull and the turret floor did not rotate with the repositioning of the weapon.

In combat, the loader was required to pick up a round from storage while avoiding the gun's breech as the turret rotated and then place the shell into the breech with his left hand. Obviously this was detrimental to the gun's rate of fire. In later models, the 100mm (3.9in) D-10T2S gun was installed with its improved fire-control system and bore evacuator. The secondary armament of the T-54 included a 12.7mm (0.5in) pintle-mounted DShKM anti-aircraft machine gun near the commander's hatch and a 7.62mm (0.3in) PKT machine gun coaxially mounted in the turret.

Specification

Dimensions	Length: 6.45m (21ft 1in) Width: 3.27m (10ft 8in) Height: 2.4m (7ft 10in)
Weight	36 tonnes (35.4 tons)
Engine	1 x 12-cylinder V-54 (later V-55) diesel powerplant generating 388kW (520hp)
Speed	50km/h (30mph)
Armament	Main: 1 x 100mm (3.9in) D10T rifled gun (later D10T2S) Secondary: 1 x 7.62mm (0.3in) PKT machine gun; 1 x 12.7mm (0.5in) DShKM machine gun
Armour	20–170mm (0.78–2.75in)
Range	500km (300 miles)
Crew	4

Staying Power

Somewhat surprisingly, the T-54/55 has been known throughout its service history for its perceived shortcomings as much as it has for its adaptability. Critics have pointed out that the tank was less heavily armoured than contemporary main battle tanks. Its layout was suspect in several ways. Fuel and ammunition were stored in close proximity to one other, potentially resulting in explosions in the case of a direct hit. The turret was cramped, hampering the movement of the crew during combat and the traverse of the main weapon and the V-54 diesel engine, built primarily of a magnesium alloy, was prone to catching fire as a result of oil lines becoming clogged with metal filings.

The tank carried a crew of four, including the driver, commander, loader and gunner. While the driver was positioned forward in the centreline of the hull, the other crewmen occupied the turret and were each seated on the left side. A single direct hit could kill or incapacitate all three.

In the mid-1950s, the T54A included a rudimentary NBC defence system and a stabilized main gun. Fire control improved further with the T-54B as the D10T2S gun was stabilized in two planes. When it debuted in 1960, the T-54C had been equipped with a loader's hatch flush with the turret and one of the machine guns had been removed.

By 1958, the T-55 had come into its own to an extent. It was distinguishable from the mid-production T-54 in that its loader's cupola, turret dome ventilator and often the 12.7mm (0.5in) machine gun were removed. The V-55 diesel engine was an improvement over its predecessor but still prone to failure. Further improvements included a laser rangefinder, improved armour protection and rotating turret basket that partially eliminated the loader's difficulties.

Proxy Wars and Revolutions

The T-54/55 main battle tank has engaged in combat on numerous occasions during its more than 65 years in service. During the Vietnam War, South Vietnamese and American Patton tanks clashed with North Vietnamese T-54s and often got the better of the Soviet-built machines. In one engagement near Dong Ha, the capital of the Quang Tri Province, in April 1972, South Vietnamese M48A3 Pattons destroyed 16 T-54s with no losses.

Elsewhere, T-54s became a symbol of resistance to Soviet domination as they rolled through the streets of Budapest during the Hungarian revolt of 1956. They played a prominent and successful role with the Indian Army in its wars with Pakistan. However, they did not fare as well against the Israeli Centurions during the Six-Day and Yom Kippur Wars. In the photo below, an Iraqi T-54/55 lies abandoned after the defeat of Saddam Hussein's army in the 1991 Gulf War.

AMX-13 (1952)

Designed shortly after the end of World War II, the French airmobile AMX-13 light tank was in production into the 1980s and exported to numerous countries. Its many innovations included an oscillating turret and automatic loading system.

Following the end of World War II, the French arms industry recovered rapidly and one if its first offerings was the AMX-13 light tank. Atelier de Construction d'Issy-les-Moulineaux (AMX) began the design process in 1946 with the intent of producing a tank destroyer and reconnaissance vehicle and modified the plans somewhat

Ammunition Storage
Since the oscillating turret of the AMX-13 could house only two six-round magazines for the automatic loading system, additional ammunition was stored externally at the rear of the hull.

Engine
The basic AMX-13 was fitted with the eight-cylinder SOFAM petrol engine. Later versions were powered by a diesel engine that improved the vehicle's range and reduced the risk of fire.

The automatic loading system of the AMX-13 reduced the number of required crewmen to three, although only 12 rounds were carried in two magazines inside the turret.

to produce a light tank that was airmobile and believed suitable for use with airborne troops.

Production of the AMX-13, named in reference to the 13-tonne (12.7-ton) weight of the original vehicle, began with Atelier de Construction Roanne in 1952 and ended in the 1980s. During the 35-year production run, approximately 7700 examples of the tank and its variants were built.

The AMX-13 incorporated components of previous World War II-era tanks while also fielding innovative equipment. The interior of the tank was divided into a forward compartment with the driver seated to the left

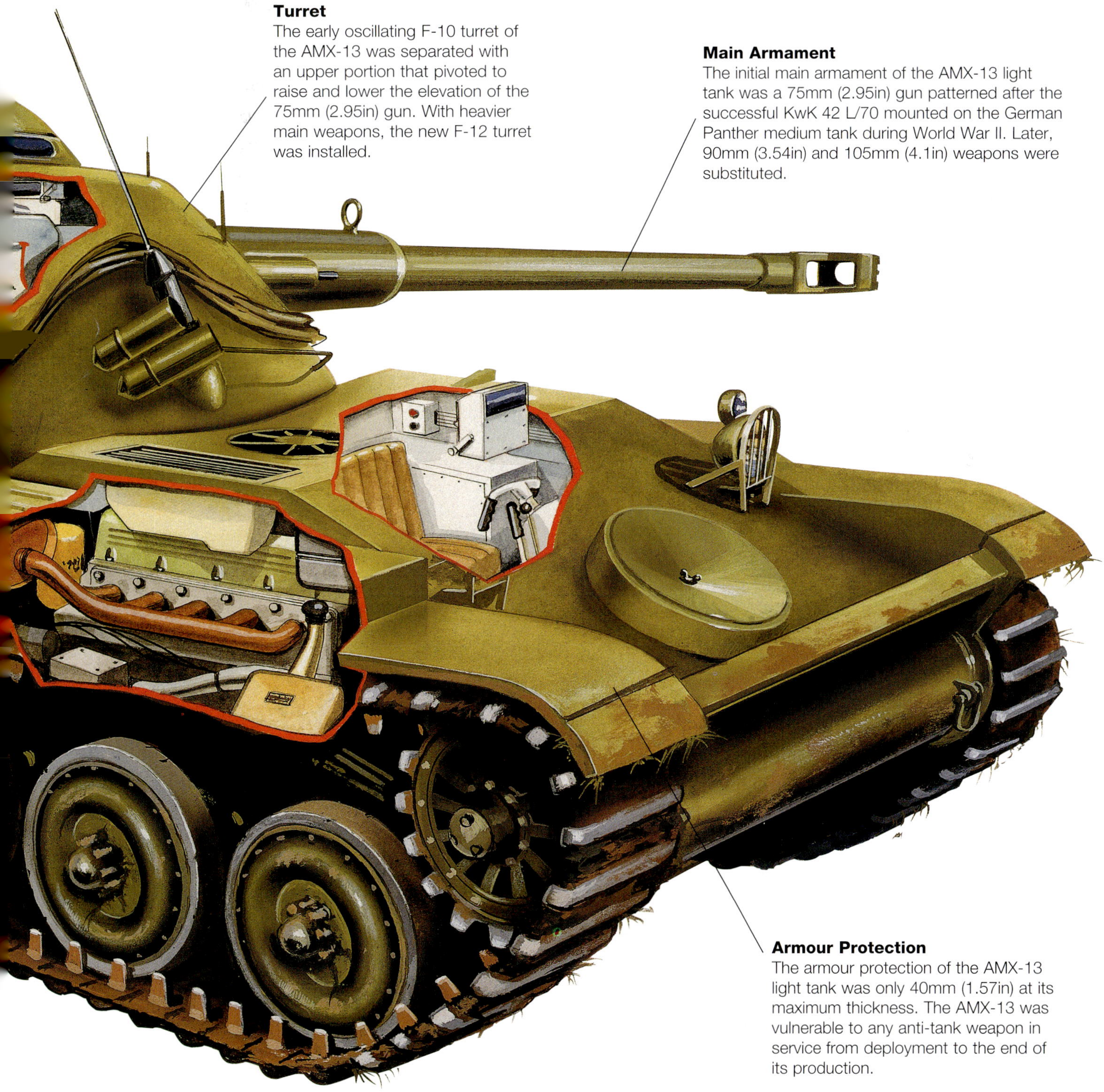

Turret
The early oscillating F-10 turret of the AMX-13 was separated with an upper portion that pivoted to raise and lower the elevation of the 75mm (2.95in) gun. With heavier main weapons, the new F-12 turret was installed.

Main Armament
The initial main armament of the AMX-13 light tank was a 75mm (2.95in) gun patterned after the successful KwK 42 L/70 mounted on the German Panther medium tank during World War II. Later, 90mm (3.54in) and 105mm (4.1in) weapons were substituted.

Armour Protection
The armour protection of the AMX-13 light tank was only 40mm (1.57in) at its maximum thickness. The AMX-13 was vulnerable to any anti-tank weapon in service from deployment to the end of its production.

The wheeled Panhard EBR armoured car shared the oscillating turret of the AMX-13 light tank. With its crew of four, the EBR mounted the 75mm (2.95in) gun of the AMX-13. Production began in the mid-1950s and approximately 1,200 were built.

in the hull and the SOFAM V-8 8GXb petrol engine to the right and running the length of the hull with exhaust emitted from a pipe near the external ammunition storage compartment. The commander and gunner were situated in a fighting compartment to the rear and inside the oscillating turret.

Specification

Dimensions	Length: 4.88m (16ft) Width: 2.5m (8ft 2in) Height: 2.3m (7ft 7in)
Weight	15 tonnes (14.7 tons)
Engine	1 x SOFAM eight-cylinder V-8 petrol engine
Speed	60km/h (37mph)
Armament	Main: 1 x 75mm (2.95in) gun Secondary: 2 x 7.5mm (0.29in) or 7.62mm (0.3in) FN1/AAT52 machine guns
Armour	10–40mm (0.39–1.57in)
Range	Road: 400km (250 miles) Cross-country: 250km (150 miles)
Crew	3

The turret itself was a departure from previous designs. Designated the FL-10, it was conceived by Fives-Gail Babcock and fitted toward the rear of the chassis to operate a fixed main gun situated in the upper half of the turret. Pivoting the upper half on the lower half of the turret raised and lowered the elevation of the main gun. While the oscillating turret may have offered a more stable gun platform, it proved problematic in mountainous terrain. The AMX-13 was at a decided disadvantage in attempting to depress the main weapon or elevate it sufficiently to clear hills and ridgelines.

The oscillating turret did facilitate the introduction of an automatic loading system, eliminating the need for a fourth crewman and improving the crew's response time in combat along with its rate of fire. However, the AMX-13 carried only two six-round magazines inside the tank and once these 12 rounds were expended the tank was compelled to withdraw to relative safety to allow the crew to reload outside the vehicle. Obviously, the crew could be exposed to enemy fire and highly vulnerable during this procedure.

Early AMX-13 models were constructed with a torsion bar suspension and the SOFAM petrol engine. During the latter stages of production, a diesel engine was added to reduce the prospect of catching fire and a fully-automatic transmission and hydropneumatic suspension were installed. The AMX-13 gained popularity as an export commodity and numerous countries that purchased the light tank made their own modifications to it.

Although the airmobile AMX-13 light tank was innovative in design, it was less than ideal in the field with its limited armour protection and traverse for the main weapon in mountainous terrain.

The original main weapon of the AMX-13 was a 75mm (2.95in) gun with a single-baffle muzzle brake patterned after the highly-successful German KwK 42 L/70 mounted on the PzKpfw V Panther medium tank. The AMX-13 was upgunned in 1966 to a 90mm (3.54in) gun and then a low-velocity 105mm (4.1in) primarily for export purposes. An improved turret, the FL-12, was concurrently introduced. Secondary armament consisted of a 7.5mm (0.29in) or 7.62mm (0.3in) FN1/AAT52 machine gun mounted coaxially in the turret and a 7.62mm (0.3in) anti-aircraft machine gun. In some cases, a third machine gun was mounted near the commander's cupola.

Overcoming Obstacles

Although the AMX-13 was light enough to be airlifted to combat zones, it sacrificed armour protection in the process. With a maximum armour of only 40mm (1.57in), the AMX-13 was vulnerable to any weapon with the exception of small arms. As heavier weapons were installed, the vehicle's weight climbed to 14 tonnes (13.7 tons) and later 15 tonnes (14.7 tons). In 1964, Cruesot-Loire assumed AMX-13 production, continuing to produce the vehicle for export after the French military had retired it from service during the 1970s. When production ceased in 1987, more than 3000 AMX-13s had been sold to other countries. Updates included the addition of computerized fire control, laser rangefinders, NBC (nuclear, biological and chemical) defence systems and night-fighting capabilities.

Despite its innovations and popularity as an export weapon, the performance of the AMX-13 in combat conditions was disappointing. Although it was intended for reconnaissance and infantry support roles, it was at a disadvantage during inevitable encounters with enemy armour. The Israeli Army deployed the AMX-13 during the Suez Crisis of 1956 and the Six-Day War in 1967; however, it was withdrawn from service shortly thereafter.

M-48 Patton (1952)

Following the American experience with armour in the Korean War, the development of the M48 Patton medium tank was undertaken. This was the third and most successful in the Patton line of post-war tanks.

In preparation for the potential Cold War battles with Soviet-bloc tanks on the plains of Western Europe and in response to their experience in the Korean War, American designers looked to improve their previous tanks in the Patton series, the M46 and M47, with a modified medium tank that was reasonable in cost and capable of accepting upgrades on a continuing basis.

Initially designated the 90mm (3.5in) Gun Tank T48, the prototype M48 was built to specifications issued on 27 February 1951. By 1953, the new M48, named once again for American General George S. Patton, Jr, of World War II fame, was in full production. The M48 was produced until 1959 and during the run more

Hull Construction
The hull of the M48 Patton medium tank was bowl-shaped and cast of a single piece as the earlier welded box-like construction of the M47 was discarded.

The M48 Patton tank was the mainstay of American armoured forces during the Vietnam War. Its turret-mounted machine guns were effective against enemy infantry in the dense jungle and the main weapon was sometimes deployed as mobile artillery.

Engine
The Continental ABDS-1790-5B petrol engine was prone to catching fire in the early M48. It was subsequently replaced by a Continental AVDS-1790-2 diesel engine that also improved the tank's operational range.

than 12,000 were built. Through the years, the Chrysler Corporation, Ford Motor Company and Fisher Tank Arsenal all built variants of the M48. The tank was widely exported and has remained in service with the armed forces of numerous countries for more than 60 years.

Reconstructed Warrior

Utilizing the earlier designs of the Patton series as a basis, American engineers revised the turret and hull of the existing M47 and eliminated the hull machine-gun position, which reduced the crew from five to four –

The service life of the M48 Patton medium tank has spanned six decades and many remain in service with armed forces around the world. The longevity of the M48 may be attributed in part to its adaptability to upgrades and cost efficiency. This model is employed by the Spanish army.

commander, gunner, loader and driver. The sloped armour was accentuated with the egg-shaped turret, which was cast in a single piece. While reducing the angle that would be susceptible to enemy shells, the turret was lighter and provided better direct ballistic protection.

Specification

Dimensions	Length: 6.82m (22ft 7in) Width: 3.63m (11ft 11in) Height: 3.1m (10ft 1in)
Weight	47 tonnes (46.25 tons)
Engine	1 x Continental AVDS-1790-2 V-12 diesel engine generating 559kW (750hp)
Speed	48km/hr (30mph)
Armament	Main: 1 x 90mm (3.54in) M41 gun Secondary: 1 x 7.62mm (0.3in) M73 machine gun; 1 x 12.7mm (0.5in) Browning M2 machine gun
Armour	13–120mm (0.5–4.7in)
Range	Road: 465km (290 miles) Cross-country: 300km (180 miles)
Crew	4

Rather than the previous square hull configuration, a rounded bowl shape was adopted and also cast in a single piece. The torsion bar suspension was retained, while the Continental AVDS-1790-5B 12-cylinder air-cooled twin-turbo petrol engine was chosen as the original powerplant.

Initially, the main armament of the M48 was the T54 or M48 90mm (3.54in) gun, which was handicapped from the start due to the lack of a stabilization system that made it quite difficult to lay the gun with any accuracy while the tank was on the move. Secondary armament included a 12.7mm (0.5in) Browning M2 machine gun affixed to the commander's cupola and a coaxial 7.62mm (0.3in) M73 machine gun designed by the Rock Island Arsenal and produced by General Electric.

Critical Corrections

Early on, the Continental petrol engine proved problematic. The engine caused the M48 to have limited range and was liable to catch fire. The petrol engine was replaced by the Continental AVDS-1790-2D 12-cylinder water-cooled diesel engine with the M48A3 that reached armoured units of the U.S. Army in 1963. Armour protection on the M48 glacis was increased to a maximum of 120mm (4.7in) with a slope of 60°. However, the tank was also vulnerable to catching fire if the turret was penetrated and hydraulic fluid was sprayed into the interior from ruptured lines.

Continuing design enhancements addressed the operational issues that surfaced with the M48. With the M48A1, a new driver's hatch and commander's cupola were installed so that the M2 machine gun could be

The 105mm (4.1in) L7A1 main gun and the searchlight sighted with the main gun and gunsights are prominently visible on this M48 Patton medium tank splashing ashore during training exercises. The searchlight generates one million candle power to illuminate distant targets.

loaded and fired from inside the turret. A fuel-injected engine, better fire control, larger fuel tanks and a T-shaped muzzle brake appeared with the M48A2. The diesel engine was introduced and came along with the production M48A3. The A3 variant also included a simplified rangefinder and a fire-control system that utilized a series of mirrors and a ballistic computer that was operated by cams and gears.

Patton Prowess

The Patton series of medium tanks was developed in the wake of World War II and became the frontline U.S. tank of the Cold War era. Improving on its predecessors, the M46 and M47, the M48 also became popular with NATO and allied countries. The M48 first engaged in combat with Pakistani forces in 1965 and suffered serious losses against the Centurion tanks of the Indian Army.

Jordanian M48 tanks were vulnerable due to external petrol tanks during the Six-Day War. The Israeli Defence Force replaced the main 90mm (3.54in) gun with a heavier 105mm (4.1in) weapon and also deployed the M48 during the conflict. Meanwhile, U.S. forces deployed more than 600 M48s during the Vietnam War and the tanks were effective in infantry support although the jungle did not offer ideal terrain.

A total of 1019 M48A3 models were built and a large number of existing M48s were upgraded to the new outfit. The U.S. Army accepted the first 600 of the M48A3 and the U.S. Marines received the balance. Many of these were deployed to Vietnam and provided excellent service in the infantry support role despite terrain that was never considered ideal for armoured operations.

Forward Firepower

During the mid-1960s, the Israeli Defence Force initiated a program to upgun the M48 from its original 90mm (3.54in) weapon to the 105mm (4.1in) L7A1 cannon, along with an enhanced fire-control system and a reduced profile for the commander's cupola. American engineers evaluated the improvements and incorporated them into a number of their own Patton tanks, designating them the M48A5.

The M48 Patton medium tank has remained viable into the twenty-first century due to its ease of upgrade and relatively low cost. Since its deployment, the tank has served with the armed forces of more than 20 countries.

PT-76 (1952)

The amphibious PT-76 light tank answered the requirement of the Soviet military establishment for a reconnaissance vehicle that could operate on land and water while also providing support for infantry.

During the late 1940s, the attention of the Soviet military turned once again to light tanks. The requirements of a new type of reconnaissance vehicle were varied. The tank should be amphibious, capable of operating on land, marshy terrain and in water. It should also be armed

The amphibious PT-76 was purpose built to traverse land and water in reconnaissance and infantry support roles. The design has proved effective, enduring for more than 60 years and remaining active with Russian naval infantry.

sufficiently to defend itself and to provide direct fire support to advancing infantry and it should of course be reliable in the field.

Numerous prototypes were developed by Soviet designers and one of these, tentatively named Object 740, showed great promise. During trials the new tank demonstrated the amphibious capabilities sought for use by the Red Army and Soviet naval troops. Its design was a unique blend of both armoured vehicle and assault boat. By 1951, the new tank was selected for production and named the PT-76. Production began in 1953 at the Volgograd Tank Factory.

Specification

Dimensions	Length: 6.91m (22ft 8in) Width: 3.15m (10ft 4in) Height: 2.33m (7ft 5.6in)
Weight	14 tonnes (13.7 tons)
Engine	1 x V6B diesel engine on land developing 179kW (240hp); water jet for crossing streams and rivers
Speed	Land: 44km/h (27mph) Water: 10.2km/h (6.3mph)
Armament	Main: 1 x 76.2mm (3in) D-56TS gun Secondary: 1 x 7.62mm (0.3in) SGMT machine gun; 1 x 12.7mm (0.5in) DShKM machine gun
Armour	5–20mm (0.19–0.78in)
Range	260km (160 miles)
Crew	3

Assault Amphibian

The PT-76 remained in production until 1959 and approximately 12,000 are estimated to have been built. Some 30 are said to remain in service with Russian naval infantry today, and during the height of its construction the PT-76 was exported to more than 25 countries. These included Soviet client states, Warsaw Pact nations and Third World countries in Asia and Africa.

The PT 76 maintains a distinct advantage over other amphibious vehicles of its time. The light tank is capable of entering and exiting water without field modification and exposure of the crew to enemy fire.

The long service career of the PT-76 is testament to its ability to carry out the purpose for which the tank was intended. The hull resembles that of a pontoon or boat with its contoured and sloped bow. Fabricated from cold-rolled homogenous welded steel, the hull is divided into two compartments. The sloped front glacis enhances the buoyancy of the vehicle and the PT-76's low profile is reminiscent of other Soviet tank designs.

The cramped two-man turret is positioned forward atop the hull with the driver forward in the centreline of the tank and the commander seated to the right in the turret and the gunner to the left. The design failed to correct a shortcoming of earlier Soviet tank designs as the commander was required to assist the gunner in serving the main 76.2mm (3in) D-56T gun, restricting his efficiency in combat.

The commander viewed the landscape through three observation periscopes and was often required to direct the driver, whose vision was somewhat obscured in water, across rivers or streams. The gunner utilized an MK-4 sight, but the main gun was not stabilized so could not fire while on the move.

The PT-76 was powered by a V-6B inline water-cooled diesel engine and was capable of speed of up to 44km/h (27mph) on land. In the amphibious role, it was driven by a pair of water jets that pumped water into the system and expelled it under great pressure to generate a top speed of 10.2km/h (6.3mph). A snorkel was fitted to assist with water crossings; however, it had the nasty habit of sucking exhaust fumes into the interior of the tank, making it potentially hazardous to its crew.

Fight or Flee

The PT-76 was quite stable in water with the exception of heavy surf. This was achieved at the expense of armour protection and with hollow road wheels to lighten the tank's overall weight. With armour of just 20mm (0.78in) thickness on the front of the turret, the crew was protected only from small arms fire up to 12.7mm (0.5in), small shell fragments and flash burn. A direct hit by anything more substantial was likely to penetrate the hull and disable the vehicle.

Still, the PT-76 packed an offensive punch with its 76.2mm (3in) gun. This was upgraded in 1957 to the improved D-56TM, which included a double baffle muzzle brake, fume extractor and bore evacuator. Two years later, the D-56TS was introduced with the PT-76B. The D-56TS was stabilized in two planes to finally allow firing on the move and the PT-76B also included better radio equipment, nuclear, bacterial and chemical (NBC) protection, improved optics and advanced electrical equipment. The secondary armament consisted of a 7.62mm (0.3in) SGMT coaxial machine gun in the turret, while some later models mounted a 12.7mm (0.5in) anti-aircraft gun as well.

Through the years, the PT-76 has demonstrated its reconnaissance and infantry support capabilities in combat. Despite its disadvantage in armour protection, it has been true to the literal translation of its name, Plavayushtshiy Tank, or amphibious tank.

Distribution and Copyright

The PT-76 (pictured below) has seen action around the world, particularly with the North Vietnamese Army during the Vietnam War, with the armed forces of Arab nations during the conflicts with Israel in the 1960s and 1970s, through counterinsurgency operations in Indonesia and into the twenty-first century with Russian troops in Chechnya.

For many years, China manufactured an unlicensed copy of the PT-76 and Polish factories built a copy as well. The chassis has served as a platform for the FROG (Free Rocket Over Ground) tactical missile system, the ASU-85 airborne assault gun and the BTR-50P armoured personnel carrier.

M-60 Patton (1960)

The armoured might of the Russian Bear raised concerns among the American and NATO military command structures. In response, the M60 main battle tank emerged with significant modifications to the earlier medium M48 Patton.

Reports of a new Soviet main battle tank that threatened battlefield superiority over anything then in production or deployed with Western armies prompted the United States to evaluate an entirely new main battle tank design or to

enhance the performance of the M48 Patton, the existing medium tank that had been in service since the early 1950s and upgraded several times.

The accuracy of the reports proved undeniable and as the Soviets were developing and producing their new T-62 main battle tank American designers began efforts to improve the frontline tank fielded by the U.S. Army. Primarily to counter reports that British Intelligence had generated concerning the performance of the new Soviet tank and of the 100mm (3.9in) and 115mm (4.5in) guns then being introduced to Warsaw Pact forces, the Americans began trials of a new model, the M60, in 1957 and steadily improved the vehicle's performance over the next two years.

The M60 Patton was the first U.S. armoured vehicle that was truly classified as a main battle tank. Although it relied heavily on the design of the previous M48, it was a marked improvement over the earlier tanks of the Patton series.

Based on the M60A1 Patton main battle tank, the M728 CEV (Combat Engineer Vehicle) mounted a 165mm (6.5in) M135 gun, a licence-built copy of the British L9A1 gun used in British engineer vehicles based on their Centurion tank.

Similar but Different

Although the M60 was in many ways its own machine, it was directly linked to the prior M46, M47 and M48 tanks of the Patton series, which in turn traced their lineage to the late World War II-era M26 Pershing heavy tank. While the chief concerns with the M48 had been its limited range, heavy weight, extreme fuel consumption and relatively thin armour protection, the M60 entered production in 1960 with a turret that was of similar elliptical shape and an interior layout that was in essence a copy of the earlier tanks, divided into a forward compartment for the driver, a fighting compartment for the commander, gunner and loader, and an engine compartment housing the Continental AVDS-1790-2 V-12 twin-turbo diesel engine to the rear. The tank's torsion bar suspension system varied during production but included an innovation with the tube-over-bar configuration. The torsion bar was enclosed in a tube and connected at one end to work as a double suspension.

The turret of the M60 was moved forward 12cm (4.7in) to provide additional space in what was already considered a relatively comfortable interior. The gunner was seated forward and to the right in the turret, with the loader above and to the left. The commander sat on the right directly above and behind the gunner. The driver viewed the field ahead through three periscopes and a night vision infrared scope. The gunner could utilize standard and infrared versions of a roof-mounted periscope and the commander took advantage of eight vision panels surrounding the hand rotated cupola.

The main armament of the M60, which was nicknamed Patton like its predecessors, was the 105mm (4.1in)

Specification

Dimensions	Length: 6.94m (22ft 9in) Width: 3.6m (11ft) Height: 3.2m (10ft 6in)
Weight	45 tonnes (44.2 tons)
Engine	1 x Continental V-12 AVDS-1790-2 twin-turbo diesel engine generating 560kW (750hp)
Speed	48km/h (30mph)
Armament	Main: 1 x 105mm (4.1in) M68 gun Secondary: 1 x 7.62mm (0.3in) M73 Browning machine gun; 1 x 12.7mm (0.5in) M85 Browning machine gun
Armour	150mm (5.9in)
Range	480km (300 miles)
Crew	4

M68 gun, a licence-built copy of the outstanding British L7A1 gun that was also in use with the German Leopard I and later-model British Centurion main battle tanks, even equipping some later model M48s. The M68 could be aimed and fired by the commander or gunner, allowing the tank to function with greater efficiency in combat.

The M60 Patton tank is considered by some to be its own main battle tank design and by others as a continuation of the Patton series. Regardless, it remains in widespread service with the armed forces of numerous countries.

Trials and Tweaks

With the M60A1 and M60A3, the original M60 turret was discarded in favour of a needle-nose configuration that reduced the forward silhouette of the tank and increased armour protection to 127mm (4.9in) on its front. The M60A3 entered production in 1977 and included numerous improvements such as the Hughes integrated laser rangefinding sight and thermal imaging night sight used by the commander, VGS-2 thermal imaging and Hughes VVG-2 laser rangefinder for the gunner and a solid-state ballistic computer. External appliqué armour was added to the hull of the M60A3 for protection against enemy anti-tank weapons that were being developed during the late 1980s.

Many M60A1 models that were already in service were upgraded to M60A3 specifications in the late 1970s. Improvements were added to both models along the way, including a track system with pads that could be replaced with relative ease in the field along with smokescreen and snorkel apparatus.

Staying Power

Production of the M60 main battle tank finally ceased in 1987; however, many remain in service with the armed forces of various countries to this day. Relatively recently, the tank participated as part of coalition forces during the 1990–91 Operation Desert Storm in Kuwait, where the M1 Abrams main battle tank was deployed as well.

Shooting Star

During 27 years of production from 1960 to 1987, more than 15,000 M60 Patton tanks, as shown in the photo at right, and in all variants were produced. The M60 was deployed to Vietnam on a limited basis, fought with the Israeli Defence Force during the 1973 Yom Kippur War, with Iranian forces during the Iran-Iraq War and in Operation Desert Storm. A few examples remain in service with U.S. forces.

The M60A2 variant, nicknamed the Starship, was modified with a 152mm (6in) weapon system capable of firing the Shillelagh anti-tank missile. The project proved to be a major disappointment with only 550 produced. Most of these were soon placed in storage.

T-62 (1961)

Only marginally improving on the T-54/55 main battle tank, the T-62 became the primary Red Army tank during the 1960s and was manufactured in large numbers to equip the armoured forces of the Warsaw Pact nations.

Although its development was intended as an improvement over the veteran T-54/55, the Soviet military establishment was later compelled to recognize that the T-62 was only somewhat successful at best in that regard. Western observers concluded that for virtually every improvement made with the T-62 an operational shortcoming essentially nullified it.

Advances in NATO tank designs and the deployment of the U.S. Patton and British Centurion series tanks prompted the Soviets to evaluate the ability of their main T-54/55 weaponry, the 100mm (3.9in) D10T2S gun, to penetrate thicker and more resistant armour at reasonable distances. When an attempt to upgun the T-54/55 with the stabilized 115mm (4.5in) U5TS smoothbore gun failed, the hull was

lengthened and the turret ring reinforced to accommodate the heavier weapon and absorb its substantial recoil. The result was the T-62, which was produced for 14 years in the Soviet Union from 1961 to 1975, from 1975 to 1978 in Czechoslovakia, and in North Korea until the 1980s. Altogether, nearly 23,000 T-62s were completed.

More of the Same?

Although the T-62 was operational from the early 1960s, it was not revealed to the West until 1965. For all the secrecy, the T-62 was far short of a resounding success as an improvement to the T-54/55. Remarkably, it nevertheless assumed the leading role in Red Army and Warsaw Pact

Despite its shortcomings, the Soviet-designed T-62 main battle tank remained in production for more than 20 years. Although it failed to demonstrate marked improvement over the T-54/55, it served as the frontline Warsaw Pact tank in Eastern Europe and with other armies around the world.

Secondary Armament
The secondary armament of the T-62 included a single 7.62mm (0.3in) PKT coaxial machine gun and a 12.7mm (0.5in) DshK 1938/46 heavy machine gun that the commander had to exit the turret to operate.

Engine
The 12-cylinder V-55 4-stroke water-cooled diesel engine was an adequate powerplant for the T-62, generating a top speed of 50km/h (31mph) on the road.

The Chinese Type 69 tank (shown above) was based on a Chinese version of the old Soviet T-54, but with many components copied from the Soviet T-62. The Type 69 became the first independently Chinese-developed main battle tank.

armoured formations and with the armed forces of nations friendly to the Soviet Union in the Middle East and the Pacific rim.

Both inside and out, the T-62 retained familiar components of its predecessor. The easily-recognizable turret, shaped like an overturned frying-pan, was retained. While it contributed to the tank's low silhouette, it restricted the movement of the three crewmen inside as well as the traverse of the main weapon. The addition of the larger gun made a cramped situation even worse. With good cross-country mobility and relatively easy maintenance requirements in the field, the T-62 did offer the enhanced main gun, with its characteristic thermal sleeve, a reinforced hull bottom for better protection against mines and rubber track pads.

The 12-cylinder V-55 diesel engine provided adequate power and an external fuel tank carrying 400 litres (88 gallons) of fuel improved the T-62's range significantly. Armour protection included 102mm (4in) of steel sloped at 60° on the upper hull, effectively increasing the thickness in this vulnerable area to 200mm (7.8in). However, by most standards this was still deemed insufficient. The manganese steel tracks were quite durable but prone to being thrown if the tank were quickly put into reverse or took a turn too quickly. Ammunition and fuel were stored in close proximity within the hull and a direct hit often resulted in a catastrophic explosion.

Specification

Dimensions	Length: 9.34m (30ft 7in) Width: 3.30m (10ft 10in) Height: 2.40m (7ft 10in)
Weight	40 tonnes (39.3 tons)
Engine	1 x 12-cylinder V-55 water-cooled diesel powerplant generating 433kW (581hp)
Speed	Road: 50km/h (31mph) Cross-country: 40km/h (24.9mph)
Armament	Main: 1 x 115mm (4.5in) U5TS smoothbore gun Secondary: 1 x 7.62mm (0.3in) PKT machine gun; 1 x 12.7mm (0.5in) DshK anti-aircraft machine gun
Armour	20–240mm (0.78–9.4in)
Range	Road: 450km (280 miles) Cross-country: 320km (199 miles)
Crew	4

Armoured Angst

In the field, the T-62 continued to frustrate those whose lives depended on its functionality. Some have described the interior of the tank as an "ergonomic slum." In true Soviet tradition, little consideration was given to the comfort of the T-62 crew.

Firing the 115mm (4.5in) gun was nothing short of an ordeal. Typically, the commander would acquire the target through his stadiametric sight and rotate the turret to the proper position. The gunner then stepped in, sighted the

A T-62 main battle tank churns up a cloud of dust along a dirt road. The lack of return rollers in the modified Christie suspension is plainly visible. However, the tank did maintain good traction at moderate speed.

target and fired the gun. The weapon then went into a détente position so that the spent cartridge could eject. The gunner was also required to lift a 23kg (55lb) shell into the top-loading breech with his left hand. Although the gun was stabilized to theoretically allow accurate firing on the move, this procedure nullified that capability. The low rate of fire – about four rounds per minute – meant that a miss with the first shot was often fatal for the T-62 at a time when most vulnerable to return fire.

Further complications with the gun included its inability to traverse while loading or while the driver's hatch was open in the forward hull. A later variant, the T-64, introduced an automatic loader, reducing the crew to three but this again failing to address the numerous limitations of turret and gun coordination.

Secondary armament included a 12.7mm (0.5in) DshK 1938/46 anti-aircraft machine gun mounted above the commander's position. A 7.62mm (0.3in) PKT coaxial machine gun was also mounted. Oddly, the commander could not operate the heavier machine gun from the safety of the turret interior. To fire it, he was obliged to open the hatch and expose himself to the enemy.

The T-62 was equipped with nuclear, biological and chemical filtration equipment and the interior of the turret was lined with leaded foam to defend against radiation. Although the process was something of an adventure, a snorkel could be deployed to ford small streams.

Long T-62 Service

Although its proponents and adversaries were aware of the numerous operational issues surrounding the T-62 main battle tank, it remained the backbone of armoured forces in the Red Army, Warsaw Pact and other armies friendly to the Soviet Union for many years. Its service record includes combat in Vietnam, Angola, the Arab-Israeli conflicts, the Iran-Iraq War and the first Gulf War.

Years after production ceased in the Soviet Union and Czechoslovakia, North Korea produced a variant of the tank. Following the capture of a T-62 by the People's Liberation Army during border clashes with the Soviets in 1969, the People's Republic of China produced an unlicensed copy designated the Type 69. Variants of the T-62 included the T-64 tank with an automatic loader, the SU-130 assault gun, a flamethrower tank and an armoured recovery vehicle.

Chieftain Mk5 (1963)

Although its origin dated back to the late 1940s, the Chieftain did not enter production until 1963. Intended as a replacement for the Centurion series, the Chieftain exhibited new frontiers in British main battle tank design.

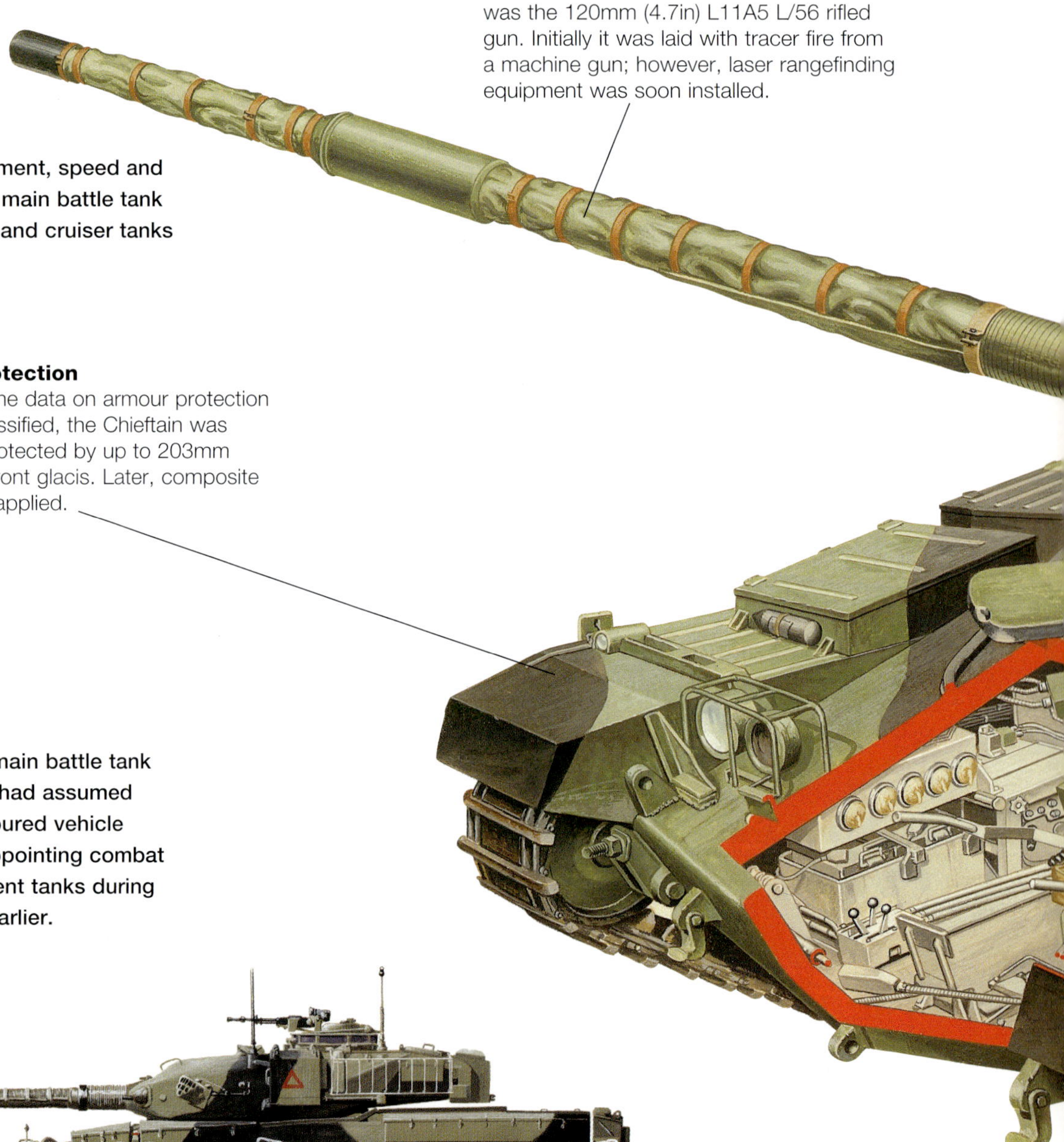

Main Armament
The main armament of the Chieftain Mk5 was the 120mm (4.7in) L11A5 L/56 rifled gun. Initially it was laid with tracer fire from a machine gun; however, laser rangefinding equipment was soon installed.

With progressively greater armament, speed and armour protection, the Chieftain main battle tank traced its lineage to the infantry and cruiser tanks of the World War II era.

Armour Protection
Although some data on armour protection has been classified, the Chieftain was reportedly protected by up to 203mm (8in) on the front glacis. Later, composite armour was applied.

With the debut of the Chieftain main battle tank in the early 1960s, Great Britain had assumed a leading role in innovative armoured vehicle design – a far cry from the disappointing combat performance of its most prominent tanks during World War II a quarter century earlier.

When the Chieftain main battle tank reached its frontline armoured units at the height of the Cold War in the mid-1960s, the British Army finally had at its disposal an armoured vehicle on par with the best of its Warsaw Pact adversaries, namely the T-54/55 and the hushed-up T-62 with its 115mm (4.5in) smoothbore gun that had created concern among NATO military experts.

In fact, British tank designers had taken to heart the lessons learned from bitter combat in World War II. Heavier weapons, better speed and stout armour protection were prerequisites to any new tank that would take the place of the effective Centurion series and allow British tankers to confront Soviet armoured units with confidence. In the Chieftain, the British achieved all this and more.

Charting the Chieftain

Specifications for the new British main battle tank were approved in 1958 and three years later Leyland Motors had built the initial prototype that would become the Chieftain. In 1963, the British Army took delivery of the first production

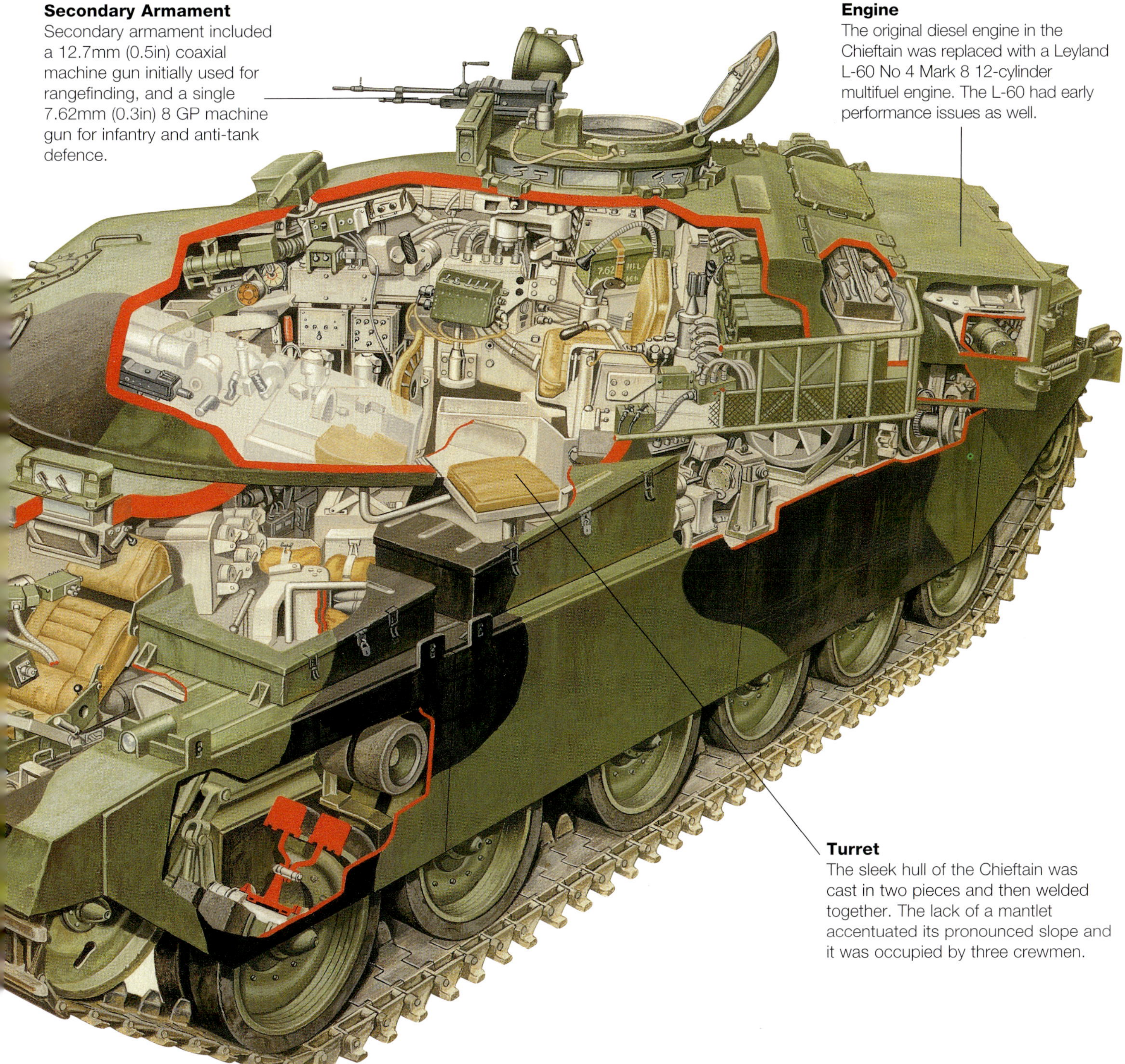

Secondary Armament
Secondary armament included a 12.7mm (0.5in) coaxial machine gun initially used for rangefinding, and a single 7.62mm (0.3in) 8 GP machine gun for infantry and anti-tank defence.

Engine
The original diesel engine in the Chieftain was replaced with a Leyland L-60 No 4 Mark 8 12-cylinder multifuel engine. The L-60 had early performance issues as well.

Turret
The sleek hull of the Chieftain was cast in two pieces and then welded together. The lack of a mantlet accentuated its pronounced slope and it was occupied by three crewmen.

The Chieftain AVRE (Armoured Vehicle, Royal Engineers) carried fascines atop a sloped rail system that deployed bundles of logs to assist in crossing shell holes or other depressions in the terrain.

Chieftain, a hulking 54-tonne (53.1-ton) beast that at once caused some concerns among field commanders about its cross-country manoeuvrability.

Those concerns were soon allayed as the world took note of the other performance characteristics of the powerful Chieftain, acknowledged in short order as the most heavily-armed tank in service anywhere until the later introduction of the German Leopard 1. Until the late 1980s, variants of the Chieftain served as the backbone of British armoured units deployed with NATO forces on the continent of Europe.

Specification

Dimensions	Length: 7.52m (24ft 8in) Width: 3.5m (11ft 6in) Height: 2.9m (9ft 6in)
Weight	54 tonnes (53.1 tons)
Engine	1 x Leyland L-60 No 4 Mark 8 12-cylinder multifuel powerplant generating 560kW (750hp).
Speed	50km/h (30mph)
Armament	Main: 1 x 120mm (4.7in) Royal Ordnance L11A5 rifled cannon Secondary: 1 x 12.7mm (0.5in) L21 machine gun; 1 x 7.62mm (0.3in) L37 GP machine gun
Armour	Classified – estimated up to 203mm (8in)
Range	Road: 500km (310 miles) Cross-country: 300km (180 miles)
Crew	4

Performance Plus

Immediately, observers grasped the significance of the Chieftain's main weapon, the 120mm (4.7in) Royal Ordnance L11A5 rifled cannon that was eventually to become the standard calibre of NATO Cold War-era tanks. Specifically, the weapon was required to exhibit the ability to penetrate enemy armour at greater range than any other tank available. Early Chieftains relied on a 12.7mm (0.5in) machine gun firing tracer ammunition to mark and range targets for the main gun; however, this was rapidly replaced with laser rangefinding equipment. The L11A5 became widely known for its penetrating power, rate of fire of six to 10 rounds per minute and the fact that it fired projectiles and charges that were separate rather than combined in a single shell. Such an arrangement significantly reduced the possibility of a catastrophic explosion.

Initially, the Chieftain was powered by a 436kW (584hp) diesel engine that was quickly deemed inadequate for the heavy tank. The next production engine was the Leyland L-60 No 4 Mark 8 12-cylinder multifuel powerplant. The L-60, however, was found to have problems of its own. The 54-tonne (53.1-ton) Chieftain was sometimes sluggish in difficult terrain and the engine was found to be unreliable, with a breakdown rate that approached 90 per cent of the engines installed. Fan drive and cylinder liner failures were addressed and piping was rerouted to improve the L-60's performance.

The Chieftain Mk5 main battle tank is easily recognized in the field with its long 120mm (4.7in) rifled gun and the characteristic slope of the front glacis and turret, which does not include a mantlet for the main weapon.

The Chieftain's armour protection was of homogeneous cast and welded nickel steel, while the turret was cast and welded as well, with steel and ceramic composite appliqué panels added on subsequent variants. Thickness remains classified to a degree but has been estimated at up to 203mm (8in) on the front glacis; side skirts protected the wheels and Horstmann suspension.

In keeping with standard British configuration, the layout of the Chieftain placed the driver forward with the fighting compartment centred below the turret and the engine to the rear separated by a firewall. In the final production variant, the Mk5, the driver was positioned in a semi-reclining seat to assist with the tank's low silhouette and the ability to fire on targets below the Chieftain's terrain grade.

The commander had a 360° view of the field through an array of periscopes and was seated to the right in the sleek, streamlined turret beneath a rotating cupola. The gunner sat below and to the commander's front, while the loader was to his left in the three-man turret. Improvements to the powerplant and the nuclear, biological and chemical defence system were continued with the Mk5. The turret did not include a gun mantlet and afforded greater concealment with the tank in the hull down position.

Desert Chieftain

The Chieftain Mk5, the final production model of the successful series, ended the line of more than a dozen variants. Export versions of the Chieftain have been deployed with the armed forces of Middle Eastern nations such as Oman, Kuwait, Jordan and Iraq. Iran ordered Chieftain tanks in the Shir I and Shir II configurations and a request for 1400 Shir II tanks was cancelled after the fall of the Shah's government in 1979.

Specialized versions of the Chieftain included the AVRE (Armoured Vehicle, Royal Engineers) vehicle and others for recovery, bridgelaying, mine clearing and anti-aircraft purposes. The Shir I was later renamed the Khalid.

Leopard 1 (1965)

The Leopard 1 main battle tank began as a joint venture between Germany and France. When the cooperative effort failed, German designers continued with the development of their own weapon.

In November 1956, only a few months following the creation of the army of the Federal Republic of Germany a decade after the end of World War II, the West German military issued specifications for a new main battle tank to replace the American M47 and M48 Patton models that had equipped its armoured units.

A joint venture with France was launched to develop a tank that both countries could deploy with their own forces and introduce to the international arms market for potential export. Eventually, the joint project failed to gain the needed cooperation. Both countries pursued a new armoured design independently. By 1961, a prototype tank was being evaluated, and in July 1963 defence contractor Krauss-Maffei had won the contract for the new German tank, christened the Leopard 1.

Production of the Leopard 1 main battle tank continued from 1965 to 1979, but the assembly line was reopened in 1981 to fill an order from the government of Greece.

The Leopard 1 main battle tank entered service with the army of the Federal Republic of Germany in 1965. It was well armed and utilized state-of-the-art technology but sacrificed armour protection for speed and mobility.

Main Armament
The British Royal Ordnance 105mm (4.1in) L7A3 L/52 rifled gun was built under licence in Germany and equipped the Leopard 1 main battle tank. A limited number of later variants mounted a 120mm (4.7in) gun.

Panzer Progress

The first operational Leopard 1 reached the West German Army in September 1965 and represented significant progress in the main battle tank designs of the mid-twentieth century. Still, however, the classic dilemma of balancing firepower, armour protection and mobility weighed on the German engineers who brought the Leopard 1 from concept to reality.

The tank was armed with a licence-built copy of the outstanding British Royal Ordnance 105mm (4.1in) L7A3 L/52 rifled gun. The L7A3 was equipped with a solid construction barrel in a single piece, a screwed-on breech

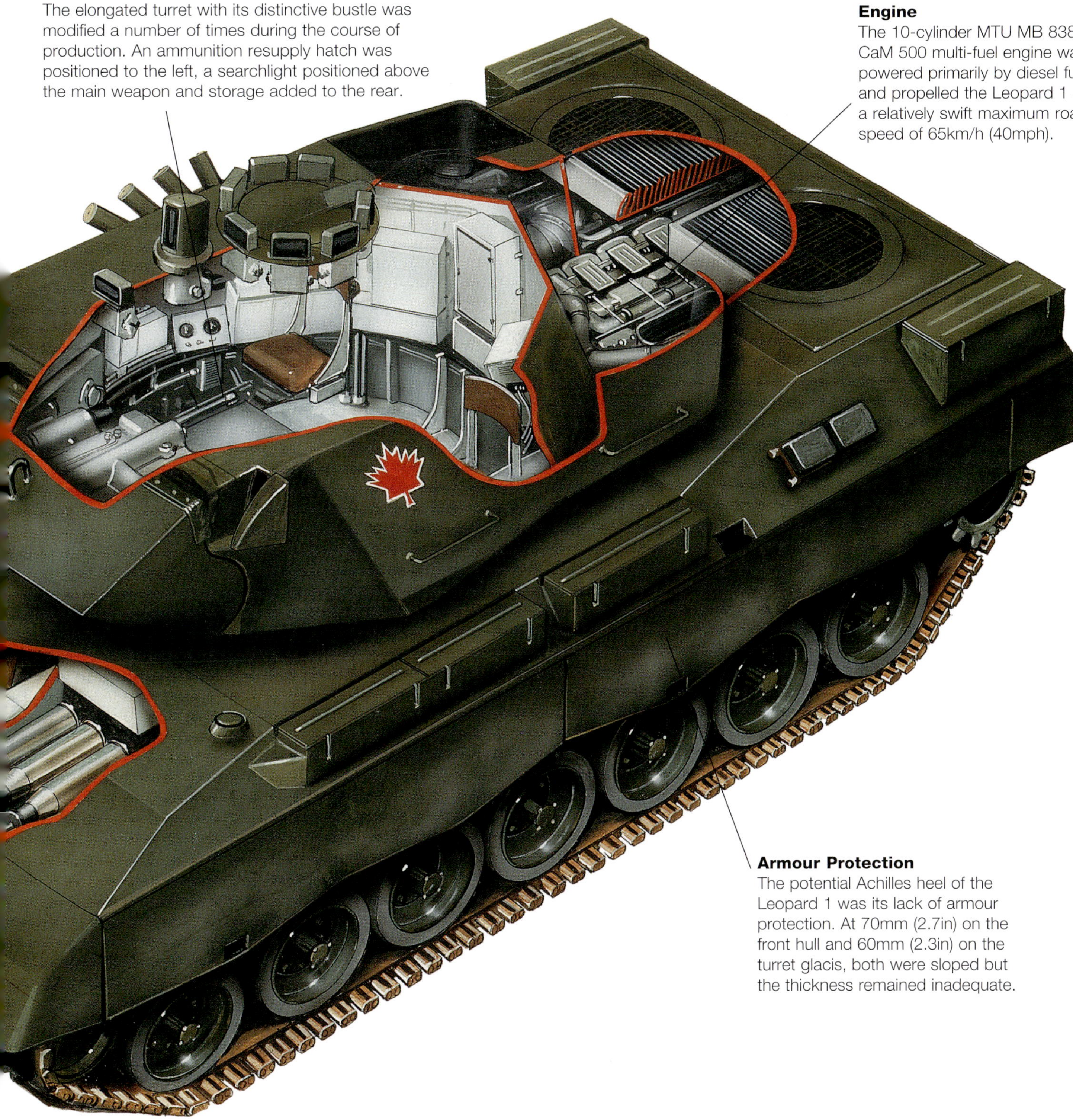

In 1971, the West German government authorized a series of upgrades to the Leopard 1, including a major improvement with the stabilization of its main 105mm (4.1in) gun. Improvements continued up to the end of the 1970s.

ring and a bore evacuator. If necessary, the barrel could be changed in the field in about 20 minutes. The weapon was loaded by hand; however, its semiautomatic breech mechanism opened to eject the spent cartridge into a container in the turret basket after each round was fired.

The MTU MB 838 Ca M500 10-cylinder multifuel engine ran primarily on diesel and delivered a top road speed of 65km/h (40mph). It delivered the best power to weight ratio of any contemporary main battle tank powerplant. Like the barrel of the main gun, the engine, too, could be replaced in approximately 20 minutes if necessary. The tank was lightweight at 39 tonnes (38.3 tons) and quite manoeuvrable in difficult terrain.

The compromise with the Leopard 1 design rested in its relatively thin armour protection, deemed by most observers as inadequate for reasonable combat survivability. At 70mm (2.7in) on the front of the hull and 60mm (2.3in) on the turret glacis, the armour was sloped to deter penetration. However, in comparison to other tanks it was less than ideal.

The Leopard 1 was served by a crew of four with the engine to the rear and separated from the fighting compartment by a firewall. The driver was seated forward in the hull to the right. The cast turret accommodated the commander and gunner on the right and the loader to the left. The commander viewed the field through any of eight periscopes that ringed the hatch atop the turret. One of these could be replaced with infrared equipment. A 7.62mm (0.3in) coaxial machine gun in the turret was originally used for ranging the main weapon, but an optical gunsight was later introduced.

Specification

Dimensions	Length: 8.29m (27ft 2in) Width: 3.37m (11ft) Height: 2.39m (7ft 10in)
Weight	39 tonnes (38.3 tons)
Engine	1 x 10-cylinder MTU MB 838 CaM 500 multi-fuel powerplant generating 619kW (830hp)
Speed	65km/h (40mph)
Armament	Main: 1 x 105mm (4.1in) Royal Ordnance L7A3 L/52 rifled gun Secondary: 2 x 7.62mm (0.3in) Rheinmetall MG3 or FN MAG machine guns
Armour	10–70mm (0.39–2.7in)
Range	Road: 600km (373 miles) Cross-country: 450 km (280 miles)
Crew	4

Production and Proliferation

During the course of production, more than 6500 Leopard 1 tanks were built and 2237 of these were delivered to the West German military. Italian defence contractor OTO-Melara manufactured the Leopard 1 under a licensing agreement. The armed forces of 14 countries, including Canada, Australia, Denmark, Greece, The Netherlands and Italy deployed the Leopard 1.

A series of improvements maintained the combat edge for the tank. Among the major enhancements was the stabilization of the main gun with a Cadillac Gage system and the fitting of a thermal sleeve to prevent the barrel from warping, improved tracks and armoured skirting to protect the suspension and road wheels in the 1A1 variant. In the 1A1A1, German contractor Blohm and Voss supplied reinforced steel plating for the turret, front hull and gun mantlet. Imaging systems were enhanced with the 1A1A2.

The Leopard 1A2 brought a more heavily cast turret, nuclear, biological and chemical (NBC) defence improvements and better night vision equipment, while the 1A3 featured a welded turret, spaced armour and a wedge-shaped gun mantlet. Computerized fire-control capabilities were upgraded in the 1A4 and even as the Leopard 2 was being introduced in the 1980s, the Leopard 1 received further modifications with the 1A5 and the 1A6, mounting a 120mm (4.7in) gun.

Leaping Leopard

The powerful 105mm (4.1in) L7A3 rifled gun mounted on the Leopard 1 was popular among numerous countries and set a standard for accuracy. When stabilized, its lethality was enhanced considerably. Manufacturer Krauss-Maffei announced that the incorporation of the stabilization equipment, including a laser rangefinder and integral thermal imaging, increased the probability of a first-round hit from the Leopard's main gun significantly. Of course, first-hit capability was prominent in the tactical deployment of the Leopard 1 considering the compromise between firepower and mobility advantages that were achieved at the expense of additional armour protection. In the photo below, the imposing L7A3 gun extends several feet beyond the Leopard 1's hull.

Stridsvagn 103B (1967)

Something of an anachronism, the Stridsvagn 103B main battle tank bore a greater resemblance to the tank destroyers of World War II than the main battle tanks of the modern era that it was supposed to defend against.

In its turretless design, the Swedish Stridsvagn 103B accounted for several other requirements in a tank that was developed and manufactured in the homeland following serious consideration of purchasing foreign armoured vehicles for the Swedish Army. In the mid-1950s, the Swedish military sought to replace its complement of aging British-made Centurion tanks. A joint design effort from Volvo, Bofors and Landsverk was judged unacceptable. A short time later, it was a radical departure from the standard that gained attention.

Engineer Sven Berge of the Swedish Arms Administration offered a turretless tank that would be economical to

Since their vehicle did not possess a turret, the crew of the Stridsvagn 103B, or S-Tank, fired its 105mm (4.1in) gun by turning the entire vehicle and raising or lowering its suspension.

Main Armament
Manufactured by Bofors, the L74 gun was similar in construction to the British L7. The L74 had a longer barrel that was locked down in order to maintain register while the vehicle was in transit.

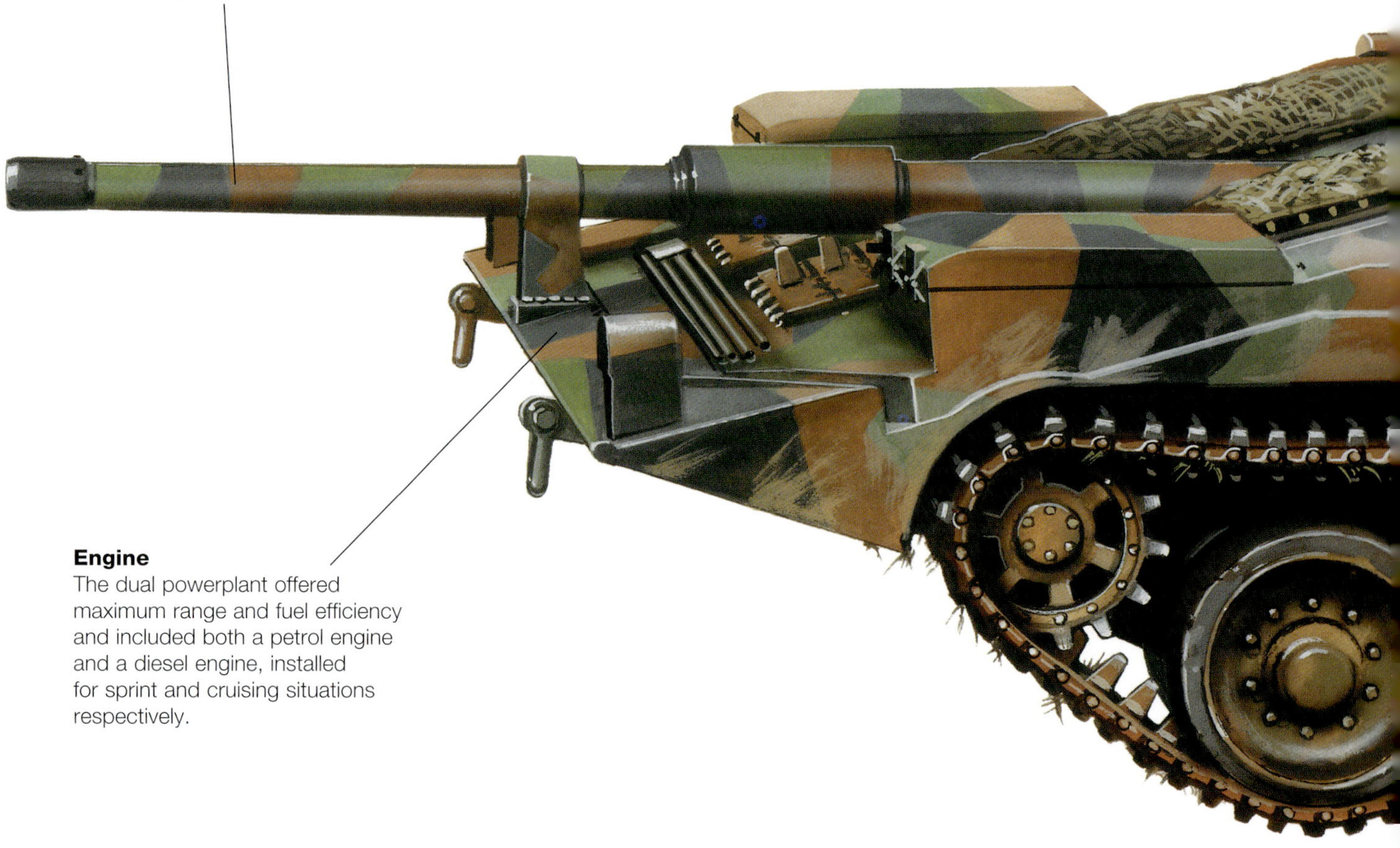

Engine
The dual powerplant offered maximum range and fuel efficiency and included both a petrol engine and a diesel engine, installed for sprint and cruising situations respectively.

produce, built in Sweden and take into account the defensive posture of the military in the context of the rolling hills, forests and mountainous terrain of Scandinavia. The Stridsvagn 103B would seem ideal for the changing climate and terrain of Sweden moving from rolling farmland in the south to tundra and high mountains in the north. It would be configured to negotiate both frozen ground and marshy, soggy lowlands.

Tailor-made Tank

The Strv 103, or S-Tank, entered production in Sweden in 1966 following nearly a decade of development. Only about 300 were built and the service life of the vehicle was a remarkable 31 years, as the last was withdrawn from service in 1997. The turretless tank did mount a capable primary weapon in the L74 cannon, which was similar to the successful British L7 gun. The L74

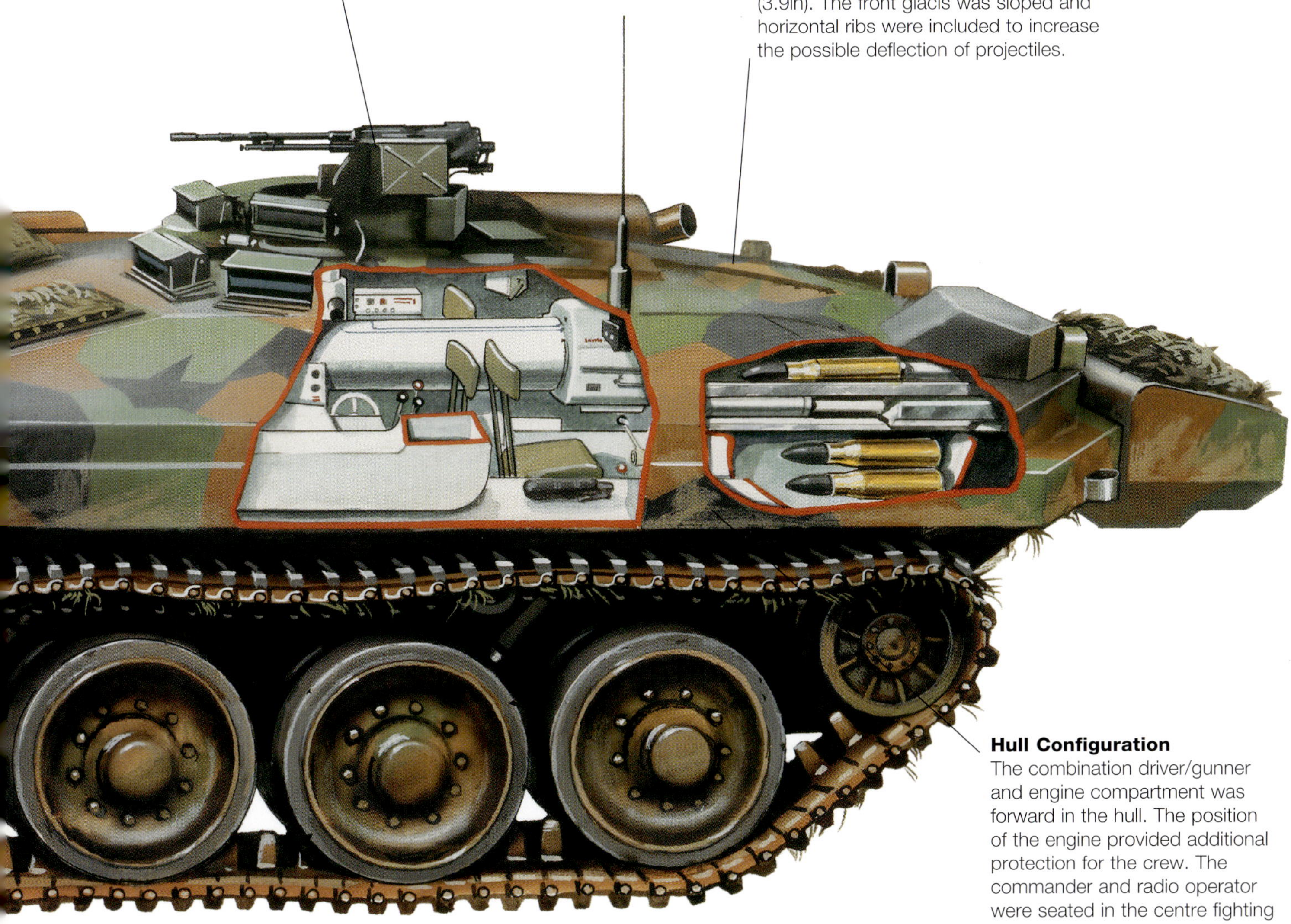

The long-barrelled L74 gun of the Strv 103 extended well beyond the length of the turretless tank's hull. Bofors, the L74 manufacturer, was one of the premier weapon-producing companies in the world.

was expertly crafted by Bofors, a long-time weapons producer based in Sweden. The Bofors weapon featured a longer barrel for greater range and muzzle velocity, as well as an automatic loading system with twin vertical breech blocks that held 50 rounds of ammunition at the ready.

The rate of fire was an impressive 15 rounds per minute and the type of ammunition could be changed with the simple push of a button. The magazines could be replenished in 10 minutes and empty shell casings were discarded to the rear of the tank.

Despite optimistic thinking on the part of the Swedish engineers, the Strv 103 did require a complicated set of manoeuvres in order for the tank to bring its main weapon to bear. The entire vehicle had to be turned and either elevated or depressed on its suspension for the gun to be laid and fired; therefore, it was impossible for the Strv 103 to fire on the move. To address the obvious combat disadvantage, Berge introduced an automated transmission, external crossbar steering mechanism and a sophisticated hydropneumatic suspension that rapidly regulated the angle of the vehicle against the terrain and horizon.

In normal conditions, the commander pulled double duty by sighting the target and then overriding the driver's steering capability by manipulating a series of tillers and turning the S-Tank into proper firing position. He then selected the appropriate ammunition and released control of the weapon to the driver/gunner for firing.

Specification

Dimensions	Length: 7.04m (23ft 1in) Width: 3.6m (11ft 10in) Height: 2.15m (7ft)
Weight	38.9 tonnes (38.2 tons)
Engine	1 x Caterpillar 553 gas turbine generating 365kW (490bhp); 1 x Rolls-Royce K60 V-8 multifuel powerplant generating 179kW (240hp)
Speed	50km/h (30mph)
Armament	Main: 1 x 105mm (4.1in) Bofors L74 L/62 gun Secondary: 3 x 7.62mm (0.3in) FFV machine guns
Armour	90–100mm (3.54–3.9in)
Range	Road: 390km (240 miles) Cross-country: 200km (120 miles)
Crew	3

Swedish Sophistication

Since there was no turret or gun mantlet to add weight to the Strv 103, more armour protection was added to

The Stridsvagn 103B was ideally suited for camouflage in the rolling terrain and high mountains of Swedish territory. It served with the Swedish military for 25 years but was never utilized in combat.

the hull, ranging from between 90mm (3.54in) to 100mm (3.9in) of homogeneous rolled and welded nickel steel. In the rolling terrain of Sweden, the S-Tank was virtually invisible with camouflage in the hull down position, perfect for lying in ambush. The commander and driver/gunner were each capable of firing the main weapon if necessary.

The tank's interior layout complemented the defensive philosophy that guided the development of the vehicle. The driver/gunner was seated forward and to the left in the hull, while the commander was beneath the cupola with driving and weapon controls. The radio operator faced to the rear and was also able to drive the tank, which functioned fully in a rearward orientation so that the main weapon could be brought to bear quickly.

The engine was placed in the front of the tank, increasing the protection for the crew. Initially, it was powered by a diesel engine and gas turbine combination. With the Strv 103B, however, concerns about power were addressed. The original petrol engine was removed in favour of a Caterpillar 553 petrol engine that complemented the Rolls-Royce K60 diesel. In the 103C, a General Motors Detroit Diesel engine replaced the Rolls-Royce K60. The combination of the diesel cruising engine and petrol sprint engine provided fuel economy and maximized range.

Stridsvagn Stability

Although the Stridsvagn 103 never fired a shot in anger, it served the defensive purpose for which it was intended admirably. For a turretless tank, it proved versatile in operation. With the 103B an amphibious flotation screen was introduced and in the subsequent 103C the tank was equipped with a bulldozer blade, laser rangefinding equipment and supplemental fuel tanks for increased range. With the 103D, thermal imaging and computerized fire-control equipment were installed. The Strv 103 remained in service with the Swedish military for a quarter of a century, until it was replaced by the German-built Leopard 2 main battle tank in the early 1990s.

Scimitar (1970)

One of a family of reconnaissance vehicles manufactured by the Alvis Company, the FV 107 Scimitar followed the FV 101 Scorpion and excelled in rapid deployment and infantry support.

During the late 1960s, the British Army issued requirements for a light armoured vehicle that could be airlifted, provide direct fire support to infantry and negotiate difficult terrain that larger, heavier tanks would have difficulty in traversing. The Alvis Company responded with a series of closely related light vehicles that fulfilled these military requirements.

The first of the vehicles was the FV 101 Scorpion, mounting a 76mm (2.9in) gun. Following in 1970 was the FV 107 Scimitar. Eventually, a family of seven Alvis vehicles were acquired by the British military and also by the armed

Deployable by air, the FV 107 Scimitar is officially classified by the British Army as a Combat Vehicle Reconnaissance Tracked (CVR[T]). Entering service in 1970, it was one of a series intended to replace the venerable Saladin armoured car.

forces of Belgium, Honduras and Jordan. About 650 FV 107s were built.

With the Scimitar, the main 30mm (1.18in) RARDEN (Royal Armament, Research and Development Establishment and Enfield) cannon might at first glance appear to be relatively weak. However, in combination with the light weight of the Scimitar at 7 tonnes (6.8 tons), an

Mounting a 30mm (1.18in) RARDEN cannon, the FV 107 Scimitar is lightly armed compared to the FV 101 Scorpion, another member of the family of armoured vehicles that carries a 76mm (2.9in) primary weapon.

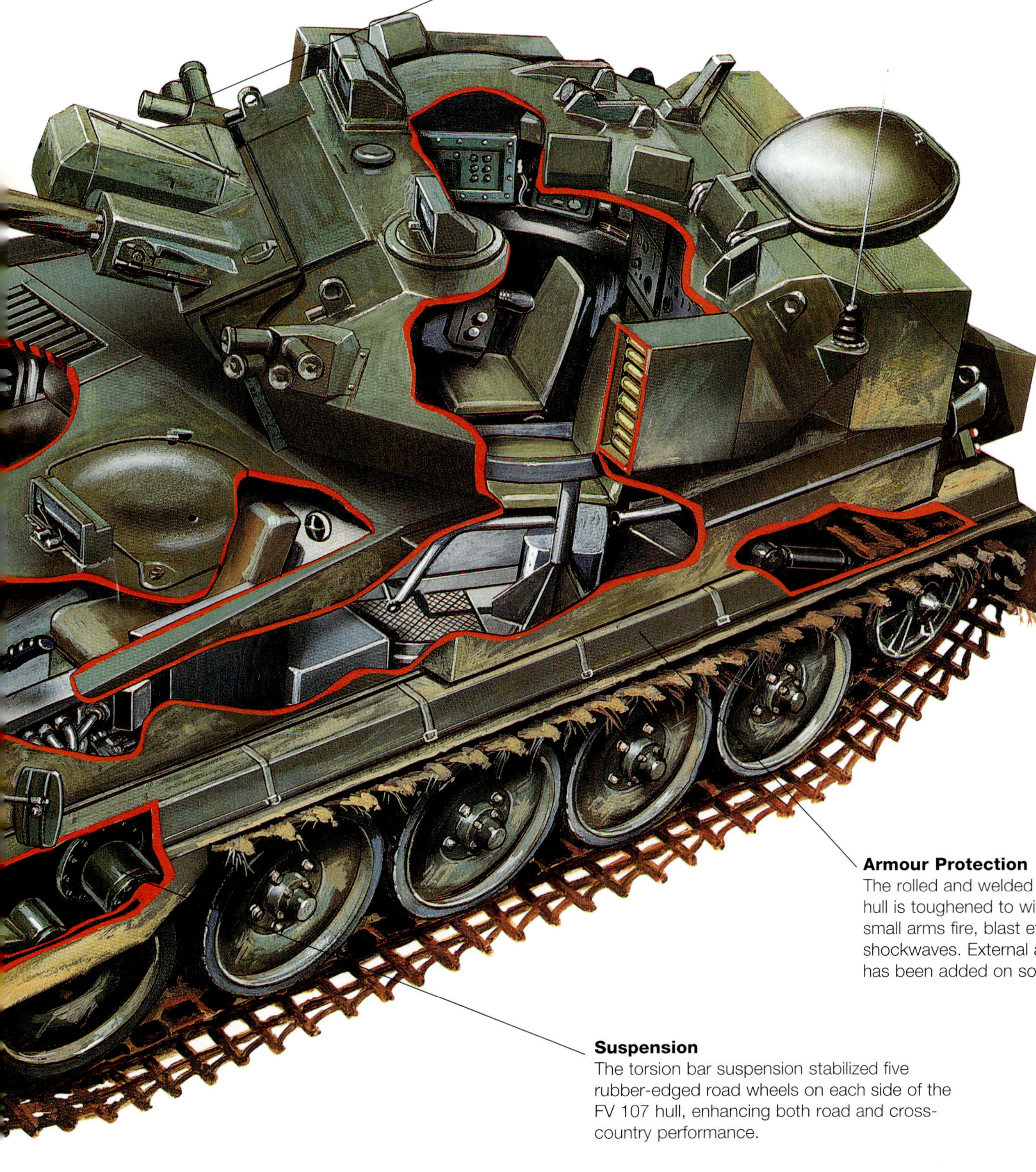

Secondary Armament
The secondary armament of the FV 107 Scimitar has been enhanced through the years. The standard package of the 7.62mm (0.3in) L37A1 machine gun or L94A1 chain gun has at times been augmented with other automatic weapons mounted on the exterior of the hull.

Armour Protection
The rolled and welded aluminium hull is toughened to withstand small arms fire, blast effect and shockwaves. External armour plating has been added on some vehicles.

Suspension
The torsion bar suspension stabilized five rubber-edged road wheels on each side of the FV 107 hull, enhancing both road and cross-country performance.

The well-armed FV 107 Scimitar deployed with British forces for the first time in 1971 as a reconnaissance and infantry support weapon. It remains in service around the world today.

excellent top speed of 80km/h (50mph), a low silhouette with a height of slightly more than 2m (6ft 6in) and ground pressure of only 2.2kg (5.1lbs) that allows the traverse of swamp, desert and mountain terrain, the firepower of the RARDEN completes a versatile package.

Specification

Dimensions	Length: 4.9m (15ft 9in) Width: 2.2m (7ft 3in) Height: 2.1m (6ft 9in)
Weight	7.8 tonnes (7.6 tons)
Engine	1 x Cummins BTA 5.9-litre (1.29-gallon) diesel powerplant generating 142kW (190hp)
Speed	80km/h (50mph)
Armament	Main: 1 x 30mm (1.18in) L21 RARDEN cannon Secondary: 1 x 7.62mm (0.3in) L37A1 machine gun or L94A1 chain gun
Armour	12.7mm (0.5in)
Range	Road: 645km (400 miles) Cross-country: 450km (280 miles)
Crew	3

Packing a Punch

The small calibre of the RARDEN gun belies its power and potential lethality. It is capable of firing in single shot or automatic mode and at a withering rate of up to 90 rounds per minute. A maximum of 165 rounds of ammunition, either sabot, high explosive or armour-piercing special effects (APSE), are available in the turret. Surprisingly, the RARDEN generates a muzzle velocity of up to 1200m (3937ft) per second, while the armour piercing rounds are capable of penetrating the side armour of some main battle tanks. It is also effective against low-flying enemy aircraft. Therefore, the presence of the Scimitar, even with heavier vehicles lurking about, is not to be discounted.

The Scimitar's secondary armament includes either a single coaxial 7.62mm (0.3in) L37A1 machine gun with 3000 rounds or an L94A1 chain gun to defend the vehicle against attacking infantry. In addition, banks of smoke grenade launchers are installed on the turret.

Rapid Transit

With a rolled, welded and toughened aluminium skin, the armour of the Scimitar is only 12.7mm (0.5in) at its thickest. However, it is capable of standing up to most small arms fire, blast effect and shockwaves. External armour plating has been applied to some vehicles on a selected basis.

The survivability of the crew in a combat environment resides with its offensive punch and pure speed. The torsion bar suspension and its rubber wheels facilitated high speed manoeuvres. Early production examples were powered by a 4.2-litre (0.9-gallon) Jaguar J60 petrol engine. This was replaced by the 5.9-litre (1.29-gallon) Cummins BTA diesel engine that could produce a top speed that is comparable to or surpasses other vehicles similar to the FV 107.

Inside Out

The interior of the FV 107 Scimitar is divided into fighting and engine compartments. The crew of three enjoys reasonable space, with the driver seated forward and steering the vehicle with a system of tillers and brake pedals. The commander and gunner are in the turret and acquire targets through computerized fire control with thermal imaging and laser rangefinding. The turret offers excellent visibility with five periscopes for the commander in 360° panoramic alignment and an optical gunsight. The driver utilizes two periscopes with either active or passive night vision sights and the gunner has two periscopes that are interchangeable with night vision equipment.

During more than 40 years of service, numerous upgrades have been made to the original Scimitar. These include additional externally mounted machine guns, passive night vision equipment, automatic fire suppression, an auxiliary power generator and advanced communications technology. Better cooling equipment has increased the service hours of the powerplant between overhauls. The RARDEN gun has received a bore evacuator.

When the potential of nuclear, biological or chemical weapons is present, a forced air system permits the FV 107 to function efficiently. If necessary, a hole beneath the commander's seat serves as a rudimentary toilet. Should the tank be locked down for an extended length of time, the crew is able to breathe normally and even cook meals.

Scimitar on the Scene

One of seven reconnaissance and infantry support vehicles developed by Alvis for the British Army, the FV 107 Scimitar continues in service today after more than 40 years. As of the spring of 2009, the FV 107 was in line for upgrade with the Future Rapid Effect System (FRES). A combat veteran, the vehicle was deployed in the Falklands War as B Squadron, Blues and Royals, providing the only British armoured vehicles used during the short conflict. During the fight to capture the Al Faw peninsula during the 2003 invasion of Iraq, C Squadron of the Queen's Dragoon Guards fielded the Scimitar. The FV 107 was also deployed in the first and second Gulf Wars, Bosnia, Kosovo and Afghanistan. As shown in the photo below, it is easily transportable aboard a flatbed trailer.

T-72 (1971)

Intended for the export market and the client states of the Soviet Union, the T-72 main battle tank was smaller and faster than other contemporary armoured vehicles but lacked the firepower and protection it needed on the modern battlefield.

Since it was designed for the export market, the T-72 required relatively little training to operate and maintain in the field. Produced at lower cost that the concurrent T-64, it was licence-built in Poland, Czechoslovakia, India and the former Yugoslavia.

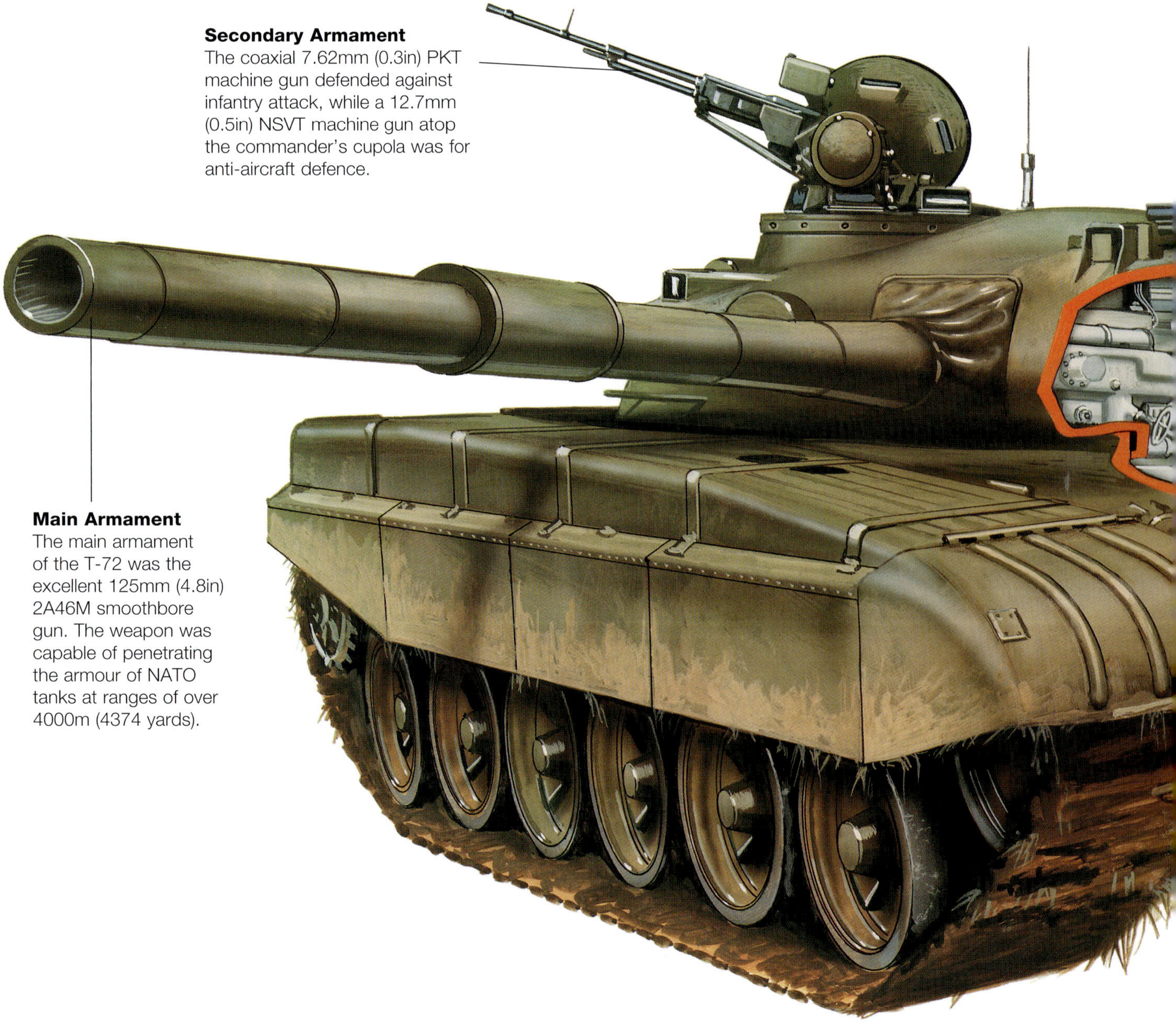

The Soviet designed T-72 main battle tank may be the best-known adversarial vehicle of its kind in the West. Such recognition stems primarily from the fact that it has been the most frequently engaged tank of Soviet origin in modern warfare. The T-72 was deployed by the Syrian Army during the 1982 conflict with Israel in Lebanon. It was the mainstay of Saddam Hussein's Iraqi armoured divisions during the Iran-Iraq War, during the 1991 Gulf War and again during the 2003 coalition invasion of Iraq.

In almost every instance, the T-72 has proven inferior to the Israeli Merkava, American M1 Abrams and British Challenger tanks it has faced on the battlefield. The essence of its less than stellar combat performance lies at least somewhat in the fact that the T-72 was developed for the export market and for reserve or second-echelon units of the Red Army. Therefore, it was developed with fewer resources than the T-64, which was a concurrent effort for Soviet engineers. Iraqi and Syrian T-72 tanks were also likely older and insufficiently upgraded to face their main battle tank opponents.

The T-72 was deployed with armoured units of the Soviet Red Army stationed within the Soviet Union, while the T-64 equipped forward units that would confront NATO tanks in the early hours of conflict in Europe.

The long-barrelled 125mm (4.8in) 2A46M smoothbore gun was also mounted on the T-64 and T-80 Soviet main battle tanks. On later models, it was capable of firing anti-tank guided missiles and a variety of standard ammunition.

Twin Soviet Sons

Both the T-64 and the T-72 were attempts by the Soviet design directorate and the Red Army military establishment to field modern main battle tanks rather than cling to the obsolescent concept of the medium and heavy tank that dated back to World War II. Indeed, the T-64 and T-72 were major improvements over the T-54/55 and T-62 tanks. They also exhibited the first major innovations in Soviet tank engineering since the legendary T-34 of half a century earlier.

There, however, is where much of the similarity between the T-64 and the T-72 ended. The T-64 did become the frontline tank of Soviet armoured divisions at the tip of the Red spear in Eastern Europe, but its innovations were never fully perfected and the tank experienced maturation difficulties that eventually cut production to only 5000 examples, ending in 1981.

If longevity is a measure of effectiveness, it must be conceded that the T-72 has smartly eclipsed its favoured sibling. The T-72 entered production in 1971 and it is still the cornerstone of the armoured forces of numerous nations while in production today. Well over 25,000 have been built.

Specification

Dimensions	Length: 6.95m (22ft 10in) Width: 3.59m (11ft 9in) Height: 2.23m (7ft 4in)
Weight	41.5 tonnes (40.8 tons)
Engine	1 x V-46 12-cylinder diesel engine generating 582kW (780hp)
Speed	60km/h (37mph)
Armament	Main: 1 x 125mm (4.8in) smoothbore 2A46M high-velocity gun Secondary: 1 x 7.62mm (0.3in) PKT machine gun; 1 x 12.7mm (0.5in) NSVT anti-aircraft machine gun
Armour	Classified; estimated up to 500mm (19.6in)
Range	460km (290 miles)
Crew	3

Fielding the Ural

The original version of the T-72, known generally as the Ural, did constitute a vast improvement over the T-62. Along with a significantly improved V-46 12-cylinder diesel engine, the T-72 mounted the outstanding 125mm (4.8in) 2A46M smoothbore gun, an automatic loading system, composite armour and improved target acquisition capabilities. The diesel engine was quieter than the T-62 powerplant, generating less smoke and vibration. The original diesel engine was upgraded to the 626-kilowatt (839hp) V-84 diesel in 1985.

The main gun fired ammunition that was capable of penetrating the armour of contemporary NATO tanks and the automatic loading system resulted in a rate of fire up to eight rounds per minute, although it often broke down with wear. Secondary armament included a 7.62mm (0.3in) coaxial PKT machine gun and a pintle-mounted 12.7mm (0.5in) anti-aircraft machine gun at the commander's hatch. Similar to the British Chobham armour, the composite protection of the T-72 tripled the effectiveness of steel at about the same thickness.

Few Creature Comforts

The T-72 introduced several innovations, including the 125mm (4.8in) smoothbore main gun, automatic loader and composite armour. However, it was intended primarily for the armed forces of the Warsaw Pact and Soviet client states.

Like the earlier Soviet tank designs, the T-72 afforded little in the way of comfort or ease to its crew of three. Divided into three compartments, the hull positioned the driver forward, the fighting compartment in the centre and the engine to the rear. The low silhouette and elliptical turret were reminiscent of the T-54/55, as were the cramped quarters. A single periscope limited the driver's field of vision and rather than a steering wheel and automatic transmission, he drove the tank with an archaic system of tillers and a seven-gear manual transmission.

The gunner was seated in the turret to the left with integrated gunsights and laser rangefinding equipment, while the commander was on the right under a rotating cupola with both standard and infrared gunsights supported by a stadiametric rangefinder. The T-72 was equipped with nuclear, biological and chemical (NBC) defences and an amphibious package that could be deployed rapidly.

Improved models of the T-72 included the T-72B with a larger diesel engine, guided missile firing capability, appliqué armour and better fire control, and the T-72M and T-72M1, each with advanced passive armour protection. The T-72S reportedly includes a new engine and explosive-reactive armour.

T-72 on Parade

In the photo at right, columns of T-72 main battle tanks parade through Red Square in the Soviet capital of Moscow. The T-72 had been deployed for six years before it made its public debut in 1977. Since that time it has seen action in numerous hot spots around the globe. During the 1982 conflict between Israel and Syria in Lebanon, Syrian T-72s proved markedly inferior to Israeli Merkava tanks and scores of the Soviet-supplied tanks were destroyed in combat. The Iraqi T-72s of Saddam Hussein also fell victim to modern U.S. and British Abrams and Challenger tanks in 1991 and 2003. This was partially due to the fact that the T-72s lacked the necessary upgrades to maintain modern battlefield viability.

Merkava (1977)

Designed and built in Israel, the Merkava has received four major upgrades since entering production in 1977. Its radical redesign emphasized crew survivability followed by firepower and mobility.

For nearly 20 years after the birth of the state of Israel, the tiny nation's armed forces depended on variants of the American World War II-vintage Sherman and British Centurion tanks. In the wake of the Six Day War of 1967, however, the Israeli military establishment was shaken by the realization that it was necessary to become as self-sufficient as possible.

France and Great Britain restricted deliveries of certain weapons systems to Israel following the June 1967 Six Day War, and General Israel Tal, a veteran of the Israeli Defence Force (IDF) and its prior armoured engagements, urged that the country's research and development efforts concentrate on a main battle tank designed and produced in Israel.

The Chariot

The Merkava program was established in 1968 with the premise that the new Israeli tank would embody the best attributes of American, British, French and captured Soviet-made tanks then in Israel's possession.

Several additional caveats were identified. The tank would emphasize crew survivability above any other

Main Armament
The primary weapon of the Merkava main battle tank was initially the 105mm (4.1in) L43.5 M68 gun. This was replaced in later upgrades with the 120mm (4.7in) MG251 and MG253 smoothbore guns capable of firing a variety of ordnance.

Engine
The Merkava IV is powered by the General Dynamics GD833 diesel engine, a substantial upgrade to the original diesel engine and capable of moving the tank at a top road speed of 64km/h (40mph).

The word Merkava translates literally from Hebrew as "Chariot." The Israeli main battle tank's variants offer the capabilities of carrying eight combat-ready infantrymen or three wounded soldiers on stretchers.

attribute. The rationale of senior commanders was that soldiers who were confident of their own survival would be more willing to aggressively engage the enemy and employ armament and mobility to their fullest.

Furthermore, the tank should be designed to wage war in the desert, primarily in the disputed areas of northern Israel, the Golan Heights and the Sinai Peninsula. Finally, the tank should incorporate as much state-of-the-art equipment as possible, exhibit a radical design that would minimize its vulnerability and perform multiple roles on the battlefield.

Israeli Military Industries led the design effort and the prototype Merkava was run out for testing in 1974. The

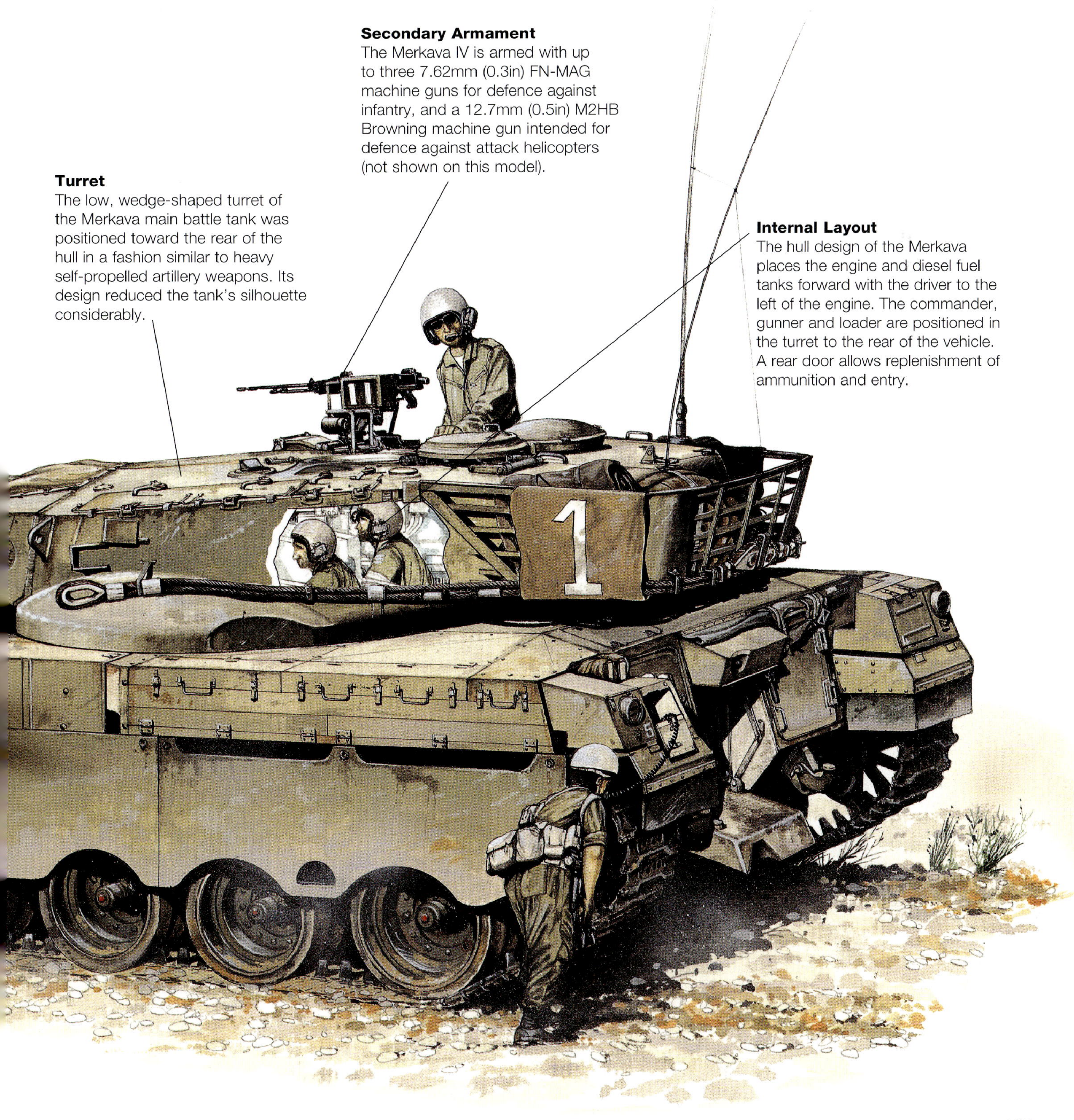

Secondary Armament
The Merkava IV is armed with up to three 7.62mm (0.3in) FN-MAG machine guns for defence against infantry, and a 12.7mm (0.5in) M2HB Browning machine gun intended for defence against attack helicopters (not shown on this model).

Turret
The low, wedge-shaped turret of the Merkava main battle tank was positioned toward the rear of the hull in a fashion similar to heavy self-propelled artillery weapons. Its design reduced the tank's silhouette considerably.

Internal Layout
The hull design of the Merkava places the engine and diesel fuel tanks forward with the driver to the left of the engine. The commander, gunner and loader are positioned in the turret to the rear of the vehicle. A rear door allows replenishment of ammunition and entry.

The Merkava series of main battle tanks was designed and manufactured in Israel, eliminating to a great extent the dependence of the Israeli military on imported tanks and armoured vehicles.

Merkava I was approved and production was initiated with IDF Ordnance three years later. By the end of the decade, the Merkava was deployed with frontline Israel Defense Forces armoured units.

Specification

Dimensions	Length: 7.45m (24ft 5in) Width: 3.7m (12ft 1in) Height: 2.75m (9ft)
Weight	55.9 tonnes (55 tons)
Engine	1 x Teledyne Continental AVDS-1790-6A 12-cylinder supercharged diesel generating 671kW (900hp)
Speed	46km/h (28.5mph)
Armament	Main: 1 x 105mm (4.1in) L43.5 M68 gun Secondary: 3 x 7.62mm (0.3in) FN-MAG machine guns; 1 x 12.7mm (0.5in) M2HB Browning machine gun; 1 x 60mm (2.36in) Soltam popup mortar
Armour	Classified
Range	Road: 400km (245 miles) Cross-country: 200km (125 miles)
Crew	4

Radical Rethinking

From the drawing board to the assembly line and the battlefield, the Merkava was a departure from conventional tank design. The engine and diesel fuel tanks were positioned forward in the hull, adding to the armour protection of classified composition but assumed to be initially of homogeneous rolled, cast and welded nickel steel later augmented by an Israeli adaptation of the British Chobham composite armour.

The Merkava turret was moved toward the rear of the hull and fashioned in a low wedge shape to minimize the tank's silhouette. The Merkava was also constructed to serve as a troop carrier or medical evacuation vehicle if necessary. It was armed with the 105mm (4.1in) L43.5 M68 gun. Following the Merkava I's combat debut during the bitter 1982 fighting in Lebanon, the Merkava II was introduced with better fire control, an urban warfare package and a redesigned automatic transmission.

Steady Improvement

In 1989, the Merkava III became operational and exhibited numerous improvements. The main 105mm weapon was replaced with the powerful 120mm (4.7in) MG251 smoothbore gun patterned after the German Rheinmetall weapon of the same calibre. The original Teledyne Continental AVDS-1790-6A 12-cylinder diesel engine was replaced with a more powerful diesel, while modular composite armour was fitted, an external telephone was added for communicating with troops in the field and laser rangefinding equipment was installed.

The Merkava main battle tank does not utilize a turret basket. The floor moves as the turret rotates in acquiring a target. The commander enters and exits the tank through a hatch, dispensing with a cupola that would raise the tank's silhouette.

By 1995, the Merkava III was again improved with NBC (nuclear, chemical and biological) defences and the BAZ fire-control system for better acquisition of targets while on the move. Later, the Merkava IIID brought better tracks of Israeli design and manufactured by Caterpillar on line.

Merkava in the Streets

Following the heavy fighting in 2006 against Hezbollah guerrillas in the streets of Lebanese towns, the performance of the Merkava IV was criticized by some observers who considered the tank too vulnerable to anti-tank missiles and somewhat slow and unwieldy in an urban warfare context. Nevertheless, the Merkava maintained its reputation for crew survivability and completed its mission.

After the 2006 war, it was announced that production of the Merkava would end within four years. Then, in 2011 it was reported that a successor to the Merkava line was in development. However, those who would retire the venerated tank may have spoken too soon. In August 2013, the Israeli government announced that production of the Merkava would resume.

In development since 1999, the Merkava IV became operational in 2004. It features a better 120mm (4.7in) MG253 smoothbore gun capable of firing anti-tank guided missiles and a variety of ordnance. The weapon is fed by a semiautomatic loading system that includes a revolving magazine of 10 rounds. A new fire-control system that acquires multiple moving targets through thermal sighting and tracking and improved night vision equipment were added along with an electrically controlled turret. The Merkava IV engine was improved substantially with the General Dynamics GD833 diesel generating 1118 kilowatts (1500hp).

The Trophy APS (Active Protection System) recognizes a threat, computes its probable impact location on the Merkava IV and deploys countermeasures to defeat the incoming weapon. The Merkava IV entered combat during the 2006 war with Hezbollah in Lebanon. Based on its comprehensive combat performance, the Merkava series is considered among the finest main battle tanks in the world.

Leopard 2 (1979)

The Federal Republic of Germany authorized the production of the Leopard 2 main battle tank in 1977 following two cooperative engineering efforts with the U.S. that ended with each country going its own way in armoured vehicle design.

When a Leopard 2A6 main battle tank of the Canadian Army struck an improvised explosive device (IED) on the battlefield in Afghanistan in 2007, no casualties were sustained among the four-man crew. The tank's commander later reported that the vehicle "worked as it should."

Perhaps no other comment could so validate the success of the Leopard 2 design, which was undertaken more than a quarter of a century earlier. The Leopard 2 that deployed with the Canadians to the battlefields of Afghanistan was the product of several contributing elements. As far back as the 1960s, the United States and German military establishments had been in discussions to embark on a cooperative venture to develop a new generation of main battle tank.

The Leopard 2 was the product of years of research and development, incorporating attributes of its predecessor, the Leopard 1 and the prototype MBT-70 developed jointly with the United States.

When the priorities of the U.S. and German military establishments began to diverge, the joint development of a main battle tank ceased. However, both countries used the experience to produce outstanding armoured fighting vehicles.

When the resulting prototype, dubbed the MBT-70, was rolled out some months later, it surprisingly laid bare the divergent priorities of the two armies. As the joint venture fell apart, the Germans decided to pursue their own Leopard 2, incorporating elements of the existing Leopard 1 and the MBT-70. In turn, the Americans pursued the M1 Abrams. Between 1972 and 1974, no fewer than 16 prototype layouts of the Leopard 2 were evaluated. Meanwhile, the Americans produced the XM-1 Abrams prototype. Through a second joint development agreement, the two countries exchanged prototype tanks.

The tanks were independently judged and found to be comparable in numerous respects. However, the Americans concluded that the XM-1 Abrams was better armoured and chose to chart their own course. In September 1977, the German Defence Ministry chose to move the Leopard 2 into

Secondary Armament
A pair of 7.62mm (0.3in) MG3A1 machine guns are mounted on the Leopard 2, one coaxial in the turret and the other pintle-mounted at the loader's hatch. Banks of smoke grenade launchers are installed on either side of the main gun.

Engine
The MTU MB 873 Ka-501 diesel engine is standard in the Leopard 2; however, the larger MTU MT 883 has been installed for trials with the EuroPowerPack upgrade.

Turret
Centred on the chassis, the Leopard 2 turret is shaped somewhat like a lozenge. Its flat profile reduces the radar signature and overall silhouette of the tank, although headroom is restricted.

The observation and target acquisition systems of the Leopard 2 commander and gunner are coordinated. Such technology combined with the 120mm (4.7in) L55 smoothbore gun produces deadly efficiency in combat.

full production. Krauss-Maffei was chosen as the primary contractor and project manager for the first 1800 tanks that were slated for delivery in five batches. In time, more than 3200 Leopard 2 tanks have been produced and the armoured vehicle is in service with at least 14 countries.

Specification

Dimensions	Length: 9.97m (32ft 8in) Width: 3.75m (12ft 3in) Height: 3m (9ft 9in)
Weight	62.3 tonnes (61.3 tons)
Engine	1 x MTU MB 873 Ka-501 V-12 twin turbo diesel powerplant generating 1103kW (1479hp)
Speed	72km/h (45mph)
Armament	Main: 1 x 120mm (4.7in) Rheinmetall L55 smoothbore gun Secondary: 2 x 7.62mm (0.3in) MG3A1 machine guns
Armour	Classified; third-generation composite
Range	550km (340 miles)
Crew	4

Tremendous Technology

The technological aspects of the Leopard 2 remain second to none. From the beginning, the tank has included the latest in both offensive and defensive systems. When the Leopard 2 entered service with the West German Army in 1979, it was undoubtedly one of the most sophisticated weapons of its kind in the world.

The original main weapon was the 120mm (4.7in) L44 smoothbore gun manufactured by Rheinmetall Waffe Munition. Upgrades replaced the L44 with the L55. The lengthened barrel of the new gun increased the muzzle velocity and range of the weapon and the likelihood of a first-strike kill in combat. The weapon was fielded specifically for use with a new kinetic-energy shell, the LKE 2 DM53, made of heavy tungsten and capable of penetrating the latest in armour deployed with Soviet Bloc tanks.

The Leopard 2 powerplant is the MTU MB 873 Ka-501 12-cylinder diesel engine, capable of delivering a top speed of 72km/h (45mph), while the MTU MT 883 engine has been evaluated as part of an upgrade known as the EuroPowerPack. The transmission is the Renk HSWL 354 and the torsion bar suspension provides good traction in open country and rugged terrain despite the broad, flattened profile of the tank. The interior layout is functional with the driver forward, the commander, gunner and loader in the turret and the engine to the rear. The turret allows reasonable movement, although head room is restricted.

Advanced target acquisition technology includes the PERI-R 17 A2 periscope for both commander and gunner and thermal imaging for the commander, which is displayed on a screen inside the turret. The driver's thermal imaging view is linked to the fire-control system and can be shared with the commander. For the gunner, the Rheinmetall EMES 15 with laser rangefinding and Zeiss optronik thermal sights cooperate with the fire-control system as well.

Leopard Longevity

Continuing upgrades to the Leopard 2 have enhanced performance in a number of areas. The Leopard 2A1 introduced the gunner's thermal sights, improved fuel filters and reengineered ammunition racks, while improved digital radio equipment was installed with the 2A3. The 2A4 included an automated fire and explosion suppression system, better composite turret armour of tungsten and titanium construction, and digital fire control.

With the 2A5 variant spall liners were added throughout the interior along with more armour and electrical controls for the turret, an auxiliary engine, improved mine protection and air conditioning. Also in the 2A5, a better gun braking system was introduced for the long L55 weapon. The 2A6 includes third generation composite armour with steel, tungsten, plastic and ceramic components and the lifesaving mine protection that demonstrated its worth in the Afghanistan conflict.

Leopard 2 In Country

The Leopard 2 main battle tank, shown below after halting during field exercises, has been deployed to combat in the Balkans and Central Asia. German armoured forces deployed Leopard 2A4 and 2A5 models in Kosovo, while Canadian and Danish forces are among those that have fielded the tank in Afghanistan. Danish Leopards provided fire support in denying the Taliban success during a flanking manoeuvre in Helmand Province in January 2008 and supported Canadian troops in recapturing the Nad Ali District in December. In February 2008, a Leopard was damaged by an improvised explosive device but returned to its base unassisted. One Danish Leopard crewman was killed in July 2008 by the massive detonation of an improvised explosive device, however.

M2 Bradley (1981)

With its roots in the Vietnam era, the M2/3 Bradley fighting vehicle did not enter service with the U.S. Army until 1981. Even then, controversy swirled around its perceived combat capabilities.

At the height of the Vietnam War, the U.S. Army was seeking a replacement for its M113 armoured personnel carrier. Combat experience had revealed that the M113 was difficult to manoeuvre in jungle terrain, its high profile was susceptible to shoulder-fired anti-tank weapons such

as the Soviet-made rocket-propelled grenade (RPG), and its armament was insufficient to lend substantial direct fire support to infantry.

Although there were clearly defined specifications for the new fighting vehicle that eventually became the M2/M3 Bradley fighting vehicle, progress was slow. Some sceptics questioned its light armour protection and the real contribution its 25mm (0.98in) main weapon could make on the battlefield. The concerns raised were largely based on the poor performance of the Soviet BMP-1 troop carrier during the Yom Kippur War of 1973. Nevertheless, the requirement that a new fighting vehicle maintain offensive pace with the emerging main battle tanks of the period and the need for rapid reconnaissance and the advance of infantry to take and hold territory remained paramount.

The Bradley fighting vehicle has been configured in both infantry and cavalry types. Its reconnaissance role is complemented by excellent firepower and anti-tank capabilities in such a light vehicle.

The M2/M3 Bradley fighting vehicle has undergone numerous improvements since entering service. One of these included the Operation Desert Storm (ODS) upgrade following the 1991 Gulf War. Improved fire control, navigation, thermal imaging and command and control have enhanced the vehicle's performance.

Brokering the Bradley

Named in honour of General of the Army Omar N. Bradley, a hero of the Allied victory in World War II, the Bradley fighting vehicle weathered controversy, Congressional inquiry and funding battles on Capitol Hill before production was authorized in February 1980 and the M2/M3 entered service in 1981, a full 15 years after the research and development that produced it had begun.

Specification

Dimensions	Length: 6.55m (21ft 6in) Width: 3.6m (11ft 9in) Height: 2.98m (9ft 9in)
Weight	27.6 tonnes (27.1 tons)
Engine	1 x Cummins VTA-903T eight-cylinder diesel powerplant generating 447kW (600hp)
Speed	66km/h (41mph)
Armament	Main: 1 x 25mm (0.98in) McDonnell Douglas M242 chain gun; TOW anti-tank missile launcher Secondary: 1 x 7.62mm (0.3in) M240C machine gun
Armour	Classified thickness; spaced laminate, steel appliqué and aluminium alloy 7017 explosive- reactive armour
Range	483km (300 miles)
Crew	3

The Bradley has been constructed in two basic configurations. The M2 infantry variant was initially designed to carry a crew of three and seven combat-ready infantrymen who entered and exited the vehicle through a rear access hatch. Later, the troop capacity of the M2 was reduced to six. The M3 cavalry version carries the three-man crew and a pair of scout infantrymen. Produced by BAE Systems Land and Armaments, nearly 6800 Bradleys have been built.

Calculated Combination

In keeping with the armoured equation that attempts to balance firepower, armour protection and mobility, the Bradley has been designed and steadily upgraded to perform scouting and infantry support missions. In combat during the Gulf War of 1991 and the invasion of Iraq in 2003, its tank and armoured vehicle killing prowess came into sharp focus as well.

The Bradley is powered by a Cummins VTA-903T eight-cylinder diesel engine capable of a top speed of 66km/h (41mph). Its torsion-bar suspension is adequate for rapid movement across desert sands and through marshy or uneven terrain with a power-to-weight ratio of 14.7 kilowatts (19.74hp) per ton. Armour protection is, out of necessity, light compared to main battle tanks. Spaced laminate armour and additional steel plating are sufficient to protect against small arms and shells up to 23mm (0.98in), enhancing the base protection of aluminium alloy 7017 explosive-reactive armour (ERA).

While it may be considered a light weapon, the M242 chain gun is capable of penetrating the armour of enemy vehicles firing armour-piercing ammunition with a core of dense depleted uranium. High explosive shells are effective against softer targets. The gunner chooses the appropriate ammunition through an automated remote dual selection system and is, therefore, able to engage multiple and varied targets in quick succession. The Bradley carries 900 rounds of M242 ammunition.

Anti-tank armament includes the proven TOW missile system carried in a collapsible rack on the left side of the turret. Seven missiles are routinely carried in combat zones. Infantry support is also available with a coaxial 7.62mm (0.3in) M240C machine gun with 800 rounds loaded and ready and 1540 rounds stored in reserve.

A Bradley fighting vehicle churns up a cloud of desert dust while on manoeuvres. Its performance during Operation Desert Storm and Operation Iraqi Freedom validated the beliefs of its proponents. The Bradley proved superb in reconnaissance, infantry support and anti-tank roles.

Veteran Variations

Following the Gulf War combat experience, an ODS (Operation Desert Storm) upgrade was authorized for the Bradley. Countermeasures against missiles were introduced, as well as the introduction of global positioning and digital compass systems, a tactical navigation system and better laser rangefinding equipment in the A2 variant. The A2 variant is also capable of interfacing with the Force XXI Battle Command Brigade and Below (FBCB2) command system. Infantrymen are accommodated with bench seating and heating elements for the preparation of hot meals.

With the follow-on A3 upgrade, FLIR (Forward Looking Infrared) sighting was installed along with an electro-optical imaging system and better fire control. Currently, the GCV fighting vehicle is in development following the cancellation of the earlier Future Combat Systems Manned Ground Vehicles programme in 2009. The successor to the Bradley is anticipated by the end of this decade.

Bradley in Iraq

The M2/M3 Bradley fighting vehicle established a commendable combat record during deployment in the 1991 Gulf War and the invasion of Iraq in 2003. During the Gulf War, Bradley vehicles from several troops of the 2nd Armored Cavalry Regiment of the U.S. Army engaged and destroyed a number of Iraqi armoured vehicles in the Battle of 73 Easting and other engagements.

Although the Bradley was found susceptible to improvised explosive devices (IED) and rocket-propelled grenades during Operation Iraqi Freedom, its crew survivability rate was excellent. In some cases, the Bradley defeated Iraqi tanks with its TOW missiles. Special-purpose vehicles based on the Bradley include a forward observation variant and anti-aircraft and anti-tank platforms.

Challenger 1 (1982)

As its complement of Chieftain tanks was aging, the British Army adopted the Challenger 1 in the early 1980s. Just a few of these tanks were built and they served as a bridge from the old to the new, more powerful Challenger 2.

In an ironic twist of political upheaval and military requirements, the Challenger 1 emerged as the primary main battle tank of the British Army in the early 1980s. The tank remained so for nearly two decades, supplanted by the improved Challenger 2, designed and built by Vickers Defence Systems at the turn of the twenty-first century.

When Islamic revolution toppled the government of the Shah of Iran in 1979, an order for 1225 Shir II tanks was suspended. The Shir II was intended as an upgrade to the existing Chieftain and appeared to be a tank without a future. Concurrently, the British Defence Ministry approved a joint venture with the Federal Republic of Germany to produce a new main battle tank that would theoretically

The Challenger 1 incorporated several improvements over the previous Chieftain main battle tank and compiled an impressive service record during the 1991 Gulf War. The upgraded Challenger 1 remains in service with the Royal Jordanian Army today.

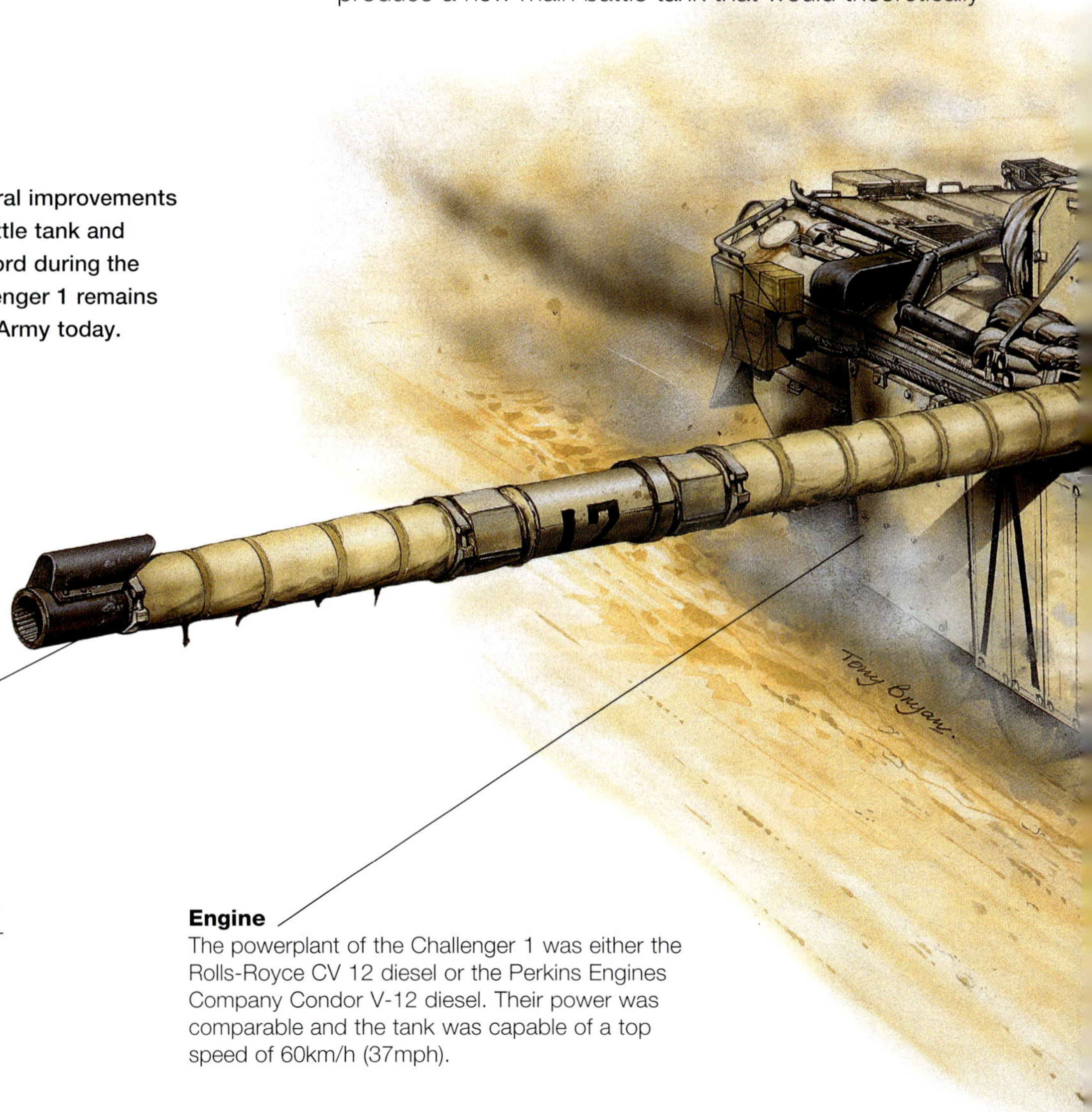

Main Armament
The 120mm (4.7in) Royal Ordnance L11A5 that had armed the Chieftain main battle tank was retained with the Challenger 1. Already known for its accuracy, the weapon's precision was improved with a new gunsight and fire-control system.

Engine
The powerplant of the Challenger 1 was either the Rolls-Royce CV 12 diesel or the Perkins Engines Company Condor V-12 diesel. Their power was comparable and the tank was capable of a top speed of 60km/h (37mph).

standardize the armour deployed by NATO countries in Western Europe.

Soon, it was apparent that the Anglo-German joint venture was headed nowhere. The British then initiated the research and development of a new tank of their own, tentatively called the MBT-80. Prohibitive cost and rapidly advancing technology, however, slammed the door on the MBT-80 rather abruptly.

Shir II Focus

Following this pair of pronounced failures, the British turned their attention once again to the surplus Shir II. Upgrading it to the standards of the British Army appeared a viable alternative while development of a new generation of main battle tanks continued. The project was approved and the "bridge" tank was named the Cheviot. This was

The Challenger 1 served as a bridge from the aging Chieftain main battle tank to the ultra-modern Challenger 2. Blending existing technology with numerous upgrades, the tank equipped armoured units of the British Army for nearly two decades.

later changed to Challenger, harkening back to a World War II-era cruiser tank.

As the Challenger was reengineered, numerous improvements were installed. However, mechanical problems surfaced with such components as the gearbox, main engine generator drive and laser-sighting equipment. These were addressed and the resolution of these issues contributed to the ongoing research to produce a new tank.

Specification

Dimensions	Length: 11.55m (37ft 10in) Width: 3.52m (11ft 7in) Height: 2.89m (9ft 6in)
Weight	62 tonnes (61 tons)
Engine	1 x Rolls-Royce CV 12 diesel or Perkins Engines Company Condor V-12 diesel generating 895kW (1200bhp)
Speed	60km/h (37mph)
Armament	Main: 1 x 120mm (4.7in) Royal Ordnance L11A5 gun Secondary: 1 x 7.62mm (0.3in) LA82 machine gun; 1 x 7.62mm (0.3in) L37A2 machine gun
Armour	Chobham composite, thickness classified
Range	Road: 450km (280 miles) Cross-country: 250km (155 miles)
Crew	4

Old and New

The main weapon mounted on the Chieftain, the 120mm (4.7in) L11A5, was held over with the Challenger. The reliable gun fired a round that used a separate bagged propellant charge rather than a cased one, adding a measure of safety against explosion. Secondary armament included a pair of 7.62mm (0.3in) GPMG machine guns with 4000 rounds.

The elongated, flattened turret with a pronounced slope housed the commander to the right, the loader on his left and the gunner forward and below. Surprisingly, there was ample space inside while the silhouette and radar signature of the Challenger were minimized. In traditional British style, the engine compartment was to the rear and the driver was positioned forward in the centreline of the hull. His recumbent seat further reduced the tank's silhouette.

The Challenger engine was either the Rolls-Royce CV 12 diesel or the Perkins Engines Company Condor V-12 diesel. Their power was equivalent and the tank was capable of a top speed of 60km/h (37mph). The No. 10 Mk.1 laser sight was intended for use in all weather conditions and paired with the GEC Marconi fire-control system it could acquire targets more rapidly and while on the move. The commander's Rankin Pullin image intensification swap sight and No. 15 day sight were upgrades that considerably improved his awareness of the surrounding battlefield.

The Challenger 1 was accepted by the British Army in December 1982. Its hydro-pneumatic suspension, supporting six road wheels on either side of the hull, functioned well in the desert during the 1991 Gulf War.

Armour Accent

With a primary focus on survivability, the most revolutionary improvement fielded with the Challenger was its Chobham armour, a classified composite that includes ceramic and metal alloys. First developed in the 1960s at the British research facility in Chobham Common, Surrey, the armour is much stronger than conventional steel and reportedly is capable of withstanding an impact five times greater than earlier protection. Chobham was also installed in the American M1 Abrams main battle tank.

Known simply as the Challenger until its replacement came along, the tank was then designated Challenger 1 to differentiate it from the new Challenger 2. Approximately 400 Challenger 1 tanks were subsequently transferred to the Royal Jordanian Army, where they continue to acquire upgrades and are called the al-Hussein. The Challenger 1 was deployed to Iraq and served with the British Army during the 1991 Gulf War as well as in Bosnia and Kosovo.

Special-purpose vehicles based on the Challenger chassis include an armoured recovery vehicle and a driver training vehicle with a fixed turret. The Challenger Marksman SPAAG is a self-propelled anti-aircraft combination of the Challenger chassis fitted with the Marksman turret, which includes Marconi 400 series radar and twin 35mm (1.37in) Oerlikon autocannons.

Accepting the Iraqi Challenge

Upon arrival in the Middle East during Operation Desert Shield/Desert Storm, the Challenger 1 received an upgrade package specifically for potential clashes with the heavy armour of Saddam Hussein's Iraqi Army. The tanks were offloaded from transport ships at al Jubayl, Saudi Arabia, and fitted with additional Chobham and explosive-reactive armour, external fuel tanks and smoke generating equipment. During engagements with Iraqi T-54/55 and T-72 tanks and other vehicles, the Challenger recorded approximately 300 victories without loss. A Challenger also confirmed the longest tank versus tank kill in modern warfare, destroying an Iraqi tank with a depleted uranium round at a distance of more than 5km (3.1 miles).

M1A1 Abrams (1985)

The M1A1 Abrams main battle tank resulted from a major upgrade to the original M1 that entered service with the U.S. Army in 1980. The M1A1 has seen combat service in the Balkans and the Middle East, amassing an impressive record.

When joint ventures with the Federal Republic of Germany to produce a standard main battle tank revealed the divergent priorities of each country's military establishment, the U.S. chose to continue the development of its own prototype, tentatively named the XM-1. The first M1 Abrams tank was delivered for field testing in 1976 and by 1980 the new tank entered service.

In 1985, the M1A1 entered production with several modifications and improvements to the original M1 design. The M1A1 was battle tested during the 1991 Gulf War and Operation Iraqi Freedom in 2003, essentially proving a number of detractors, who pointed out its high per-unit cost and possible mobility issues, quite wrong.

One of the finest main battle tanks in the world, the M1A1 Abrams incorporates numerous offensive and defensive innovations. Among these are classified armour protection, a U.S.-made adaptation of a German Rheinmetall 120mm (4.7in) smoothbore gun and a powerful gas-turbine engine.

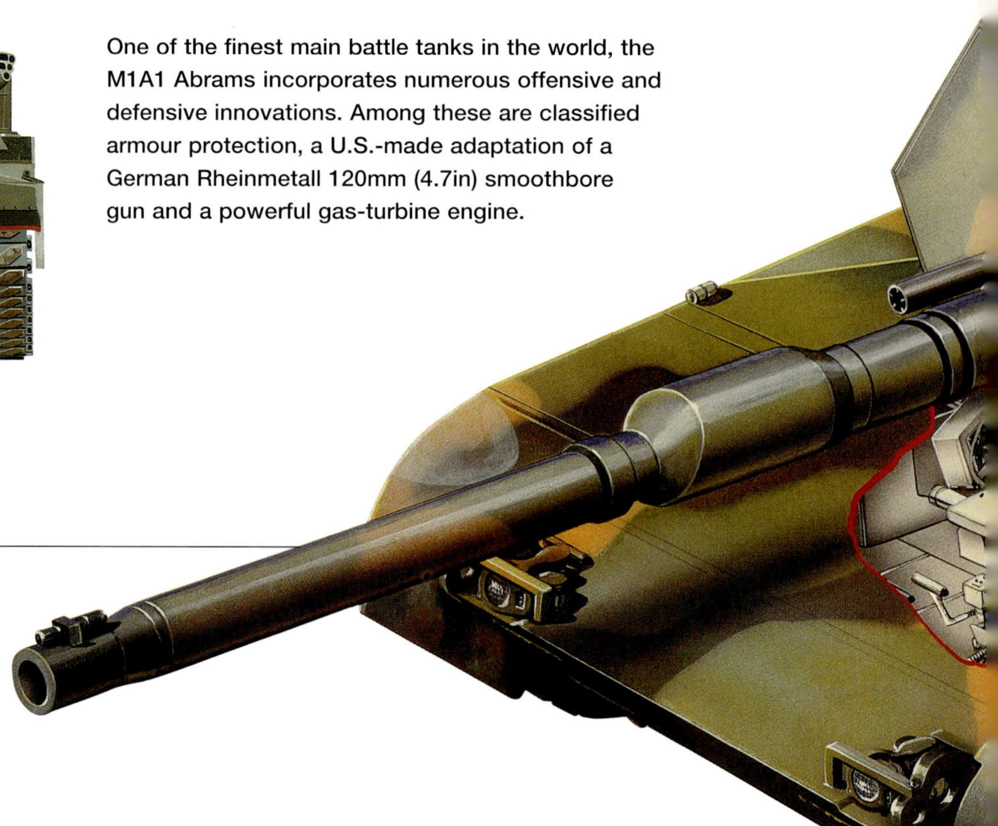

Main Armament
The 120mm (4.7in) M256 smoothbore, adapted under licence from the German Rheinmetall L44, arms the M1A1 Abrams, replacing the 105mm (4.1in) M68A1 rifled gun, derived from a British Royal Ordnance design, that was mounted on the original M1 main battle tank.

The M1 Abrams series of main battle tanks has been in service with the U.S. Army and Marine Corps for more than 30 years. Numerous upgrades and modernization efforts have allowed the Abrams to remain one of the most formidable land combat systems in history.

Adaptable Abrams

Perhaps the most notable improvement fielded with the M1A1 was the substitution of the 105mm (4.1in) L/52 M68A1 rifled main gun with the 120mm (4.7in) smoothbore Rheinmetall L/44. The German weapon was deemed superior in firepower and capability to deliver a variety of ordnance; however, it was considered overengineered by American standards. The U.S. obtained a licence to produce the weapon from Rheinmetall and proceeded to produce a version with fewer parts, including a coil spring recoil system rather than the original hydraulic recoil. The Americanized gun was named the M256.

Secondary Armament
A 12.7mm (0.5in) M2HB machine gun is mounted near the commander's hatch atop the turret, while one 7.62mm (0.3in) M240 machine gun is installed coaxially in the turret and another on a skate mount atop the loader's hatch.

Ammunition Storage
Separated from the crew compartment within the turret, ammunition is stored to the rear in armoured boxes. The storage area is protected by explosive-reactive armour with its top panels designed to blow outward in the event of a direct hit.

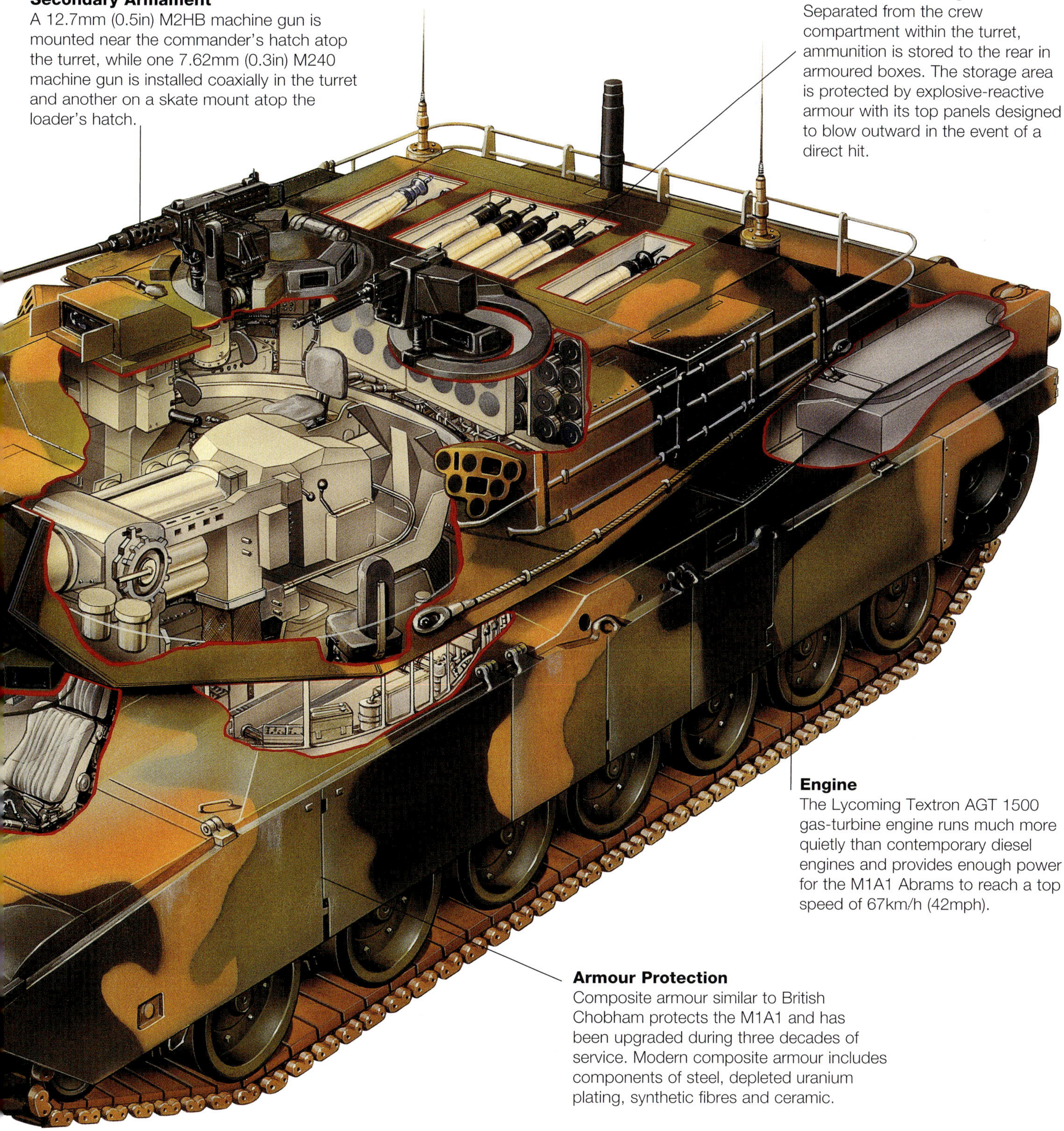

Engine
The Lycoming Textron AGT 1500 gas-turbine engine runs much more quietly than contemporary diesel engines and provides enough power for the M1A1 Abrams to reach a top speed of 67km/h (42mph).

Armour Protection
Composite armour similar to British Chobham protects the M1A1 and has been upgraded during three decades of service. Modern composite armour includes components of steel, depleted uranium plating, synthetic fibres and ceramic.

Modernization programs have maintained the battlefield edge for the M1A1 Abrams. Through the years, upgrades have included a nuclear, biological and chemical (NBC) defence system, enhanced armour protection, a better suspension and improved target acquisition equipment.

The M1A1 powerplant essentially broke new ground in armoured vehicle propulsion. Rather than the diesel engines that had powered tanks for more than half a century, the Lycoming Textron gas-turbine engine has developed a reputation as reliable in extreme climates and runs considerably quieter than its diesel counterparts. With the gas-turbine engine, the tank reaches optimal cruising speed in just a few seconds and friends and foes alike have come to call the M1A1 the "Whispering Death."

Specification

Dimensions	Length: 7.92m (26ft) Width: 3.66m (12ft) Height: 2.89m (9ft 6in)
Weight	57 tonnes (56.1 tons)
Engine	1 x Lycoming AGT 1500 gas-turbine powerplant generating 1120kw (1500hp)
Speed	67km/h (42mph)
Armament	Main: 1 x 120mm (4.7in) L/44 M256 smoothbore gun Secondary: 2 x 7.62mm M240 machine guns; 1 x 12.7mm (0.5in) M2HB machine gun
Armour	Composite appliqué over homogeneous rolled and welded nickel steel
Range	Road: 500km (310 miles) Cross-country: 300km (180 miles)
Crew	4

Early production M1 tanks were outfitted with a version of British Chobham armour, many times stronger than homogeneous rolled steel or appliqué steel plating. In 1988, the rolled and welded nickel steel hull of the M1A1 was fitted with appliqué composite armour of depleted uranium encased in steel, ceramic, synthetic fibres, rubber and other components. Its actual protective capabilities remain classified. However, in combat in Iraq no recorded penetrations of Abrams armour were made by the guns of Soviet-made T-72 or T-72M tanks.

The original requirements for the M1 Abrams tank were in anticipation of a ground war with Warsaw Pact forces. Acknowledging the overwhelming numerical superiority of the Soviets, American military planners stressed the ability of their weaponry to acquire enemy targets, shoot first and equalize an otherwise significant disparity of forces. Emphasis was initially placed on such priorities as crew survivability, surveillance and target acquisition, first-round hit probability and acquisition and firing time.

Targeting Technology

No fewer than a dozen upgrades to the M1A1 have taken place during the last 25 years. Target acquisition improvements include the addition of Forward Looking Infrared (FLIR) equipment and Far Target Locating sensors, thermal sights for secondary armament and sophisticated computer upgrades. The digital fire-control computer assimilates data from laser rangefinding equipment and produces an accurate firing solution based on the bend of the barrel as determined by a muzzle reference system, other angle measurements and external sensors that transmit information on weather conditions.

The layout of the M1A1 Abrams is functional and the turret has received particular attention as upgrades and the introduction of new equipment have impacted available space. The driver is positioned forward in a reclining seat to reduce the tank's silhouette. His three periscopes allow for night vision and operation in adverse weather. The gunner, seated on the right inside the three-man turret, utilizes a Hughes laser rangefinder, which has been documented to identify targets and facilitate kills at more than 2.5km (1.55 miles) and a single axis GPS-LOS visual system. The loader manually loads the M256 gun and replenishes ammunition for the secondary armament of one 12.7mm (0.5in) and two 7.62mm (0.3in) machine guns. He is seated to the left in the turret. The commander, seated to the right in the turret, views the field through optics and six periscopes.

During a seven-year production run that ended in 1992, approximately 4800 M1A1 Abrams tanks were completed.

The advanced technology of the M1A1 Abrams includes the commander's thermal imaging and computerized weapons management station, a highly sensitive fire-control system with enhanced target acquisition, global positioning, navigation equipment and onboard diagnostics.

Today, approximately 4400 remain in service with the U.S. Army, while the U.S. Marine Corps operates about 400. The tank has been exported to Iraq and Australia and has been built under licence in Egypt.

M1A1 Abroad

Although it was initially conceived for combat in Europe, the M1A1 Abrams main battle tank achieved field superiority in the desert of the Middle East. Its purpose to destroy enemy forces on the modern battlefield utilizing firepower, mobility and shock effect was fulfilled during the 1991 Gulf War and Operation Iraqi Freedom in 2003.

During the Gulf War, only 18 Abrams tanks were put out of action. Of these, nine were total losses, while nine sustained damage primarily from mines and returned to service. No Abrams crewmen lost their lives. In 2003, American M1A1 tanks destroyed seven Iraqi T-72s in an armoured clash south of Baghdad without loss to themselves.

AMX-56 Leclerc (1991)

Entering service in the early 1990s, the AMX-56 main battle tank gave France a main battle tank on par with the performance of other contemporary tanks such as the German Leopard 2 and the U.S. Abrams M1.

In search of a main battle tank to replace its obsolescent AMX-30, which dated to the 1960s, the French government evaluated and ultimately rejected tanks of American, Israeli and German design and embarked on a joint development programme with the Federal Republic of Germany that collapsed in late 1982. Eventually, this resulted in a commitment to a French-made main battle tank.

Concentrated development of the AMX-56 Leclerc, named for General Philippe Leclerc (1902–1947) who led the Free French 2nd Armoured Division during World War II, began in 1983 and by the end of the decade the first prototype was delivered. Production by Groupement des Industries de l'Armée de Terre Industries (GIAT) began in 1990 and nearly 900 of the modern tank and weapons

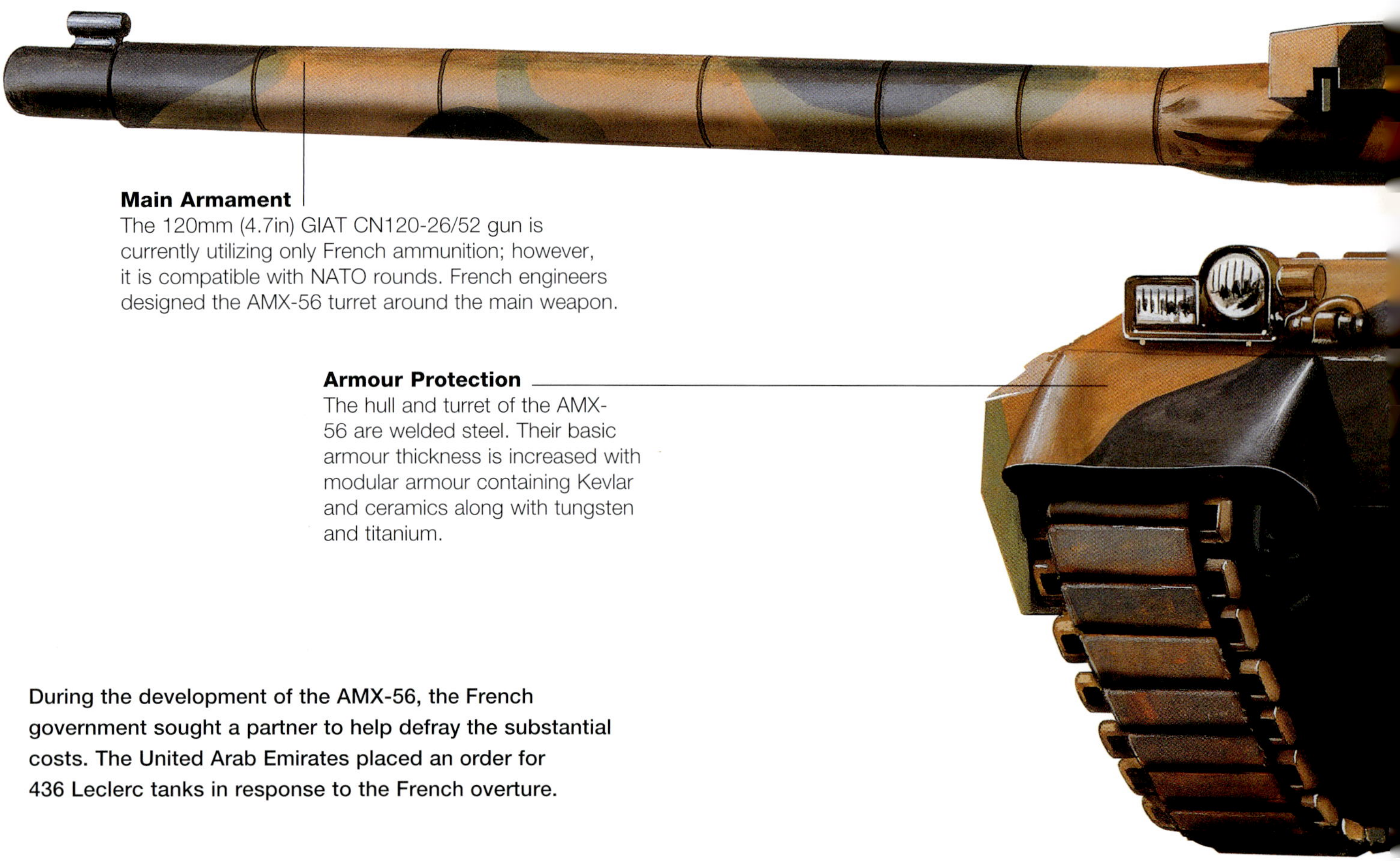

Main Armament
The 120mm (4.7in) GIAT CN120-26/52 gun is currently utilizing only French ammunition; however, it is compatible with NATO rounds. French engineers designed the AMX-56 turret around the main weapon.

Armour Protection
The hull and turret of the AMX-56 are welded steel. Their basic armour thickness is increased with modular armour containing Kevlar and ceramics along with tungsten and titanium.

During the development of the AMX-56, the French government sought a partner to help defray the substantial costs. The United Arab Emirates placed an order for 436 Leclerc tanks in response to the French overture.

system have been built for the French Army and the armed forces of the United Arab Emirates.

French Fusion

With an eye toward mobility and defensive as well as offensive capabilities, the Leclerc weighs 51 tonnes (50.1 tons), substantially less than other main battle tanks, both West and East. The resulting power-to-weight ratio is impressive at 21.1kW (28.3hp) per tonne and the tank's top speed is 71km/h (44.1mph). The 12-cylinder SACM V8X-1500 diesel engine is supplemented with a Suralmo-Hyperbar gas turbine supercharger and the Turbomeca TM307B auxiliary

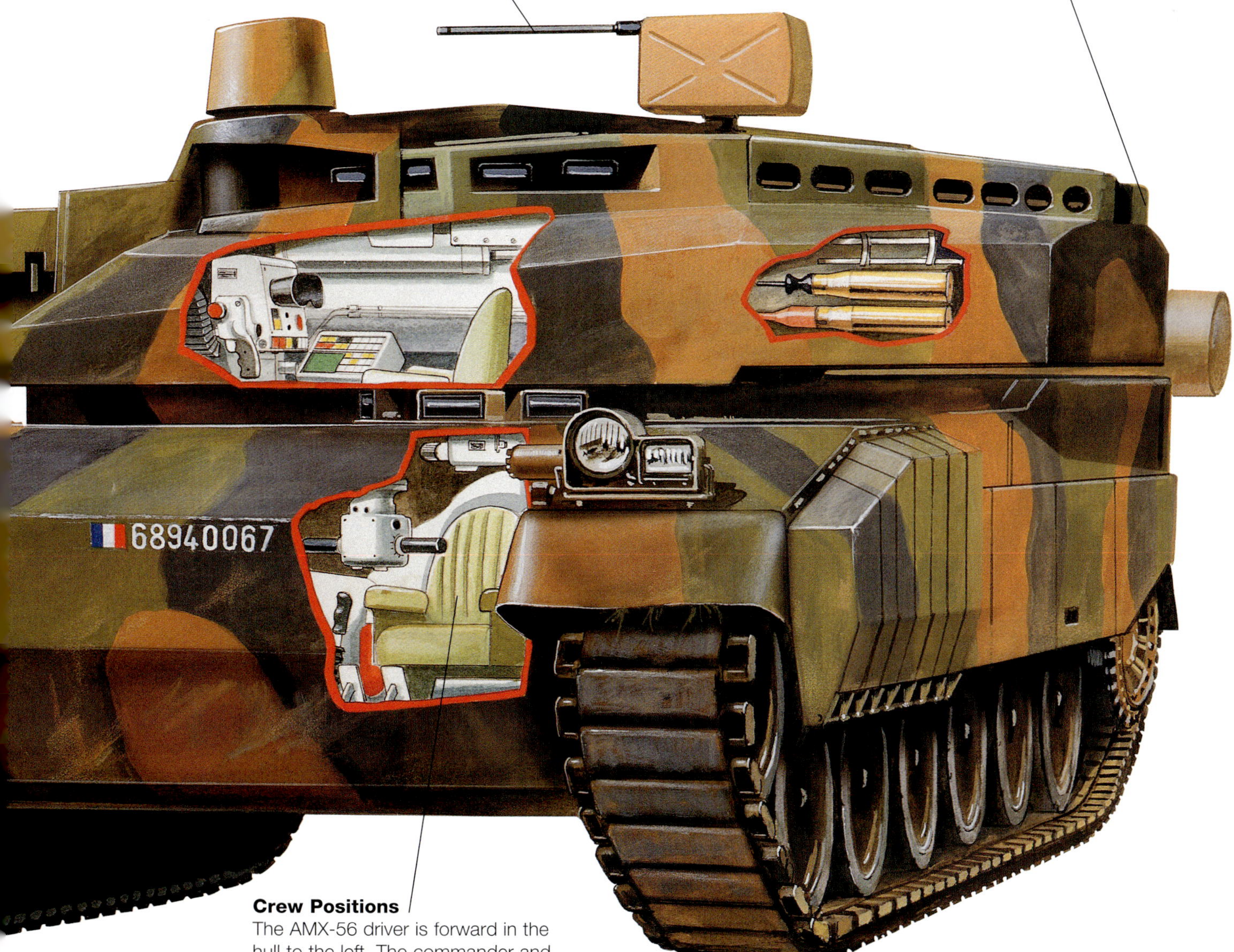

The AMX-56 Leclerc entered service with the French armed forces in 1993 and production ceased in late 2007. However, the assembly lines will be reopened if the need should arise.

power unit. The suspension is hydropneumatic with six pairs of road wheels, the idler in front and the drive sprocket to the rear. The SESM ESM 500 automatic transmission includes five forward and two reverse gears.

Specification

Dimensions	Length: 6.88m (22ft 7in) Width: 3.71m (12ft 2in) Height: 2.46m (8ft 1in)
Weight	51 tonnes (50.1 tons)
Engine	1 x 12-cylinder SACM V8X-1500 diesel powerplant with Suralmo-Hyperbar gas turbine supercharger and Turbomeca TM307B auxiliary power unit generating 1120kW (1500hp)
Speed	70km/h (43.5mph)
Armament	Main: 1 x 120mm (4.7in) GIAT CN120-26/52 gun Secondary: 1 x 12.7mm (0.5in) coaxial machine gun; 1 x 7.62mm (0.3in) turret-mounted machine gun
Armour	Welded steel with SXXI composite and explosive-reactive armour in AZUR upgrade
Range	Road: 550km (330 miles) Cross-country: 350km (210 miles)
Crew	3

The entire engine can be replaced in the field in only 30 minutes and an exhaust system cools emissions to reduce the heat signature of the vehicle. A pair of external fuel tanks, 200 litres (44 gallons) each, increases the tank's range.

From the defensive perspective, the Galix combat vehicle protection system, developed by Nexter and Lacroix Tous Artifices, consists of nine 80mm (3.15in) grenade launchers affixed to the turret and capable of firing smoke, fragmentation or infrared grenades. The KCBM defence apparatus includes infrared jamming gear and missile and laser "paint" warning equipment to alert the crew if their vehicle is fixed by enemy targeting systems.

The AMX-56 is protected by series 3 SXXI composite armour with tungsten, titanium and other components. The AZUR version of the Leclerc is configured to enhance urban survivability and efficiency and includes additional explosive reactive armour and composite protection, side skirts and bar armour to protect against rocket-propelled grenades and other close-in missiles. Extra armour protection is installed for the engine, designed particularly to defeat improvised petrol bombs, such as Molotov cocktails.

Offensive France

The 120mm (4.7in) GIAT CN120-26/52 gun is the main armament of the AMX-56. It is readied either manually or by an autoloading system with a total of 40 rounds carried, 22 in the autoloader magazine, 18 stored in the hull and one in the firing chamber. Manual loading may be accomplished from inside or outside the turret and the need for a crewman specifically to load the main gun is eliminated. Engineers recognized the difficulties that other nations had experienced in fitting main weapons into cramped turrets or upgunning to

Seen here on desert manoeuvres, the AMX-56 is powered by a supercharged 12-cylinder diesel engine with an additional auxiliary power unit. The AMX-56 may also be specially outfitted for optimal performance depending on the prevailing climate.

larger weapons. Therefore, they opted to design the AMX-56 turret around the GIAT CN120-26/52 gun.

With a rate of fire up to 12 rounds per minute, the gun is reportedly capable of 95 per cent accuracy at such a pace. It is equipped with an automatic compressed-air fume extractor and thermal sleeve to reduce warping of the barrel. The weapon currently utilizes only French ammunition but is compatible with standardized NATO rounds as well.

Tropical refit

The AMX-56 has been specially equipped for the tropical climate of the United Arab Emirates, which has received at least 436 of the French main battle tanks. The tropical outfit includes an 1120kW (1500hp) MTU 883 diesel engine along with the Renk HSWL295 TM automatic transmission. The Leclerc Battle Management Equipment package consists of the HL-80 command sight and a battlefield management system similar to the French tank's HL-70 sight and FINDERS system. With sophisticated target acquisition, the AMX-56 commander and gunner are able to each track up to six targets and engage them successively within a 30-second timespan.

The FINDERS (Fast Information, Navigation, Decision and Reporting) system enhances overall AMX-56 performance, providing up-to-the-minute global positioning and directional data with a colour map display and allowing the tank to identify itself, other friendly tanks and hostile armoured vehicles simultaneously. Digital fire control allows target ranging up to 4km (2.5 miles) distant and effective identification at 2.5km (1.5 miles). The Nexter Terminal Integration System, called Icone (ergonomic communications and navigation interface), works with the EADS defence electronics system to exchange digital information with higher command and reproduce it on a computerized map.

Leclerc Abroad

The AMX-56 has yet to engage in tank versus tank combat. However, it has been deployed with United Nations forces in Lebanon, where at least 13 were stationed until 2010 and in Kosovo, where 15 of the tanks maintained an armoured force capable of both offensive and defensive operations.

T-90 (1992)

Although the T-90 main battle tank had been intended as an interim upgrade to the venerable T-72 and the T-80, it has been in production since early 1993 and in service with the Russian armed forces since the late 1990s.

Although the new T-99 combat platform is reportedly slated for deployment by 2015, when the T-90 main battle tank entered production in early 1993 the debut of any new Russian tank design was indeed sometime in the distant future – and the military establishment of the Russian Federation knew it. The T-90 was intended as a short- to mid-term improvement over the aging T-72, constructed mainly for the export market and the T-80, which proved a disappointment in combat conditions during the First Chechen War between December 1994 and August 1996.

As the Russian government considered the high cost of research and development, a revision of the T-72 was determined to be the best alternative. The employment

The Russian T-90 has resulted from cost constraints, the need to retain manufacturing jobs and the overriding necessity to field a main battle tank that is comparable to Western designs. Its service life is now expected to extend beyond 30 years.

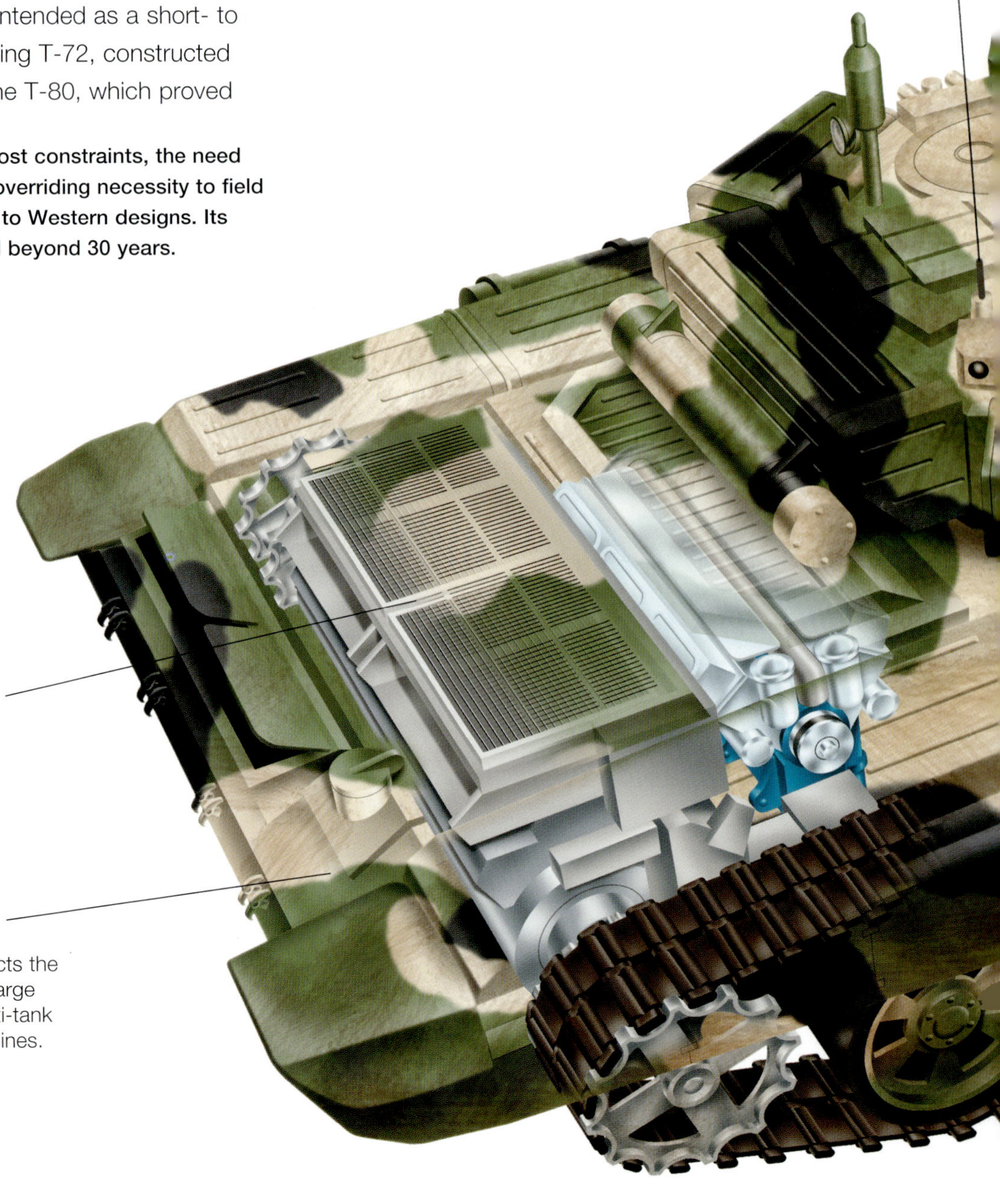

picture in Russia was grim at the time and production of the T-90 would also preserve manufacturing jobs in two cities, Nizhni Tagil, where the latest versions of the T-72 were built, and Omsk, the home of T-80 production. Kartsev-Venediktov was designated the principal design firm and the production itself was directed by Uralvagonzavod. The per unit cost of the T-90 was originally estimated at £1.5 million, or approximately $2.3 million, and this was believed to have escalated due to rising costs of raw materials.

The T-90 main battle tank, originally intended as an interim design, will likely serve with the Russian ground forces and naval infantry units for at least 30 years before its relegation to reserve formations. The new T-99 combat platform is expected to debut in 2015.

Russian Revolutions

The T-90 is visibly similar to its predecessors in the long line of Soviet-era tanks that culminated with the T-80. Its elliptical or clamshell-shaped turret and characteristic low silhouette continue to afford little comfort to the crew. The T-90's restricted headroom is somewhat compensated for by the installation of an automatic loading system for the main gun, dispensing with the need for a fourth crewman.

Nevertheless, by NATO standards the turret of the T-90 is cramped and ergonomically dysfunctional. The commander is seated to the right inside the turret with the gunner to the left, while the driver is centred and forward in the hull. Each crewman is equipped with thermal imaging and laser rangefinding equipment to direct the vehicle, acquire targets and lay the gun accurately. Typically, the driver is further tasked with serving as a field mechanic capable of performing basic maintenance and repair without removing the T-90 from a combat zone.

Explosive-reactive Kontakt-5 armour covers the turret and hull of the T-90 and is often easily recognized in brick-form appliqué. The Model 84 V-84MS 12-cylinder multi-fuel diesel engine powers the T-90 at up to 60km/h (37mph).

Holdover Firepower

The 125mm (4.8in) 2A46 smoothbore gun, a highly-modified version of the Sprut anti-tank gun, had been mounted in the earlier T-80 and was retained in the T-90. The 2A46 fires a variety of ordnance, including the Refleks 9M119 AT-11 Sniper, a laser-guided missile that is effective against aircraft and armoured targets. Secondary armament consists of a 12.7mm (0.5in) anti-aircraft machine gun mounted near the commander's hatch and a coaxial 7.62mm (0.3in) machine gun.

In a defensive posture, the T-90 excels with an effective array of countermeasures known as Shtora-1, or Curtain. The Curtain components include laser early-warning sensors to alert the commander in the event that the tank is

Specification

Dimensions	Length: 9.53m (31ft 3in) Width: 3.78m (12ft 5in) Height: 2.22m (7ft 3in)
Weight	46.5 tonnes (47.2 tons)
Engine	1 x Model 84 V84MS diesel powerplant generating 626kW (840hp)
Speed	60km/h (37 mph)
Armament	Main: 1 x 125mm (4.8in) 2A46 smoothbore gun Secondary: 1 x 7.62mm (0.3in) coaxial machine gun; 1 x 12.7mm (0.5in) anti-aircraft machine gun
Armour	Steel composite augmented by Kontakt-5 composite with protection equivalent to 1350mm (53in)
Range	550km (340 miles)
Crew	3

"painted" by opposing target acquisition systems, infrared jamming equipment and aerosol grenades that obscure the vehicle from sight.

Radiation lining coats the tank's interior, while nuclear, biological and chemical defences are active. Mine-clearing equipment reduces the likelihood of damage from such ordnance or an improvised explosive device. The driver's seat is welded to the roof of the hull to reduce the concussion in the event an explosive is detonated inadvertently. Bulldozing equipment allows the T-90 to dig its own revetment and quickly assume a hull-down attitude.

Indian Initiative

The government of India purchased a number of T-90s in response to the purchase of the T-80 by its rival, Pakistan. The export version was designated the T-90S and the Indian Army has fielded more than 600 of the modern tanks with a 736-kilowatt (988hp) 12-cylinder V-92S2 diesel engine but fewer state-of-the-art technical systems than the standard issue Russian T-90. The situation has since prompted the Indian government to seek contract bids to upgrade the T-90S with customized improvement packages.

Variants of the T-90 include the aforementioned Indian T-90S, known as the Bhishma, the command version designated T-90K, the T-90A, which has been nicknamed the Vladimir in honour of chief designer Vladimir Potkin who died in 1999, the BREM-72 armoured recovery vehicle, the MTU-90 bridgelayer, the BMR-3 mine clearing vehicle and others.

T-90 Deployment

The T-90 main battle tank shown below clearly displays the blocks of additional Kontakt-5 ERA that have been placed on its side skirts for additional protection against anti-tank weapons, mines and improvised explosive devices (IEDs). During its service life of nearly three decades, the T-90 has been deployed with Russian forces during the Second Chechen War in 1999 as Dagestan was invaded by Chechen fighters. It also entered combat during the brief but fierce fighting that ensued with the Russian invasion of neighbouring Georgia in 2011. Most reports indicate that the T-90 stood up to hits from Chechen anti-tank weapons without significant damage.

M1A2 Abrams (1996)

Building on the successful combat record of the M1A1 main battle tank, continuing upgrades include the prominent M1A2 package. Significant enhancements to the tank's computer systems and thermal imaging capabilities have been completed.

The demonstrated battlefield superiority of the M1A1 Abrams main battle tank during the 1991 Gulf War prompted U.S. military planners to evaluate the option of continuing upgrades to the existing platform rather than employ vast resources in the development of a new weapons system. In 1996, the government owned and operated General Dynamics Land Systems Tank Plant in Lima, Ohio, initiated the upgrade of 1000 M1 Abrams tanks to the M1A2 configuration. Most of these tanks had been in service for more than a decade at the time.

Entering service with the armoured battalions and cavalry squadrons of the U.S. Army beginning in 1998, the improved M1A2 Abrams was considered a viable option to the costly development of a new main battle tank.

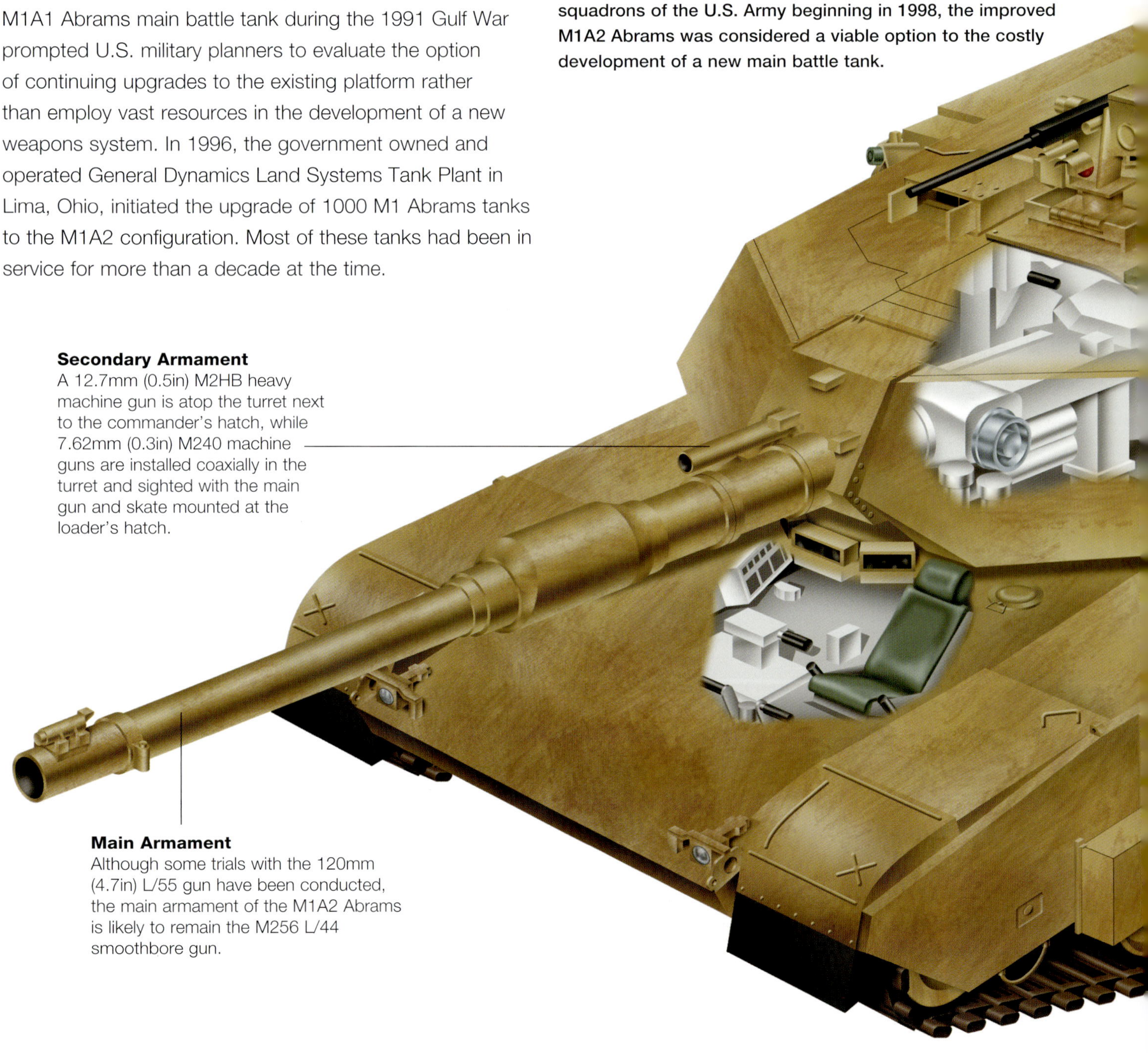

Top-tier Technology

Between 1996 and 2001, more than 600 upgrades were completed at the Lima Army Tank Plant (LATP) facility in Ohio, and a relatively small number of M1A2s were built as new. The improvements of the M1A1, including the installation of the 120mm (4.7in) M256 smoothbore gun

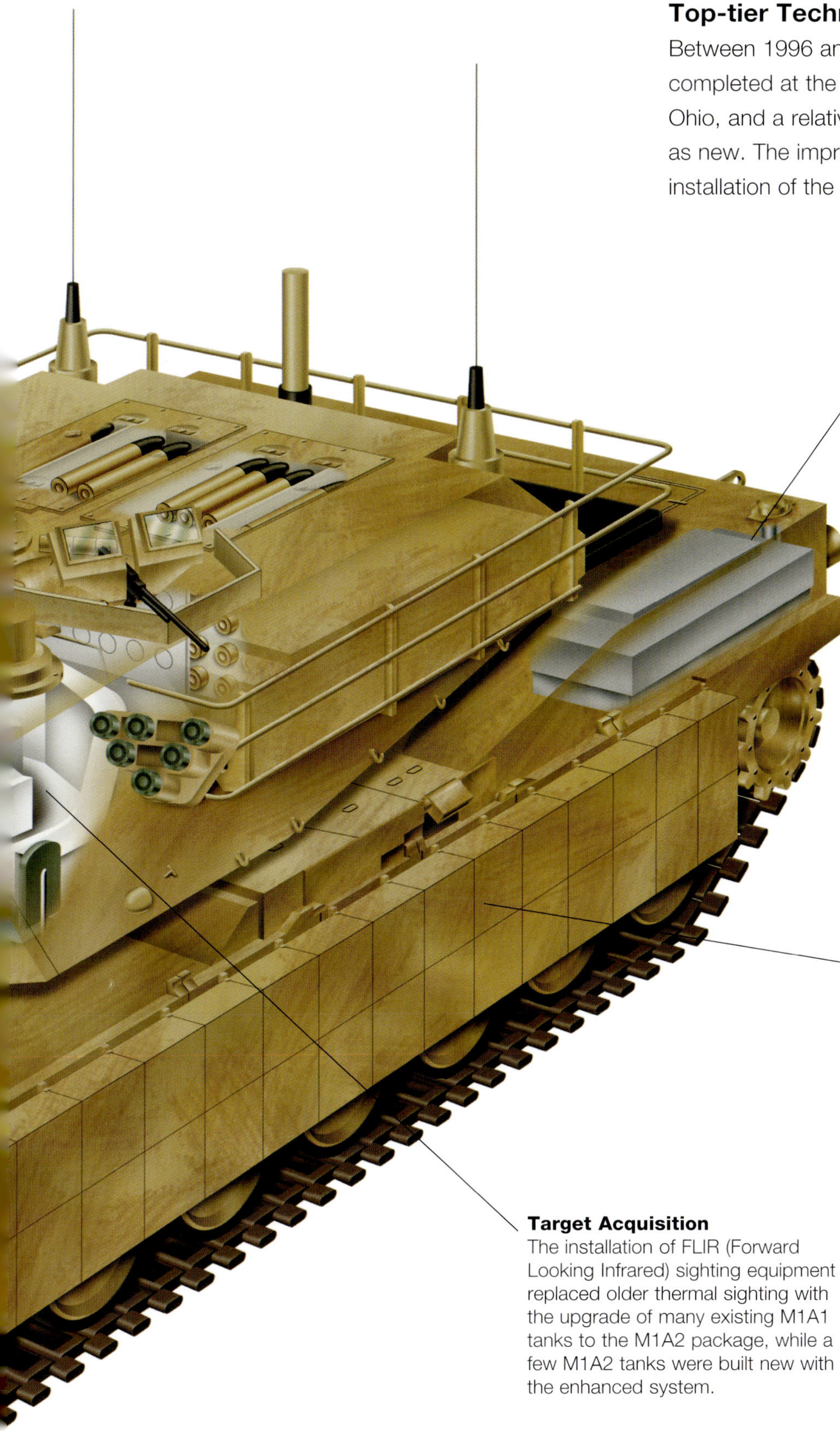

Engine
The AGT 1500 gas-turbine engine has been out of production since 1992 and development of a replacement engine, the LV100-5 gas turbine, is underway. The gas-turbine engine is substantially quieter than a standard diesel.

Armour Protection
A third-generation composite material based on the original Chobham armour includes plates of depleted uranium and offers protection equivalent to as much as 960mm (37.7in) of rolled homogeneous steel.

Target Acquisition
The installation of FLIR (Forward Looking Infrared) sighting equipment replaced older thermal sighting with the upgrade of many existing M1A1 tanks to the M1A2 package, while a few M1A2 tanks were built new with the enhanced system.

Specification

Dimensions	Length: 9.83m (32ft 3in) Width: 3.66m (12ft) Height: 2.37m (7ft 9in)
Weight	62 tonnes (61 tons)
Engine	AGT 1500 Lycoming gas turbine powerplant generating 1118kW (1500hp)
Speed	Road: 67.6km/h (42mph) Cross-country: 54.7km/h (34mph)
Armament	Main: 1 x 120mm (4.7in) M256 smoothbore gun Secondary: 2 x 7.62mm (0.3in) M240 machine guns; 1 x 12.7mm (0.5in) M2HB machine gun
Armour	Composite appliqué armour with equivalent protection estimated up to 960mm (37.7in) of homogeneous rolled steel
Range	426km (265 miles)
Crew	4

The M1A2 Abrams included numerous upgrades to the proven M1A1 main battle tank. Rather than embark on a program to produce a new tank, the U.S. military establishment opted to continue the modernization of the existing Abrams design.

adapted from the Rheinmetall L/44 and retooled under licence for simpler manufacture in the United States, an improved turret, nuclear, biological and chemical (NBC) defences, a heavier suspension and better armour protection, were complemented in the M1A2 with further enhancements.

The M1A2 was equipped with a commander's independent thermal-imaging viewer, thermal-imaging gunner sights, better navigational and global-positioning equipment, thermal-imaging and integrated display systems for the driver, a comprehensive weapons station with a thermal imager and a digital colour terrain map display.

The U.S. military maintained its priorities of crew survivability and early target acquisition linked to accurate fire. Therefore, prominent among the M1A2 upgrades was the installation of the Raytheon two-axis GPS-LOS primary sight, replacing a single-axis sight in the M1A1, to significantly increase the probability of an accurate first round hit. In February 2001, General Dynamics Land Systems began work on a contract with the U.S. government to fulfil a contract agreed upon in the late 1990s. A total of 240 M1A2 tanks were to be supplied with a SEP (Systems Enhancement Package) by 2004. The SEP package includes the U.S. Army Force XXI Battle Command, Brigade and Below Program (FBCB2), a digital battlefield command information system that works with radio interface equipment and allows a shared view of the battlefield among cooperating tanks, along with coordinated combat management.

Other improvements include faster data processing with full colour map displays, thermal temperature management that maintains an interior temperature below 35° Celsius to minimize the risk of sensitive equipment overheating, an auxiliary power source protected by armour and second-generation FLIR (Forward Looking Infrared Sighting). In 2006, DRS Technologies was awarded a contract for U.S. Marine Corps M1A1 tanks for the Firepower Enhancement Package (FEP), which included better laser rangefinding equipment, a precision lightweight global positioning receiver and the FTL (Far Target Locating) apparatus with amazing accuracy up to 8000m (26,246ft).

Although research has been conducted to evaluate the benefits of replacing the L/44 gun with the longer Rheinmetall L/55, such a programme may not be initiated. The L/44 is stabilized in two planes and is accurate on the move. It also fires a variety of ammunition, including armour-piercing rounds with cores of depleted uranium that have been deemed more efficient in penetrating power than other rounds. The L/55 has been utilized in Europe and fires armour-piercing rounds with tungsten cores.

The existing AGT 1500 gas-turbine engine has served the Abrams well for decades; however, it may be replaced by an even quieter LV-100-5 gas-turbine engine developed jointly by Honeywell and General Electric that emits no visible exhaust.

TUSK

The TUSK (Tank Urban Survival Kit) system may be added to the M1A2 in the field, eliminating the need to return to a maintenance depot for refitting. TUSK has become more relevant considering the potential for combat in urban scenarios, such as in narrow streets and among buildings. The system includes slat armour on its flanks to defend against rocket-propelled grenades, better explosive reactive armour and better armour plating for the side skirts that protect road wheels and suspension, particularly against mines and IEDs (improvised explosive devices). The loader's 7.62mm (0.3in) machine gun is equipped with a thermal sight and the commander is capable of firing the 12.7mm (0.5in) machine gun from the safety of the turret interior. An external telephone allows the tank to communicate with supporting infantry.

M1A2 Forward

The M1A2 Abrams main battle tank, shown at right traversing a dirt road during exercises, demonstrated superior firepower, armour protection and mobility during Operation Iraqi Freedom in 2003. The M1A2 served as the spearhead for the swift campaign across the desert and into urban warfare settings during the battles for control of such cities as Baghdad and Nasiriyah. The improvements to the Abrams series are intended to extend the service life of these main battle tanks to approximately 70 years, or sometime around 2050. The prototype of the new M1A3 Abrams is expected to be ready for field testing sometime in 2014.

Challenger 2 (1998)

Although retaining the name of its predecessor, the interim Challenger 1, the Challenger 2 main battle tank is almost completely new as only five per cent of its components are common with the earlier tank.

More than 150 modifications to the chassis of the Challenger 1 main battle tank were incorporated into its successor, the Challenger 2, an ultra-modern highly technological weapon system that has emerged as perhaps the finest fighting vehicle of its kind in the world today.

While it retains the Challenger name, the new main battle tank is, in virtually every category, a remarkable upgrade from its predecessor.

Only about five per cent of the older design, mostly associated with its automotive components, has been

The Challenger 2 entered service with the British Army in 1998 and rapidly established itself as one of the world's finest main battle tanks. Its deployment to hotspots in the Balkans and the Middle East has confirmed its wide-ranging battlefield capabilities.

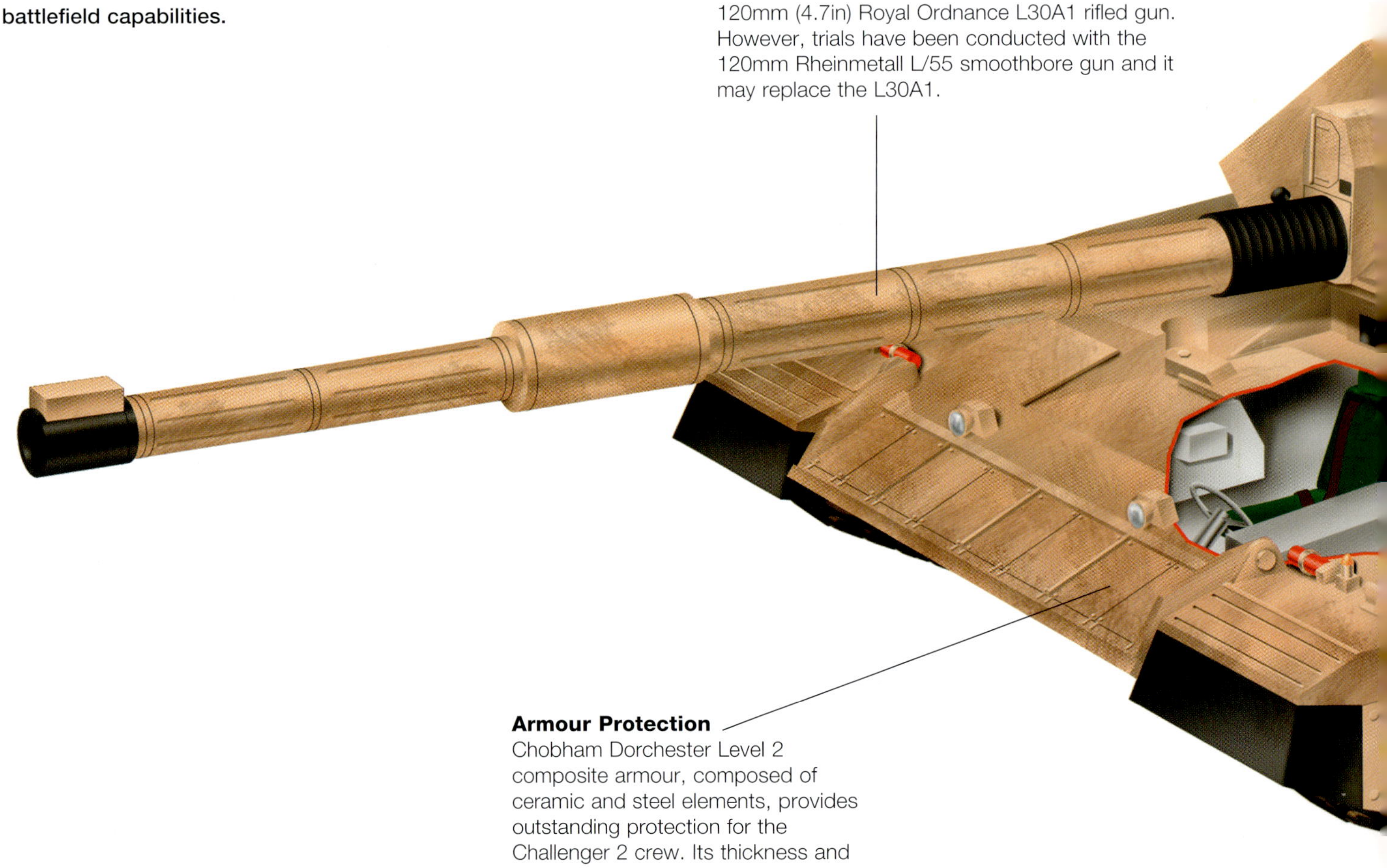

retained in the Challenger 2. In 1986, Vickers Defence Systems initiated a project to replace the Challenger 1 and during this process the company merged with Alvis. Subsequently, Alvis Vickers became BAE Systems and the project was continued by the BAE Land Systems Division. Thus, the Challenger 2 is the first tank built for the British Army to be designed, developed and produced by a single principal contractor since World War II.

Challenger Change

The Challenger 2 layout is similar to earlier British tanks with the engine situated to the rear, fighting compartment in the centre and the driver seated forward in the hull. The commander is seated in the turret to the right of the main gun with the loader to the left and the gunner in front and below. The concept of an automatic loading system was eventually abandoned in favour of more efficient

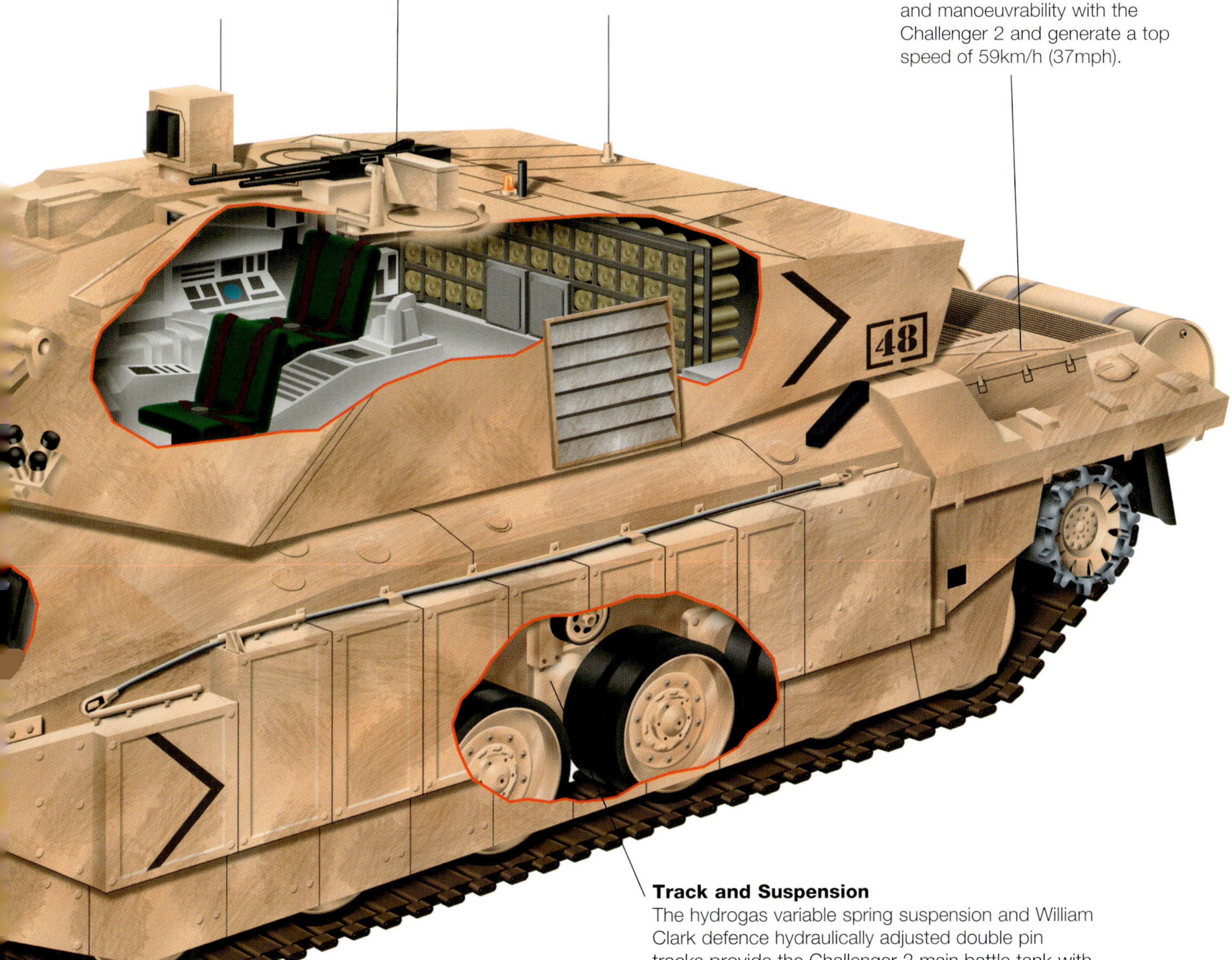

The Challenger 2 main battle tank combines firepower, manoeuvrability and armour protection in one of the most advanced vehicles of its kind in the field. The tank has been deployed in Iraq, Bosnia and Kosovo.

around-the-clock operations and to avert the risk of mechanical failure.

The original main weapon was the 120mm (4.7in) Royal Ordnance L30A1 rifled cannon. Its electro-slag refined steel construction is complete with a thermal sleeve to prolong barrel life and minimize warping during combat operations, a bore evacuator and a chromium barrel lining to increase the interval between changes. The fire-control system is manufactured by Computer Devices Company of Canada and complemented by stabilization controls that allow firing on the move and an electronically-controlled turret that is capable of 360° traverse independent of the hull. The turret and gun are both controlled with solid state electronics rather than hydraulic lines that are vulnerable to battle damage and could catch fire.

Manufactured by Thales, the TOGS II (Thermal Observation and Gunnery Sight) offers thermal imaging and night vision technology. Both the commander and gunner see thermal images on their sights and on monitors. The driver utilizes the Thales Optronics passive driving periscope for night vision and is also equipped with a thermal rear-view camera. The commander's position is further equipped with eight periscopes for all-around viewing and a panoramic SAGEM VS 580-10 gyrostabilized sight with laser rangefinding equipment for laying the main gun.

Under the auspices of the CLIP (Challenger Lethality Improvement Programme), the British Ministry of Defence authorized field testing of a new main weapon to potentially replace the L30A1. Trials were completed in 2006 and the replacement of some Challenger 2 main weapons with the 120mm (4.7in) Rheinmetall L55 smoothbore gun may have already been completed. The L55 is the same main weapon that equips the German Leopard 2A6 main battle tank.

Secondary armament consists of a 7.62mm (0.3in) Hughes L94A EX-34 chain gun mounted coaxially in the turret and a 7.62mm (0.3in) L37A2 GPMG machine gun attached to the loader's hatch.

Speed and Defence

The Challenger 2 is equipped with stealth technology to avoid detection by enemy forces and equipment to prevent jamming of its communications. Improved composite

Specification

Dimensions	Length: 8.3m (27ft 3in) Width: 3.5m (11ft 6in) Height: 2.5m (8ft 2in)
Weight	62.5 tonnes (61.5 tons)
Engine	1 x 12-cylinder Perkins Caterpillar CV-12 diesel powerplant generating 890kW (1200hp)
Speed	Road: 59km/h (37mph) Cross-country: 40km/h (25mph)
Armament	Main: 1 x 120mm (4.7in) L30A1 rifled gun Secondary: 1 x 7.62mm (0.3in) Hughes L94A EX-34 chain gun; 1 x 7.62mm (0.3in) L37A2 GPMG machine gun
Armour	Chobham Dorchester Level 2, classified properties
Range	450km (280 miles)
Crew	4

Equipped with stealth technology to avoid detection by opposing forces, the Challenger 2 main battle tank is capable of closing with the enemy rapidly, acquiring targets and achieving a first hit while maintaining concealment.

Chobham Dorchester Level 2 armour, a combination of steel and ceramics, provides outstanding protection for the crew and its actual thickness remains classified. Nuclear, biological and chemical (NBC) defences are fitted and five L8 smoke grenade dischargers are positioned on the sides of the turret. The Challenger 2 is also capable of making smoke with the injection of diesel fuel into the exhaust manifolds.

The powerplant of the Challenger 2 is the reliable 12-cylinder Perkins Caterpillar CV-12 diesel engine that is capable of generating a top speed of 59km/h (37mph). An export variant, the Challenger 2E, is powered by the Europack and transversely mounted MTU 883 diesel engine with the HSWL 295TM automatic transmission. Hydraulically-adjusted double-pin tracks designed by the William Cook Defence company are easily maintained in the field and allow for the solid traverse of difficult terrain, while a hydrogas variable suspension provides excellent cross-country stability.

Solid Combat Performance

In addition to the British Army, the Challenger 2 is also operated by the armed forces of Oman. It has also been extensively tested by the armies of Greece, Qatar and Saudi Arabia. The Challenger 2 achieved an excellent combat record during Operation Iraqi Freedom. Only one Challenger 2 was destroyed in Iraq and this was by friendly fire from another Challenger. Two Challengers were damaged by improvised explosive devices and a rocket-propelled grenade. However, after action reports also indicate that on occasion the Challenger 2 absorbed multiple hits from rocket-propelled grenades and an anti-tank missile but sustained little damage.

Glossary

armament The standard or customized weapons that a machine is equipped with.
artillery Long-distance weapons of heavy firepower; the armed forces who use such weapons.
battalion A body of troops numbering between 400 and 1000 who are prepared for battle.
cavalry Soldiers who fight in armoured vehicles.
chassis The base frame of a machine.
coaxial Specifies that something has a common axis.
composite Consisting of multiple parts or materials.
cupola A turret that has a mounted gun.
deploy To mobilize troops for military action.
heavy tank The biggest and most expensive tanks, having the strongest armour and firepower.
hull The outer shell of a machine that houses its main operational components.
infantry Soldiers who are trained in face-to-face combat.
light tank A small tank with light armor that moves rapidly and is often used for reconnaissance.
medium tank The most widely-used and cost-effective tank that is designed to be mobile, but with heavier armour than a light tank.
nuclear, biological and chemical (NBC) defense system A system of protective measures for surviving nuclear, biological and chemical hazards.
onslaught A destructive offensive that makes much progress.
ordnance Mounted guns, or a group of soldiers who are trained to use them.
powerplant An apparatus that generates electrical power for a vehicle.
reconnaissance Special forces collecting information or identifying a target ahead of main forces.
retrofit To go back and apply a new feature or accessory to something that has already completed manufacturing.
service life The amount of time that a particular model of something fulfills its primary function.
sortie A transition from a position of defense to attack.
sponson A protrusion on the side of a vehicle to which a tank's gun is often mounted.
superstructure A structure built on top of something else; for tanks, this structure is on the hull.
suspension The system of wheels and supports that cushions a vehicle's body from the ground and allows it to move.
transmission The component(s) of a vehicle that carry power from the engine to the wheels.
traverse To move across/through a space.
turret A protective space/barrier from which a mounted weapon can be fired.
upgun To upgrade a gun or weapon.
variant A newly adapted version of something.

For More Information

National World War I Museum and Memorial
100 W. 26th Street
Kansas City, MO 64108
(816) 888-8100
Website: https://www.theworldwar.org
Exhibits and special events educate the public and commemorate the many lives lost during WWI.

The National WWII Museum
945 Magazine Street
New Orleans, LA 70130
(504) 528-1944
Website: http://www.nationalww2museum.org
Digital collections, exhibits, and shows offer a glimpse into the lives of Americans during WWII. Explore life during the war effort through letters, recruitment posters, weapons, models, film, and other artifacts.

The General George Patton Museum
4554 Fayette Avenue
Fort Knox, Kentucky 40121
(502) 624-3812
Website: http://www.generalpatton.org
Exhibits at The General George Patton Museum include collections of tanks used in World War II and the Korean War, General George Patton memorabilia, physical and digital archives, and other artifacts.

AAF Tank Museum
3401 U.S. Highway 29B
Danville, Virginia 24540
(434) 836-5323
Website: http://www.aaftankmuseum.com
AAF Tank Museum has an extensive collection, with items ranging from international tanks, artillery pieces, flamethrowers, rocket launchers, and more. Exhibits display various pennants, banners, flags, pins, and other symbols and insignia, as well as a broad range of military attire.

U.S. Army Ordnance Museum
2601 Aberdeen Boulevard
Aberdeen Proving Ground, MD 21005
(410) 278-3602
Website: http://www.ordmusfound.org
U.S. Army Ordnance Museum exhibits historically important equipment that is relevant to the US Army Ordnance Corps.

National Museum of the United States Army
2425 Wilson Boulevard # 230
Arlington, VA 22201
Website: https://armyhistory.org
Scheduled to open in 2018, the National Museum of the United States Army will provide a comprehensive portrayal of the traditions and history of the Army.

The U.S. Army Center of Military History
102 4th Avenue, Building 35
Fort McNair, DC 20319-5060
http://www.history.army.mil/
The U.S. Army Center of Military History records the official history of the army in times of peace and war.

Museum of American Armor
1303 Round Swamp Road
Old Bethpage, NY
(516) 454-8265
Website: http://museumofamericanarmor.com
The Museum of American Armor replicates the sights and sounds of American forces during World War II to preserve and exhibit this seminal chapter in history.

Websites

Because of the changing nature of internet links, Rosen Publishing has developed an online list of websites related to the subject of this book. This site is updated regularly. Please use this link to access this list:

http://www.rosenlinks.com/WMPM/tank

For Further Reading

Barnes, G.M. *Weapons of World War II: A Photographic Guide to Tanks, Howitzers, Submachine Guns, and More Historic Ordnance.* New York: Skyhorse Publishing, 2014.

Bishop, Chris. *The Encyclopedia of Weapons of World War II: The Comprehensive Guide to over 1500 Weapons Systems, including Tanks, Small Arms, Warplanes, Artillery, Ships and Submarines.* London: Amber Books, 2014.

Bishop, Chris. *The Illustrated Encyclopedia of Weapons of World War I: The Comprehensive Guide to Weapons Systems, including Tanks, Small Arms, Warplanes, Artillery, Ships and Submarines.* London: Amber Books, 2014.

Clausewitz, Carl von. *On War.* Princeton: Princeton University Press, 1989.

Forty, George and Jack Livesey. *A Complete Illustrated Guide to Tanks & Armoured Fighting Vehicles.* Leicester, UK: Lorenz Books, 2014.

Forczyk, Robert. *Tank Warfare on the Eastern Front 1941-1942: Schwerpunkt.* Barnsley, UK: Pen and Sword Books, 2014.

Haigh, Richard. *Life in a Tank.* London: Forgotten Books, 2016.

Hartman, Ted. *Tank Driver: With the 11th Armored from the Battle of the Bulge to VE Day.* Bloomington: Indiana University Press, 2014.

Haskew, Michael E. *Modern Tanks and Artillery 1945-Present* (The World's Great Weapons). London: Amber Books, 2014.

Haskew, Michael E. *Tank: 100 Years of the World's Most Important Armored Military Vehicle.* Minneapolis: Zenith Press, 2015.

Haskew, Michael E. *Weapons of War. Tanks: Inside & Out.* New York: Rosen Publishing Group, 2011.

Holder, Nick. *The Royal Ordnance Factory at Hayes: The Story of a World War II Gun and Tank Factory at Hayes in the London Borough of Hillingdon.* Museum of London Archaeology Service, 2011.

Jackson, Robert. *101 Great Tanks.* New York: Rosen Publishing Group, 2010.

Kaplan, Phillip. *Tank: Heavy Metal at War.* New York: Skyhorse Publishing, 2016.

McNab, Chris. *A History of the World in 100 Weapons.* Oxford: Osprey Publishing, 2014.

Nishiyama, Takashi. *Engineering War and Peace in Modern Japan, 1868-1964.* Baltimore: Johns Hopkins University Press, 2014.

Roach, Mary. *Grunt: The Curious Science of Humans at War.* New York: W. W. Norton & Company, 2016.

Sommerville, Donald. *An Illustrated History of the Weapons of WWII: A comprehensive directory of the military weapons used in World War Two, from field artillery and tanks to torpedo boats and night fighters, with more than 180 photographs.* London: Southwater Publishing, 2012.

Spilling, Michael. *Weapons of War: Tanks & Armored Vehicles 1900-1945.* Leicestershire: Chartwell Books, 2013.

Zaloga, Steven. *Armored Champion: The Top Tanks of World War II.* Mechanicsburg, PA: Stackpole Books, 2015.

Index

Page numbers in *italics* refer to illustrations.